The Temptations
of Big Bear

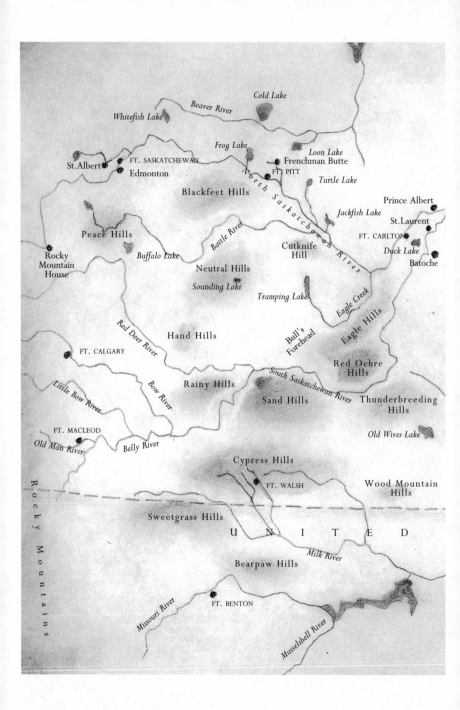

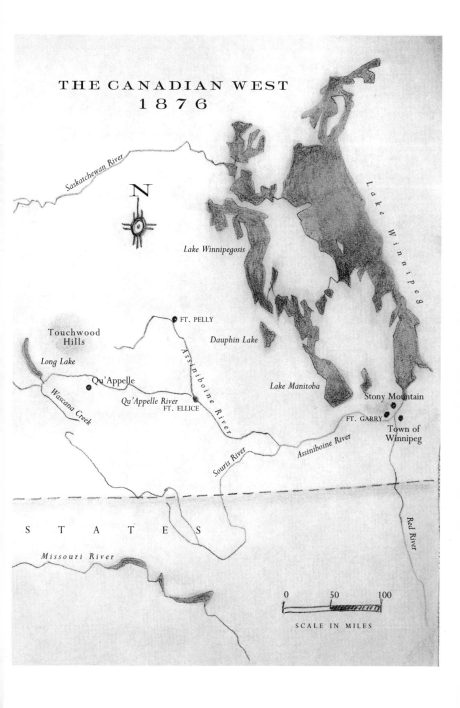

THE CANADIAN WEST
1876

Saskatchewan River

N

Lake Winnipegosis

Lake Winnipeg

Touchwood
Hills

● FT. PELLY

Dauphin Lake

Long Lake

Assiniboine River

Qu'Appelle ●

Wascana Creek

Qu'Appelle River
FT. ELLICE

Lake Manitoba

Stony Mountain ●
●
FT. GARRY ●
Town of
Winnipeg

Souris River

Assiniboine River

S   T   A   T   E   S

Red River

Missouri River

0   50   100

SCALE IN MILES

THE TEMPTATIONS OF BIG BEAR

Rudy Wiebe

SWALLOW PRESS
OHIO UNIVERSITY PRESS
Athens

No name of any person, place, or thing, insofar as names are still discoverable, in this novel has been invented. Despite that, and despite the historicity of dates and events, all characters in this meditation upon the past are the products of a particular imagination; their resemblance and relation, therefore, to living or once living persons is to be resisted.

FIRST SWALLOW PRESS/OHIO UNIVERSITY PRESS EDITION, 2000.

Swallow Press/Ohio University Press, Athens, Ohio 45701

Copyright ©1973 by Rudy Wiebe
Published by arrangement with Alfred A. Knopf Canada,
a division of Random House of Canada Limited, Toronto, Canada.

Swallow Press/Ohio University Press books are printed on acid-free paper ⊗ ™
09 08 07 06 05 04 03 02 01 00   5 4 3 2 1

LIBRARY OF CONGRESS CATALOGING-IN-PUBLICATION DATA

Wiebe, Rudy, 1934-
    The temptations of Big Bear / Rudy Wiebe.—1st Swallow
    Press/Ohio University Press ed.
        p. cm.
    ISBN 0-8040-1029-3 (alk. paper)
    1. Big Bear (Cree chief)–Fiction. 2. Cree Indians–Fiction.
    3. Canada, Western–Fiction. I. Title.

PR9199.3.W47 T46 2000
813'.54–dc21   00-033843

Maps by CS Richardson

This story is for Tena and Adrienne and Michael and Christopher, who helped me unearth it.

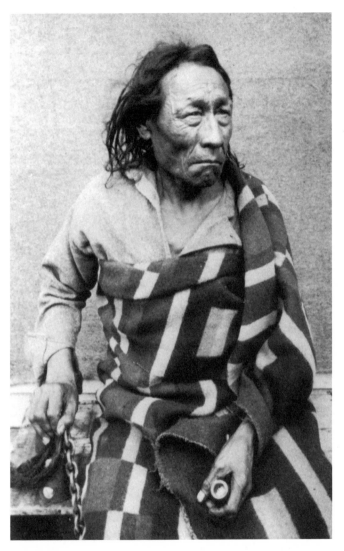

Big Bear outside the North West Mounted Police barracks.
Regina, Saskatchewan, September 1885.

Edgar Dewdney, Lieutenant-Governor and Indian Commissioner of the North West Territories. Ottawa, Ontario, April 1883.

Cree camp on the prairie, south of Vermilion, Alberta. Taken during Canadian Pacific Railway survey, September 1871.

Big Bear and his band trading at Fort Pitt, Saskatchewan, October 1884.
A full description of this photo—the first ever taken of Big Bear—can be
found on page 210.

Standing, from left: Four Sky Thunder (Kah-nee-o-keesikow-paniss); King-
bird (Okeemow Peeaysis), Big Bear's third son; Iron Body (Napasis); Big
Bear (Mistahimaskwa); Angus McKay, Hudson's Bay Company; Otto
Dufresne; Louis Goulet; Frederick Stanley Simpson; Constable Alex
McDonald. *Sitting:* Matoose; Constable H. Rowley; Corporal R.B. Sleigh;
Corporal H. Edmonds.

Big Bear, after his surrender, with (standing from left) Sergeant Smart, and Constables Colebrook, Nichols and Sullivan. Prince Albert, Saskatchewan, July 1885.

Group of nine taken in the square of the North West Mounted Police barracks at Regina, Saskatchewan, September 1885. *Back row:* Constable Black, N.W.M.P.; Rev. Louis Cochin; Superintendent Richard Deane, N.W.M.P.; Rev. Alexis André; Beverly Robertson, Big Bear's defense lawyer. *Front row:* Horsechild, the youngest of Big Bear's five sons; Big Bear; Police Chief A.D. Stewart; Poundmaker.

Big Bear (left) and Poundmaker in the Manitoba Penitentiary at Stony Mountain, 1886.

Poundmaker. Regina, Saskatchewan, September 1885.

Big Bear in the Manitoba Penitentiary at Stony Mountain, 1886.

Contents

God who made the world and all that is in it, from one blood created every race of men to live over the face of the whole earth. He has fixed the times of their existence and the limits of their territory, so that they should search for God and, it might be, feel after him, and find him. And indeed, he is not far from any of us, for in him we live, and move, and have our being.

—Acts of the Apostles, 17:24–28.

Fort Pitt,
September 13, 1876

I

Sweetgrass had signed the treaty. The Honourable Alexander Morris, P.C., Lieutenant-Governor of Manitoba, the North West Territories and Keewatin, looked down his long wide nose again, past his mustache and the clerk's serge shoulder at the heavy X on the paper. Heavy, and broad enough to break the steel pen when it struck, as he had thought then. Break it, old man, hold it like a gutting knife and break it and every one of these Cree will do it in ceremony and we'll have one great splattered original with — twenty-nine pens? Not enough between Pitt and Carlton, more likely Fort Garry, to get it finished.

How many quills could a wild goose — feathers for an X!

Once he would have thought those twenty-seven His X Marks under Sweetgrass and James Seenum made little difference, but no longer. Not after the several hundred thousand square miles to which he had finally and forever extinguished, as the Prime Minister liked to say it, all native rights. In his four years they added up to something a little over three hundred and fifty thousand; these final one hundred and twenty thousand — who could tell exactly, larger than the entire British Isles — won with no more than a few embraces endured and shots fired in celebration, rolling wood and prairie land lying as it seemed now at his booted feet. Who could imagine

so much land? Even ignoring all that disappeared in blue distance beyond the treaty boundaries which he himself had only
seen as squiggles of rivers on paper and would never see otherwise; even after driving over it at an unending trot day after
day along trails winding up and down and right and left and
through and over under the relentless sky, he could not. It
sometimes came to him when the long snake of their party
emerged, and again immediately vanished, into the gorge of
sky and land, that despite everything done in the name of
brotherhood, the Queen, the Great — thank God others
would have to concern themselves with the continuing justice
of it, thank God.

Two hours surely, and more to get wound and hung with
baubles? He had said nine-thirty. He stood motionless, refusing to draw his watch. Oh wild democracy, twenty-nine chiefs
for less than a thousand Indians and any fly-by-night like that
Saulteau at Carlton talked while the rivers ran even if praises
be he was finally rejected with his impossible 'I want ten miles
around the reserve where I may be settled' — ceremony was
all. The police band: that was a mistake, for the sake of half a
day to have them ferrying equipment over the west ford. How
had he made such a mistake? McKay, Christie certainly should
have reminded him, at least the council tent, and the flag
despite its bent poplar pole....

He stood, hands folded behind his back; looking over the
curly head of his clerk through the triangle of tent door. The
land sloped in benches to the flat about Fort Pitt. Nothing of a
fort, really; a disarranged clump of log buildings with four-
sided shingle roofs, a port of call halfway between Carlton and
Edmonton worried by weather almost into hovels, even the
Company's. But the land lay scooped out, beautiful. The huge
river turning past the tiny peaks of the buildings, coils of it

spinning in circles like suns, its grey water so thick, so heavy with silt it seemed to bulge up out of its bed, lean against hills. And trees on the diagonal slopes, not only in the deep ravines like the South Branch or the Qu'Appelle where the buffalo browsed them, but here like spines up tilted ridges too, poplars and fading yellow birch like sprouting grass impossible to ride through, and spruce in the crotches of streams, black spires laid on beaver lakes. Who would sign away such land? As if they had a choice.

"Is it something, Mr. Kerr?"

The clerk managed the fallen ink bottle into his fingers now and lightly pushed himself erect. But there was no dignified way to extricate his long legs from those of the tiny table; with a lurch he lifted it off, set it aside completely, and stood up.

"No sir. Not at all." He was flexing his foot, head down. "It's, just my ankle, just a — twinge is all." Abruptly he seated himself on his stool and hoisted the table back.

"Dr. Jackes tells me," the Governor's smile drew down the corners of his heavy mustaches without betraying itself in his tone, "you hurt it last night. During the Indian dance, I think."

The shoulders hunched, the pen dipping with excessive care into the bottle.

"Yes sir. I don't usually trip up, in dances."

"Perhaps it was the blanket that tangled you. I am given to understand the squaws enjoyed your imitations of them, immensely."

The pen was so careful with the last 'His X Mark,' as if that were more cumbersome than 'See-kahs-kootch' just completed. The Governor turned on his heels, eyes up along the ridge of the council tent.

"Mr. Kerr, have you been back to Perth recently?"

"I joined up with Colonel Wolseley's Expedition, 1870 sir, First Ontario Rifles, and, after the west...."

"I was born in Perth myself," the Governor said sardonically. "Of course, there aren't any squaws there to . . . dance. Traditionally, of course, an Englishman only *watches* natives dancing."

A surge of red finally crossed Kerr's face, "Of *course* I'm Irish." But vanished as quickly. "Dancers! The best dancers in the world have to be French halfbreeds. After the buffalo hunt any evening in the firelight, the dancing oh wooo —" he laughed, rasping his breath in through strong teeth. "With the green hides for a floor!"

"You've been with them?"

"I lived on the Saskatchewan, yeah."

"When?"

"A year, four years ago."

"Then you know the man they call their president, that Dumont?"

"Gabriel, I slept in his tents with his family! What a man! He taught me the buffalo hunt, he and Ambroise Fisher. 'They come, *les animaux*,' it would go through the camp like lightning, and at sun-up we'd be running them, between the Saskatchewans. Long valleys of them."

"Well, there weren't any near Carlton."

"Yeah. That fall herd should be coming north. I asked Gabriel at Carlton but he just shook his head, they have to go farther and farther into Blackfoot coun —"

The Governor had wheeled on his polished heel, "Dumont was at Carlton, now, during the treaty?"

"Yes sir." Kerr held the tightly rolled leather of the treaty he had been copying. His curly black hair was cropped round about his ears like fur. "Didn't you —"

"Well," the Governor said, his voice again quite under

control. "Well. Nothing. He will have to leave judicial decisions to the police now, that's all, now that they're here. The government has settled that."

"Gabriel's real good," Kerr's young face was hunched together earnestly, "and he don't need nobody to help tell his people keep the law. He does it himself. Once when some Cree messed up the buffalo running —"

"The police are here now. Indians or halfbreeds, it makes no difference."

Kerr was twisting a tassel of treaty leather in a long, thin spiral. "He was going to talk, to you. He told me, about the land but then you said.... " His voice dropped.

"What?"

"It was, that — the 'two hands'...."

"Ahh," said the Governor; had Kerr dared look up at that moment he would have seen mustaches lifted in a smile. "Monsieur Dumont knows when to show himself to talk. I said the French halfbreeds can't take with both hands, land both at Red River where they've been given plenty but won't take it, and here on the Saskatchewan. They must know once and for all what they want."

"But they just want to hunt the buffalo!"

"Then let them come and talk about it."

"He wanted to. At first." Kerr's head swung up and their glances met like gun bolts snapping into place. "Sir, Gabriel Dumont is a really straight man. He don't talk English, and he'll never talk where he's not wanted, he's hardly one for talking at all. He does things."

"Then let him be careful what he does. If he has some just claim, he can present it in the proper manner to the North West Council presently constituted, but *all* native claim has now been extinguished and any —"

A racket of buggy wheels driving closer caught the Governor in his rhetoric and he broke off, feeling slightly foolish; to lecture one young man, white, in this empty…horses trotted by so close the buggy following blocked the tent entrance. It halted there to a bellow, its body rocking between high wheels under a broad brown face circled completely by black hair merging into a full mustache and beard that spread over the gold buttons of a bulging coat. Commissioner the Honourable James McKay had his own four hundred pound sense of when ceremony was unimportant.

"Forget your quick goodbye, Alex," he leaned in gigantically, "they're not coming now."

"We sent to them at eight-thirty, and I've been —"

"And I've been at the camp, seeing to it, dropping hints about the time," McKay swung down thrusting the doorway wider, moving his bulk easily, "and then it was like something run through the lodges, here, just look." He had the Governor's shoulder, was pulling him out past the buggy wheel. "There on the ridge across the river — the ravine, see the notch there?"

"Yes, yes, well, more Indians? Good."

"Not just 'Indians', that's — take my glass," the short brass telescope was in the Governor's eye almost before he could raise a hand. "Find the lead horse, half down the ridge, then the fourth back, a bay, and the man short, without feathers. See him?"

"Hey!" Kerr exclaimed. "Yeah, that's — riding fourth, no dress up, that's Big Bear!"

"Goddam right Big Bear, I told you he's the real wild power of the Plains Cree and he'll talk for every Cree and Assiniboine and Young Dog on the south plains doing what they all should be doing, killing buffalo, not sitting here chewing bacon."

"There's plenty of ... " oddly, while it drew a spot closer, the telescope seemed at the same time to push that spot back into a kind of greyish-ringed haze; the Indian swaying gently with the bay horse, "of time to hunt, it's good he ... " as if he were very far away, barely moving in a flat, constant green circle at the end of an unbelievably long tunnel, "he's in time, good, to make treaty. Sweetgrass and the others —"

The Commissioner was farther on the slope, waving his huge arm like a banner across the river. "The first thing is don't let his looks fool you, he's no Company or Missionary old woman like Sweetgrass. And he won't throw his arms wide and kiss you either. Wait till you hear his voice."

The Governor lowered the telescope. "He's that one last fall that refused to talk to Reverend McDougall about the treaty we were coming to make."

"George, God rest him, couldn't give one twist of tobacco to The Bear." McKay's head dropped forward like a bull buffalo in charge, "'We want none of the Queen's presents. When we set a fox-trap we scatter pieces of meat all around, but when the fox gets into the trap we knock him on the head. We want no bait; let your chiefs come like men and talk to us.'"

"I just wrote him a letter. ... "

"A letter!"

The three men, clerk, Governor, commissioner, stood side by side. Staring across the flat over the stove pipes and roofs of the Hudson's Bay Company at the long line emerging from the bluffs above the river. The motion was so deliberate, so inevitable that each horse and rider seemed to hang still on the open ridge slanting to a cusp of poplars down, behind a fold in the earth. One by one, as if on parade, in single file they moved and when the lead horse with its moulded rider merged down into the trees even the seeming motion disappeared in relation to itself, in relation to the sky, the sage gleam of the river, the green land now tinged brown and gold in the September sun. One figure, another, and another, vanished but at the top of the ridge there was always one more so the line simply remained, drawn against those three elements and wavering a little but there, drawn, and only as they studied one bit of that line, squinted to almost see the thin spiral of dust rise like ashes upward from the poles of the travois, was there a flicker of motion downward from the notch of blue sky, downward into the earth beyond the water.

"George McDougall wrote he was a conjuror too?"

McKay was muttering, "He wants to see you. He sent a messenger ahead."

"Of course."

"It'll take a while for them to cross, you might as well go down again."

"Tell them I'll see them at three. And the police, send a runner to the west ford that we won't leave till tomorrow sun-up."

"I did already. And the band come back."

"The tent?"

"Leave the flags up but we'll take that down, the band means more. Make it four. Them others won't come without him now," McKay's left arm swung an arc at the lodges among the spruce of the creek and merging into the poplars up the ridge behind them. "The Bear isn't rushed."

"It's only the third month on this one, who's rushing?" Morris heard the tiredness in his own voice. Instead of sonorous declamations of farewell, the fall morning had run to nothing but questions, silly little questions; as if after four years of signed and multi-copied treaties he now discovered himself still quite alone and re-arranging surfaces. He had known what was needed, for years, what... the clerk was staring at him. There was nothing for it but jocularity. "Well, Mr. Irishman John Kerr, Perth, Ontario and St. Laurent, Saskatchewan Territory, you now have time to make another copy of the treaty, on the solid comfort of the Factor's table. Come along."

McKay rumbled, "Waste time making it," but he was in his buggy and already so far down the slope that no one but himself and his horses and a crow pecking at a bead in the grass heard; the crow erupted from under the horses with a squawk. "Damn trader glass," said the Honourable James.

II

"My heart rises like a bird to see you once more."

Sweetgrass grasped the Governor's hand, his kind old face thrust forward, his voice clear and high so that Peter Erasmus, translating, inevitably fell into the same cadence to carry his English to the stiff scarlet rows of policemen at the foot of the flagpole. On the flat where the council tent had stood and up the slopes around were five or six hundred Indians and beyond them on the ridges warriors sat on horseback, outlined against the sky. Sometimes they seemed to move through the sun directly. The Governor did not like his position; having marched up the slope to the flagpole at the head of his party, the band tootling quite impressively at last into the vast air — all that repetition of only three tunes — he now faced straight into the lowering sun. By some oddity he had never before been on a council flat at this time of day; the Indians circled before him seemed not so much human as innumerable mounds the earth had thrust up since morning; there was a strange yellow and blackness about the still, brilliant air, a kind of crystal lack of shading that made alert thinking seem silly.

As if there were only inevitabilities into which all, irresistibly, moved. He shook his head; the outlined smile on the old face before him smudged, wavered, and he widened his own smile, gesturing in apology with his head at the sun; shifting to his left. Sweetgrass understood. With half a step the Governor had cut off the sun against the chief's raven headdress; he must concentrate. He must.

Sweetgrass continued: "The Great Spirit has put it in our hearts that we shake hands once more, before all our brothers. That Spirit is above all, and under His eye every person is the same. I have pity on every one who lives by the buffalo. If I am spared until next year I want you, who has come to us from the Great White Queen, to act for our good: to protect the buffalo. We must hand in hand protect the buffalo. I am thankful. When I hold your hand I feel the First One is looking on us both as brothers. May this earth here never taste a white man's blood. I thank God I can lift my head, and when I take your hand and touch your heart, as I do now, let us be one. I have said it."

Sweetgrass' brown hand rested a moment beside the gold buttons of the Governor's dress uniform, then it pointed upwards and a rumble of agreement moved over the hillside. The Governor, still holding the chief's right hand, looked about his circle slowly, smiling: the curve of seated chiefs, Commissioners McKay and Christie in blue dress suits, the lines of police whose brass instruments blazed; in ceremony now, his mind perfectly clear. Though he had seen such panorama often, he was again impressed. A wild people coming in kindness. If there was some way this scene, the feeling of this world could be captured for the Prime Minister. Or even for the Court in — that was too much; what could such crudities, such make-shift jumble, indeed, such stench mean to highbred sensibilities. But a Canadian; surely, there was a courtliness about this unbred old man — well — his eye moved slowly across the chiefs again. They wore the coats and huge medals they had received on signing the treaty; a few sported beavers, one a woman's floppy hat, but most had the usual tangled motley of feathers and skins and string and sticks and bones — except one. He sat in the inner circle draped in a buffalo robe. The Governor stared across the leveling light. Big Bear's shoulder-length hair was held out of his face by a thong; his head down as if in thought.

Governor Morris: "We have come together and understand each other. My heart is glad that you have all seen the right way. I had written a letter to Big Bear and Bobtail and the other big chiefs on the plains with the buffalo, but Big Bear is here now. I am happy to tell him personally that the treaty is for them too, it was made as if they all were here."

As the interpreter spoke Cree, the expression on Sweetgrass' face slowly loosened until there was nothing to be seen at all except folds hung in blank immobility. The Governor knew he had broken decorum; he did not need the growl of McKay's pretended cough to confirm it. Sweetgrass dropped his hands, turned, and shuffled to his place in the circle. It seemed he hesitated a moment, his red coat bright against the dark robes and blankets of the people spread up the hillside, then he faced around and sat. When he had settled himself, his lean buttocks shifting slowly to find comfort, he glanced up across a quarter of the circle; nodded to Big Bear.

But Big Bear sat. After a time the usual murmur of people ceased, even the sounds of the camp far along the creek and over the ridges — a child's cry, the sound of a dog, or a horse — silence so deliberate that the Governor, though he clenched his mind against it, against so much as flexing his body to ruffle it, knew with a lurch that every stretching second drained him standing at attention farther into insignificance. As if a hand had wiped over the hillside and its shadow struck them all, forever, into undifferentiated stone. He had to break the — sneeze, swipe at a fly, some understandable, natural movement. He was still standing — so speak the usual formulas into this black and yellow — the seated man was blurring into focus because his head was lifting. The light hung there, split down the long shale divide of nose, the mouth opening gigantically, black.

"I find it hard, to speak."

For nearly a month now every Cree had sounded the same to the Governor. He had found it best to concentrate completely on Peter Erasmus' words, but now he found his head turning into blackness, slowly down into the enormous, strange depths of that incomprehensible voice.

Big Bear: "There is a stone between me and what I have to say. It is no small matter we were to consult about. And now I see only these red coats, these shiny things. There is a stone."

The Governor had opened his mouth as translation proceeded, and McKay jerked his sleeve; but he was not going to sit down while they talked to themselves.

Sweetgrass: "My friend, let there be nothing between you and your words. Speak. We wait to hear you."

Big Bear: "The stone is my people. I have come to speak for my people, far on the plains hunting our food. I expected the chiefs would have waited until I could speak for my people."

Sweetgrass: "Long ago we sent the message to them. The message to the one who stood for the Queen, the winter after we made peace with all Blackfeet. When we heard our lands had been sold to the Company, and we didn't like it."

Big Bear: "I never sent a message."

Sweetgrass: "When we heard that about the Company. And we didn't like the Americans bringing firewater. That year of the terrible starvation, when a quarter of us died of the White Sickness that came with our hunters and the Blackfeet from the Missouri. Now we have the police; they keep the Americans out. There's the doctor to help us against the White Sickness. And the one who stands for the Queen has come with an open hand, to feed us when we have no food. We have taken his hand."

Big Bear suddenly laughed; the resounding laughter of a man who has a happy thought. "Not long ago the Hudson's Bay Company sold rum and when I was young I drank it, and so did you, my friend. Long before we made a short peace with the Blackfeet! We drank all night with our friend James Simpson and weren't ugly or cut anybody up. We sang songs, quietly, and remembered the hunts. The great hunts that we had then when we needed them, the buffalo covered the prairie." He stopped an instant, and the Governor understood his voice changing to a harder, wilder depth as his look flickered about the seated chiefs. "The buffalo, it seems there is only one left. James McKay I know, and Mr. Christie; I've traded with him and he has given me Company flour when my people were hungry. But who is this 'Governor' standing there? I have never seen him before. Has anyone? Will we ever see him again?"

Governor Morris: "I am the Representative of the Queen. As my blue coat shows, and as Mr. McKay and Mr. Christie have told everyone here, I am her Head Councillor in this territory, as they also are councillors. When you hear my voice you are listening to your Great Mother the Queen. She tells you 'I love my Red Children as well as my White. I know it is hard for them to live and I have always helped those that live in need in other parts of my Dominion.' We have agreed about what the Queen is willing to do for you, so that you never need go hungry, as Sweetgrass has said."

Big Bear seemed to be pondering Sweetgrass as if the interpreter was simply a medium, a bird flying by perhaps.

Big Bear: "Councillor?"

Governor Morris: "Yes. I am her Head Councillor."

Big Bear: "The Queen speaks to us?"

Governor Morris: "Yes. You have heard her voice, whom God bless and preserve long to reign over us."

There was a momentary silence.

Big Bear: "The White Queen is — a woman."

Peter Erasmus jerked; he glanced swiftly at McKay, who had grunted at the word, then began to translate just as a high shriek rose from somewhere far back in the crowd. It could have been one of the young men forked so easily on their restless horses along the high ridge, but as it lifted and grew to suddenly return like echo from the hills across the river it was obvious no one human voice could raise that cry. The last English syllable vanished as in a deep underground rumble that burst into immense laughter bouncing from person to person until the hillside was rocketing with sound. Even the inner circle of chiefs grinned. But the Governor, the commissioners, the police stood rigid with darkened faces. The Governor swung about to Erasmus, his voice shivering,

"Tell that — that — I didn't come here to have my Sovereign Queen insulted by some big-mouth savage. Either they stop immediately or —"

McKay and Christie both had hands on his arm, speaking swiftly under their breath. Erasmus, confused, said nothing. There was no need; the chiefs were all studying the Governor and Sweetgrass raised his hand until slowly the sound died.

"My friend," he said in his soft clear voice to Big Bear, "this is the one who speaks for the Queen. She is the Grandmother. Her councillors wear blue coats and her police and chiefs wear red coats so that whenever we meet we know we are meeting friends. We have accepted his hand, and we wear her red coats."

Big Bear slowly arose. The Governor had regained control of his face once more; McKay gestured, Kerr came forward with three folding chairs and the Governor and then the two commissioners seated themselves. The sun, now low on the hill, threw their shadows in long blocks across the policemen standing at attention with their coiled and spiralled instruments still aloft, still gleaming.

Big Bear spoke more deliberately than ever, his voice as loud. The buffalo robe built him huge against the sun.

"Yes, you wear her red coats. And you have given your hand."

There was a long pause but he said nothing further. James Seenum, seated beside Sweetgrass, said:

"I think The Great Spirit, under whom we all live, put it into their hearts to come to our help. It is all becoming so different, I do not know. I feel as if I saw life when I saw that one saying they would help us. Think of our children."

"Yes, you have given away your hand," said Big Bear again as if he had not heard. Then he turned and deliberately named the Wood Cree, "And you, Seenum, have been touched by the water of the missionary John McDougall who sits here among you." His finger swung to a bearded man. "He advised you to give your hand. And you, Sweetgrass, have been touched by the water of the missionary who wants us to call him 'father,' and he named you 'Abraham.' They have come from somewhere, we do not know, and they say they talk for the One Great Spirit. Good. I am not a disobedient child. I have always been the friend of the white man but I was never a Company chief, or a Missionary chief. I am chief of the River, the First

People. It is a hard life I and my children live. And now I no longer understand and feel as I once understood when I did not see so many white men before me who spoke for so much that none of us ever needed to feel or see before. The White Queen is our Mother. Good. I am not a disobedient child. She will feed us when we are hungry. Good. I am thankful for food. She is our Mother under The Great Spirit. Good. Under the Spirit as missionary McDougall there says? Or the other one says, Lacombe? Or as I say? I throw back no man's hand, but I say I am fed by the Mother Earth. The only water I will be touched by comes from above, the rain from The Only One who makes the grass grow and the rivers run and the buffalo feed there and drink so that I and my children live. That we have life!"

Big Bear's voice was a tremendous cry echoing over the valley, and again with the interpreter; as if again and again in any language the words of themselves would refuse to stop sounding. And over them suddenly there broke the sharpness of hooves. A horse had vanished on the ridge above and was running as if shot from a bowstring, its head stretched straight, its tail bannering, running as if by itself. Nothing in the beautiful demonstration of ceremonial riding given when the Governor first arrived at Fort Pitt had matched this, as it appeared, unconscious, intense, pointed speed downward suddenly unleashed. But for hooves drumming one would have thought the animal did not touch the ground. It ran, down. Below the police however its direction turned; towards them; drumming diagonally across the tilted earth with no shift in speed. Clearly now there was a naked leg hooked over its back, an arm through its streaming mane. As it shot past below the two rows of policemen with their faces rigid before them, their steady stares crossing each other at the flagpole and passing on somewhere against the sky, the muzzle of a gun lifted under that straining neck. The bullet had passed up between the rows, beneath the flag and over the Governor's head before the crack above motion and hoofbeats snapped him into understanding what had happened. At least he had kept his face under control, thanks to that mesmeric speed. The horse disappeared north, among the tent poles along the creek. He hissed over his shoulder to McKay,

"Macleod, get Macleod to get whoever that was!"

"Listen," McKay whispered, "listen to them. I wonder, Macleod should maybe get his name, yeah, but —"

"That's dangerous!"

"Just listen."

The Chipewyan chief, The Fish, was speaking in his ponderous Cree as if they had not just sat in silence, watching. "We have all taken his hand. We all think it is for our good. That is all."

Big Bear: "Stop. Stop! My friends!"

His right arm swung over the seated people, longer and longer out from the clutched robe as if in its urgency that incredible voice, the pinched thrust-forward face, would leap the entire man out at them stripped.

"I have not seen this Governor before. I have seen Mr. Christie many times. I do not know what the Company has to do with the Grandmother —"

"Mr. Christie has nothing any longer to do with the Company," Morris interrupted as the sentence began in translation. "He is no longer with the Company. He is now the Queen's Commissioner."

For the first time Big Bear looked at the Governor. There was not a flicker of change on his face; it was the perfectly impersonal look with which he might have studied a trail he wished to remember, a rock whose detail needed some deliberate thought to scar on his memory. Finally this look moved an instant to Christie, to McKay, and then more slowly about the circle of the chiefs; it returned to the Governor.

Big Bear: "I heard the Governor was to come, and I said that I shall see him. When I see him I will make one request. There is something that I dread. To feel the rope around my neck. It is not given to us by The Great Spirit that Redmen or Whitemen should spill each other's blood."

The Governor stared about. "What was that, that about the rope? Repeat it."

Erasmus gestured to McKay for corroboration, "That was just the way he said it, 'There is something that I dread. To feel the rope around my neck.'"

"But who's ever said anything about ropes, eh? About hanging?"

"I dunno," McKay muttered.

"He's obviously a coward."

Christie snorted, "He's no coward! I could tell you stories, he's got more Blackfeet scalps than —"

McKay interrupted, "He's no coward, nah! I dunno, but sure, he knows that's the way we punish killing. The police have made that clear enough if they didn't know it before, but he sure did. That's the worst insult for a warrior to get it like that, I dunno. Maybe he means our law, the whole thing. It's beginning to rub him. Like you can't talk without pictures, I don't think he was even talking to you there, when he said it."

"What?"

"He was talking to them other chiefs. Look at them."

The Governor looked. They all sat with bowed heads as if they had again all remembered a single thing. He settled more erectly in his chair. He had personally negotiated three treaties that gave his country more lands than any one negotiator in history, anywhere on earth, bloodlessly, and no one man would stand in the way of the fourth and largest. From the very beginning, except for a few minor malcontents, the big chiefs had been happy, sometimes like Sweetgrass even effusive in their gratitude for what the Government was agreeing to do for them. They were afraid, as who could blame them, of the terrible smallpox, and even more of the vanishing buffalo. Whatever this Big Bear meant — so he was no minor chief, so he spoke for perhaps eighty perhaps as many as a hundred lodges, six or eight hundred people out on the prairie — it was clear the Queen's will had to be laid down for him, once and for all. He gestured to Erasmus.

Governor Morris: "It was given us by The Great Spirit, man shall not shed his brother's blood, and it was spoken to us that he who sheds his brother's blood should have his own spilt. There can be only one law at a time; the law here now," he gestured behind him to the lined police, "is the Great Queen's. The good Indian needed to fear no Indian law; the good Indian now needs to fear no Queen's law. He will be safer than he ever has been for the redcoats are here to protect Indians and whites. Look at the Blackfoot Confederation. The American traders were taking their fur and giving them nothing — only whisky which, when they drank, they didn't know what they were doing. They stabbed their friends and sometimes killed their own children. Two years ago the Queen's redcoats came and punished those traders and sent them back where they belonged. Last summer the Blackfeet were able to buy two thousand horses with their robes, robes that before would have gone to the Americans for whisky. That is the way things are."

Big Bear: "I have said it. There is something that I dread. To feel the rope around my neck."

Governor Morris: "Why are you so anxious about bad men? The Queen's law punishes murder with death. No one changes that, not the Queen nor her Councillors. I cannot change that."

The chief's raised hand fell, his face lifted and he spoke directly to the Governor.

"I find something very bitter in my mouth; I cannot swallow it. Our tongues should be sweet today."

Governor Morris, smiling: "Mr. Christie has already handed out many sweet things! To those who made their marks, with all their families."

Big Bear: "There are many things left undone. It does not taste good to leave them like that."

Governor Morris: "Left undone! I don't know what is left undone!"

Big Bear: "I must see my people before I can say more."

Governor Morris: "Haven't the chiefs here told you the conditions of the treaty? They have. I have been here eight days and we have agreed on everything. The Cree are the principal tribe of plains Indians; this has been the fourth time that I have met my Cree brothers with a treaty in my hand. And standing here on this — uh, sitting — on this ground I cast my eyes to where the sun rises, down to the great lakes and I see a broad road leading from there to the Red River, I see it stretching on to Fort Ellice, I see it branching there, one to Qu'Appelle and Cypress Hills, the other to Carlton and on to here, Fort Pitt, and to Whitefish Lake and on into the far land of the Chipewyans. A broad road, and all along it I see the Governor and the commissioners of the Queen taking the Indian by the hand, saying, we are brothers, we will lift you up, we will teach you the cunning of the white man. All along the road I see Indians gathering, I see gardens growing and houses building. I see them receiving money from the Queen's commissioners, I see them enjoying their hunting and fishing as before, I see them living as they have always lived, but with the Queen's gift in addition. I met the Saulteaux at the North-west Angle, the Cree at Qu'Appelle, at Ellice, at Carlton, and now at Fort Pitt. They read my face and through that my heart, and said my words were true. They all gave me their hands on behalf of the Queen. What they did I wish you to do."

Big Bear spoke heavily into the long hush, "I am glad that we will be helped, so much. And always there is the land."

Governor Morris: "I am glad to see you thankful. And of course, the land —"

James McKay erupted into loud Cree: "The Willow People wanted to lend us the land for four years, but we aren't here to trade for land. We aren't buying land! We aren't here to make peace because we have never been at war! All we want is to protect you and your lands from the white settlers that are coming, who'll build houses in places you want to live yourselves. So we say, choose the places where you wish to live. They will be reserved to you forever. Otherwise, when the Queen's white children come no one will be happy."

Big Bear: "No one can choose for only himself a piece of the Mother Earth. She is. And she is for all that live, alike."

James McKay: "The Queen Mother must care for all her children, not only her red ones."

Big Bear: "The Governor says we will live as we have always lived. I have always lived on the Earth with my people, I have always moved as far as I wished to see. We take what the Earth gives us when we need anything, and we leave the rest for those who follow us. What can it mean, that I and my family will have a 'reserve of one square mile'? What is that?"

James McKay: "Since you are a chief and have a large family, you will receive land in proportion. All your band can receive land in one place."

Big Bear stared about his circle. "Who can receive land? From whom would he receive it?"

The question they had not spoken; which they had perhaps suppressed, or in the moments of excitement perhaps forgotten even in their endless discussions, wrote itself with a paint like hunger on every face. The land lay before them, shading with the seasons of sun and rain, overcast and snow, eternally variable and forever again the same. Who indeed could give it?

But the Governor nodded to McKay. The questions had always before been there, somewhere; perhaps never so sharply put but certainly lurking under all the little queries and bickerings, and once or twice even spoken aloud by some rash, some contrary nobody like that Saulteaux with no following who could momentarily look a month or year down the road. But the old chiefs knew; they were afraid for their people before surveyors, settlers, sickness, whisky traders — the Pacific railway was now halted in scandal but if anyone, anywhere, found a spot of gold on this river, the deluge was unstoppable by man or government or God himself — there was so obviously nothing these natives could do before such scourges, all as one impossible to their way of life. The old chiefs knew. Here there simply remained to do what had been done often before: be immovable, repeat everything once more in a good farewell speech. And shake hands. He arose, began again to say what he had long planned.

Governor Morris: "I wish Big Bear to tell Bobtail and the other headmen with him now on the plains, to tell them what has been done, that it is for them also, just as if they were here. Next year they and their people can join the treaty and they will lose nothing. Of the treaty. I wish you to understand, fully, and to tell the others. The North West Council is making a law that will protect the buffalo, and all men, Indian and white, will obey it. The Government will not interfere with the Indian's way of life, it will not bind him. We only wish to show you how to live from the soil, to make a living on the reserves. Your poor you must help yourselves, as we all do, and only when Providence should send a great famine or pestilence over all Indian people will the Queen help feed and clothe you. So it is with all the Queen's children. They must all work for their food.

"And now I have done. I," the Governor was turning to them all spread before him, smiling to say his last great words. But Big Bear still stood, and again with his naked arm high; the palm a black bar thrust into the flaming sun about to settle on the ridge. Erasmus gestured his quandry to the Governor, for the chief had spoken. The Governor hesitated; again the deep voice.

Big Bear: "I do not understand. What is this 'North West Council'?"

Governor Morris: "The Great Queen's highest councillors in these territories; they advise her on what laws must be made. They wear blue coats, as you see."

Big Bear was studying the blue-coated McKay, who suddenly smiled hugely.

James McKay: "There isn't a horse strong enough for me to run the buffalo now; I can only sit in a chair before a table, or in a special wagon I made for myself. And talk, certainly."

Big Bear spoke softly following the laughter that greeted the humour of friend and half-blood brother: "Ahh. You remember the great run we had once, south from Sounding Lake that carried us all day into Blackfoot country. The year the land was as if The Only One snowed buffalo."

James McKay: "The Company never had so much good pemmican."

The Governor stared from one to the other as Erasmus steadily translated; he said in an undertone, "My Honourable James, the sun is very low; campfires will suffice for that."

McKay gestured almost impatiently, not turning to the Governor for the chief had spoken again in the usual council tone.

Big Bear: "When the White Queen makes a law for the buffalo, it's good she has such a councillor. But I see only three blue coats; perhaps there should be a few more of them, since all," he lifted his head slightly to the hillside, "will have to obey this law. Whatever it is."

Governor Morris: "Oh. Of course the Councillors will consult with the chiefs before the buffalo law is passed. Of course."

Big Bear: "That I do not understand. Of course. I come from where my people hunt the buffalo and I am told that the treaty is such and such. I and my people have not heard what the treaty says and already nothing of it can be changed. It is already done, though we never heard of it. I told you what I wish. That there be no hanging."

Governor Morris: "What you say cannot be granted; why do you keep talking about bad men? The law is the same for red and white."

Big Bear: "That may be. But itself, it is only white."

There was a long pause.

Big Bear, softly: "I am glad we are to be helped, but why don't the chiefs speak?"

The Fish: "Sweetgrass has already spoken for us all."

Big Bear: "And when am I to speak for my people?"

Governor Morris: "You are doing so now."

Big Bear: "You must forgive me, I cannot seem to understand anything here. I have not spoken of anything this treaty speaks about. I have mentioned one very big matter, and another, and about these I have heard only that they will not be granted. These matters all go only one way. About the treaty as it is I have not been able to say anything yet."

The Governor allowed himself no look to heaven. He sighed and began again with careful, tireless diction, speaking sentences precisely and pausing at the end of each for interpretation.

Governor Morris: "The basic treaty as it stands is that which three years ago the Saulteaux and Swampy Cree accepted at the Northwest Angle. There were four thousand of them there, you are a handful compared to that, and after long deliberation it was good to them what I said and they made their marks. Two years ago the Cree and Saulteaux at Qu'Appelle agreed to it in Treaty Number Four, and last year the Swampy Cree and Saulteaux at Lake Winnipeg. And this summer we came to you with the same treaty, Number Six. It is the same as the others. We negotiated many days and added and changed some clauses at Fort Carlton, as Big Child and Star Blanket wished. Then they and Red Pheasant and the others and later also The Beardy, who at first had many objections too, made their marks. Now here at Pitt these chiefs have spoken. They have deliberated many days; they have asked the Reverend John McDougall and Peter Erasmus for advice. And then they have all signed. They all agree it is good."

Big Bear: "Star Blanket is a chief. Sweetgrass is a chief. I also am a chief."

Governor Morris: "The Queen has not and will not negotiate and change the conditions of the treaty with every single chief."

Big Bear: "The land is one for us all, so we must all talk and agree."

Governor Morris: "Yes. And I think you are not wiser than all your brothers."

The flag clicked noticeably against its pole; the hillside was bright, but long shadows were spreading up the river. The Governor continued:

"Whether you make your mark or not, the white men will come. Whether you take a reserve or not, white settlers will take land and the Queen Mother will say it is theirs. We can do no more, these words to which so many chiefs have set their marks, on this leather, are our last words. If you cannot give me your hand now, you may do so when you have spoken with your people, and it will be as if you had done it today. It will not be made hard for you."

While Erasmus translated the last sentence, Big Bear began to move in a sacred way; as if he held aloft the Pipestem, though his hands were empty; he did not even raise them where he stood. He turned full circle from the People seated on the north slope, then east to the rigid policemen and the Governor with his party, south to the People, and finally west to those on the hillside against the red sun. Before Sweetgrass his formal turn seemed to hesitate; then he completed the circle and sat down in his place. His robe was about his shoulders, he had become no more than a mound against the light. The Governor sighed, waited a moment for a possible word, anywhere, then began once more to end it.

Governor Morris: "And now I have done, I am going away. The country is very large; there is room for all. It is too large for one Governor and another will be sent in my place. I hope you will receive him as you have done me, that you will speak frankly to him and give him your confidence. He will live among you, already at the ford on the Battle River they are building a house for him, and for a judge to interpret the law also. All will be for the best.

"Indians of the prairie and forest, I bid you farewell. I do not expect to see you again, face to face. My heart is happy that you have listened to me, to the words I bring from the Great White Queen. When I return to my home beyond the great lakes I will often think of you and will rejoice in your prosperity. I ask God to bless you, and your children forever. Farewell."

The seated chiefs arose, a deep sound of agreement, of approbation spreading across the hill. They stepped forward, shaking hands, making short statements of satisfaction and farewell. When their circle was complete, Sweetgrass took the Governor's hand once more and lifted it high.

Sweetgrass: "O Great Spirit, our Master who has power and all things, I speak to you. Look on this parting. I beg good life for us all. I beg your blessing on us who are often hungry; who are often afraid; who do not understand. I beg for us all good life. As long as this earth stands and this river flows."

McKay signalled. The North West Mounted Police band quickly hoisted its instruments into position and, with a stagger, began 'God Save the Queen.' The whites stood rigid, the adult Indians respectfully motionless as always, but as the afternoon lengthened the children had begun to flit about between the seated People, quite ignored by them, and now they drew closer to the flagpole. Their eyes goggled at the strange contortions of the gold-stripes' faces, at the fantastic sounds blaring at them. They had heard these blasts at the end of every council, but they were too wild to recall clearly and they heard them again as for the first time. The children stared, openmouthed.

The sounds ended and the hillside spread, everywhere. After a time the Governor became aware again of Big Bear, still seated. He stood looking at the stubborn chief through the People walking, running between them; McKay and Christie stood at his shoulder. Suddenly Big Bear got up and faced them. Not a feather in his hair, nose one long blade, his face a pattern of lines powered together almost black by sun and wind. He was walking forward, holding out his open hand. Smiling, the Governor took a step.

Big Bear: "I am glad to meet you. I am alone and my River People are on the hunt; the buffalo come and People must follow. I do not throw back your hand, but I accept nothing. I am not a disobedient child. I will tell my people what I have heard here."

Governor Morris: "Yes, yes, very good, and you must all come next year, and it then will be as if you had done so this year. Yes. I have travelled over seven hundred miles already just to see you, and talked for many moons. The Queen and her Councillors in Ottawa want the very best for all their children."

Sweetgrass: "It is for the good of our children. I want to dig up a small piece of land to grow food. We should all do that."

As Erasmus translated for the Governor, Big Bear turned to Sweetgrass. And his hand rose to the sun, one gigantic red ball sliced through by the knobbly line of the ridge.

"My old women should have it ready now," he said, almost laughing. "Buffalo cow tongue, maybe a few humps."

"Ah-h-h," sighed Sweetgrass. "Yes. Yes."

They were walking away, leaving the Governor and his party at the foot of the crooked flagpole. Through the indistinguishable black shapes of their people riding, running across the slopes and benches of hillside, they were walking slowly on the shoulder of the hill together.

III

John McDougall: The Holy Scriptures say it is the fool who multiplies words without knowledge.

Mention the treaty and there is no end of such words, from "lazy savages, given our money every year," to "everything they had, how could you take part in that, John McDougall?" Let me tell you, my father spent his life on the Methodist mission frontiers of the north, first in Canada, then in Manitoba, and finally in the North West where he died. I, his eldest, was child among the Ojibway and Saulteaux, youth among Swampy and Wood Cree, and man among the Plains Cree. In 1873 my brother David (the trader, he had no calling to the Church) and I built Morley Mission for the Mountain Stoneys on the border of the Blackfoot country where not even the Hudson's Bay Company had dared establish a permanent post. From Edmonton House on the North Saskatchewan to Fort Benton on the Missouri, five hundred miles as a bird flies over grass and rivers, there was exactly one other white habitation, the mission of the Roman Catholic Scollen (American whisky runners are neither white nor red; they are Abomination). I have ridden fifty miles in a forenoon and been as ready for as many more after; I have slept through blizzards with little beyond a blanket about my shoulders and a low fire at my feet. If my rides for supplies from Victoria Mission to Red River or from Morley to Fort Benton sound unbelievable even to the police, who laboured over these trails themselves, how can I help it? Every day of my life I have thanked God in my prayers for the body He gave me. So when I hear words about the Indian treaties, I take a long look at where they come from.

Has he ever tried to swallow buffalo liver steaming from the carcass, and sprinkled with gall for taste? Has he ever tried to translate a single word into another language? What would he do with "treason," with "the Queen, her crown and dignity" among a people who have no concept of state and even if they had could not imagine a woman having state dignity, much less a crown, whatever that might be?

Everyone knows everything that should have been said, now.

Let me tell you, in June of 1874, when my brother and I returned from two months and nine hundred miles of ox trail to Fort Benton for supplies we found that our father had arrived with a letter from the Canadian government asking me to explain the coming of the Mounted Police to the plains tribes. The police would set out from Fort Dufferin in early July. I arrived home at midnight; by noon the next day I was riding for the commission instructions two hundred and twenty miles away in Edmonton. I have been in the North West since 1862 and as far as I know no Ottawa politician has ever understood travel on the plains.

No one who has not had the experience can understand what horses fed on southern Alberta grass can accomplish, if ridden properly. In hardly a week I was back and immediately with the Stony chief Bearspaw I departed for the plains. Not even when the smallpox cut down over half the Blackfoot had the Plains Cree been able to conquer the confederacy, though in 1870 they tried at the Belly River, the biggest Indian battle ever to take place on the Canadian plains. But what no other Indian could do with bow or gun the Americans without a thought had done with the bottle. All the plains chiefs understood now; only white men could protect them from the American whisky runners; the chiefs listened. But there were always the savage young men astride their beautiful horses. They wanted glory.

David had to return to Fort Benton for more supplies and our wives and children were again alone above the Bow. I had been gone forty days when I met the last small party of Bloods in the border country. I finished the final arrangements for the return trip with my companions and, instead of sleeping, took two horses and rode north alone that very evening. At midnight I crossed the ford of the old north trail where Fort

Macleod now stands. The early autumn moon was almost full and the plains to my right, the humped-up foothills to my left came to me in a glow as if a silver mist were drifting down upon me from heaven itself. Out of the morning lightness the sun slid up like a bloody stone; it left exactly the same colour edging the snow on the mountains as I rode over the last foothill and saw our fort below. What a joyous evening! One hundred and forty miles of trail in twenty-four hours' riding.

Each family had a two-room area within the fort, but while we men were gone all lived together. My Elizabeth told me that only the evening before two Siksika men burst in at our door after the children were asleep. Both were gruesomely painted, and armed, and our dear wives were numb with fear. They had only a breech-loading shotgun I had left for bird shooting and of course they had no thought to try and use it. After a moment Mrs. David began to sing "All Hail the Power of Jesus Name," and then it came to my wife she should slip away and get our Stony cook who could speak Blackfoot. "I don't know how many times I sang that one verse," Mrs. David laughed, though she shivered still. "It was all I could remember, and they walked around me, looking, but didn't touch anything." When the women came back our cook persuaded the men to leave, but no one in the fort had slept that night any more than I on the trail.

Who could doubt why I had suddenly felt I should ride through the night? We read Psalm 121 together and I was in the midst of prayer when the outer gate creaked. I was barely up from my knees when our door burst open. In the flare of light from the kitchen fire all we could see was rifles and paint.

I turned my back to them, reached for the candle and deliberately bent down and lit it at the fire. Then I turned and went to the door. Their leader had taken one step in at the door and still stood in exactly the same position. When I lifted the light I knew why he had stopped so suddenly; not five days before that I had been in his camp on the plains a hundred and fifty miles east and from there, as he knew very well, I had travelled south with my party. Now here I was.

"Come," I said in Blackfoot, and gestured. Holding their guns carefully they crowded in; there were twelve of them — I would have hoped not quite so many — and they sat down on the ground all about the three walls of our kitchen. My wife and Mrs. David had risen and sat in their chairs before the fire, but from their expressions I do not think they would have been able to walk into the next room where the children slept, even had I ordered them. No more than any other Indians are Siksika warriors cold-blooded murderers; now that nothing had happened the instant they entered there was, I knew, some chance for hope. But several had short handguns, and two repeating Winchesters.

I placed the candle in its holder on the table and sat down beside my wife's feet, more or less in their circle. Beyond a few words I speak no Blackfoot, and they knew that too. There was silence. They looked at me and I looked at them.

Suddenly one spoke, in Cree, "When did you come?"

"Just now."

The speaker said something to the leader who, after a further moment staring at me, murmured back.

"He asks," said the Cree speaker, "when do you sleep?"

"When there is time."

And I laughed as I said it, without a trace of humour. God knows I felt it for an instant stronger than ever before, though I never mentioned it to my father and all the years I worked with him I do not know if he ever felt it, what these squatting men had reason enough to feel towards us. They never rode over the country like I; they had no empires to organize. You may believe me that as I sat there, the touch of my wife's foot bringing me the tremor of her body and the firelight glazing those, other, fantastic bodies and slowly the smell gathered of horses and sweat and buffalo grease and a distant tinge of wildness, almost as of sweetgrass crushed under running horses' hooves, and it seemed I was again riding the North Trail which Bring Down The Sun told me all Indian peoples had made when they first came from the north more generations past than he could know: there was the land, beautiful immensity. And I remembered Captain William Butler. On his official tour of inspection in 1870 he told my father: "It is humiliating to an Englishman that so fine a country should be totally neglected."

Believe me I am not one to let my mind wander, especially when surrounded, but the dark sullen face I saw so close now behind the ochre streaks, so much closer than at the camp where he was a minor councillor and had not condescended to get off his horse to hear what he already knew I had told more than enough of his people, such a face and such a body hewn down as only a horse and wind can hew them on the open prairie, I could not but love him for that he must and would forever hate me.

Into that long silence after my little laugh the door again opened. Doors are bother enough for Indians, leave alone the whiteness of knocking. In the darkness there stood five Stoneys. They stopped on the threshold when they saw the Siksikas and for a time they looked at the guns, the breech-clouts tied tight for action. I got up.

"We saw you ride over the hill, John," Chiniki said. All Indians call me by my first name.

"You're welcome," I said, though for a moment I could

have wished them far away. The Siksikas began to lean their guns against the wall; my Elizabeth reached forward and swung the kettle over the fire. "We were all just going to have tea," I said.

Believe me, that was exactly the problem. Something as supposedly innocent as tea. It strengthens you so much better than water. Or tobacco; it tastes so much better than the inside scrapings of willow bark. Or steel knives. Or horses; how can they be compared to dogs? Guns were never anything but a curse to the prairie peoples; they would have been useful for stalking but with a good horse to run buffalo the old ball-and-powder flintlocks were incredibly dangerous during a flat-out gallop. A man with a bow could put three arrows behind a running shoulder in the time one with a gun could perhaps get off a single shot that might as easily blow off his hand as knock over the beast. The Sharps rifle, that could kill buffalo up to distances of a mile and so made running them obsolete, barely reached the Canadian Indians before the herds were wiped out. They needed guns for nothing except to more conveniently kill each other. Or whites. And of course, human nature being what it is, such convenience becomes very shortly the greatest necessity of all.

So what can anyone, Big Bear included, think I would say at the treaty at Fort Pitt in 1876? The Cree had always treated the white man as a brother, they intermarried and lived together, but the Blackfoot confederacy for centuries hated whites as halfgods, halfdevils capable of any good or evil they wilfully chose to visit upon them and so to be feared, flattered, or killed as possible. And now the words I gave them about the police had proven true; the traders had fled, the police were absolutely just. They had found Commissioner Macleod so admirable that Bullhead, giant and often drunk chief of the Sarcees, gave him his own name, and the place where headquarters was built quickly changed names from "The-place-where-the-north-trail-crosses-Oldman-River" to "The-place-where-Bullhead-lives." The prayers that concluded every meeting I had with the prairie bands in 1874 — they prayed in their fashion as fervently as I; most whites find it impossible to imagine how deeply every Indian action is rooted in his, albeit almost completely false and most tragically limited, faith in The Great Spirit — were so movingly answered. The Queen's law had come, what could I say?

Acting both for the Canadian government and the church, my father had instructed me to attend the treaty. They found his body on Sunday, February 6, 1876; on Saturday, April 29 my son, whom we named after him, was born; in accordance with the treaty timetable sent me, I was at Fort Carlton in late July. After waiting a week, the message came that the commissioners would be one month delayed. Chief Bearspaw of the Stoneys was with me and I wanted very much for him to understand about the treaty with the Crees but now there was nothing for it but return to Edmonton and return later. Bearspaw rode back six hundred and sixty miles, while I could come only to treaty for the upper river bands at Fort Pitt. When I arrived September 2, on the hills and along creek ravines stood the lodges of at least one thousand Cree. Perhaps a thousand more could have been there, and those the most savage who lived on nothing but buffalo and Blackfoot raids, the ones with Big Bear who most needed the highest official explanations, but governments never explain their delays. The final results of this one were seen in 1885.

The first man I met in that teeming camp was Peter Erasmus. Big Child and Star Blanket, Peter told me, had their sons track him far south on the plains where he with James Seenum's band was on the buffalo hunt; they wanted him to interpret for them at the Carlton treaty. (That was Peter's last buffalo running, but neither of us dreamt it at the time.) Governor Morris had declared that the government paid for translation, but Big Child insisted that either they paid for their own man, to give them the words personally, or there would be no talk. The commissioners could hardly like that, especially gigantic James McKay who was half Cree himself, but they had to agree. And when I heard Peter make intelligible that official English, I doubted I could have done better myself.

But I prepared myself. I made careful note of all the Governor said and on September 8 when a messenger came to my tent, asking me to come to the Indian council, I was ready with a prayer on my lips. They asked me to sit between Sweetgrass and James Seenum. (Big Bear was quite wrong when he said I had baptized Seenum; he was baptized a Methodist by the Reverend Henry Bird Steinhauer, our Ojibway missionary to the Cree and who was father to my first wife Abigail.) Beside Seenum sat Peter, and I knew he had already been explaining for more than a day. Rarely, not even the many times I have preached the Gospel, have I felt such a weight upon me as I did then, looking around the motionless faces of that dark council tent.

Sweetgrass had loved my father. My father often said that Indians baptized as Papists usually showed only the best and rarely any of the worst qualities of that sad heresy. So it was with Sweetgrass, or Abraham if you will, who smiled and said,

"Two summers ago this young man came to tell us of the coming police. Everything he told us was true. Last summer his father told us of the one who speaks for the Queen Mother who would come to deal with us justly; that no more poles would be put in the ground or land measured before he came to deal with us. And now the Governor is here; yesterday we heard what he had to say. This young man's father is no longer here to counsel us, but him I know as one white man who has an Indian heart. Peter Erasmus has told us what happened at Carlton; I want John to tell us in his words what has been said here so we can fully understand."

I thanked Sweetgrass and his council for their confidence, then I began. Since Her Majesty desired to open for settlement the territory they now roamed, she wished them to consign that territory to her and her successors, forever, on the following conditions:

Her Majesty agreed to set aside reserves of land for them in a ratio of one square mile for each five-member family; to maintain schools if they desired; not to deprive them of their habitual hunting rights; to distribute monies of five dollars per person every year, with fifteen dollars for each councillor and twenty-five dollars for each chief; to provide ammunition and twine for nets every year to a sum of fifteen hundred dollars; to supply each Indian agent with a medicine chest; to provide each family working at cultivation with four hoes, two spades, two scythes and one whetstone, two hayforks and two reaping-hooks, two axes, one cross-cut saw, one handsaw, one pit saw and the necessary files; also one plow for every three families, and to each chief, for the use of his band, one chest of carpenter's tools. Further, to supply each band with enough wheat, barley, potatoes and oats to seed the land actually broken, as well as four oxen, one bull and six cows, one boar and two sows, and one handmill when the band had sufficient grain. Each chief should receive also, every three years, a suit of clothing; also on signing the treaty, a flag and a medal, and as soon as convenient, one horse, harness and wagon. Finally, should pestilence or general famine overtake any band, the

Queen, on being satisfied of the same by her Indian agent, would relieve that calamity with all due speed. On their part, the Indians agreed to choose their reserves and behave themselves according to Her law, as good and loyal subjects of Her Majesty the Queen.

Sweetgrass then put out his hand, to my shoulder. "I thank you John," he said, "for every word. When you speak, I hear my own voice, and I want you all to hear his words this way. Now John my grandson, I have one hard thing to ask you."

I would not have thought that old, old man would have had such strength in the hand that tightened on my shoulder. Believe me, within my heart I praised God for the confidence that he, at that time praised by the Hudson's Bay Company as the wisest of the Plains Cree chiefs — "when you speak I hear my own voice" — the incredible confidence he placed in me. But Sweetgrass knew I had never acted in any other way than was consistent with a minister of the Methodist Church. A Canadian patriot and loyal to my Queen. Who could know that within nine years I would stand on that very spot and see Fort Pitt devastated? Stand there as chief guide and chaplain to the Canadian troops pursuing the Plains Cree who had wrought the devastation? Some of whom sat there motionless, facing us in that very tent. The heart of a policeman dried on a stake. Who could know? But was not the dread of that in us both — in how many seated there — as his grip tightened? Yet what word could he expect. Or Big Bear. To such a question.

"I want you to go further," Sweetgrass said in his mellow voice, "and forget you are a white man. You are one of us. You understand every word and you are one of us. John my grandson, what do you say?"

The winter before, before Christmas 1875, I was out for over two weeks on the plains and saw not one single buffalo.

Our hunting party faced starvation, and David and I rode sixty miles into a blizzard one day to reach Morley and send back supplies to the rest. For New Year 1876, my father and mother returned from the Highwood River where they had been visiting the Siksika; he told me he had expansion plans for another mission that spring and also that the buffalo were coming up country between the Bow and the Red Deer. Shortly after New Year's I began preparations for a fresh meat hunt. The weather grew steadily colder and I was so short of men that father would have to help. We left Tuesday, January 18. Father drove a four-horse team on the bobsled, my cousin Mose and I followed with a string of single horse sleds and leading the buffalo-runners. Hector, a Stony, joined us with a sled next day.

By Friday we were only half loaded and, since the buffalo were moving steadily to the hills, we left the prairie and camped by a knob on Nose Creek where there was shelter and wood. On Sunday we rested, as always, and could see from our lookout the herds moving westward. Monday morning we were up in the leaden daylight — there was no sunrise — and though I immediately located a small group of buffalo, my unshod horse refused to run on ground frozen glassy between drifts. I picked a fine farrow cow and, from one knee, knocked her down with a long shot. I straightened her for skinning, waved to Hector and tried my second runner. He ran, but slipped badly on his first turn and I just had time to get my leg up as we crashed down. By the time Hector came up, and my father too, I could hobble about. They tried to deter me but I had one more plan. On one sled was Tom, old now but in his prime a fine buffalo horse. I went back and unhitched him; when I looked out, another small herd had come over the rise. Tom started with a will; though we had another fall, it was not so severe and soon I had five more good cows scattered over the plateau. That was enough, it was very cold and we had to skin fast. There was barely light left and I remember we only had five small biscuits to eat. Father insisted I have three; I would not have it so finally he broke the odd one in two. It was long after dark when we were loaded, and we were about eight miles from camp.

There are certain things never to be washed from the memory. Over the ground, snow ran in drifts before the wind but overhead the stars shone bright as ice. Hector was leading, the four single horses and their sleds followed, with me on the last. My father rode beside me, sometimes he dismounted and walked. We thanked God for the day; we talked of the future. My father was especially happy about the orphanage he planned to begin that spring because only if we began our teaching with infants could we ever, ultimately, win over their race from its red heathenism. At the top of a long hill, about two miles from camp, we gave the sled horses the run and I was parted from him for some time. We crossed the frozen creek and began the long incline when he galloped up beside me.

"I will go ahead," my father said. "See about Mose and get supper started for when you come." He pointed ahead to a bright star. "That star is right over our camp, John," he said.

I looked up, and answered, "Yes, Father."

And he rode on up the hill into the darkness.

That was the night of Monday, January 24. On Friday we found his horse; saddled, trailing the lariat rope. It was Sunday, February 6, after ten days of search by every man in the area, including the entire Mounted Police post at Fort Calgary, that his frozen body was found. A halfblood not with us came upon it while chasing a buffalo, put it on his sled and brought it to our camp. I lifted the blanket. His face was perfectly natural. It seemed to hold an expression of conscious satisfaction.

When he felt death upon him, he had found a level spot and properly laid himself out, limbs straight and hands folded up on his breast.

A man called Shaw had brought about seven hundred cattle through the mountains from Columbia Lakes that fall, 1875. These laid the foundation for Alberta's ranching industry. He was wintering them on the Bow and in late February when we again had to ride for buffalo, Shaw rode beside me and said:

"John, your father's gone. You surely won't remain in missionary work any longer. This land's all empty, look at it. I see nothing but progress here from now on, so let's work together in the stock business, you on this side of the mountains and I on the other. I'll give you half my stock, right now, so we can start on an equal basis. What do you say?"

We were at the base of a long hill, on the top of which stood a great rock like a sentinel. I galloped up the hill and, with some difficulty, climbed the rock. There, stretched at full length, lay the body of a man wrapped in buffalo leather. The space was so narrow I could only stand with one foot on either side of the dead warrior and out over the land, black on the fierce white snow, I could see a few, solitary, buffalo.

Sweetgrass. Shaw. Big Bear. How could anyone not a fool expect me to say anything else? The answers were different, but truly they were exactly the same. Who can not know there was only one word I could say? That I had to feel a deep satisfaction when I had spoken it?

IV

"Come my grandchildren," the voice of an old man chanted over the camp, penetrating in the smoke-ravelled air, "come with me, Sun is going to sleep."

Gradually, from among the lodges, the bushes and across the face of the hill children began to materialize running, running towards Red Bone calling them. Big Bear paused outside the circle of his camp; not even the meat smell could hold them, the children of the River People as intense and silent in their running as the animals they had been stalking in play, many five and six years old but none seven or eight or nine. The White Sickness, yes. He had come to his own father's voice once, calling those same words up hills bare as women's breasts above Jackfish Lake, and his father's voice came to him small and naked, *All living has soul and the greatest of all living is Sun. It is good to pay respect when he comes back to the circle of Earth to rest.* Trying, it would not come to him when he had last thought of his father's words; they were air, ground he found under his feet when he awoke, but watching a tiny boy trundle steadily through trampled grass toward the sound leading to some sandy hill among the trees — Horsechild, his youngest son under the crust of dusty mud — he felt sadness rise like mist about his knees.

"But it's a good sadness," he said aloud to Lone Man, who had come up beside him. "Knowing."

His tall son-in-law looked at him; whatever it was, it was not the immovable, sodden heaviness everyone felt facing whites. Lone Man turned slightly to the pole below them where the flag was gliding down, into the red and gold cluster.

"Talking to them," Big Bear said, "the medicine is always bad."

Lone Man said, "Maybe somewhere a sickness would find itself that would kill them all here and then they wouldn't come anymore."

Big Bear laughed aloud. "That would be a sweet medicine! River People don't have it of themselves."

"Like Whiteskins," Lone Man muttered.

"Let's eat," said Big Bear, and on that sweet turn they entered the ring and walked towards the chief's lodge set in its centre. Steadily through the evening life of women, dogs, children, through the air thick with stench and cooking and meat-drying fires. A bay horse tethered by the central lodge hunched together and staled as they came by; they both stopped. Their eyes moved over the strained, beautiful flanks of the mare.

"Yes," Big Bear said after a moment. "She does that too much. Something's poisoned in her."

Lone Man nodded; he fingered his hand gently across the mare's haunches, now relaxed. On the first raid after he had married Nowak-keetch he had presented Big Bear with a Siksika scalp; that was the only reason he could talk to him at all, and it was impossible to question him, certainly about a horse. He said merely, "It's too bad."

"Yes," said Big Bear again, as if they both did not know that every time the mare was in heat he tied her to his tent peg and allowed no horse near her. It almost drove the stallions mad; as if his riding a mare, fast though she was, were not inexplicable enough. "And now she has worms," he toed aside some droppings. Long white strands twitched in the falling light. "I've given her to my oldest woman. She'll dig anything out of her, good."

Lone Man's face remained immovable. Big Bear did that almost every day, deliberately make jokes which were impossible for some person to laugh at. Lone Man had never spoken of or to Root Grubbing Woman, his mother-in-law, and he never would; he never so much as thought of her, as was proper, and it occurred to him that Big Bear had at this moment decided to give the mare to his oldest living wife just to force him to do so. Even if it meant he himself had no horse whatever. As it did. Lone Man kicked a white dog aside and pulled back the lodge flap; Big Bear bent to enter, and he followed.

Into the coned warmth of the lodge, a thick weighed darkness of roasting meat and women and firelight and fur; soft darkness of leather and people sweat; darkness moving like raw yearling buffalo hung headless, turning in the complete circle of living and solid sweet immovable and ever changing Earth; darkness of fat's slip and dripping, of birch bark curling light, a darkness soft in flares of burning blood like the raw heat of woman tunnelled and spent for love.

"Good liver," said Sweetgrass.

The only sounds were of fat's burn, and eating. Teeth against bone, meat tearing, breath rasping through nostrils, teeth in meat, lips and tongues and throats sucking, teeth against teeth. Meat chunks continued to drop from the gleaming carcass turning softly lower, knives above greased arms reaching from the round smoky dark. Slabs of hump, of ribs, of haunch. The soft mound of woman rounded about a black kettle at the edge of the fire, and sound the orange bright flash of fat and of eating, tea slurped through a broken tooth.

"Good testicle," said Seenum.

Two hands move in the orange darkness. *Mus-toos-wuk!* Sounds die as the flat left hand sweeps through dark to dark: the herd as wide as the horizon. Another wave, slightly rippled now, and the buffalo are in motion, soon grumble like a thunderroll over the undulating land. A bobbing right arm: the rider. The bobbing arm gains gradually, cleaves down, stiff; and the herd parts as the hands separate and again the left hand is the herd, the right the rider running, running over the rippled land. The right thumb rises up, turning as the hunter reconnoitres, chooses the best cow, then the left hand extends as one clumsy beast humpling along, curving slightly left as the right, more pointed now with the thumb flat along its top, drives nearer; always nearer. The two hands bound side by side, one humped, one arrowlike but running as one so close they seem to kiss in the smoking air. Right eases back, left forward as if to cut in front and 'Pssst!' Left hand is a fist tumbling over and over to sink at last shuddering motionless and right has already wheeled away, thumb high and waving. Slowly from the left again rises the flat hand, undulating, and in an instant right has flattened once more, scooped through a hollow and up towards that smoking orange horizon. Moving together inevitably, deadly.

"Good run," said Big Bear.

Kingbird sat at the entrance so it was easy to slip out of his father's lodge. The moon was still down but soon there would be more light than the stars only. The lodge glowed from inside; the patterns of seated men and the dangling bones which were all that remained of the yearling played on the worn leather. Without a shared coup to his credit — he hadn't even made a buffalo run — he should hardly have been inside with that company but any time he could edge in Running Second could always get him something to eat. Never enough. He could not remember having enough to eat in all his fifteen years; when the camp had meat he ate until he fell asleep and when he awoke he was hungry again. That was normal, like everyone else he knew. He had to get a runner.

The white dog he had kicked aside was looking back, draggle-tailed, from the protection of dim distance. He bent as if to his moccasin, found a clod at his feet and in one motion threw it. It splattered, but the sound was enough to send the dog slinking. For a moment, strangely, nothing seemed to move among the lodges, the small fires barely greying up into darkness, the lodgepoles crossed like many-legged fumbled Xs around the bend of whitening sky. Kingbird followed the dog, but it wasn't there; his father's bundle hung on its tripod, facing Thunderbird painted on the back of the lodge: the darkness moved, lifting its head and the mare nickered. He was around the bundle, beside her, rubbing her ears. She nuzzled him and slobbered softly against the naked skin of his belly. A beautiful horse; and he had heard in the indefinable movement of information that was any band's camp that his father had now given her to Root Grubbing Woman. His old half-mother wouldn't do anything but make another travois beast of her; now if his father had given her to Running Second there would have been no question of demeaning her to dragging baggage. She would have been his by morning, she'd have been bred by evening and after — he could have traded — but his thoughts stopped there. At the moment he could not have thought of questioning what his father had done but if a reason were needed, as it was not, he might have thought of one why Running Second had no travois horse and the older wife now two. And Root Grubbing Woman's son Little Bad Man laughed at him already, more than enough.

Kingbird liked the mare's lips on his skin; he liked her warmth, the press of her teeth against him. He rubbed his right hand along under her mane, down her neck and shoulder to her chest. Muscles flowed under her hide like a hard slipping river. Her skin fluttered as his hand brushed down her leg; there was a crusted cut inside her knee. Gently he nudged around it and she stood, patient to him. He took the piece of buffalo fat he was sucking out of his mouth, ran it gently over the crusted blood; worked it slowly until the wound was soft, coated with fat. Down beside her knee and chewing again, tasting faintly her blood and sweat, he could look along the level of the ground at spruce beyond the lodgepoles sticking into the sky; shadows flickered on walls, flames, but the lodge at his back sounded only slurping tea. Above him hung the great barrel of the horse's belly, breathing, her lips against his neck. He lifted himself erect slowly, his left hand along her back to her loin, his right gently up the curve of her belly, back between her hind legs. His hand could sense the warmth of them before he touched them, a firm warmth like brushing against his mother, and then his fingertips touched her teat and her nose bumped, bumped on his buttocks. Not hard; like nudging her colt, so he lifted his hand under her again. This time her teeth and he stepped back. Rubbed himself, feeling the line of her teeth on his arm, laughing at her silently, his left hand still up along her loin. The grey stallion had often been tethered like this beside the lodge and as a little boy he had discovered that if he touched the dangling penis the horse suddenly became perfectly quiet. His father appeared behind him once while he was feathering softly down that great swinging rod, "A little better than nothing," he had said, laughing aloud. A Blood had the stallion now, if he was still alive. His father had given him to a warrior rubbed out on his first raid.

Good, good, his eyes and his hand on her loins had been telling the mare, so that's not where it's right, good, so wait, we'll get there. His right hand slipped round against the back of her hind leg, burrowed slightly and rubbed down with the hair, then, lifted and rubbed down gently again. Each movement brought him a little higher, a little further around up her flank, his rub widening as it rose to include gradually his whole right hand down her smoothed hair, her giving muscle, while his left slid up over the curve of her loins and down. Gently, slowly he felt the tension build in him like a bow bending to the pull; his whole body drawing forward into the anticipation of his hands as they gradually and unceasingly moved and he felt the mare as if broadening under his left hand, seeming to lower herself and spread wider, slacker till the muscles under her skin seemed to shimmer over blood singing as his right hand moved ever higher; up under the tail he felt lifted to him. Lightly down the inner fold of her, and then he brushed her at her soft root. She stood rigid, shimmering, and under his left hand lowered still, widened immensely down and apart as his left hand circled, cupped the thick smooth base of her tail, down as if she planted and set herself down into the very earth; while his right hand brushed softly over her drooping centre, spongy and warm and pursed against his shivering fingers. His left arm was rammed, holding him stiff against the ferocious pressure jamming higher in him; held him hung over something bottomless, aching as if viced between his shoulder and the mare's rigid tail. Then his right fingers brushed a damp fold, slipped, and his left arm collapsed, he fell through it as if split, his right plunging by a membrane with a brush softer than sweetgrass down into a hot, boundless, swirling swamp. The mare screamed brilliantly.

A spruce branch stripped savagely over his face before he realized he was running.

Kingbird collapsed against the spruce, bounced, slid aside and fell flat, laughing. In complete silence he lay on the needled ground, his blood pounded wildly on in his soundless laughing. From all around the hills and the flat below by the fort stallions were answering the mare's cry; if someone had been drowsing off over his tea that would have pulled him up again, stiff. Or anyone else in the valley. The tree above him moved, he rolled over and a spray of stars peered through the shadows above him. The ground was good, scratchy and soft on his neck with the smell of needles and roots and the flared brilliance of the mare over his right hand and his legs and belly had flowed away like warm water. He stretched his arms out above him, against the moving branches; Matoose would be with the horses, what a thing to tell him. His arms collapsed across his face as the tree's murmur faded and he was asleep.

But awake instantaneously at the sound, his hand on the knife in his belt but otherwise motionless. The rim of sky was brighter now; the slur of bushes in the rising wind, it wasn't that. As he listened, sorting noises, waiting for that trigger-sound again, he slowly gathered his body together so that when he heard his feet were under him, he was moving toward it, crouched, moccasins soundless on the spongy moss there. His face relaxed, smiling, because there was only one person in the camp who grunted like that.

But when Kingbird crept near the small opening among the spruce he could not understand what he saw. The wide, solid outline of the half-brother was unmistakable, but he seemed low, and jerking, as if ramming himself unsuccessfully upwards against the night sky. Slowly Little Bad Man's great chest and head tilted forward, still heaving, where his arms reached and then Kingbird saw a shape on the ground over which he was curled, thrusting against. In the ground darkness Kingbird could recognize nothing; such a seeming shape as he slowly distinguished under that big body, clamped to it by those arms. Kingbird was only seeing, eyes all his concentrated senses; he balanced on the tip of comprehension, rocking on his hocks, when like an axe-blow the man's drumming rhythm broke with a final grunt snorting through his nose and he toppled aside. For a long moment there was the dark mound of them there, and the slowing saw of breath. It was only when Little Bad Man stood up, stretched and vanished without a sound, seemingly without even a motion, that Kingbird realized his half-brother had been mounting a woman kneeling as if he were a stallion.

He knew it was a woman for he could now see her skirt pulled up far beyond her laced moccasins. He watched from his cover; her breathing softened until he could no longer hear it, and she lay quite motionless. After a moment he crept forward. She lay as in the bend of her kneeling, simply toppled on her side, her legs fallen tight together with her leather skirt still crumpled up high on her buttocks behind. Her arms splayed as if she had abandoned them; her face down in the dirt, away. But he knew who she was by the porcupine quill tie, her hair; tomorrow Little Bad Man might add her to his lodge, if he had liked her. Leaning barely an arm-length away, Kingbird found himself wondering very strangely whether the girl had felt what happened to her. She lay as if it made no difference whatever, breathing quietly, perhaps asleep against the ground. Why hadn't she carried her knife? Her thighs gleamed, he had only to pull them up — his hand lifted, hesitated, then curled around to touch — the smell of the mare pricked him. He leaped and ran. Between trees and bushes to the slough where Matoose herded the horses, cutting through bushes like the leap of his heart, silently laughing.

In the central lodge the rows of men were still seated about the fire. Big Bear's long pipe was deliberately moving the circles now; the great leather pouch of tobacco Sweetgrass had brought would last several rounds. Some men had left when the buffalo was finished, but more kept coming in the door opposite. Big Bear knew them all and he did not think of them now. At the head of the fire, his wives gone and an old server tending fire and tea kettle, he was content to sit with his robe thrown back and his eyes shut; to smell his friends about him, smoking, breathing in the thick smoky air of the lodge. Drinking black tea. He sat gratefully thoughtless, almost dozing.

A sudden shuffle roused him; beyond the fire someone stood. Shouting, "I smoke no woman's tobacco!"

Big Bear squinted a little, then closed his eyes again. He had seen the pipebowl leaping at the edges of the smoke and from the voice knew very well what his nephew looked like as he waved it. He never hesitated to speak in council and always with the same violent, very changeable absoluteness. Though this was no council and no one would make it one. Big Bear opened his eyes to Sweetgrass; said carefully loud,

"I'm always happy when a buffalo presents himself. I have never asked where he comes from."

Sweetgrass had already swallowed the woman insult. His red coat was gone and he sat in the folds of a new red and white blanket smelling of Company with the big silver medal where his stomach turned from his chest; he kept facing outward the side with the sunrise behind a commissioner shaking an Indian's hand, the crown and sharp nose of Victoria Regina against his skin. The gifts of friends, like the gifts of The Spirit, were simply accepted with gratitude; sometimes some friends were other friends' enemies: these were life matters certain young people, even those with three or four wives, sometimes found it convenient not to understand. Sometimes chiefs found that convenient, too; he understood. There was a small scuffling as Little Poplar stepped between the Worthy Young Men, the lodge clapped with his exit.

"I hate!"

Only the sigh of tea, of smoke savoured and slowly exhaled. The old server pushed coals together and laid sticks in precise patterns about the kettle. Soon the fire awoke again and the faces in the lodge gleamed as if rising up shining out of darkness. Big Bear lifted his head then but after one swift glance around he closed his eyes. The power of that word stood on their faces as if each had spoken, long and carefully, and the warmth from the fire lapped against his slightly sweating skin like those thoughts, nudging and nudging him. That one word suspended, turning. He did not know who would reach out with the next, but silence lay in him like a sodden lump. For a moment it seemed he should still be young and seated across from his chief at this eating and he simply stood up and followed that one word out and with it rode south to the hunters. The moon was rising, under the mare's delicate hoofs the plains were washed incandescent. The band followed; a very much larger band than had forded the river that morning. He had no horse.

His hand touched a tiny foot. Horsechild had eaten until he fell asleep, slumped down behind him on the robes. His face must be creased against the willow backrest. As he gathered this from his son's foot in his hand, Big Bear heard The Fish on his left clear his throat; begin to speak in Chipewyan. He had to open his eyes; the signs for Sioux and Cheyenne, pointing south. He closed his eyes again and after a time Lone Man said,

"The Cheyenne and the Sioux killed many Bluecoats in the time the eggs are hatching. They rubbed out hundreds, every one of them on a hill by the Little Bighorn, south of the Missouri. You've heard this."

The Fish signed agreement, adding, "We heard nothing after that."

Lone Man said, "Little Pine has heard more."

Big Bear looked across a quarter of the circle to his old friend. Little Pine was one with him of the Battle River People, but he hunted only the plains. Often he took his band far south, sometimes to hunt with his brother-in-law Piapot and the Young Dogs and Assiniboine around Wood Mountain, sometimes beyond the rim of the Blood country by the Cypress Hills, fighting and stealing horses there, down to the

Missouri where he had seen fire-boats huger than three Company York boats piled man-high with whisky barrels churning up against the river spouting smoke. When he heard of the treaty his band had come north, but he had left them all on the hunt with many of Big Bear's band near the Neutral Hills and alone had come north to see. He would not sit in the chiefs' circle before the White Queen's flag; he sat up the hill, his seamed warrior face black. He had not said a word since they forded the river below Pitt. And suddenly Big Bear knew he wanted to hear his voice, very much.

But Little Pine said nothing still; he kept his head, set with four eagle feathers, down. Only his hands lifted and he made several swift signs.

"If they killed all those soldiers," signed The Fish, "why are they running?"

Little Pine sat motionless. Sweetgrass said,

"You remember our great chief Broken Arm from the Peace Hills, everyone under the Sun knew him. The Bluecoats once invited him to their main camp very far away, farther away than the big lakes, far by the Stinking Water. He came back and told how he saw so many Whiteskins, and even black Whiteskins, that if all the People were as many as the buffalo when the plain is covered, even then we would be only as one fly to the numberless flies of Whiteskins. Horseflies included. They breed like that, there is never an end to them."

Seenum no more than The Fish could now understand, and he said in Cree, "Running?"

"I think there may be too many," said Sweetgrass, "even for the Sioux and Cheyenne to kill them all."

The Fish gestured to Lone Man, who said,

"Yes, they killed all those Bluecoats in one band. And there are many bands of them that fight with each other, but Whiteskins don't like People to kill them. They can do it for each other, like Broken Arm said."

Little Pine spoke suddenly, "Those soldiers ride everywhere, fast, fighting. They never have women or children with them and they never stop it. They're just made to fight."

The Fish clapped his hand to his mouth in astonished disbelief. Little Pine was looking at him, and laughed drily.

"I'll tell you. All summer they fight and in winter they have something like women in their camps. They have holes like women but they can't cook or have children. They just lie in their lodges and those soldiers stand in a line with presents to mount them. Then in summer they want to do the same with our real women."

"Ahh," The Fish understood that. "There was one like that once near us with the Company. He wouldn't live with those he mounted."

"Or the police."

Everyone stared at Little Pine. Finally Sweetgrass said, "I haven't heard."

"I think they're men, and I haven't seen any women with them."

Nothing could be said to that either. After a moment Seenum said, "The treaty is good. The Governor will give it to the Queen Mother and she'll see my mark, and know me."

Little Pine did not bother to laugh. He said, his face tilting down, "The Cheyenne and Sioux have made so many marks on treaties they can't remember some and they all last till Whiteskins say they're over and then they have to be talked again, and changed. Or they fight."

"We have given our hand to the Queen Mother," said Sweetgrass in his soft voice. "The Bluecoats have no Mother, as my grandson John told us. They only have a Father by the Stinking Water."

"Are this Father and this Mother man and wife?" signed The Fish.

"No. Long ago they killed each other, and then the Father killed many of his own people and now he has very good trained soldiers to kill the Sioux and Cheyenne."

"But how can the one Great Mother...or Father...and if they are...."

The Fish stared about. The soundless feeling welling in the lodge blundered up in Big Bear as he kept his eyes steadily on the livid coals, the inarticulate confusion he knew was on The Fish's bony, on Seenum's flat, square face, and on his own, for which no one there could shape sound or any combination of sounds leave alone a recognizable sign because there was no order in the white world. They talked of nothing else but there was no order; only a kind of inevitable devouring, as in the years before his father's grandfather the People had met whites in the forests far east of the big lakes and now they were here still pushing, pushing, an insatiable gigantic beast wanting without bottom. *Come back to the circle of the Earth.* He could hear the wind rising outside, hear it brush the leather of the lodge, click it against the poles and the smoke from the fire stood like a swaying slender tree praying upward into sky. The mare had been silent since her one scream; the silence in his lodge was for him too close. He felt the bowl of the pipe against his arm; Sweetgrass had filled it again and an ember lifted to him in a split stick. He let the sweet smoke pummel gently in his head, wrapping his tongue in it and as he opened his mouth to release it the lodge flap moved. His second living son Little Bad Man came in, and then Little Poplar, too. The smoke rose from him, diffusing gently up, and suddenly he felt happy as he hadn't since they rode down the river hills that morning and saw the Queen's tent and the canvas of her police. Though he had known they would be there.

"I will not die," Big Bear said, "until my teeth are worn to my gums."

He grimaced hugely, mouth wide, and a swell of laughter went up as he ran his finger about the line of his strong teeth.

"Near The Forks a badger had his home under my lodge. When we came he was not at home, but he returned while we lived there waiting for the buffalo and often at night I could hear him doing his work in the ground. One day I killed him, but as he died he turned on his back. So I didn't eat him; I took out his entrails but left the blood and the next morning I looked inside him. And I saw what I've said."

Big Bear put the pipe between his teeth and puffed quickly, shortly. Through four small puffs of smoke rising he lifted the pipe arm-length above his head, pointing it first behind him to the north where his bundle hung, then east, south and west. The men watched; he had mentioned The Forks of the Red Deer and South Saskatchewan rivers and he made the smoke offering because that was where, years ago, he had received his bundle vision; many of them had ridden behind him when he wore it on his neck, and they knew its power. So did the Bloods and Siksikas. He held the pipe across his knees then, between long draws that drew the tobacco down tightly in the bowl. Lone Man followed his voice with his hands.

"I was hunting a wolf before we came here. The buffalo had crossed the river toward us and we were waiting at the Tramping Lakes where they like to drink; the day after this we had the first hunt. The wolf had very big feet and left white hairs in the bushes. I followed him and when I came around the sand hills that are south of there I heard something. I looked all over the hill but saw nothing, and then I looked to my feet and I saw a little man. He was smiling, I saw that. The hill was really like a round small house and the little man stood at the door. The door opened and a second one came out and leaned against the doorpost. They were dressed with hard boots and dark clothes that button, not like People. Their hair was curly, but yellow, and their eyes hollow behind noses and mouths that came out like snouts. I was not dreaming, and I stared so hard at them that I don't know anything that was inside the open door. The first Little Man said,

"'Give me your bow.'

"'No, I can't.'

"'Give it.'

"'No, I can't. I'm hunting a white wolf.'

"'Then we'll wrestle for it.'

"'Oh, I never wrestle.'

"But he asked four times and I agreed. I put down my bow and got ready; the Little Man took off his black hat which had a hard, stiff peak. Then we wrestle. His arms are too short to go around my middle but he jumps and squeezes me there and they are like a rope drawn tight by a big horse. I lift him up and swing him around to throw him; I throw him, but he is on his feet. He has my leg and throws me but I always land on my feet too. I can hear Second Little Man snorting in his snout but I'm sweating because First Little Man is all over like the itch when the leaves come out. At last on one of his spins he trips over my leg and I put him to the ground.

"'Hie-ho!' Second Little Man is very happy. 'That's good, you're beaten.'

"'I just stumbled over his leg,' says First Little Man. 'Now, again.'

"And his arms are there again before my breath comes back. That was a tough little man, I hope I'll never meet him again. I was just about finished, I could hardly stand when I tripped him again and held him. Second Little Man was laughing all the time by the door.

"First Little Man covered his yellow hair with his hat and said, 'I guess that's enough, you beat me twice. But only because I stumbled over your leg. So I'll show you something.'

"He turned and then I saw an opening like a cave in the hill which I hadn't seen before. The sun was very bright but I couldn't see into it. He beckoned, so I picked up my bow and followed him; I had to bend down almost to my knee but he walked in very straight. Soon all the sunlight was gone and I could not see him so I said,

"'This is as far as I go. What have you to show?'

"His voice was right beside me, where I could hear him still walking in his hard boots. 'Just ahead, there's a light,' he said and I saw that, though I hadn't noticed it before, and when we came into the chamber I couldn't see where it came from. There was no sunlight and the air stank like the White Sickness. My eyes could not even see the little man, though I was staring all around, and then his voice spoke right beside me and I could make out the top of his hat with the pale curls sticking out around it and his nose covered with holes like that too.

"'Look in front of you,' said First Little Man.

"At first there was nothing but the reddish stinking darkness. I was still breathing hard from wrestling, though I could not hear him breathe, and there did not seem to be enough air there for me. The harder I breathed the less there was of it, as if I had taken almost all when I came in and now there was nothing left but stink and when that was gone there'd be only nothing. Then in front of me I saw a shape, and another beside it, and another until I saw six coming towards me; at first they seemed coming far away like out of a long thin hole in the ground but soon they were close enough I could see heads and bodies and legs, and then I saw they were People. They were stiff up and down and they wore black clothes like Whiteskins but I could see they were River People. Those were River People, their hands behind their backs and their heads twisted to the side as if their spirits had been jerked out at their necks and their necks frozen. They did not seem to be standing, they just were there in a row coming closer and turning a little as if air turned them. I could see the circle like a burn around each crooked neck and their faces were swollen thick full of blood and I could not recognize anyone. But it seemed to me I knew each one of them.

"The little man's hand touched my knee. 'Come,' he said, and I bent down and he took my hand and pulled me out into the bright air and sunlight. He said there,

"'You should have given me your bow.'

"The second little man was still standing by the door. His face was all knobs and ashes from the Sickness and he held his hat against his knees with both hands, laughing. He had no more breath than I, but his was from laughing. Then they both went in and shut the door. I saw the door close and there was nothing but sand. I looked, but I couldn't find the cave either. There was nothing there, not even the wolf tracks, nothing but sand."

His pipe was empty on his knees, and the fire had died to a glow. Suddenly a flame crept around a curl of fresh bark. The Fish stood up in his place, a beaver skin folded in his raised hands.

"I thank Big Bear," he said in slow Cree, "for everything he has told us today."

He laid the skin before Big Bear and, followed by his councilmen, left the lodge. Seenum stood up, heavy and broad.

"I too thank Big Bear, for what he told us."

He removed the yellow-striped blanket from over his shoulder and folded it carefully upon the beaver skin. The great gold buttons of his red coat glinted and winked as he left with his councillors. Then Sweetgrass was on his feet.

"I thank The Almighty Spirit for what we have heard." He lifted his hands high towards the seated chief and for a moment it seemed as if the kindly old man who before the snow fell would be dead of a gunshot would shout something, that he grew massive and filled the great black cone of the lodge. But he said nothing, nor did he move, and the flames died in their bed and Sweetgrass spoke softly into the silence.

"There is a black buffalo runner by my lodge. I give him to Big Bear."

After he too was gone, Big Bear sat for some moments in his place. The firelight rose as Running Second came in with Root Grubbing Woman, piled on a few birch sticks. The chief was looking expressionlessly at Lone Man, and suddenly Lone Man had to smile. It was as if a black stallion stood there between them. The lodge was tight with men and it did not appear as if any were about to leave for their sleeping robes. More were coming in, filling the places of the Chipewyan and Wood and other River People. Kingbird came in, eyes bright across the fire and Twin Wolverine, his oldest living son, had been there all evening; suddenly Big Bear laughed aloud. Even Little Pine looked up.

"Let's eat," Big Bear said. Immediately there was laughter and talking. Root Grubbing Woman returned in a moment bent under a gigantic haunch of buffalo; it was all she and Running Second together could do to hang it from the rope above the fire. Horsechild had jerked erect at the word "eat," and Big Bear was gently rubbing his head with his fingertips.

"Eat," he said to his last son. "When Sun wakes we ride to the buffalo."

TWO

Between The Forks and the Missouri, 1878–1882

I

"The plains are large and wide. We are the children of the plains, it is our home and the buffalo has been our food always. If the Police had not come to the country, where would we all be now? Bad men and whisky were killing us so fast that very few, indeed, would be alive today. The Police have protected us as the feathers of the bird protect it from the frosts of winter. I am satisfied. I will sign the treaty."

So spoke Chapo-mexico, translated Crowfoot, head chief of the Siksika and what was left of the Blackfoot Confederacy on Friday, September 20, 1877, at Blackfoot Crossing on the Bow River. His words were echoed by Mekasto, translated Red Crow, head chief of the Bloods; second only in reputation, he was also second only in deference paid to James F. Macleod, Commissioner of the North West Mounted Police and named with David Laird, the new Lieutenant-Governor of the Territories, as Special Indian Commissioner to negotiate the last of the prairie treaties, Number Seven. Said Red Crow:

"Three years ago, when the police first came to this country, I shook hands with Stamix-otoken at Belly River. Since that time he made me many promises. He kept them all — not one was ever broken. I entirely trust him and will leave everything to him. I will sign with Crowfoot."

Bearspaw, speaking for the mountain Stoneys who had been Christian since 1840, said through John McDougall that he was pleased with the treaty and hoped the commissioners would give them as much as possible, as fast as possible.

So David Laird could bump two hundred and eighty-six miles across country to his almost complete headquarters above the Battle River content. He had factual data that would look just fine on the Annual Report, 1877:

The number of Indians paid was as follows:

Head Chiefs	10 at $25	$250
Minor Chiefs and Councillors	40 at 15	600
Men, women and children	4,342 at 12	52,104

Not quite $53,000 for a bit more than fifty thousand square miles of grass and hills. A down payment actually, but complete with rivers, valleys, minerals, sky — everything, forever. Rotting buffalo.

Well, almost content. On August 28 he had seen the first buffalo north of the South Saskatchewan, and a few every day after to the Red Deer; but the herds were very small with almost no calves. Once these plains had been black with two immense herds whose cycles some told him were as predictable as the sun; others swore that only when you saw them did you know they would come. Sometimes the eastern herd came north through Wood Mountain in the spring, across and up the northward flowing South Saskatchewan River and eventually turned south again down the Souris Valley and over the Missouri in the fall; often a western herd came past the Cypress Hills in fall and north along the Red Deer and the Bow rivers, wintered in valleys and started south along the foothills in the spring. Only bone piles were left of the eastern herd; nothing had come up between the Saskatchewans as far as Carlton since 1874. And the western herd seemed merely stragglers now among its skeletons in marshy hollows and carcasses decaying into tainted, sweetish air. Laird could build no hope whatever in the buffalo ordinance; he would write in his report, "After ten years it is feared the buffalo in Canada will have become nearly extinct," which Ottawa would think unbelievably pessimistic and history prove absolutely wrong by eight years.

Almost content. The telegraph might have informed him that the day after he arrived at Battleford in unseasonable snow Chief Joseph and his Nez Percé had surrendered to General Howard in the Bearpaw Mountains, thirty miles from their attempted refuge in his territory; that Crazy Horse, Oglala Sioux general of the bloodiest red victory over white soldiers had been killed on September 5 at age thirty-five. But Crazy Horse would have reminded him of Sitting Bull, and he needed no reminder of that Sioux trying to plead a refuge, a home for five thousand followers from the Queen he insisted on calling "my Great Mother." Macleod had left for the Cypress Hills immediately after Treaty Seven to try and settle matters; the American negotiator coming north was, of all possible men, Alfred H. Terry, the general in command of George Armstrong Custer on June 25th, 1876. The telegraph would inform Laird promptly enough after this October 17 meeting at Fort Walsh that Sitting Bull had refused so much as to shake hands with Terry; had further insulted him by having a woman harangue him: "I wanted to bear children over there but you never gave me any time. I came to this country to raise children and have a little peace." Considering, it was just as well Chief Joseph made his famous speech in Montana Territory: "I want to have time to look for my children and see how many I can find. From where the sun now stands, I will fight no more forever."

Sitting Bull and his Sioux would be gotten rid of, somehow, south where the Long Knives might slice them as fine as they legally wished. There was no way, however, to get rid of Big Bear and Little Pine. They belonged in Canada and had as yet surrendered nothing and Assistant Police Commissioner A.G. Irvine reported their personal followings now numbered over two thousand, to say nothing of stragglers.

And the wild Plains Cree, like the wild Teton Sioux, were in Cypress Hills country. There was only one blessing: these last untamed survivors of all plains Indians were traditional enemies.

Big Bear had not appeared at the first annuity payments under Treaty Six, and that too could only be seen as blessing. The 1877 payments were to be made at Fort Carlton and at the time set several thousand Indians were assembled but no supplies or money had arrived. Explaining that the season had been too muddy for freighters to get through from Red River neither fed nor impressed anyone with the way the Grandmother's councillors kept her solemn affirmations; expensive temporary supplies had to be quickly purchased from what the Hudson's Bay Company had on hand. Laird decided to make the 1878 payments on the hunting grounds; it was personally inconvenient but it saved money.

Almost none of Big Bear's band came with him to Sounding Lake in August 1878; they were far south of The Forks with Little Pine, hunting buffalo. While payments were being made to those on the treaty lists and a small herd of beef was vanishing, Big Bear argued day after day. He was speaking, he claimed, not for his band only but for those who had already said they surrendered the land forever. Before Government came the land gave everything they wanted; the Company had traded with them and they lived where and as the land wished. Now this Government said it had taken the land. He had considered this for two years and could not yet understand how that was possible, but, if it was, Government must provide for them. Now it was obvious to anyone watching the traders who appeared at the payments like leaves in spring that the papers the People received at treaty provided almost nothing. Twelve together might get one gun, two one bag of flour, one almost a blanket. Land was not like paper; wind did not blow it away nor water rot it. Whatever the Governor could carry with him as a gift he could have for the Government, but not land. Laird finally replied he could, of course, change nothing in the treaty ratified long ago but he would inform Ottawa of what the chief had said. On the night before the Governor left some bullets whistled over his tents. Inspector Walker and Sub-Inspector Francis Dickens marched their police to the Cree camp for a brief talk. Next day Big Bear said what he would say several times, annually: he would wait and receive the Grandmother's reply from her chief Councillor. But for him, Laird like Morris vanished after one meeting; he never saw either again.

II

The horses, flanks streaming water from the river, humped themselves frantically up the cutbank. Stones broke loose, sage lunged by in leaps, down. Barrelled muscles bunching between his legs and then exploding, leap upon leap, Kingbird let himself open one long, high shriek that stretched him and his horse over the lip of the bank where the prairie dropped flat before them. The others scrambled behind him, the lodges of the camp drifting smoke into the dusky morning air across the grey coils of the Red Deer below, and he drummed yellow-ears, foaming flat out along the rim. He could see women tiny around the lodges, the little boys left on the wedge of sand waving, the wide valley spread westward with the grey river looped across from bank to bank, yellowing cottonwoods splattered against grass inside its loops and the long parallel lines of People country north and east behind him. He lifted his arm once, to Horsechild far below, then the land shouldered them gone and yellow-ears ran hard between the stones and cactus, up a tilt. Where a long ravine cut in front of him he turned south, pulled down to a canter. One good whoop was enough crossing into Blackfoot country.

A horse ran near him and he felt Miserable Man's white blaze; yes, and far behind Thunder's pinto; but that was all. He signalled then, and Man knew nothing, turning to look also. Thunder signed east, the V where the rivers met below the camp. Iron Body and Round The Sky were riding around that way.

They had come fast over a small rise without much care, but it had not seemed as if anyone was too near across the river. But now the land dipped and rose south to a long straight ridge a mile or more before them; fast up that rise and then careful, very careful. Kingbird pulled back until the pinto was close, then he touched yellow-ears and his stride lengthened; wind in his ears, the sunlight bright over the autumn grass. The sky laughed, Iron Body had let him lead here. A rabbit leaped from behind a rock and zigzagged out of range.

On the ridge they slowed and rode parallel to it, just below the line where their heads would show to a rider on the other side. A hawk laid a giant circle over them, and it felt good; he grinned back to the other two and rode up. The long horizons were empty, everywhere; as far as they could see west and south the grass and cactus of a narrow plateau folded down into the tight valley of the South Saskatchewan River. They scouted a ravine, then dropped their horses into it and slid to the ground. Thunder accepted Man's flintlock, climbed back out and found a good point on the ridge, behind a stone.

"That rabbit would have tasted good," Miserable Man said. The three horses were below them, heads down in the grass still greenish there. "Fat."

"That means a long cold winter, yeh," said Kingbird. He could see a triangle of water below them, and the steep face of the opposite bank; it didn't seem like a very good place. But Miserable Man said nothing; the ravine was so steep he sat almost upright stretched against the slope, smiling. A very big man, with his face rooted over by the White Sickness.

"We better eat more then."

"You'd make it now," Kingbird gestured to the other's bulging stomach but then he sensed it, and Man too, just before yellow-ears raised his head. And Thunder called above them like a rabbit hit by a hawk. Kingbird had the rifle and they were crawling up to the level of the prairie.

"Forget it," Iron Body said behind them. "You're dead already."

He was standing with his rifle in the ravine below the horses; Kingbird slid down, grinning, only a little ashamed. "I knew it before the horses moved."

"But you went up."

"That was Thunder, how did he. . . . "

"Sky, with the horses." There was nothing to do but laugh.

So they were together then, and riding at a steady trot. Kingbird felt even better in the sunlight warming to noon; he didn't think anyone could have known Body sooner. Lone Man perhaps. And his father, well, he would have known every track Iron Body's grey left just after he left it, if he had needed to. Someday; perhaps.

"Across The Forks," Iron Body said, trotting beside him, "we saw a Young Dog riding. Just as he rode down to the river, but he was alone, I think."

"All alone?"

"I think so, like a messenger."

Even if it had been a Blood war party, their camp with all the warriors there was too big to more than annoy. Body cantered ahead, left, to skirt the edge of the deep Saskatchewan valley they were following south; Thunder was somewhere beyond a ridge, on the right. They rode for two days, steadily, always near the river and not pushing their horses; they saw no Blackfeet, which they had expected, but they saw no buffalo either, which they had not. The People had been hunting well enough north-west, but all they had now of fresh meat was three fat rabbits Man almost blew out of existence with his overloaded flintlock and by morning of the third day when Sky signalled "Antelope!" ahead they were all slack-bellied ready for a hunt, no matter how hard. There were only three, their rears tiny white spots across a long tilt of prairie. The hazy sun was past its height before they got around them downwind, the horses heaving up and sliding down the tight ravines of the river slashed vertically in places five hundred feet down to the water cutting tight under the cliffs of its gorge, but it was all in a day's hunt and the grey gladly stood motionless on the rise downwind where Body felt it was right to show himself, motionless for half the afternoon as the antelope hesitated closer. They were apprehensive but also too curious to live longer, and the three guns sounded almost as one, two lay kicking. The marksmen sprang over the slight ridge where they had lain as motionless as the rider sat, frantically cramming bullets or powder and balls but the survivor was gone like a dull white flame. Thunder, Kingbird, Round The Sky leaped about, slapping each other, laughing. Who had missed? Iron Body said, "Forget it," and fingered his good medicine; Miserable Man was already inside an antelope, stuffing his face with hot bloody liver.

For the rest of that day and most of the fourth they ate, rested, in a good camp by the river where there was grass and dry sticks that burned without smoke. It grew colder. Towards evening they painted themselves and were ready for Blackfeet. After a long session in his medicine tent, Red Bone had told them an enemy camp, probably Siksika, would be a certain distance from where Bullshead Creek joined the river; it might be as far beyond as the spring, or perhaps only a short distance below, where the medicine man had once lost his hat swimming, he could not quite understand where, but it would cost them one of the horses they brought back. He liked buckskins himself.

"I thought he liked little lame mares," Thunder said. "That's what he always rides."

They all laughed, and Sky said, more kindly,

"Everyone rides what he can get."

Above their valley camp the river looped east before it took its last turn west, so when they brought the horses up to Miserable Man on look-out they rode west across prairie. The night air breathed steadily colder; Kingbird thought he smelled snow on the wind rising from the distant mountains he had never seen. Sometimes in summer when the sun burned the land his father told him of those mountains with water running from under ice all year long, the snow laid in wedges on rocks where neither trees nor even grass grew and the clouds often walked low and covered them, yet hot yellow water, stinking and boiling like a kettle, ran out of the earth melting the very snow to steam in winter. His father had seen those spirit places, well, his father had seen everything and the dust of buffalo running or clouds piled over the prairie sometimes looked like those mountains, he said, though the mountains were always straighter, not so round. Hard, very hard. The clouds were now straight lines; there was almost no light and the black slab rearing ahead might have been the hard mountain about to close them, in its maw.

"It's good if it snows," said Round The Sky riding beside him. "They'll stay close to the fire."

There was the heavier darkness before morning when they came to a coulee and Iron Body gestured them down. Dry, its clay bottom cut into buffalo wallows. Now on foot; Man would stay with the horses, Body and Thunder scout back along the river they had paralleled, Sky and Kingbird west to the spring; if the Siksikas were across the river, as well they might be among the bushes of south gullies, they would come back for the horses to swim across upstream; if anyone had to scatter, they would all meet Man with the horses opposite Bullshead Creek. Sky doubled a string of dried buffalo meat and two ropes around his middle, his robe on his arm; Kingbird took a robe and his rifle. It was a little slower but much warmer running across the land, grass crunching soft and certain. He ran at Sky's shoulder; the wind and the clouds and the folds of the land in the leaden cold told him everything he needed to know though Sky had been here before.

Before dawn lightened behind them they were at the spring; that Kingbird could not have known, though the bushes he smelled soon after they started down would have told him; otherwise north ravines this wide were as bare as the table prairie. The biggest part of the spring seemed almost at the valley floor; they could not see or smell a camp and of course there was nothing to hear, especially in the steadily tightening north-west wind. It was too dark to see tracks around the seepage, but they could feel them deep, the water crackling ice at their frozen edges. Horse tracks, and plenty of moccasins too. Women. They burrowed in among tight bushes that rattled a few leaves; chewed dried meat; waited. Kingbird wished they could make a tiny fire to melt more beargrease to rub on his naked torso. They lay with their eyes down the tilt of the ground, and even in his robe with Sky against his back he began to feel the cold working at him. They waited.

He was awake instantly at the sound; Sky barely moved against him. Women's voices, chattering Blackfoot before he knew he had his eyes open and understood the morning was heavy grey, down so low the edges of the ravine dissolved into mist below them; women with their buffalo paunches for water, chattering, there seemed more than could be counted on two hands. One by one emerging up out of the mist, bundled against the cold, one even carrying a cloth bucket the Company traded. Kingbird wished now he had listened more carefully when his father tried to teach him Blackfoot; a few were talking about horses, he thought, but he couldn't understand. Sky was grinning, the flap of his robe over his head, fingers talking incomprehension too. So they waited while all those big fat women, some of them young too without tattoos and steaming a little they were so warm, filled themselves and their bags at the seepage hole and went off, laughing the silly laughter of women. But when they had gone there was one still there; she stood a furry column by the muddied puddles, then she set down her bags and started up the slope. To where they were lying.

Kingbird felt Sky stiffen with him. Stupid woman, get back and heat your man's tea! But the woman came on, unaware, directly to their bushes. If her eyes worked she must see them.

Her feet suddenly stopped, her robe twitched; she had squatted and was making water. Kingbird could see along the bottom of her smooth muscled flanks, the spiral of steam rising off the ground. Hear and smell, so close he could stick out his tongue and touch her, WUH, the leaping warmth in his body grabbed violently down and he would have been on her, run her up his pole before she could snatch a scream — bear-grease! — Sky's hand clutched his neck. Sky's painted black cheek and nose were against the ground too, eyes staring, but his fingers in Kingbird's hair said everything necessary until all that skin lifted, vanished with a fall of robe and King-bird slowly slackened: one of them is doing it somewhere, all the time.

That heat and silent laughter held them until they word-lessly agreed to try the mist, just as between the wind up from the valley they heard. Two horses. The mist darkened, there they were with one such boy up as Kingbird himself had been not many autumns before, getting to ride horses mainly to water. The brown was nothing but the grey had legs like a run-ner, and a chest too. Unfortunately the boy already knew too much; he kept his face up the ravine while the horses drank, looking easily against the wind. A knife was impossible but the grey was really horse and Kingbird put his sights on the boy holding the tethers in his left hand, scratching himself in the crotch with the right, forever looking around. Sky touched him — sure — the grey was good but not worth it. So the Sik-sika boy went off still scratching.

In a short time they knew they should have followed him; the morning did brighten but with a kind of white density that closed them in even more as the wind increased and soon snow began to sprinkle. Driving snow would have been just fine, had they known where the horse herd was. No one came to the

spring again, and they still could hear nothing. But the women
— more than ten lodges. A very small camp for Siksikas.

"We could come back with Body and the others at night," said Kingbird.

"Maybe they found more."

"Yeh."

"When it stops snowing in the evening they could track us at a gallop."

"A night's start."

"If we got it."

"What do you think?"

"It will stop before evening."

"And not melt for another day, maybe two?"

"Yeh," said Round The Sky and pulled his legs under him. "We might as well finish the meat."

"Anyway, who wants to just sit," said Kingbird, gnawing. "I should have drilled that."

"He's no good for coup, scratching kid."

"Two horses."

"Huh," said Sky, cramming his wide friendly mouth full, heavy brows crinkled at Kingbird. "The Only One provides a full belly, an enemy camp asleep and a nice snowstorm getting thicker and one shoots a kid can't get himself warm and stiff yet?"

"My father lent me yel —"

"It's small, how many buffalo runners would such a camp of People have?"

"One or two."

"Yeh, and Siksika's maybe four, five. Maybe one good one, really *good*. Now, your father is Big Bear, your first raid you get a great runner, now that's a gift, eh?"

"Yeh. But where's the herd?"

"The best runner isn't in the herd."

"Hey!" said Kingbird, almost aloud. The bushes, still leafy, were beginning to sift snow now, melting on his shoulders, but he didn't feel anything. He understood what Sky was saying, exactly; the Worthy Young Man's immense generosity.

"You take the gun?" he asked, excitement crowding his throat.

"You don't want noise yeh!" and they both laughed in silence together; Kingbird pushed the gun to him, gave him the nine bullets. They knotted their robes about their middles and they were ready. Round The Sky touched Kingbird's knife hand.

"Only great men have fine horses. Taking a fine horse is the best coup. The valley is narrow here, a few trees east near the river. I think that's where the herd is." Then he crawled out from under the bushes, stretched in the driving snow, vanished up the side of the ravine.

The snow was not melting; Kingbird's tracks were sifted over in the time it took to study the land. When he gained the spot where the first women emerged he could make out the conical darkness of lodges; that close, even the dogs curled up still. There was nothing for such a day — nothing but a great runner! Sky said there were trees in this valley, then obviously these had made bad camp; the river bank kept off neither wind nor snow. He slid behind the first lodge, heavy leather: someone was snoring; he could hear when he placed his ear against the leather. A man, and he must be very old to make noise. He moved and beside the next lodge, smoke rifling out level at its peak stood a horse hipshot, hunched against the snow.

His body moved for him like a swift soundless streak. He was there, left hand over nostrils, right to the tether rope for one jerk off — the rope was not around any lodge peg. His heart staggered his whole body, almost alarming the horse. The rope disappeared under, into the lodge — he would have given the owner's leg one beautiful jerk! After a moment he could fumble his knife out; he cut the rope as carefully as if it were a sleeping snake, straightened, pulled gently. The horse turned, reluctant, against the wind, but without a sound like a trained horse should. After a few steps he tugged it into a trot. He was already beyond the spring when he thought to look at it.

The horse blinked at him, sprinkled with snow. Dark brown and a blaze longer than Man's. The legs could make a buffalo runner, yes, it must be. He rubbed the flat of his knife along against the hair-grain of its back; almost a sore. The more he looked at it, the less certain he was about this being the best horse in a camp of Siksikas. Nothing at all behind him; this was nothing, just a boy snatching meat from old blind women. He looped the rope about a bush well out of sight above the waterhole, and went back down.

And as he moved, around the back of that encampment through hard whistling snow, breaking the wind on his bare chest, suddenly he felt the heat of power manhood churning in him, lifting him like a shadow from lodge to lodge — when he stopped and looked back at his tracks, they disappeared in the whiteness springing up from trampled grass — he was being brushed by The Spirit invisible. The Only One had given him his beautiful day; Sky had known it. There were Siksikas here, lots of them, breathing and muttering and cooking meat so that he salivated and sometimes a woman screeched a sound through the lodge leather, but he was invisible. Moving under The Spirit. He moved as if he were watching himself, separate and he did not find the brown and the good grey. He hunched down, listening to hide being scraped steadily, again, waiting for stillness to come before he moved and a Siksika came past the turn of the lodge in front of him. A big buffalo robe over his head, going somewhere in what seemed the protected circle of his camp and Kingbird crouched there bare in raid paint and he could have reached up and opened his throat, zip, with not one sandpiper chirp out of him. He was big like a cottonwood in the snow. Zip. The runner, he wanted the buffalo runner, greater coup than any size bloody scalp; he dropped his hands and waited. Then fast behind the next lodge.

He saw a buckskin but now he studied it. It was pegged out, and its backbone lay gaunt with a ridge of sores along it; glistening whiteness, as if they were working them with hot grease and the snow cooled them in patches. The lodge was marked over with power signs which his father could have read; perhaps a medicine man too powerful to lose the horse. Give old Red Bone such a horse to cure, all sores and medicine maybe too strong for him! Snow wasn't even melting on its back, a silly joke, such a thing for good words. He moved, past dogs curled breathing under granular snow, past more and more lodges until he felt himself giant, the length of his body singing and driving the whole valley under his feet into the snow and with the next lodge he would have laid a circle around that camp of stupid sleeping and now helpless Siksikas. And there, as he knew he would, he saw the horse.

A bay and very big. Through the snow bigger than any horse should possibly be. A stallion, arched neck turned away from the wind, great haunches and a chest that would outlast any buffalo running the land, standing in the lee of the lodge next to the one where the old man snored. He could feel the shadow of the river cliffs just beyond though he could see nothing — a bad camp, almost against cliffs; The Spirit had made them feel the storm coming and be careless with the spring so close. Thankfully he slid past, completed the circle to the first lodge and then looped back to the bay.

The stallion stood and saw Kingbird there glistening naked in the snow. Barely moved his one great eye, unblinking, streaked slightly with yellow; as if he had stood there forever, frozen streakily white waiting for him to come finally. Power lay over them, lifting them like a river together with the sun flames over summer land and buffalo mountains thundering dust thin voices of his father, dancing. A rope hung down the stallion's jaw to the snow behind a sharp mound. Then Kingbird became aware of tobacco smoke. A wisp unravelling up in the whistling air, and a robe covered with snow over a head and a hand closed and sitting there with his horse in the cold was a Siksika smoking. The rope in his hand.

His father had told him they cared only for their horses. Something touched him, motionless understanding, seeing another curl of sweet smoke, something near sadness to kill such a horseman. As he smoked. But that thought was less than a twitch; his knife was up while the bay stood for him, eye one great unblinking roundness, and then in one stroke he knew what Sky had said. A greater way, and given him by the circle: the greatest way of all.

He took half a step, that was all, cut the tether at the ground, so gently against the snow not a flake stirred, then looped the short line around the stallion's nose and he was up, on his back. The horse had not shifted a muscle even to raise his head; Kingbird saw beyond the arched neck that Siksika mound below him, puffing, and a finger-length of nice braided leather curled an instant on the snow. That great stupid stupid enemy he had humiliated forever: his tension exploded. Erect he jerked the stallion, wheeled, screaming the River People's warcry. Screamed and screamed to batter the lodges and bounce off the cliffs and his knife scooped down to that robe flying up and tugged, barely, but the stallion was already striking stones down the ravine like no mount he had ever forked, up he could hardly check him to circle and slash the rope of the brown off the bush and they were on the plains running west into the snow as fast as the brown gelding could run. With blood still on his knife tip.

Toward evening the snow faded; the west lightened, arched suddenly red in sunset as he signalled the coulee from the north-west. Nothing answered; was there. Miserable Man must have had to move during the snow but some strange tracks — seven, eight ponies, that could be Sky — were not quite covered. He lifted his leg to rest sideways on the stallion that would make him a Worthy Young Man, reading these things on the snow; the gelding stood head down, almost blown. Then he rode slowly north-east, following the trail. A rib bone set on end, a buffalo shoulder blade dusted with snow; he scooped the blade up as the bay walked. A curly cloud in ochre: it was Sky, with Siksika horses. He rode a great circle north-east and then south, but he did not know the country and made a cold camp that night, the horses feeding at ropes' length. When the sun stood clear two handbreadths over the prairie he rode out on the height above the South Saskatchewan River opposite Bullshead Creek where a medicine man had once lost his hat or perhaps the Great Serpent appeared to Kausketo-opot. What he saw there now made him forget both legends and friends.

A long line of scarlet riders was splashing toward him into the ford. A Blood was leading them, and one scarlet didn't stay on the ford ridge; it floundered into deep, swift water and the Blood threw a rope around the horse's head and pulled him back up, the scarlet dragging along. The rest followed very close. Behind them on the Bullshead flat was a huge camp — Bloods? — and directly below Kingbird was another. Many

were the peaked square tents of Whiteskins, but across a small
dry wash and under cottonwoods stood the lodges, he recognized them like a thunderclap, of River People. They were not
in circle, rather the fighting half-moon and in the open centre
a big Assiniboine warrior tent; beside it was a lodge with a
flaming ochre sun — Little Pine, and beside that his father! He
had been at The Forks. Kingbird watched the police ride up,
towards the square tents, and he wheeled down behind a ridge.
Galloping out on the valley floor he found a thicket among the
cottonwoods; the bay was really too bright and big to hide, but
there was nothing for that. He began to run through the wet,
almost vanished snow, across the valley.

Many years later the then retired Colonel A.G. Irvine would
peer down the dusty tunnel of his memory at those October
days when he had been North West Mounted Police
officer-in-charge at Fort Walsh. He would not mention
Sub-Inspector Francis Dickens; he would remember what
happened on the South Saskatchewan this way:

"In 1878, Big Bear, the Cree chief who figured so prominently in the 1885 troubles, had stopped the Government
surveyors from carrying on their work. Complaints of this
were brought to me. I selected twenty-six men and we proceeded to the scene of the trouble, taking our Winchester
rifles with which we had just been equipped. Previous to this
we had used the Snider carbine.

"When we arrived at the south branch of the Saskatchewan
about where Medicine Hat now stands, we found a large
number of Blood Indians camped there. They had heard
that Big Bear had been hindering the surveyors and they
knew that we were going to interfere. They perceived also
that we were equipped with new rifles and, putting two and

two together, came to the conclusion there was going to be some fun.

"The Bloods and Crees having always been deadly enemies, the chief of the Bloods asked to be allowed to join me. I withheld my answer till the following day. As it was late in the evening when we arrived at the river, I considered it advisable to camp there, as fording the south branch was somewhat dangerous at any time and would be more so after dark.

"The scene in the camp of the Bloods that night is one I will never forget. The braves held a war dance; all were stripped to the breech clout, and between warsongs they alternately recounted their many deeds of valour occasionally mentioning the name given me by Chief Crowfoot, Big Buffalobull. It was certainly a beautiful sight to see these fine, well-built children of Nature dancing in the light of the fitful campfires of buffalo chips.

"The next morning I told the chief it would not do to take the tribe but I would take him and his chief brave, to which he gladly consented. The Indians then showed me the ford, and we got over safely. When we reached Big Bear's camp it looked ominous. The women and children had all been sent away, which among plains Indians is always a sure sign that they expect some fighting.

"I ignored Big Bear and went to the surveyors' tent. When I sat down the Bloods took their places on either side of me. Big Bear followed with a large number of his braves, to talk to me. I did not waste many words with him, but told him if he interfered with the surveyors, who were servants of the Queen's Government, as I was, I would have him arrested, taken to Cypress Hills, and locked up in the guard room.

"As I was talking to him a Siksika rider arrived from Fort Macleod with letters for the surveyors. The Bloods and Siksikas are really the same people and common enemies of the Crees, so when Big Bear saw this courier hand papers to the surveyors and saw the Blood chief and his brave beside me, it occurred to him that there was a concerted action between the Bloods, Siksikas and police to attack him, and he calmly and submissively consented to allow the surveyors to go on with their work; and they never afterwards were interfered with by any of the Indian tribes.

"I believe if it had not been for these fortunate coincidences, that we might have had some quick practice with those new Winchesters."

When Kingbird got across the wide valley, pulled his robe across his shoulder and walked into the camp, the fire lay dead in his father's lodge; there had never been either women or children there. The men were across the wash, in front of the Whiteskin tents. Big Buffalobull sat in his beautiful jacket, legs lying in front of him like polished logs in his horrible shining boots; all were drinking tea. They obviously hadn't started to talk yet and after watching for a time, until his father sitting with Little Pine on his right began to stuff the pipe, Kingbird was prepared for a long wait. Someone touched him. Round The Sky; he had rubbed off all his paint.

"The snow's already gone," said Kingbird. They were both laughing silently and so they both knew it was still good. Very good.

"It didn't snow as much here," Sky said, looking across the council circle. "Too many Blackfeet here."

"Yeh," said Kingbird, and they edged out of the crowd. Iron Body in yellow warpaint was at the edge of the wash adjusting his rifle sights for short range. "I got one great runner, and a brown gelding."

"Hah!" Sky and Body exclaimed together. "I got seven, mixed," said Sky.

"Did you hear me?"

"Yeh! Otherwise I'd have got more. I was leading away the sixth, there were only two boys under one robe, and then I heard you and just roped another one, not caring for noise, and then the Siksikas came yelling and shooting and grabbing anything and seeing nothing, trying to get after you so fast, and I got all seven down the valley, they never come near me I think."

"That's the trouble having so many horses," said Body. "You get excited and don't see what's gone."

They were laughing together in the warming sun, a yellow leaf drifting by from the cottonwoods. "All Thunder and I found," said Body, "was this camp. I think we should get back to those horses, now."

"What about this?" Kingbird looked at the crowd.

"Someone should stay here. If anything is starting, come fast."

"Maybe The Only One would give us a fight yet too," Kingbird said wistfully.

"I don't think so, Big Bear isn't wearing anything around his neck," said Sky. "But I'll watch."

Round The Sky was right, and after that became obvious they five ran the nine horses back to The Forks and were in camp there for half a day of glory and Happydance by the women before Big Bear returning with the warriors overshadowed them. The story, as it was told wherever People lived to the great glory of Big Bear and Little Pine and the River People, was that scouts for Little Pine's hunting party, which included some Young Dogs and Assiniboines, discovered white men pounding sticks into the ground near the creek. All the warriors rode with Little Pine to look, and Little Pine

did not like what he saw. They rode down and told them
to stop; this was the People's country, they had signed no
treaty, no white had a right to measure anything in it. The men
said courteously that they were of the Government and
were actually not measuring much, they were just looking at
rocks. At this Little Pine exploded in complete fury. He had
heard from the Sioux what happened when Whiteskins started
"just looking" at rocks, tapping them with iron hammers and
drilling long thin poles out of them: suddenly white madmen
poured in like sand and ripped and hacked and rooted the land
until everything was dead, not even a worm could live there
afterwards. Here there would be nothing like that! The
Whiteskins got mad then and sent to the police at Fort Walsh;
Little Pine sent a Young Dog to Big Bear at The Forks. In
the meantime Bloods arrived, and then Siksikas too. That
snowy morning when the warrior tent stood in the half-circle,
after drinking tea and smoking, came the great negotiated triumph: the thirty-six police would return to Fort Walsh, the
surveyors return to Battleford for winter, the Indians disperse;
Big Bear would settle the matter with the Governor when the
leaves came out. The Governor was to bring him some other
messages from the Grandmother and her Councillors at that
time anyway.

That was how Kingbird heard it at The Forks, the way it
was told in the lodges of the People and relived by boys at
play everywhere. He thanked his father for yellow-ears and
gave him the great bay runner, and then Big Bear gave Kingbird the black stallion Sweetgrass had presented to him the fall
he died. When they saw this happen, the Assiniboines were so
pleased that twenty warriors and their families decided to stay
with Big Bear that winter. So at last Kingbird had a runner, and
a mare besides he could keep or give someone; Round The Sky

had two horses. Iron Body had two for leading a good raid, Miserable Man one for guarding the horses and Thunder one also. The brown with the blaze could run buffalo; they gave him to Red Bone.

"Why not give him the buckskin," said Thunder. "She's a mare."

Everyone in the lodge laughed at that, and Iron Body gave Thunder the better of his two horses also.

III

The rabbit on the prairie above The Forks had, of course, been right: 1878–9 was a hard winter. That October snow was barely gone when another roared down and stayed. Stranger still, the chinooks refused to come from the mountains; the wind sometimes warmed a little, the clouds arched upwards over the sinking sun like a great burning land and the little boys ran among the People in full cry, "Ahh-ahh, it comes, it comes!" But it never did; the beautiful air breathing warmth in dark winter seemed no more. Above his smoking camp Big Bear sat in the sky's circle on Bull's Forehead Hill facing west, the drifts angled down into the two valleys, pointed islands and loops wiped level, the rivers' buttes folded down like frozen blankets about him: a white land, yes, and this was his place he had seen often in his many winters, and felt without chinooks. But when he contemplated what he found here, though the land appeared the same, something was wrong with it. As if just under the edge of his vision a giant blade was slicing through the earth, cutting off everything with roots, warping everything into something Whiteskin clean and straight though when he tried to stare down, get under it to see, it looked as it always had, seemingly. When chiefs had given the land away, why should the round sun shine or the chinook blow? Whites were always warm and fat in their houses, they no more needed the chinook than the buffalo.

His River People and the bands of Metis wintering with them had food and warmth because they still had some buffalo. The great beasts were wintering among the brush and trees of the wide Red Deer. A small herd trickled north early in the Breeding Moon and they all worked to try and keep some of them in the valley, rode regularly along the north buttes of the Red Deer, set narrow fires there to turn them if possible; winter came suddenly and many stayed. He had thought then, let the next herd go north, this is for us here. They slaughtered them carefully, no stampedes or jumps, the young men were allowed no wild runs across the prairie which soon became impossible anyway in the snow. The animals were lean, almost none had fat enough for pemmican so they shot them as needed, only early in the morning among the trees a few at a time so *mus-toos-wuk* could not catch the scent of blood and hurt himself running. And there had been no more, it seemed; by the mid-winter Big Bear began to hear children crying, far north among the People, south and west among the Blackfoot confederacy. Even before runners, then a few hunters came and were welcomed and ate to ride back to their camps, travois loaded with such meat as their ribbed horses could drag. It seemed there had been only that first, small herd. Otherwise not even stragglers.

He heard many children in the north crying as he sat where once on the edge of manhood he had received his great vision. One evening in February he did not return. Running Second crossed The Forks at dawn and found him sitting, naked except for a breech clout, on his robe covered with fine, fresh snow. She guided him down to the lodge; there he went immediately to his tobacco and prepared three small packages. He sent one west to Crowfoot, one south to Red Crow, and the third east to Sitting Bull.

He smoked himself then, mixing in plenty of red willow. Like The Wallowing One before her, Root Grubbing Woman had gone over the river to the Sand Hills; Big Bear often missed her huge easy efficiency and the heavy warmth of her breasts about the back of his neck at night. She put a man warmly to sleep. Running Second worked hard, always, but he had had to take another woman; his daughters were married and no chief's household could be served by only one woman. And there were so few hunters now. The Magpie was very young and Running Second could teach her about work, but at night he did not much like her yet. Not like he had thought he would. She looked better from the back bending over the meat pot, stirring in a rhythm, then she felt under a robe. Tight and firm everywhere, though round enough; it would take him a little while to hammer her soft into something livable. But when late in the Goose Moon Crowfoot and Sitting Bull sat beside him at his fire, seeing their eyes finger around her as she bent and left made him warm happily despite Red Crow. He passed his pipe to Crowfoot.

"I thought she was your granddaughter," said Sitting Bull in Blackfoot.

Crowfoot pulled smoke into himself. "She's too young for that," he said, and they laughed all together. Smoked thankfully.

Horsechild slipped through the door and stood, staring across the lodge. He had heard endlessly about these great men, their coups and bravery, they were almost as great as his father the women said though he had no conception of that: they both limped when they walked in their beautiful clothes. But they didn't have many feathers. The big Sioux was so great he had left the Long Knives country before he killed them all. Long Knives with blue coats. Suddenly he wondered if his father had ever killed one. He moved around and found his place, where if he wanted he could touch his father. He peered out at the strange men, one and the other, a Sioux and a Siksika so close to a Person, smoking, the laughter slowly drying up into scars on their sun-blackened faces as they silently smoked one after the other. Lifting the pipe high too, to the four directions. When his father took a breath and spoke, he still could not understand the words.

"Sometimes when I meditate and look," Big Bear said in Blackfoot, "the sun no longer looks round. It's starting to look as if it had four corners."

"Ahhhhh."

"I want my children who aren't born yet to see our round sun."

"Ahhhhh."

"It came to me it's time for the People and Siksika and Sioux, and the Bloods I thought, too, to smoke together and talk about land."

"Red Crow sent me the tobacco. I talk for all the Blackfeet," said Crowfoot.

"Ahh. Yes."

Horsechild was exploring inside his nose with his finger; he studied what he found there and then carefully swallowed it. The Siksika sat like a motionless rock when he spoke but the big Sioux was agreeing with whatever his father had said; he had never seen anyone by their fire who did not, so why was his face getter blacker? He could not understand.

"The Only One, Who gave us the earth."

"I have never signed away land, to anyone," said Sitting Bull, fumbling a little in the unfamiliar Blackfoot and using his hands easily. "I was raised at Red River hand-in-hand with the Red River halfbreeds and the red soldiers left me alone but those bluecoat soldiers wouldn't let me live there. My father was rich, I never starved, I had meat and robes to give to the hungry and poor, but the soldiers kept pushing at me. Whenever a Whiteskin wanted my land, they always said he could have it, even the Black Hills which as you know is the centre of the world and was to be mine forever. So finally I rubbed them out. But they kept after me, shooting, till I came to this country. Yes, it is time. That's why I have come."

Crowfoot said slowly, "Here we have never been rubbed out with soldiers."

"It's not bad when you're young," continued Sitting Bull. "You just rub them out and go home and there's plenty to sing and dance and uniforms with fancy braid to put on."

The Siksika sat like a polished stone but Horsechild could see his father agreed with the Sioux; they two sat for a time in silence, looking into the fire as if they saw happiness there, far away in the small flames. Probably they would do nothing but sit and talk and talk, as always. He got up and pulled his robe up; then he went out into the stinging grey daylight.

"The trouble," Sitting Bull said, "is they never do it properly. They never give you any rest to heal up and get your horses bred and hunt meat. They do nothing but fight and fight so even if you kill them and then ride away from one place, you never get it back. If you ever see that land again there are whites on it, scratching and tearing up the grass. Those soldiers don't stop at shooting warriors either. They know women and children hardly ever have anything to shoot back, so that's safer. After a while it's no good. American soldiers have nothing to do but kill."

"Here they have never rubbed us out with soldiers," Big Bear repeated after Crowfoot. "There are other ways."

"Yes," said Crowfoot. "And that's why I have come, to talk too. My people are starving because someone has stopped the buffalo from coming north this winter. Here and there our hunters find a few lonely buffalo, and now children cry at night for hunger. What will my people eat in spring?"

"I heard them," said Big Bear sadly. "But we kept only some small herds near The Forks, and they are almost gone, there are none left for our people in the spring. The animals did not come."

They sat, and now they were waiting for Sitting Bull. Big Bear wished Horsechild had not left; he had liked him there, behind him, warm and breathing. He leaned forward and placed some sticks across the fire.

"If Louis Legare didn't trade at Wood Mountain," Sitting Bull said heavily, "many of us would be dead now. We are riders, and I am trading our horses now. For flour. The buffalo did not come, the Cypress Hills people are living by the police. Flour one day, then none the second, then salt bacon, then none. They are hungrier than we."

"In the north," said Big Bear, "the ones who farmed like the Government wanted them have now eaten everything out of the ground. They've asked for their payments now instead of next summer, and what will they do then if there are still no buffalo?"

"They are still on the Missouri. Plenty, but those soldiers were burning along the line all autumn. To keep them south."

"Ahhhhh," said Big Bear.

"And that is because of the Sioux," Crowfoot said rigidly. Big Bear could see why that hard face, nose beaked like a great eagle, could lead and talk for the warrior Blackfeet. He was one to terrify Whiteskins. If only.

Sitting Bull was staring across Big Bear at Crowfoot. His

huge bulging eyes hardening down to black arrow-points; there was another. A spirit and a face to help build a wall against White Grandmothers and White Fathers. Terrible as they were, now there had to be walls, walls. If only.

"No one needs to tell me it's because of the Sioux," said Sitting Bull, and the black rage seemed to slowly harden up into his face. "They want to make me go back, to throw away my life and sit on a piece of land as big as my ass and listen to the wind howl and rot eating that stinking salt pig! Never!"

Big Bear knew it was time to speak. He had known there could be nothing but disaster once these two sat face to face thundering; the very power that roared from them made them less than nothing when Whites could use them against each other. He wished now that Running Second would come, now, to make tea, and she entered as he thought this; then he was talking very carefully, not as easily as he would have in Cree, but well enough.

"The People," he said, "as we call ourselves, are many. We are not so different from the Sioux. We, like you, began in the forests and some of us, the Swampy People, like the Santee Sioux, still live in the forests and hunt moose and beaver. Some of us, the Wood People, live in the forests but go like the Yankton Sioux to the plains for the fall hunt. And our own people, the Plains People, the Teton Sioux. We want only the plains and our whole living is buffalo. We have our own stories of why we are like this, but perhaps it is because The Only One in His goodness gave us all land, wherever we wish to live with it, and also gave us the horse to kill buffalo by running if we wanted that. All that is for People came from The Only One. And then there are Whiteskins. They push us, trading us guns and we push too. I sometimes ask That One if He also sent us these whites. They have traded us some good things, I know, but it is hard, though I know that everything — would He really do that to any Person? I sometimes...."

And then he stopped for a moment and watched Running Second dump tea into the kettle. He always liked to see it fan black from the lip of her small bag. Anticipating it. Smell. He could not quite voice to these dark men what had come to him sometimes as a glimmer of terror as he sat above the camp and watched the great lights play over the face of earth, at night infinitely beautiful and terrifying in their absolute disregard for prayer or pleading. Those ghost dancers. As he sometimes thought then, holding his eyes open, his will rigid against them until their edges smudged, crumbled at last. And the thought came nevertheless: perhaps The Almighty Spirit has nothing about whites; despite what the missionaries keep saying He Only is theirs too, whites are for themselves, good sometimes even as the People are but always white and always unto themselves white. Perhaps even for That One. But he would not readily think that; only in moments of extreme exhaustion and cold, and such a thing could not be said here now. Must not. There would be time and place for — oh pray not.

"I think," he continued, not looking up for he could feel bodies and minds intensely listening, "that the Teton Sioux and the Plains People are great Peoples, great in their many groups and bands. My People have used guns to push against the Assiniboines and Siksikas and Bloods, the Sioux against the Cheyennes and the Crows, from whom we raided our horses. That is so. And some became our friends and brothers, the Assiniboines who are almost Sioux, the Cheyennes, and some we mostly fought, the Siksikas and Bloods, the Crows. Perhaps because they were as strong as we. Everyone needs good enemies to become a good man."

Slipperiness was under him, and he feared it, but it had to be walked. Tried.

"There is a difference, between my People and the Sioux. There are many but I want to talk only about this one. For a long time the whites we met were traders with the Company, long ago with two, but now only one. Mostly the People liked them and did not say no when these took their beautiful daughters. From this was born our half-brother, and the Teton Sioux knew them on the Red River. The buffalo hunt."

He looked at Sitting Bull steadily. Slowly he smiled and that big face answered in the firelight.

"Yes," said Sitting Bull. "On the great hunts as they were there then we always fought them. For years before I was born, until we made The Great Peace."

"Why did you make peace?"

"Enough fathers had no sons. And the buffalo were going away, west."

"And Whiteskins?"

"Yes. The Santees killed hundreds, but there were finally too many."

"Yes," said Big Bear slowly, "a man makes peace with his enemies because a greater one is pushing him. Yes."

Here was truly glare-ice, but he had courage to face Crowfoot too.

"And I," he said carefully, unaware of the tea smell rising in the lodge, "I — all Blackfeet are great warriors. Until we had guns we could never cross the rivers though these plains were covered with buffalo and we starving among the trees. The true greatness of Blackfoot warriors is they know a single willow, strong as it is, can be broken, and so the Siksikas and the Bloods and the Piegans and the Sarcees have given each other their hands. And they hold them still. I am of the River People;

I have taken Teton coups on the Missouri and run from them at Pinto Butte; I have killed Siksikas on Ribstone Hill and attacked them and seen my friends, my son, die fighting the Bloods at Belly River when Piegans rode over us. I know your People have wailed because my medicine was strong, and I won't enrage you by telling the long list of my deeds for which the River People honour me as yours honour you for what you have done against my People and half-brothers. These were warrior acts and I did not wail for my son when he sang his last song like a warrior. That is the way life is, and it is our good life, and I have prayed day and night this past winter when I heard children crying from a pain we have all known, often, but now with the end of everything we have ever lived standing at the end of it, prayed our Only One *give me back those days*. But I see now they will not come. Never. I see that. Unless we all together make a life circle with our hands and face the Whiteskins as one."

Big Bear did not want either of them to say anything; he wanted them to keep their words inside their heads until his own thoughts hammered in their heads, nothing more, but Sitting Bull was already speaking. He was not one to wait in any council for speech and once begun he could not be interrupted, though Big Bear heard him with a darkness rising higher and higher in him.

"Two years ago," said the chief of all Sioux, "I came to the Queen's land; many of my people were already here, and more came with me. I was rich from trading and from what I had taken at many battles which I all won. But I had no powder or bullets. I even tried to get buffalo by roping them and stabbing them with knives. The police have always allowed me only a little, enough to hunt and during the last winter there has been mostly nothing to hunt; the lodges are almost empty. I am trading the horses and after that there is nothing. But my spirit is the spirit of the Sioux and though some are dead, my warriors are still many. I have two thousand warriors ready to fight when the leaves come out. Yes. I spoke otherwise at the Rainy Hills but I say now, kill every Whiteskin back to the Souris River on the east, south to Missouri and the Cheyenne River to the mountains, north to the Saskatchewan and the Red Deer to the mountains. That is our land, there we care for the buffalo, there we live brothers. I am ready. That is what I say."

Running Second's round face peered at Big Bear over the tea tin; he signed to her and in a moment she came with cups of the black tea. He had considered killing too, often. He studied Sitting Bull intensely; trying to see it. To kill by bullet and knife and club — anything, choke them — every white unless they fled beyond running water: sometimes it was given him to see as if he stood precisely on the edge of it flat and upright, and if it was a buffalo he would kill or a horse he would take it came so motionlessly close into the frame of his vision that individual hairs curling in sweat laid themselves open before his sight. He had waited for this also, sometimes prayed so endlessly it at last froze into conviction: he would not see it. Never like this man, his squarish battered face glistening in the memory of such wars fought and one more coming in raging joy. The hot cup burned in his hand, and Big Bear suddenly understood Crowfoot had not said a word. Understood this only when Crowfoot said,

"Here the police have never killed anyone. They have given us food. No Blackfoot will kill them."

"Yes," said Sitting Bull slowly. "They have helped me too, and my heart is always good except when I see a blue soldier. We'll tell the police to go away just before we start."

"They won't go."

"Then we'll rub them out."

"They have fed us. They are good men."

"Yes, good men, but always *white* men!"

He heard his apprehensions dropped like a rock in his trail, and it seemed to Big Bear every white man he knew and had known and some of whom he loved because they were good, stood there stacked up in front of him. Just to see them all was to be battered bloody. But they were not rock either, for rock was the oldest, eternal grandfather of all things who stayed in his place and you could be certain of him. Whites were only certain in changing; unless they took an Indian woman and she dragged him to a stop — maybe the only way to hold them tight was by the penis? — they kept on wanting some thing here or there and then another and wanting to change still another forever that kept them running forever and frantic. They never had rest. Surveyors sticking in poles with wires and government agents sending messages and missionaries talking talking to stop stop stop stop and settlers ripping up land and knocking down trees and wolfers dashing about scattering poison and killing wolves and buffalo. Even the police were always packed down under things they had to do right now, to go, to make some person do something. It ran in his head like a sore, they were always moving though no one had died at the old place — maybe whites quickly made a place sick? — one fort and then another, build this, tear that down. He had tried to unravel this desperate placelessness — they built houses that couldn't move and yet they seemed always moving placelessly — many times, and inevitably again it ran him into that hemmed-in ache. He shook his eyes clear, to look at Sitting Bull who knew so many things about whites. So many more than any Person would ever want to know if only he could help it.

Sitting Bull had swallowed some tea. He said, "I have nothing to do in this country except think. I came here two springs ago, and talked peace with you and your adopted Cree son Poundmaker in the Rainy Hills, and I think now that some of what I thought then isn't the way it is. I have always tried to think there were good and bad Whiteskins, as there are good and bad People. I thought the ones that killed my women and children and did not let me rest were bad whites, so what I had to do was rub those out until just the good ones were left. Then everything would be good for the Sioux and everybody. It always seemed to me there were a lot of very bad whites, that they might even rub me out before I got to mostly the good ones, but the police showed me my thinking was all wrong. The police chiefs I know are all good straight men; they share their food with me always when I have none, they punish whites for the same things they punish us, in the same way. They are straight men. *But*, they are white."

Big Bear and Crowfoot sat motionless, staring into the Sioux's face where sweat stood in small, black beads.

"Even the best white men," said Sitting Bull, "can at last be nothing but bad for People. The police keep me from starving, yes, but they will not let me have land that helps me live. They cannot, they say, because my land is where the Bluecoats prowl. The land here is the Queen's. Who is this White Queen? Who is this White Father in this Washington? I ask. How is it they are so big? The good white men who are police tell me something I have never heard: those two have divided everything that is between them, this part mine, this part yours, and I belong to the part where the White Father in Washington has soldiers that want to kill me. The police say they cannot help that. But I say if they are as powerful as they say they are and if they were People, *they would help it*. No!

There are no good and bad men any more. As I once thought. The way it is now, there are only People and Whiteskins."

Into the long silence following Crowfoot spoke at last, with very deliberate dignity.

"Three years ago when Sioux and Cheyenne danced the Sun Dance at the Little Bighorn, your chiefs sent tobacco to me. You had seen a vision of soldiers falling into your camp and you invited me to come with my warriors to kill the Bluecoats and then you would come north with me to kill the police. I sent your tobacco back, though in the confederacy we had two thousand warriors and many wanted to smoke it. I have given my hand to the Grandmother's commissioners. We will not fight her police, and then we will never have to fight her soldiers."

"But your children are crying with hunger."

"The treaty says we will be fed when there is famine."

"The treaty!" Sitting Bull spat. "I have seen treaties signed by commissioners in the name of Whiteskin government that said they would give rations *every* day, not just in famine. And they would build *everyone* houses, food and houses is what the treaties *said*." And he spat again, violently into the dark emptiness of the lodge.

Confrontation, and nothing but anger and finally rage would grow there; Big Bear had ordered his thoughts again and said quickly, "We have all fought, many times, and killing will not fill our stomach now. We know that. If we fight soldiers or police we will be wiped out because there always seem to be more of them, with endless bullets, and People always have only a certain number of warriors and cannot make bullets. We need Whites so we can kill them! They are stupid, yes, but I do not think that much. How many bullets do they trade us now? And once we started fighting they would trade us none at all. If we got every bit of powder in the country now and didn't fire one shot to celebrate, we still wouldn't have enough to kill all the soldiers that would come once we had started. The Sioux have showed us that. Also, I think there is no point talking to police. They are good men, mostly, and very brave and they do what they're told. And the Government agents too. Why talk to someone just carrying more paper around? We must talk with one voice to their head men, and the Grandmother herself so she will change the treaty."

"I know enough chiefs who talked to that Father in Washington," said Sitting Bull glumly. "They come back different. Every white is the same, no matter what he calls himself, big or little. He wants more, everything, and the more People talk to him the more of everything they lose. There is only one way: kill them or get rubbed out."

"The Sioux should know," said Crowfoot. "Some of them have killed soldiers until they had no land left at all. I will not let that happen to —"

"I did not send you tobacco," said Big Bear quickly across the fury rising in Sitting Bull's face, "and you did not come here for us to quarrel. We have each done things we thought best for our people, one signed the treaty, one fought the soldiers, one did not sign the treaty. Nevertheless, we are all in the same trouble. I say we must now stand together to face the Whiteskins. I see that the buffalo are almost gone; they were given us by The Only One, and He is taking them away. I hear their footsteps still where we once saw great herds to every horizon: at Sounding Lake and at the Tramping Lakes and over the land I hear them, but more and more now their sound comes from where The Spirit has taken them, down in the land to Him where we and the whites can no longer abuse them. I think they will soon be all gone and we will have to try and live without them, unless we find the way of That One again. The whites," he hesitated, momentarily broken away by that black thought, but he forced himself to speak quickly, surely, what he wanted with all his being to be so,

"The Spirit must have sent these whites to us so we must find the way He wants us to live with them. We see we cannot fight them. Fighting is good in raids, and makes men, but we know it cannot be His way for us to do nothing but kill. One only becomes more manly by killing other men and I don't think American soldiers are men: they have deliberately killed too many women and children. I don't know such a word for them as they are then, I think The Spirit has given us none, but if men again and again cut up small children, they cannot any longer be men. That's about all that can happen when you fight to wipe out, and I won't let that happen to my People either. But I say, the treaties as they now stand are bad. They were always made by the same whites talking to a few People here, a few People there, saying, 'Those others have taken the hand, are you wiser than they?' And there was food there, lots of sugar; and tobacco. So they signed and didn't understand what was happening. We must be all together, with one voice. We must change the treaties. They take too much that The Spirit has given, and return nothing."

"The Blackfeet were all together at Bow River Crossing," said Crowfoot. "And there were Plains Cree chiefs there too, taking the hand."

"There are some who have not." It was not a good answer; it was a very bad one and he knew that even as he could not stop saying it.

"The Blackfeet know you as 'the leaderless people'."

Big Bear laughed aloud, quickly before his rage could leap to his face. "That's because my People are so free," he said as if easily, "they wander everywhere in bands as small as they please and —" but he got himself stopped at last. He was going to say "and take orders from no one; a chief leads only by wisdom," but before this Siksika, in this place, that certainly had to be swallowed into silence. And he did it, painfully, with the last of his tea, praying.

By the time Running Second and The Magpie had the buffalo hump hot for eating, Big Bear thought he could see their round beautiful world coming nearer again. Every month Sioux warriors with their families trickled south and Big Bear was careful to say nothing of that, nor of the great reputation which with every inactive month melted also. It was enough to prod gently at what was least likely to embarrass for no one knew better than Sitting Bull that any confederation could only improve what he now had: nothing. It was Crowfoot, angered by the River People blocking the buffalo — the insult of his tacit refusal to believe so few had come north Big Bear carefully ignored; far stronger than insult was Crowfoot's almost studied ignorance of the buffalo going away altogether; at least he would not acknowledge it in this lodge, which was not so strange — angered by the Sioux for being there at all, five or six thousand of them each day devouring game and buffalo and police supplies that could as easily have fed the Blackfeet another day as well: Crowfoot was the problem. Crowfoot was a proud haughty man, as every great chief must be, but now white hunting parties and travellers, whenever they wanted to see a 'great' chief, asked at Fort Walsh to find Sitting Bull; it had once been Fort Macleod for Crowfoot. Only three years after the Big Treaty with all those whites writing down every word and sending it everywhere on the talking wires when the Great Blackfoot Confederacy gave its bloody hand to the nice old Grandmother and Crowfoot said all those beautiful stupid things — bird feathers, yes, to pull off and throw away before they stink in a fire — Big Bear drew out his patience as if it had no end, almost beginning to smile to himself, eating. If this could happen, some White-skins for a few days might want to see not a Sioux or a Black-foot, but a Person. Little Pine was the only other great chief who had not given his hand and he was too angry and old, he cared nothing for whites as long as there was a buffalo left. To speak of who must lead this confederation was the last possi-ble matter to wreck them: better it should never be thought. Big Bear even refused to think that he, with the most scattered and varied tribe of them all, with the least acknowledged posi-tion, must have the greatest difficulty convincing his people that confederation was needed. He had never taken any hand and he spoke as leader of all the Plains and Wood People. If he could work these two men to understand with him there was nothing That One would not give him to do: he saw that like the evening star glowing through the first darkness. And he had the great arrogance of Sitting Bull convinced, though Crowfoot sat, carefully nasty with insult still, proud as if he was some kind of special being that need not work together with anyone to gain the best for his people: perhaps, it came to Big Bear, he has talked too often, too long, to whites who have told him too long of his greatness. He lets priests take children away to schools. Perhaps Crowfoot cannot com-pletely think Blackfoot any more. Looking at Sitting Bull, Big Bear saw his thought mirrored on the Sioux's face: here we have another graciously invited away, fattened by the White Father beside the Stinking Water; he comes back where he belongs and all the white soft bread and white soft sheets and white soft blankets on white soft beds have juggled loose the pins in his head. The tightness is gone. But Crowfoot was not, yet, quite unpinned; he clearly loved his tall adopted son

Poundmaker of the Plains People and finally seemed in grudging agreement by evening as they went outside, urinated, looked at the bright cold stars and came back in to eat. So Big Bear dared what would make the confederation complete, the most dangerous of all. He sent for Gabriel Dumont, head chief of the Metis, to come eat with them.

"There is some things I think," said Dumont, wiping the buffalo fat from his chin down into his straggly black beard. He and his people had also been at The Forks all winter and eating enough. "We can fight them in two good ways, from trenches like we used to fight the Sioux in the summer hunt on Red River, or running them like buffalo, like you did on the Little Bighorn. Between us we have the best riders in the world, we just need more guns and horses. Now, while we get that we have to talk to this Government, maybe we don't have to kill too many. The chiefs at Carlton asked them to talk to my people about treaty, but they never have. We write letters but they say we don't have the land as we live on it, they won't help us if the buffalo are gone. We have no treaty and soon we'll have no land. Nothing. More and more letters are written, but nothing. Here is the other thing I think. While we get ready to fight we have to talk to this Government together. But we can't talk white, none of you can and I can't. I talk Cree and Blackfoot and Sioux and French, but not white. You have to talk white or it helps nothing."

"Ahhhhhh."

"The one thing I think, we need one Person who talks white."

"Ahhhhhh."

"Louis Riel is at St. Joseph now, on Red River."

There was complete silence. Then:

"Louis Riel had to run away from the Grandmother."

"Louis Riel is no Person."

"When Louis Riel steps over the line the police take him."

"Louis Riel prays only to the white Spirit."

"He prays to the same Spirit I pray to!" shouted Dumont suddenly.

"Ahhhhhh."

Horsechild looked up, startled. He was at his usual place when there was meat in his father's pot; he had just snapped a short bone against one of the fireplace stones and was putting a jagged end into his mouth. The Magpie disappeared like a cold whisper behind him, and his mother continued to poke with a stick the fire licking the black kettle. The voices of the men he could not understand went on faster, growing louder, their gestures all about the round rim of his looking growing more excited and soon they would be furious. Horsechild did not like the big Metis chief. Hair grew out of his face as black as the pale-faced priest who always went through camp like a terrible, stooped-forward crow peering about for scraps to peck up, to stuff somewhere under his skirts. He sucked on the broken bone, snaking out the marrow with the curl of his breath, faintly salty gobs of blood catching on his pursed lips and hanging there while he looked through the smoke at his father surrounded by the great men talking louder and louder like boys. Only a few hairs pushed out of his father's face, a very few on his upper lip and around his chin and he had watched him many times twitch them out, one by one pinched between the huge nails of his fingers. His father sat now quite unmoving. His lips clamped together so hard they looked a straight thin line under his nose and the veins on the sides of his head glistened thick as branches, his eyes barely a slit. As if he was staring into a blazing light that had been coming straight toward him for a long time from far away but which he had not quite faced until the sounds in the lodge rose a little higher, and then suddenly stopped, all together.

IV

Edgar Dewdney:
                Department of Indian Affairs

Private and confidential
                                    Ottawa 19th December 1879
My dear Sir John.

   The official reports of both my travels and for the year have
gone in to Vankoughnet and I herewith give you the private
reactions you asked for. You will notice my official report has a
good deal more of everything, including the Indians we have
had to feed, our continuing legacy from Mackenzie's North
West policy. What there was of it.
   After six and a half months in the North West I must hon-
estly say that I believe the re-election of our party on October
17, 1878 and your re-organization of Indian matters into a full
department under the Department of the Interior with yourself as responsible minister saved our territory from a disaster.
It seems Laird's office was almost totally unprepared for the
starvation of the past year. Once fires began to burn along the
border (set of course by American soldiers), the depleted buffalo herds would not move north even if General Miles' troops
had not patrolled the border continuously all winter. As they
did, Superindentent Walsh informed me, and he is certainly
the most competent Indian handler we have in the North
West. He almost had Sitting Bull convinced that the Americans would keep their word and give him a decent reservation
but the first time the Sioux moved a mile across the line in normal pursuit of buffalo and disturbing only dust they are run at
and fired upon by Gatling guns! Washington policy obviously

is: experiment with your latest weapon on your Indians. I understand that through his Excellency a strong official protest has been registered and it cannot be too strong for such acts are barbarous; the Plains Indian has nothing but the buffalo. No one, least of all I, would advocate confronting the Americans because they believe in handling natives with a strong hand, but these policies are now costing us money and must be vigorously protested. Our police and agents have worked very hard on the starvation and developed a workable system whereby they give out rations for one day only on alternate days, but you will note that the total cost is still very high especially when we are unprepared and forced to buy from local suppliers. Indians are accustomed to an almost pure fresh meat diet and it is hard to imagine how debilitating flour and salt bacon are until you observe life in a begging camp. Debilitation is not of course all bad, for it checks their desire for fighting, but you might note the scrofula and death statistics. We will need much more beef and it is available in Montana for a price, but it will still be immeasurably cheaper than trying to maintain a standing army like the Americans. Didn't their newspapers report it was costing them an average of two million dollars per redskin killed? We could give them a bargain: cut that in half for a lump payment on Sitting Bull and his 5000 Sioux and be more than enough money ahead, though we fed them forever, to build the Pacific Railway! That's a dream for one's cups, I know, and all the world knows of Lemonade Lucy's present regime in the White House. But surely President Hayes imbibes privately?

You must excuse me, but it is the holiday season.

Everything about Sitting Bull is bad and I can see our only policy is to continue pressuring him, he must go back. Walsh's handling on the spot is good: keep them from complete starvation but offer no hope for land and at the slightest misdemeanour of any Sioux make the arrest and give him a public trial and always jail him if the offence in any way allows. Walsh has informed me that several leading chiefs including Sitting Bull's own adopted brother, his war chief Gall, have just recently returned to American territory and to understand how significant that is let me elaborate what I discovered on my long journey across the plains last summer.

You remember that in May I called to your attention the March 24 issue of *The Saskatchewan Herald* where a long item detailed very disturbing matters under the title "News from the Plains." It got its substance from a letter by Father Lestanc the priest who travels with the St. Laurent Metis camps wherever they move, and said, "all the tribes — that is the Sioux, Blackfoot, Bloods, Sarcees, Assiniboines, Stoneys, Crees and Saulteaux — now form but one party, having the same mind . . . the Indians consider the treaties concluded with the Government are of no value, and that the Indians should not be imprisoned for offences against the law. They also seem desirous of securing Sitting Bull's assistance to obtain another and better treaty." Subsequent reports by Inspector Crozier tended to support Vankoughnet in his opinion of "editorial inflation," but on closer interview with Crozier and also some Indians I discovered several matters we should both know, though I doubt officially.

The first is that one great confederation of all Indians very nearly came into existence last winter. It was the unlikely achievement of one Cree chief brought to Government attention years ago and of whom the *Herald* said, "up to this time he cannot be accused of uttering a single objectionable word, but the fact of his being the head and soul of all our Canadian plains Indians leaves room for conjecture." Neither

Father Lestanc nor the editor Laurie, who on these matters is an informed man, would use such words lightly: "head and soul" and after I talked with this native several times I am convinced they are correct.

He is Big Bear, the Plains Cree chief who now alone of all their ancient chiefs has not signed treaty. He is almost a foot shorter than I and in no way prepossessing of feature for he must be nearly sixty, though in copper age is very hard to tell and his face pulled into gaunt sharpness over its bones. Macleod told me he has a bundle from the Great Parent Bear, that is he is guided in war by the most powerful spirit helper known to the Cree, and that this bundle made him until recently the absolute terror of all the Blackfeet. He looks innocuous enough, sporting no scalps or any kind of decoration on his scarred chest, which I must admit appears to be at least the proportions of my own. But I believe that now it is his voice, and his perception, which draws more and more people to him. His voice would be unbelievable in Parliament. The deep rich timbre of it alone, forget all sense (so rarely needed anyway) would devastate any opposition, including Blake. Could we but teach him English, even French — forgive me!

In 1874 this man would not even accept what he saw as a compromising present from Rev. George McDougall when he travelled the plains explaining the treaty then planned and in 1876 at Fort Pitt Alex could not persuade him to sign because "he could feel the rope around his neck." He has obviously no personal fear of anything, and it is difficult to translate such picture language, but I agree with the late James McKay, that the phrase referred to the much wider claims of the whole white law against the Indian. He does not argue for a great deal more food, now, like almost every other native I met begins his case and then can be simply talked down to a lesser amount;

rather he says he wants to see how the treaty will work out. Also, what glimmering he has of the underlying principles of Government behaviour seems to convince him that they cannot be right. Since we agree there is One Great Spirit over all, then That One has given Indians and whites to be what they are, and why then must Indians change? Whites want to farm, good, let them farm in their place and leave the Indians alone to hunt in theirs; whites say horse stealing is a crime, good, but for Indians it is an act of great manliness since it is very dangerous and a man who cannot protect his horse or does not have friends to help him do so obviously cannot afford to have one. His concept of life is of course pagan and simplistic in the extreme, but oddly enough in argument the mind of this stubby native seems as logical, almost civilized as any Oxford debater. His system once conceded, within it he cannot be touched. It is acutely embarrassing to be sucked into facing him on his reasoning and fortunately the slow process of interpretation provides extra time. Our first meeting took place, not inappropriately, on July 1 in the Fort Walsh square behind smudges meant to keep mosquitoes at bay but in debate it seemed here was an opponent not unworthy of your-self. For I feel I must disagree with you, Sir John: all Indians are *not* alike.

Several times since returning from the North West I have found myself straying almost into hyperbole, as here. I think now it is because I felt on the plains even more than when I was hacking out the trail across British Columbia years ago that here for me was indeed God's great, good plenty. There are terrors on those plains of course, and emptiness will forever keep it as Butler has it, "the great lone land" but at almost any point one can gain some elevation and see and see. It is all so vast, so laid out in unending curving lines that you can begin to lose the sense of yourself in relation to it. Believe me, Sir John, it can drive a small man to madness, this incomprehensible unending at any point seemingly unresisting and unchecked space. To control, to humanize, to structure and package such a continent under two steel lines would bring any engineer headier joy than the lyric prospects of heaven. The man you find who can do it will be a man indeed and I envy him, as certainly every engineer will ever after, but old Big Bear has lived into his own understanding of that land and sometimes while I was out there his seemed the more beguiling prospect; it may, in the end, last much longer than steel. When we parted at Cypress Hills on July 4 he told me something which the three day trail to Fort Macleod more than pounded into me; I was still awake early one morning (my back was getting worse again also) and I got up and went out beyond the tents to watch the sun rise. I stood erect as the rim of the sun came up and I could see how right he was. "When the sun rises on this land," he said, "the shadow I cast is longer than any river."

To be more precise. As Laird discovered at the treaty payments at Sounding Lake in August 1878, there cannot be anything more bullheaded than an Indian you let sense he has hold of something. Out of a twig he will then talk a tree that could lever the world. At this Big Bear is little less than superb and it was wisdom on David's part to resign as Indian Commissioner, who must never be thought of by the natives as a mere messenger between themselves and Government. Added to that was the surveyor affair two months later on the South Saskatchewan. If the men had actually admitted they were exploring how far east the coal extends along the river and incidentally noting levels for a possible railway (They were at the spot long enough to discover it is by far the best crossing known so far on the Saskatchewan if you ever consider a southern route, both for moderate elevations and shorter distance and though there's no coal it would be small matter to run a branch to the Belly River deposits and supply a main line. No railroad man will want to depend on wood or Ohio coal.) we might already have had a small war last October — just in time for your swearing in! The chief that first stopped them was Little Pine, a relative of Big Bear's, but possible gold is not quite so volatile as a certain railroad and Big Bear managed a compromise by adding another point to his spring agenda with whom he then supposed would be Laird. And for the fact that Big Bear was unable to lift his big lever this spring we may thank the long memories and short foresight of the Blackfeet.

Father Lestanc informed me privately he was certain both Crowfoot and Sitting Bull were in Big Bear's camp early last March, and further that Gabriel Dumont whom the St. Laurent halfbreeds call their president had gone to the Cree camp about the same time. Crozier investigated the rumour and could discover nothing untoward, but the halfbreeds were camped near the Cree all winter at Red Deer Forks. Lestanc gave me to understand that except for some crucial issue intervening we might now be facing all the Plains Indians *and also the halfbreeds under Dumont as one front united in their demands.* Even Riel's name kept coming up. The day I arrived at Fort Benton, November 10, on my way home I heard Riel himself had been there a few days before, trading robes for ammunition. It seems he is no longer chopping wood in the breaks and the authorities suspect him. I would suggest you send a note to a person in Washington you will know best and ask they give Riel something to do as far away from the Missouri as possible. For feeding Sitting Bull so long they owe us as much. I could not of course get anything out of Big Bear on this issue but Crowfoot inadvertently gave me some evidence. He told me at the Blackfoot payments, "If you drive away the Sioux and make a hole so that the buffalo can come in, we won't trouble you for food." It is fortunate he seems to blame only the Americans for the shortage of food; if he saw as clearly as Big Bear we would be sending more than sugar to the North West.

Crowfoot I believe wrecked the confederation either because his hunter mind still believes a herd will suddenly appear, as it always used to, on the next horizon or because he cannot forget old Blackfoot wounds from Sioux and Cree. He still thinks only Indian and by fortunate circumstance his people have gotten one large reserve instead of many scattered little ones and so hopefully he will continue to think so. It seems to me that for some time now Big Bear, in relation to Government has not thought Indian, that is in terms of individual band status, but he thinks now in terms of total power. He seems to understand that we, say what we will about the "good Grandmother," at the moment have all physical as well as moral power and the Indian has none because he has thrown both away. I believe Big Bear may understand that the present treaty is both the Indian's damnation and his only possible hope, for in making it at all, instead of simply wiping them out as the Indian himself certainly would have were he in our position, we have made a moral commitment to the Redman. The present treaty is too inflexible, however to help them in their condition, today. So it must be changed. I believe Big Bear realizes that red moral power, once mustered would outweigh any other kind of power we would willingly apply and that the strongest moral stand they now can make is to unite under his leadership, *who has never yet signed any treaty with any white*. He is a complete untouched pagan. To sit on the ground there in his lodge is to face a man who seemingly contains so complete an assurance of and confidence in his own self-ness — that is not a good word but you understand I'm struggling — that he cannot be moved by any, mere, white words. All chiefs of no matter what tribe must, he implies, understand his wisdom in not signing, and I think starvation might have pushed them into it already had not our agents gotten rations out and above all were they still not so held by their hopeless hunter optimism and not so torn by individual and tribal bullheadedness, all of which it seems nothing but death will ever quite wipe out of them, death or several generations should they live so long. Sitting Bull had simply everything to gain, talk or fight, and I think Big Bear did not dare bring his Cree in with the warrior Sioux without the balance of the Blackfoot Confederacy. As Walsh says it, "The veterans of the Custer fight would have been sufficient to walk over all our Indians and Crowfoot and Big Bear know that." In any case I cannot believe Big Bear wants to fight. He wants whites to leave him alone. He understands what Sitting Bull for all his experience is just now beginning to comprehend: in the long run they can only lose by physically fighting us; we have all that power. No, when he talked to me Big Bear knew it could hardly matter that his warriors' guns were empty if eight thousand hungry women and children covered the hills and valleys around Fort Walsh.

Fortunately he did not have them at his back when he came, though the procession was impressive enough with about one thousand three hundred Plains Cree coming from The Forks north and the Milk River Ridge west where they had been in Blood country shooting some fat buffalo. It was a little after "the leaves came out" which is his favourite time for talking because the land is happy and everyone feels new and good, he says. I refused to argue one word with him, or debate. I told him what Alex said three years ago: it was impossible for the Queen to negotiate with one chief alone. The law is one law:

the Queen's. He said that in the United States treaties were being renegotiated all the time and I replied I had heard that but it seemed to me such negotiation was invariably to the detriment of the Indian. At that he smiled and said,

"But we, we live in the land of the good Grandmother."

To which I responded with a similar smile and assured him we did and for that very reason the treaty was unchangeable. At Walsh we spoke three more times (I believe he found me as intriguing as I him) and he was most curious to try and understand about the "Big Headchief" in Ottawa and I tried to explain the relationship of the Queen, the Governor-General, yourself, the parliament, the Lieutenant-Governor and myself but I think the niceties of hereditary and appointed and parliamentary balances of power must remain beyond any Indian. He is noted as a sorcerer, George McDougall once wrote he was at least half Saulteaux (which might partly explain his intelligence), and he told me he believed in The Only Spirit who gave to everyone the wisdom to choose a man of greater wisdom than himself for him to follow. So I hope you will excuse me for not mentioning either the Queen nor his Excellency after that and speaking of you who leads us. He expressed a wish that someday before he died he might meet you and I said I wished that could happen. Which I do. But he would not sign.

Macleod advised that the treaty payment supplies be piled very openly in the fort square and the continued sight of that plus the traders in the village (a whole raggle-taggle place has mushroomed in front of the police fort) trading at what were excellent Walsh prices for their few new hides, and also the prospect of the accumulated annuities which I pointedly hinted might not be available again nor our providing daily rations of beef while I talked with Big Bear, proved too much for some. I'm sure the collapse of that larger plan also helped some decide for the old chief Little Pine and Lucky Man, a somewhat younger one, signed and were promptly paid all back monies from 1876. Little Pine began the surveyor business and was at Fort Pitt in '76 but I knew nothing of Lucky Man until Crozier explained he was a Big Bear councillor. At a council Big Bear apparently said as in passing that he certainly felt with those who wanted more food and so by the simple device of piling up a few tons of flour and beef behind an open gate we created a chief with about two hundred Indians. Perhaps we can use that method again to effect. My official report to Vankoughnet includes Big Bear's statement he was too ashamed to sign when so many lodges had left him. You should know that subtracting Little Pine's thirty-four and Lucky Man's twenty-five lodges some one hundred remained with him — a delicate sensibility! He also said he would take treaty at the general Sounding Lake payments but Macleod thought the Cree would not be north by the middle of August. In this assumption (Macleod has the soundest assumptions about natives in the North West. We may thank him that Crowfoot never forgets certain things and never remembers others) the police commissioner was quite correct for Big Bear was not at Sounding Lake.

For on July 3 he announced he had heard there were buffalo on the Missouri near the mouth of the Milk River and he and his young men were going there to hunt. A strange fact I noticed was that most of the men of middle years, including his oldest son Twin Wolverine who has no personal following, took treaty with Lucky Man while most of those who stayed out were younger warriors, notable among them his younger sons Little Bad Man and Kingbird and also his nephew, Lucky Man's son-in-law, Little Poplar. The latter must have a good many fathers-in-law since he already has four wives and concerned for little but a fifth, and is believed to be Big Bear's ruling spirit but unofficially I doubt that. It is often useful for them to have some wild younger men in camp. Pray God we won't need to face that combination too soon: old experience and young energy. If the North West is to be at all habitable we must work to keep that, like the reserves of major Cree chiefs, separated.

Further proof that Big Bear remains "head and soul" of the Plains Cree at least came in Crozier's telegram to me from Fort Walsh: "Little Pine and Lucky Man bands crossed south to Milk River." It was dated July 12, ten days after Big Bear stood beside his friends and watched them make their marks on the treaty and looked away across the barracks square not saying a word.

He will wait now; he says waiting has lived with him all his life. And as long as he can wait he will continue to draw every discontented straggler and perhaps even some treaty chiefs, for all such of any energy had their people on the plains this past summer and will be there as long as a single buffalo is left. Crowfoot was in Montana too, and his adopted son, The Cree Poundmaker. The latter has much influence in the north.

In one of our sessions Big Bear said the Spirit Above All was punishing them for signing away his gift of the land by removing the buffalo. How a hunter can deny the rotting corpses and bones everywhere is beyond my comprehension but he insists they are being taken into a hole in the ground and will reappear if and when the Indian has the land back. Such a superstition backing his platform for one very large and united reserve as the Sioux briefly enjoyed in the U.S. and which I understand was part of the confederation concept, should really elect him "prime minister" if Indians followed any logic discernible to us but fortunately their concept of individual liberty goes beyond all democracy; it is anarchic, and this the missionaries have not much affected — Christianity seems in part actually to support it — but they have done us splendid service breaking down heathen superstition and hopefully Big Bear soon finds himself out of tune both with the old freedom and the newer logical beliefs. We are rid of him until the buffalo are gone on the Missouri, but I must impress on you that the buffalo are finished, forever. The northern herd is now so small and with every remaining wild Plains Indian harassing it along the Missouri basin it seems inconceivable to Macleod that it last two years, three at very most. By then we must have Sitting Bull out and our northern reserve Indians settled growing their own food for our treaty lists show there are in total some six thousand (that includes Young Dogs, Assiniboine and Plains Cree) who will not willingly choose reserves until all hope of buffalo is gone and we must make it harder and harder for them now to receive the annual payments or any supplies unless they choose and settle. Otherwise when Big Bear brings back his reputation of never having accepted the Queen's hand he will be the rallying point he almost proved this spring. The Blackfoot Confederacy we can keep perfectly under control with priests and police as agents when they return; they have signed and chosen reserves. It is the Bear and his wild Cree that must concern us. All we need then is the halfbreeds again, and Louis Riel already brooding in Montana.

Which is a dreadful note on which to end a letter so close to Christmas and once again I apologize, though unfortunately for no joke. I believe you will understand me. I have not been easily intrigued by an old heathen on the plains. It is I begin to glimpse your vision of the essential keystone to the arch of

Confederation, and it is a land worthy of any man's aspirations. I enjoyed even the awesome barrenness of the Thunderbreeding Hills in late September, where a long day out of Fort Walsh we met five of Big Bear's carts loaded heavily with meat. I had shot two bulls, one magnificent that very morning and unfortunately we did not see the chief as he was far off the trail skinning a cow they told us, but his son Little Bad Man rode beside the carts. He was beyond doubt the purest example of red savage I met this summer, about thirty and powerfully broad like his father, immense mahogany face under roached hair and his naked arms and chest splattered all over blood from butchering. While we stopped one of those prairie thunderstorms came like black lightning over the hills and for a few moments we were lashed with cold water while just beyond, not a quarter of a mile away, the sun was dazzling on the long white dunes. But this Little Bad Man told us nothing of the summer hunt, only they would dry this meat for winter. He has neither the mind nor voice of his father thank God.

By the by, if you should decide the railway is to remain close to the border (God forbid Laurie in Battleford sniff such a thing!) so as, for example, to prevent lines from the United States siphoning off freight as the St. Paul now will surely do out of Winnipeg, I might have some information about a possible site for the capital. Officially I know nothing.

It will be my great pleasure Christmas Eve at the club where I hope you will be prepared to receive a presentation, a great shaggy one. And I promise to say not one word further about the North West unless to describe the beauties of its sunsets and its maidens. The Cree have two notable reputations, one concerning their low intelligence and the other their beautiful modest but by no means intractable women and from the evidence you will know I have with some pain gathered this summer (even while wearing that Porous Back Plaster I could at times barely move) I would judge both evaluations absolutely correct. I'll talk nothing of politics. Unless of course you directly ask.

Believe me,
My Dear Sir John,
Your Faithful Servant
Edgar Dewdney

v

The grass shimmered in the morning air along the line between sky and land. Out of that line the lodges developed, another feature of the land forming against space, against shouldered hills and an ultimate suggestion of mountains. But more ancient than the blue-green hills were these lodges, their weathered poles reaching swallowtail through smoke-blackened vents, out from the smoke grey and rubbed white of their base clutching at, rooted down squatly into the earth. From that scattered grey and whitish line a shape spread, dark and gradually bumbling up until it broke apart, flaring wide into pieces whose running sound was the beating of the earth itself as they grew larger, gigantic, their shadows passing over like hawks or eagles. Horses and men drumming over the land.

Their speed slackened until it was no more than a canter, then a walk under the giant summer sun. They seemed to be riding a flat halfcircle south though soon the plane of the land hid them from the camp and when they had completed their bend back the western hills lay in front of them still like blue dust riding the heat upon the prairie. Down through a forked dry gully, the horses' hooves spraying green and black and pale yellow insects into clatter, and then on a broad level expanse until it became a long incline that would break down sharp at the horizon. They stopped, two riders slid down and went forward on foot. Soon they seemed above the horsemen, but their dark thick shape gradually merged and downward into green, shorter and shorter until it vanished altogether and again only the line of land and blue sky remained.

The two men lay spreadeagled against the ground and looked into a slight breath of air, down across a hollow that opened wide towards the west as if once scrapped by some giant, hard river. The lip of its banks curved to level away north and south; directly west lay the Bearpaw mountains, their slopes tilting up gently green to the black piled about their tops. Almost as black as the buffalo feeding on the hollow below, tiny blobs on the immensity of land.

"Poor *mus-toos-wuk*," said Big Bear. "Just sixteen."

It was not really a comment on the smallness of the herd; Kingbird understood that as he scratched himself behind his ear where an ant had crawled. "There's just eleven cows for those four bulls," he said, and then thoughtfully crushed the ant between his teeth. A tiny squirt, almost like trader salt.

"One calf. The cows are barren, there's something with them. And when do they feed together so quietly in summer, no bull sniffing around or bellowing?"

Kingbird answered nothing; he had already spoken too lightly. The buffalo grazing half a mile up wind did seem small now, almost lonely, quiet as if lost against the spread land. They had not appeared that way when he discovered them, to his great joy, and galloped back to camp savouring already cooked tongue and brains at last, at last.

"Once we couldn't see the end of them," murmured Big Bear almost dreamily, "now we'll have to try killing every one of these and that will be the end of it." Kingbird wasn't listening very hard because the tiny brown spot which was the calf had turned from grass to butt steadily against the largest cow. Beautiful meat, suck. His father continued, "If we run them right perhaps all sixteen could be given us. We need them all."

"There's that calf there," Kingbird grinned, "we could get a few more and raise them like Whiteskins raise cattle."

Big Bear was crawling back from the ridge; Kingbird watched a bull moving behind the cow but the muzzle did not lift. The bull was just walking as if that cow had no smell. Kingbird scrabbled back and when they were far enough to walk again his father said,

"It took a good scout with luck to find these early in the morning but it's always dangerous to talk like whites. Soon one might begin thinking like them." He flung his arms wide to the sky, the land, and the men beyond them seated in the tiny shade of their horses. "The buffalo is of the world as The Main One gave it to us. He eats and runs and bellows anywhere, he is angry and can't be talked about like a castrated thing that's tied up as soon as it drops from its mother and won't move unless you beat it with a club."

Kingbird felt so ashamed he had to close his eyes for the very grass stared at him. All the happiness of discovery and racing to camp flat-out and leading the hunters, the pounding happiness of the buffalo run itself vanished; his legs cramped to carry him, anywhere, out from under the sky.

Big Bear said, "There is no joking left with buffalo."

"I don't think . . . " said Kingbird heavily, "I won't go on the run. I'll go away, bring the rest of them."

His father was pleased; Kingbird knew by the way his shoulders shifted, the soft way he answered immediately, not looking back to him, "Running Second knows how far buffalo run when there are some. I think Little Bad Man and Little Poplar and their People in the Bearpaws would like to hear about these sixteen."

Kingbird loped ahead, swung on his black and galloped back where they had come; the other hunters watched but said nothing. Big Bear said, "He thought Little Bad Man would want to know. There are sixteen and we should take them all, eleven cows, four bulls and one calf. They are well bunched and grazing in the long hollow below there, and we can run them west in a long line. The runners in the centre, the others ride wider outside and ahead so when they turn across to get outside too far the outside men follow. I'll be there where I was for the signal and then we'll run them."

"I would have gone to the Bearpaws," said Lone Man, still looking after Kingbird, now a motionless spot.

"He thought it better he should go." All the men were standing, the horses steadily jogging their heads in the heat and Big Bear turned his face to the sky.

"Our Father, The Main One, I have to name you first. All things belong to you. Look on our hunting. All Spirit Powers, I beg a good life for our People, I beg your blessings on everything. Forgive us for being hungry, I thank you that you have let us see food again. I ask you for a good running, that we can kill all the eleven cows and the four bulls and the calf also which I think is female. I cannot ask more now because it is time to hunt."

They were all mounted then, stringing out, those on slow horses trotting south and north to get in position on the wings. Big Bear left his bay runner to Lone Man and walked back, crawled to the crest where he had lain with his son and looked again down the valley to the buffalo and the mountains beyond. Where Chief Joseph of the Nez Percé had spoken. He

lay against the ground completely, and the earth warmth grew
in him and slowly each sound and movement and colour and
wispy smell of the living world worked in him: one bull pawed
dust over himself; an eagle lay upon the blue sky; a wolf studying
the calf twitched slightly on his belly stretched behind sage; an
ant carried her egg past his nose as a gopher emerged from his
burrow, staled, and then quivered erect as he became aware of
the long shadow motionless on the ground beside him; grass
singing sweetly. Spread there completely alert but empty
except of the hunt, the total consuming unconscious joy of one
more run merging with *mus-toos-wuk* given once more to the
River People, at last before him again, sixteen only and hardly
more than one belly-stretching meal yet everything for life
and this moment that could ever be asked, everything for this
moment while the iron road crawled steadily between him and
where he was born, nailing another straight line behind the
Grandmother's straight police to fence him in, square him in
against the innumerable bluecoats whose fires and patrol haz-
ing kept the few buffalo south of the Missouri beyond where
he could venture among Blackfeet and Sioux and Cheyenne
and Gros Ventre and Crow, surrounding them against the iron
already nailed down straight there, devouring the last of them
in the final moments of all their savage summers. But these sixteen he would surround and devour. He felt that cow's round
heart beat, the calf licked so beautifully creamy thumping
against her udder, sucking, the bird's beak slip a grub from her
hide and the relief of cool air brushing that infernal itch; he
saw the gopher come to his body in spasms, flickering, until
the whiskers of its twitchy nose brushed his eyebrows where a
fly sat, the earth and urine smell of it stood in his nostrils like
the sweet crushed grass tearing steadily, rhythmically between
the cow's teeth, her grumbling belly. Then the gopher was

gone in the mirror flash far to the north. He felt the grass patterned against his chest and after a time the dried green blades flickered Riel's words, "They squeeze us between them until we all run out like water," and there came another flash, from the south. He moved then, heavily, crawling away upon the ground, walking to his stallion. He mounted, looked down the curving line of the hunters, he lifted his hand. Lone Man's carbine exploded and the bay stallion went up over the crest in four giant leaps like Big Bear's hunting cry ululating back to him from the riders of his surround.

He was the curl of a giant wave breaking down upon and racing up the good beach of earth. The running hooves drummed him into another country, calling and calling, and it came to him he had already spread his robe on the Sand Hills, the air in his nostrils beyond earth good, the buffalo effortlessly fanned out before him in the lovely grace of tumbleweed lifting to the western wind. The gashed wounds left in the cows' shoulders and flanks by hunters they had once and then again outrun dripped brilliant red in the rhythmic bunch and release of their muscles, simply beautiful black crusted roses in the green and blue paradise of their running. Dust, bellows, shrieks, rifle explosions, grunts were gone, only himself and the bay stallion rocking suspended as earth turned gently, silently under them in the sweet warmth of buffalo curling away on either side. There were only two now, one bull and the great cow intent in the rhythm of drums, of himself and his runner and suddenly the bull broke, stumbled, rolled out of it like legs snapping and then there was only the cow, floating strong, floating nearer wave by wave, growing large until beside him streamed the tufted stick of her tail, the rolling leap of muscle in her hindquarters and he felt life surging like sweet water within her, her heart in that violent, happy thunder as she ran true the great curve of earth, as he drifted to her shoulder and his arrow for an instant pointed her like the giant constellation of the wolf road points the sky at night and instantaneously it grew in her, the feathers grew in the coarse streaming hair of her shoulders tight against her thin wiry summer curls and her rhythm rippled momentarily, then her heart staggered and eagle feathers flamed again, stood as if the first triangular flower of them had burst into double blossom. Then the bay had to swing sharply aside or he would have pitched over her, falling.

He stood where her head furrowed into the torn grassy ground, and he prayed, asking forgiveness of the Great Buffalo Spirit, thanking for what had been given, for the tongue, for the blood, for fat and bone and meat and hide, for sinews and the hollow cups of her hooves. In the circle of sun and sky and earth and death he stood complete. Then he bent to her front leg, wrestled her onto her side. His arrowheads from her shoulder, painted blood side by side. He heaved over her hindquarters and she settled her mountainous body down for him with one long sigh. He knelt beside her, cut off her teats one by one, slowly drank the warm blood and milk that came there. Her warmth upon the earth, the heat of life and happiness overcame him then and he had to sit down there, feel her heat mould him, curl him up within itself against the fulfilled dome of her belly shining against the sun.

A coyote stood on a rise in front of him; standing so close he could see the saliva drip from his lolling tongue. Coyote's mouth hanging open, laughing. Always laughing. After a time he knew he did not like this laughter and that he would soon be close enough to make it stop. Coyote was gone where he stood, and then Big Bear saw what he was laughing at. A fountain of blood growing in the ground there like a prairie lily opening upwards and swelling higher as if it grew soft and thick, and higher so he put out his hand to stop that. For an instant the fountain died, sucked back to almost nothing as his fingers approached and then suddenly it burst up between them into his face and he had to fall back. The sky above him was flaming red, red slimed him completely, wherever he looked he saw all merging to red in the spray of the fountain he slipped and floundered desperately, down on his knees, to squash down into the earth again, the mountains, the hills, the ridge where the women and children were coming with the travois and pack animals to cut up the meat and pack it to camp, the entire plain where the men were bending over four-teen scattered buffalo and a calf, waving and riding to hurry the women, singing, praying, to the mountains where he saw through a thick crimson film Little Bad Man and Little Poplar and those others coming with Kingbird, all dripping red, run-ning red in welts down their faces from the fountain squirting irresistibly between his fingers. On another rise Coyote laugh-ing openmouthed. The whole world had changed to blood. It fell like water over him on his knees and through it he saw, far away, two men coming towards him. He knew they weren't Little Men because they didn't wear hard black hats; he opened his eyes. Lone Man and Iron Body had dismounted in front of him. He looked around very carefully, then he could stand up.

"We got every one," Iron Body said.

"Yes," Big Bear said. There was no way at the moment to thank them and certainly never in words. And letting him, alone, run the best cow. He tried to smile at them, then he bent down and fumbled for a grip on the hide of her neck. His fin-gers seemed to slip, but after several tries they held and he drew a long cut through her hide. "I may have fallen asleep, though I wish I hadn't. I didn't feel a rope." And to them star-ing he seemed in sleep still, muttering and doing so perfectly such woman's work.

He wanted to forget what Coyote had laughed him into seeing, just as he had never wanted to remember what the Little Men had laughed him into seeing long ago — Coyote was even trickier than Little Men — but those memories scaffolded together something he could not lose even in the astonished laughter of his women arriving to see his cow whitely skinned and the giant joys of butchering shouting up everywhere on the hot plain. Early afternoon Little Bad Man and his group got there to join the feasting. All they had found in the Bearpaws was one bear not large enough for a mouthful each; Little Bad Man showed his father the mangy summer hide.

"That would be a good name, if you ever need another," Big Bear said. "Little Bear."

His glowering son looked away. Big Bear could see he thought he was joking again, joking at best for if anyone had been listening it would have been ridicule pushing a child into its place with them beside that gleaming hill of cow meat he had opened. He had not intended that it sound that way, the name had simply come and a name that came like that was good but it could gather no meaning if Little Bad Man refused to feel for it. He looked to the low mountains; the cow had carried him quite close. "That would be a good place to live," he added then to try and find this third son who seemed to have been glowering more and more in the years they hunted south of the Cypress Hills, "if it had game and wasn't on the wrong side of that straight line, they told the Nez Percé."

Little Bad Man, short and broad like himself but with a huge head that seemed to overweigh his great chest, grunted.

"So how is it any good?" was all he said, and turned to slice himself another hunk of raw liver.

By evening everyone in the re-united camps had eaten his fill; there was even some of two bulls and a cow left over for breakfast. Big Bear sent his crier through the camp and the Worthy Young Men and Warriors and Blades of Grass gathered for council. They had a long hard session and when it was over they had accepted his advice, against Little Poplar though Little Bad Man said nothing, that they must now start working back towards the sure police supplies at Fort Walsh. They could not go further west: it was the largest hunt they had had since leaving the Cypress Hills in the Moon of Laying Eggs. They would make a slow loop east to the mouth of the Milk River; there would be antelope, a buffalo here and there, and always wild turnips and other roots. In the Hills and Wood Mountains the saskatoons would be turning purple; perhaps there were buffalo there. Big Bear still had plenty of his teeth left but sitting in the circle of his council it had come to him very clearly, though he said nothing directly in order not to discourage anyone, that this had been the last buffalo run he would ever make.

VI

NOW THIS INSTRUMENT WITNESSETH, that the said "Big Bear," for himself and on behalf of the Band which he represents, does transfer, surrender and relinquish to Her Majesty the Queen, Her heirs and successors, to and for the use of Her Government of the Dominion of Canada, all his right, title and interest whatsoever, which he has held or enjoyed, of, in and to the territory described and fully set out in the treaty commonly known as "treaty Number Six"; also all his right, title

and interest whatsoever to all other lands wherever situated,
whether within the limits of any other treaty heretofore made or
hereafter to be made with Indians, or elsewhere in Her
Majesty's territories. To have and to hold the same unto and for
the use of Her Majesty the Queen, Her heirs and successors for-
ever. And does hereby agree to accept the several benefits. . . .

He had never liked Fort Walsh. Pounding its logs into the
ground here showed that the police, no more than the American
whisky traders who had squealed to and fro every summer
with their oxcarts until the wolfers killed so many drunken
Assiniboines on Battle Creek, cared nothing whatever about
the Spirits of the Hills. Why should Walsh care about sacred
places? He was just a white soldier by another name, his men
stood in soldier's straight lines like poles getting screamed at in
front of the pole with the Grandmother's rag on it; he didn't
need a hill for vision when he had all the bullets in the country,
he just needed hard boots to kick Sitting Bull sprawling out the
door onto that hard-tramped ground, some said it was out of
this very room where Big Bear now stood hearing the good
quiet murmur of Peter Houri's voice explain what the paper
said on the table. But he needed no words; that summer on the
plains had already spoken in overwhelming detail, spoken
more clearly than he would ever have wanted to hear, than he
needed to if he could help it, as if in some hole of his thinking
he had not already heard it long ago without being able or
quite wanting to push it into the ears of his people, all forced to
hear with him that summer, stunned.

He liked the room even less. Sitting Bull — perhaps he was
out of the American jail by now and sitting on that ass-big bit
of land they had reserved for him — Little Pine and Lucky
Man had made their names in this airless cornered room. Men

were stuffed tight around him. He had been looking through that square glass across the parade then too; a policeman passed from one straight edge to the other in their rigid way as if his legs and arms swung jointless, as if under his flat little red-and-gold hat he was pounding a trail across every grain of the whole earth. His spur glittered away and slowly there came the bottom rim of the sun, out under the sagged winter clouds and the edge of the roof, shining level at him through the pale afternoon and suddenly the clouds' rounded bellies, the hills, the walls and flagpole and parade and roof, the very room was washed with a wet, shining gold. The lamp on the table, the fire licking around the hearth vanished and the faces of the men surrounding him shone from below as if they stood in golden crystal snow. He saw the three men who had ridden with him, Twin Wolverine, Lone Man, Piapot, smiling at him as if their dark gnarled faces were suddenly hammered out in gold.

"He knows," said his oldest living son. "That the paper is good."

And Big Bear was thinking about the sun. How often in endless coming and going over the incomprehensible bigness of the world he had heard of as a boy from his grandfather and then from Broken Arm, and all the whites whom one hardly bothered to believe much, or could, how often had Sun had to look down upon what they saw that summer? They had been hunting north, hungry, and camped near Old Wives Lake after surrounding a few antelope where the hills grew wild peas and good roots. They were half a day north of the lake; The Magpie, like every untrained wife he had ever had, burst into tears when he wanted to camp beside the lake so he had to walk well out from the lodges to hear the laughter of the old women killed there long ago, whose spirits from the water still mocked the Blackfeet for falling into their trap. The sound of ancestors under a clear moon rested him more deeply than any sleep. He was standing in motionless prayer as the sun rose upon the land and after a time he became aware of something, stranger than he had ever heard in his life. The People came out of their lodges, hearing it, too, that sound as of something unearthly shrieking in spasms very far away in the north. It went on and on until the young men could not be controlled, they were armed and ready to confront whatever that was; Red Bone reluctantly agreed, perhaps, nothing came to him, so they rode north, the women already wailing behind them. They rode through the summer morning, the sound gradually louder and soon others too, spastic clangs and whistles and screams and finally pounding until he would only have had to look at them to wheel them all around, racing for space and silence. But the sun shone, Wandering Spirit was riding beside him, face rigid as a stone, and beyond him Twin Wolverine and Little Bad Man somewhere and he himself wanted to know. In all his long life he had never heard nor could have imagined such a sound, it still seemed far away and they were all mounted on horses strong from the thick grass that no buffalo was grazing now. It was too unnatural to move him in any way but curiosity; he had not put on the bear claw or sung his bundle song. From every new rise they studied the land dented with hills and topping a long incline they saw something far down a valley. For a moment it seemed a huge worm far away, pawing — if a worm could paw — something stiff up around its head as it crawled along, a slug trailing slime in the sunlight, but then he knew what it must be and he was laughing, sitting on the bay stallion laughing though he felt no happiness whatever. It was the iron road. Of course whites and their iron road. Then he led the warriors in their long gallop, almost a charge with

Wandering Spirit beside him, down the valley until the dust around its head became men and the one sound differentiated into a hundred, each more violent than the other. A policeman he did not know rode out, told them they could not approach with loaded guns and then agreed immediately when he said he was Big Bear. They rode as close as any of them wished, as they could control their horses, but he could not understand what he was seeing any more than he could understand the scurry of huge horses pulling wheels and men so covered with smoke they seemed black yet who never got in each other's way. So he soon turned away, the tangle confusing him and the sounds unendurable, as if intent now to split his awareness into unfindable pieces. Behind him a rifle cracked and the warriors streamed away from him to the hills. He looked back; the policeman waved, so all was well and he nudged the stallion into gallop after them. On the rise they stopped to breathe their horses; seen from there the head of the worm had already crawled behind a shoulder of land to the west.

"I shot it in the penis," Kingbird was saying.

The warriors pulled their mounts around him; hiding their mouths in disbelief, some already laughing.

"Did that have one?" said Miserable Man. "I wish I'd seen it."

Kingbird was laughing aloud, "That slippery thing near the ground going in and out, just like a man doing it."

"Yeh, I saw that, but there wasn't any —" Miserable Man's big face turned slackly from one to the other, "To itself?"

Big Bear said quickly, "The bullet didn't stop it." Everyone craned about to stare as if they had not remembered him. "Whiteskins can do anything, even to themselves."

Miserable Man clutched himself, almost fell from his horse in his howling laughter. The endless ribald variations that they flung at each other riding lasted all the way back until the Thunderbird came up and over suddenly very loud and black and they rode wet into camp to tell the now quiet women and children.

The Magpie lay warm against his back in the washed summer night, but he could not sleep. What he had seen would not leave him, the men and horses clawing along the heaped earth, and especially that huge black thing belching smoke and shrieking and moving itself by its fire which he had not even been able to describe to the women in parts, leave alone whole, because there was nothing like it he had ever seen or remotely imagined. Its wheels stood as high as the Red River carts of the Metis so it was a kind of wagon, yes, but — that seemed the very least of it; sometimes it shuddered horribly, as if it would tear itself to pieces snorting black smoke into the air, shrieking as it scraped itself over the steel. There seemed some burning devil frothing in it. Through his head swam Kingbird's funny story, and it did not appear in the least funny now. The shining rod thrusting in and out over the ground gouged up wide into a ridge, back and forth. It drifted away, came again, drifted, but he could not fumble it into any meaning for himself. He pulled The Magpie closer; she turned obediently under the robe and laid her leg over his, sleeping and holding him. She was not fat enough yet, nor very soft, and there did not seem to be any child in her that he could find. He looked at the sky past the swallowtail of his lodgepoles until it lightened finally into dawn. It came to him that he must take Horsechild and his women to see the iron road.

When he informed the others they decided all the women and children must see; by noon they had loaded camp and were in motion though many of the women wailed in terror. They travelled north-west for three days, by the second they could hear it and needed no scouts and about noon on the third they came upon it. The travois horses almost stampeded as they rounded a hill and the women refused to move closer so they retreated up the hillside and sat, watching, the smaller children huddled around them. Now the bay stallion seemed uncontrollably shivering, as if dreams had come to him also and Big Bear left him and walked down through the soft grass with Horsechild, and everyone who wished to, following. He told the boy to hold his ears shut, to concentrate on looking or the sounds would hurt him; so they were able to sit for some time beside a stone on a little ridge watching that pass. On either side as far as they could see the ridge had been slit through by two gigantic cuts. Men with teams drove along the cuts and dropped wood, laying it across the mound between them, strangely for there were only horses' tracks on it and little sticks with tied rags, then other teams again opposite each other with men hoisting off long pieces of iron, laying it soft on the wood, giant men in dirty shirts hammering, and before he had worked any of this to comprehension little carts with two men humping up and down and another pointing about, yelling like a policeman on parade, had gone by on the iron and the huge thing he understood now was the fire wagon with a man in it came hissing and jerking closer on the iron they had just been hammering around. He stayed until he was sitting there alone and that black belcher almost in front of him, sometimes shuddering and moving forward, sometimes staggering back, and he saw the man who had painted his face black as if he was returning from a war peep out of it, looking in all directions; he stood up and began backing towards his people, keeping it in front of him though he saw it would not go off its iron track. Then over all the sounds he heard his name.

It was Peter Houri from Fort Walsh; beyond him near the worm came a big Whiteskin wearing a tall black hat and limping with a stick. The Indian Commissioner.

"Whitebeard Dewdney is Governor here now," shouted Houri after they had greeted each other. "He wants to talk."

"I thought he said he spoke only for the People."

"He still does that, but he's Governor now too."

"Are those two things one now?"

"I can't say," said Houri. "I don't know about that."

Big Bear contemplated, far to the north-west, the Thunder-breeding Hills.

"I want to talk too," he shouted finally. "We travelled three days to see this, what they are doing, and —" there was a short piercing scream from the machine, another, and he looked back quickly towards his people. Not a single face was to be seen up the slope, as if wind had flung a spotty ragged blanket over the hill. "We have had no hunting for four days."

"Yes, they lay it very fast," said Peter into a relative quiet, but he was studying the hillside and it was clear he had understood.

That evening the Governor drove into camp. Two dogs almost as large as small horses ran behind his buggy and the famished camp dogs immediately began tearing them to pieces when enough boys arrived to happily hammer them with clubs and they retreated to a defiant distance, howling and slavering. Peter Houri and the driver wrestled the Governor's dogs into the buggy, their red hair slashed wet everywhere, and patted them while tying them gently down under the seats.

"They are very big," said Big Bear, very polite. "They must eat more than —" but Houri, settling his clothes into place again, signed to him and he stopped so only the first words needed to be translated.

"Yes," Dewdney said. "The great Governor-General Lorne gave them to me when he visited the Territories here last summer. The son-in-law of the Queen Mother, he lives in Ottawa now."

Big Bear was suddenly aware of his own son-in-law Lone Man, who had been contemplating with him the shivering rumps of the two gigantic red dogs sticking out from under the buggy seat, now turn abruptly with his hand to his mouth as though he were choking; but he himself was able to keep his face straight. Because the actuality of the Grandmother had become clearer to him; she even had a child that had a husband who walked on the plains, so she must have had a man in her at least once. He had heard from whites of course, many times, that she had an enormous number of children and many of them were alive too, but seeing such big dogs helped.

"I wish he had visited me," he said, smiling. "It could have been time for a White Dog Feast," but Peter Houri was signing, stop, stop! as both Lone Man and Twin Wolverine walked away very fast.

"He would have been happy to feast with you," Dewdney responded without comprehension, limping forward heavily on his cane, "but you were not on this side of the Line."

"We had to hunt near the Musselshell then."

"I hope you had good eating from the cattle this afternoon."

"They taste almost as good as buffalo."

"Mr. Van Horne, the Big Boss building the railroad, sent them. He couldn't come now, he's very busy and goes away tomorrow but he said he'd be very happy to meet you and take you on his train to our new town we are building at Pile of Bones on Wascana Creek."

It was a cloudless evening and the women had a blue chip-fire burning before his lodge; they sat down, Houri adjusting a folding chair for the Governor. Big Bear replied,

"I have sent thanks for the cattle, and the other good things. He must be a great chief to have such good food, and lots of it, to feed so many men. I have seen that twice, and I don't want to see any more of his railroad."

The Governor's face leaned above him, his eyes peering intently from under the stiff black rim of his hat; thick beard looped down the sides of his face and up under his nose, hung at his jowls almost like the dogs' dewlap except it was sheet white. When the translation was ended he had quietly said,

"It will never go away."

They smoked, drank tea, talked of small things and while the light burned away in the sky the River People came nearer from their lodges until they surrounded them, as always silent mounds motionless upon the ground. Finally when only fire-light remained the Governor asked him again about the treaty; surely he could see that their life as free commoners had come to an end, and Big Bear replied he had made a vow at Sounding Lake when speaking to the Governor Laird that he would wait and see how the Government that spoke for the Grandmother kept its promises to those who made their names on the treaty. That was four years, the land had given them to live and now the vow was complete. He would accept her hand this year. Tonight? The treaty could be drawn up immediately. No, the scouts had come in reporting there were some buffalo at Wood Mountain and they wanted to hunt them. But he would give his hand before the year was out? Yes. Where? In the Cypress Hills. And then again, strangely, the Governor showed his wisdom; he asked, said nothing more about treaty, as if he understood at last this agreement had actually very little, if anything, to do with the Government's trying to keep its records and its many little promises in order. Rather, from inside his coat he brought a large flask whose silver shape seemed to dance and change, beautifully, in the firelight.

"This is against the law in my Territories," he said, "except on the greatest state occasions. Such as this one."

He unscrewed the top and handed it to Big Bear. The brandy soared through him like fire. He handed it back, the Governor drank and handed it to Wandering Spirit on the ground to his right. It passed from one councilman to the next, even Little Poplar and then Little Bad Man tipping it back, and finally returned almost empty. Peter Houri took a swallow, the Governor accepted the flask and, with a quick twist, sprayed the last drops over the fire. It flared up, yellow-red an instant against the ring of glistening faces, then died again to its tiny blue flickering. There was small coughing, a clearing of throats.

"You are building a new house for the Government, Where The Bones Lie?" Big Bear asked.

"We will soon, yes. The railroad crosses the creek there."

"I have sometimes lain on that hill, and watched numberless buffalo. And the women, making pemmican."

"There are largely tents and mud there now, but will you come and see it? I invite you, as soon as you can."

But Big Bear sat for a time looking into the fire. A nighthawk in flight whirred over them like tiny bones rattling, then a silence so heavy lay around and over them the Governor suddenly shifted his weight, loudly, in his chair. Big Bear said from the ground,

"Since this is a great occasion in your Territory, I wish to tell you two things." He continued after a time, "One is of the paper in Battleford that makes words about me and sends them anywhere. I hear these words, and two months ago when Peter Erasmus came to tell me you said I and Piapot and Lucky Man had to choose reserves north of the railway, I sent my own words with him to that paper. I lived south of the Line but have held no secret meetings against the Grandmother, as it says I have. I trust Peter Erasmus and I told him I could have had meetings, American traders and Louis Riel asked me for them but I didn't do it. Riel wrote a message to American papers which said I was a good chief and whenever young men came to my camp with horses stolen from whites I let responsible men know where the branded horses were so the owner could identify them. This is true, though no Montana paper would take these words, as Riel told me. Once, when I took such a horse away from one of my young men he was so enraged he beat me with a stick. I let him, and he stood ashamed. We don't fight with any whites, and I don't want the young men to keep their branded horses because I know with whites that is stealing."

"And your young men no longer steal from the Blackfeet?"

"River People have always raided Blackfeet. It's too bad my young men weren't near the Missouri last year when Crowfoot traded all his summer robes for horses because then his people would have lost them honourably, not while they were lying sick from whisky in their lodges and the traders stole every one of them back."

"I haven't heard that about Crowfoot."

"He may not tell you."

"I did hear you kept Healey, the sheriff at Fort Benton, a prisoner in your lodge for two days."

"Otherwise he might have been killed. He rode in to us with guns to take some robes that the traders said a few young men had traded for whisky."

"Had they?"

"It's true our young men steal, but the American traders started it. We once trusted them. And the Blackfeet, when we complained that our horses were gone the police said, 'Don't you know where the Blackfoot camp is?' I asked them, 'Do you want us to break the peace?' but the young men heard this and they want to make warriors of themselves, who can blame them, so I don't know where it will end. I'm not talking about Blackfeet, I'm talking about these police. Once we could trust them and when we recognized one of our stolen horses we would go to them, but we have never yet got the first one back when a white man was sitting on it. Our word to them is as the wind. But let an American or any white say, 'There are some of my horses in the River People's camp,' the police come at once and all the man has to do is point, 'This, that horse is mine,' and the horse is taken at once without any question about where we got him."

"I am very sorry," Dewdney said heavily, "to hear this about the police. I assure you I will speak to the officers."

"This is a great occasion and I cannot talk now about why we have had to learn to distrust so many whites, nor about the police that lead our women into the bushes. I was talking of another thing."

"Does that happen often?"

"They have no women and ours are beautiful. I was talking about the Battleford paper that makes words about me not giving my hand to the treaty; it speaks where it knows nothing. I have told you of my vow, and I sent it that word with Peter Erasmus also."

"The newspaper at least has nothing to do with the Government," said Dewdney. "The man who makes it is honest and speaks what he hears from reports, but he has nothing to do with me and my chief in Ottawa."

"But you see those words?"

"Yes."

Big Bear pondered a moment. "I think then it's not so easy to say, the paper has nothing to do with the Government. As long as a paper is there it speaks words whenever you want it to, and they are always the same and people believe words they hear too often. That's the way words are; power."

"Do you read the Cree Syllabics?"

Big Bear smiled faintly, "I knew that once. But when I looked at the paper it always said only what the missionaries said, so I forgot them."

"But they can say any word in your language! Peter could write down everything we say here and you could hear it again long after we are apart. Wouldn't that be good?"

"I will keep hearing every good word said here. But with the paper and the Government I think it may be like the Hudson's Bay Company and with the railroad. You say the Government has nothing to do with either of them and so that must be true, but I can't understand. The words I hear probably come from the paper that knows nothing, the ones that say the Government gave the Company and the railroad a great deal of money and land, but, when I see them, they always seem to be wherever the Government is. There are so many things I don't understand, perhaps we will talk about some of them before I die, but there was a second thing I wanted to say to you here on this great occasion. I want to tell you how our People used to make treaties in your Territory."

Dewdney was moving his hand. When Big Bear looked up he said, "I thank you for your hospitality, and I want very much to hear this other thing you have to say. But could I ask a question?"

"Yes."

"Did Louis Riel talk to you about the Territories?"

"I held no secret meeting with him. He is very unhappy about his people in the North West and he told me the Government had not kept its promises to them, or to my people either. I held no secret meetings and he does not have to tell me about my people. I will give my hand to treaty this year."

The Governor seemed about to ask something further, aloud so Peter Houri could repeat it aloud to the faceless humps that surrounded him, but he hesitated, then suddenly lifted his long right leg over the left. Elevated against the night sky by the crossed sticks of his chair, he seemed gigantically black in arranged columns; only his whiskers glistened like flaring snow beneath the thick tall column of his hard hat. He said nothing.

"Once a band of Sioux fought against whisky traders and then came north," Big Bear said. "They came to Where The Bones Lie on the creek and there they made their camp. From the hill they could see the great buffalo herds move to and fro, and the chickens had danced and were resting on the plains, letting the lilies bloom. The land was covered with spring but in people there was only fear because the northern bands of the People and Saulteaux had come down, and the western Assiniboines too, wearing yellow paint to make war on the land where their fathers had hunted. The Sioux raised their Greatlodge there where the water was good also for horses, and grass, and one day one of the People came to them and begged admission. He passed the test, and the Sioux chief asked him to sit beside him at the head of the fire. Then the guest stood up to speak in the camp of his enemies. 'The whole earth,' he said, 'is one, and every man my brother. The First One sent us buffalo for our food, our shelter. There is enough for all, the great and small of any band. It is bad to kill one another, and I say let us live with peace.'

"Then every man in the Greatlodge stood and shouted, 'It is good! It is good! We will live with peace.' The Sioux chief stood and made the treaty words so that each was clear, and every man took his knife in his left hand and cut into his right and then took his brother's right hand in his, saying the treaty words as their blood joined. Messengers rode to every band, all people came until no one could not see the end of them from the hill. Old men and young gathered wood and buffalo chips into piles on the prairie and women brought meat so that the smell of its roasting was sweeter than sweetgrass or roses after the rain. The smell moved beyond the horizons and in every language the message came: Come, come and eat, and girls with braided hair and clean buckskin dresses trimmed with otter fur carried wooden platters covered with great roasts of meat and pemmican. The men seated themselves on the ground.

"The first man of the People who had come passed the pipe, and as the smoke rose and they breathed it he thanked again, for everything. They ate, and drank a drink of herbs they knew, and all joined in the peace treaty in the same way. The Sioux chief then wished to speak. He was very old, and ill. He tried to rise but could not, and the man of the People took his arm and helped him to stand. His words were: 'In Minnesota we fought for many years for peace, but the whites came and Government made us take a reservation, and still we had fighting. We built houses to keep warm in winter, we dug in the earth and grew potatoes and grain, but the soldiers came with knives on their guns, they killed all my brothers, my wives, and my eight sons too. Not a drop of my blood runs in any human being, and it is all thrown away. They burned our houses in the winter and the places where we had stored our food and they assaulted our women and fouled a river where we got fish and water so we died of stinking sicknesses. Then I left Minnesota in search of peace and travelled with these few people south, very far, as far as the Rio Grande River, searching —

but the threads of my life are finer than a spider's. They will break quickly, someone else must finish my words. I have found this peace, but there is so much to do and so little I have done.'

"He sat down on the ground. From everyone there rose a great cry for him, the great Wabla-dota who had come north to them from his wanderings and found peace. He fell back, he was already in the Shadowland, and he died the next day. He was buried with Greatlodge honours by all the bands, on the hill Where The Bones Lie."

The shadowy Governor slowly placed both his black boots flat upon the ground. They barely shone in the firelight. Big Bear said,

"That is what I wanted to tell you about treaty. And also ask you a thing."

"Yes?"

"I vowed four years ago that if I would make my name on the paper, the Governor would be there too. It's good you are now the Governor."

"Ah yes," said the Governor, and his chair squeaked. "I have very many things to do now, as you will understand, but I also want to be there when you do. Yes. Tell me, in your story of the treaty between the tribes, I have never heard of this Sioux Wabla-dota, but would I know that Cree chief?"

Peter Houri did not have to interpret the anger that leaped into Big Bear's voice, though he faithfully gave his words,

"No! I have never liked treaties. I let the eagle go in his own way, and the bear in his!"

Peter Houri was speaking English in his quiet voice. He must have said that aloud, again, for the shadow of his words seemed to be bumping around the cornered room and Lone Man and Twin Wolverine and Piapot were looking at him strangely. As Peter's voice stopped, so did all the whites look at him. Under the squared log walls of Fort Walsh. The sun had gone out and small light from the lamp stank.

"The treaty is paper," said Piapot, signing to Houri not to translate. "I signed it seven years ago and they've paid me and given supplies every year and I haven't chosen a reserve yet. Paper burns in any fire." His old friend Piapot, who had never got the good chief paper he wanted so much from the Company. He sometimes spoke half in wisdom but he had set up his lodge in front of the railroad, sat there smoking and refusing to move so that two very young policemen whom his young men could not provoke into fighting could come and make themselves great forever by kicking down the lodge about his ears. Yet sometimes Piapot spoke a half-wisdom, though he himself rarely knew which half was which.

"It is of satisfaction to me," said North West Mounted Police Commissioner Irvine, "that you agreed yesterday to come in and conclude this matter. Fort Walsh has been the headquarters of the North West Mounted Police for seven years and it is most fitting that you, the last of the Plains Chiefs, make your surrender here before the site is abandoned and headquarters transferred to Regina. I anticipate no problems and this is satisfying." Big Buffalobull, yes, whose back could not have bent since he dropped from his mother, if indeed that was the way he had happened to become. Who that spring had mounted seven pounder guns at the corners of Fort Walsh, stationed his men with rifles at every loophold and commandeered every pound of bacon and flour, every grain of powder, every bullet in the T.C. Powers store in the settlement and stacked them on the parade square and closed the gates because two hundred men had come riding with Big Bear to explain their guns were empty and their bands had no food.

"We have all said it, it is necessary," said Twin Wolverine. "I don't think they'll give the money again from the years before; it's almost too much now, they won't give that much again." Lone Man stood behind him, taller than anyone in the room, his robe worn shiny to the leather, his good dark face creviced by long rides that no longer had anything at the end of them. Silent.

"I have not the slightest doubt," said Indian Agent Allan Macdonald, "that this adhesion will be of the greatest benefit to the Canadian Government and to the public at large. And also to yourself and your band in what has already been and promises to be an even more difficult winter." To Big Bear he looked like another soldier; the Governor had too many things to do, he said, in Winnipeg; however when the leaves came out he was moving to his new place to live Where The Bones Lie.

"Yes," said Big Bear, and lifted his naked right arm.

All the whites had been through every ceremony necessary for their proper execution of treaty several times. So Big Bear simply said, and did, everything they required that

eighth day of December in the year of our Lord one thousand eight hundred and eighty-two, in the presence of the undersigned witnesses: Peter Houri; Louis Leveillee his mark; Pie a Pot his mark, chief; A.G. Irvine, Lieutenant Colonel, Commissioner N.W.M.P.; John Cotton, Superintendent and Adjutant, N.W.M.P.; Augustus Jakes, M.D., F.C.S., London, Surgeon, N.W.M.P.; Frank Norman, Inspector, N.W.M.P.; A. Shurtliff, Superintendent, N.W.M.P.; W.R. Abbott, Sergeant-Major, N.W.M.P.; W. Routledge, Corporal N.W.M.P.; Allan Macdonald, Indian Agent, Treaty No. 4
Big Bear (Chief), his mark.

"We didn't smoke the pipe," Twin Wolverine said, riding beside him through the granular stinging snow up the bent valley.

He had not thought The Only One would permit such blackness to be found in him; opening endlessly; he had never known all that could be there, and he could not stop himself.

"What more do you want?" he cried to his oldest living son. "I am an old man and it is no longer given me to feed my people. What more can you want?"

THREE

The Battle and the North Saskatchewan, June, August, 1884

I

Maintain the right to always get your man: by 1884 the North West Mounted Police had been patrolling the prairies, an area of three hundred thousand square miles, for ten years. Their total strength now stood at 518 officers and men and 355 horses; they had already performed most of the unprecedented acts of bravery which would eventually make them almost as useful to adventure romance as the Texas Rangers (never quite, for in ten years they had not yet actually shot and killed a single Indian). Commissioner Macleod began the legend at the fort he named after himself by handling American whisky traders and the Blackfoot Confederacy, and with fine newspaper coverage Superintendent Walsh continued it at the fort he named after himself by handling the refugee Sioux, but the basic method was trained into every green constable. It consisted mainly of nerveless confrontation. As if the Grandmother's law were so impartial and serene above any mere human question or resistance that the very pronouncement of it by one of her polished scarlet-coated officers was power sufficient for any arrest, in any situation.

The North West Mounted Police were not all handsome, clean-cut, and six feet tall. Some told barrack-room stories that would have made a Victorian daughter blush; more got drunk on the whisky they confiscated. Some were young Canadians wild for adventure, others British regulars looking for jobs when imperial wars were scarce and who believed that the proper job for Indians, as for Untouchables, was to have them sweat polishing high boots. Some, like Inspector W.D. Antrobus in May 1884 at Battleford, were humiliated; his horse was frightened by Plains Cree at a begging dance and ran away with him, his white helmet rolling in the dust. He returned for it later with an interpreter and remonstrated the People for "vexing" him and tried to order them out of town in half an hour or all would be arrested. They noticed his knees shaking, perhaps with anger, and laughed him out of countenance so he had to leave fast again, on a buggy this time. His interpreter, William McKay, told him, "You make a damn fool of yourself, talking to them that way."

Assistant Commissioner Crozier, in command at Battleford, also told Antrobus something about that. Crozier knew very well how the great reputation was wearing between government rigidity and Indian starvation; in November 1882 he had had to affect a much too spectacular arrest from under Crowfoot's nose when one warrior, Bull Elk, had defied Inspector Francis Dickens over some steer offal at the Blackfoot Crossing treaty payments. In 1883 he watched the last of the buffalo Cree come north to become, presumably, farmers on reserves they had yet to choose and though he could not know that he would be in command at Fort Carlton on March 26, 1885, if he was a man of even the faintest premonition, the summer of 1884 must have been preparing him.

When the leaves came out in 1883, of the 13,000 Cree signed under Treaties No. 4 and 6 over 5,000 were not on reserves; they were officially known as "wild and stragglers" and most of them existed around Fort Walsh. These the

Indian Department and the police had to sort out, supply with food, and get moving towards appointed places north of the railroad. Piapot, with 582 in his band, chose the Qu'Appelle Valley; they were given the luxury of travelling crammed into two railroad cars but unfortunately that train jumped the tracks, several were injured and Piapot had a further black impression of what Government intended for his people. Little Pine, with 421 followers, said he would take a reserve near Battleford but as they began moving north he heard another rumour of buffalo and turned south for one last hunt. The rumour was, of course, false. Eventually Lucky Man started north, and so did Big Bear; they arrived at Battleford on July 20, 1883 with fractions of their bands, 120 and 200 River People respectively. Big Bear had said he would like a reserve somewhere in his old hunting area of Fort Pitt where there were trees for fire wood; since the buffalo were taken, he could no longer burn chips either. He carried a piece of Government House, Regina, paper dated Maple Creek, June 12, 1883:

> Memo of what the Commissioner promised to
> Big Bear, provided that he left for the
> North and settled on his Reserve after the
> arrival of the Carts from Winnipeg.
> To have a good three-roomed house built on
> the Reserve for Big Bear.
> To supply him with six Carts and harness and
> Two Ponies, as he has only four of his own.
> Buckboard, Pony and harness, on leaving a chest
> of tea, fifty pounds of Sugar, twenty-five
> pounds of Tobacco.
> Shot guns with Ammunition. A suit of Cloths

at once as he has not received his chiefs
Clothing, it having been sent north.

But Big Bear did not select a reserve after the carts arrived from
Winnipeg. After seven years in the south he had many friends to
visit along the North Saskatchewan; some like Red Pheasant
had been struggling on their reserves since 1877, and lately
starving. The white settlers around Battleford saw him for the
first time (they had heard often) and decided he had "the square
face, big nose and glazed eyes of the untamed Indian." By the
end of September he and the 360 People now in his personal
band were getting settled to winter between Fort Pitt and Frog
Lake; there he was in turn visited by Sub-agent Thomas Quinn,
Indian Agent John Rae, Assistant Indian Commissioner Hayter
Reed, Indian Inspector Wadsworth, and by the Deputy of the
Superintendent General of Indian Affairs himself, Lawrence
Vankoughnet, an Ottawa civil servant who controlled the
department for his friend Sir John A. Macdonald. After several
years of surplus, the national economy was again sliding toward
depression and the Deputy knew he must cut expenditures. He
declared, "The benefits [of the treaty] are altogether on the side
of the Indians, and they are to be made to do their part of the
work." Passing through Fort Pitt on his way to Edmonton he
told Big Bear that he would either take his reserve within one
month or get no more rations.

But Big Bear took no reserve. He and his band cut wood,
freighted for the Hudson's Bay Company between Fort Pitt
and Edmonton; he visited his friends Little Hunter at Saddle
Lake and Seenum at Whitefish Lake. When Lieutenant-
Governor and Indian Commissioner Dewdney arrived at Fort
Pitt as the leaves were coming out in 1884, Big Bear told him
he had an invitation from Poundmaker to visit at Cutknife

Hill; he did want to see Poundmaker, Crowfoot's adopted son and a young man so close to his own heart, so he had decided to accept the invitation and fulfill his vow of making the Thirst Dance there. The Governor was disturbed; hadn't Sub-agent Quinn told him that the Government did not want them to indulge any longer in such — ah — performances, especially not the Sun Dance? Big Bear seemed surprised. The River People, he said, called their main worship of The Only One, Thirst Dance. He had made a vow to dance; the young men had already taken tobacco everywhere to his friends along the Battle and the North Saskatchewan, everywhere with the message "Come! Help me make this! And all your people," and everywhere it had been smoked as the New Moon appeared; the Thunderbird had given consent to his vow. He must make the Thirst Dance.

II

For a week the River People had been gathering at Poundmaker's. Little Pine, Lucky Man, Strike Him On The Back, Red Pheasant, Young Sweetgrass and Moosomin's bands were there, as were the Assiniboine bands of Bear's Head, Skinny Man and Mosquito from the Eagle Hills, living in a half-moon centred by Big Bear's lodge on the creek flat above the Battle River. Prayers and songs had been completed under the new moon, the vigil kept. Through the clear darkness light became, creeping over the land's black shoulders until the river rose on the valley like the serpent that lurks swivelled in the earth, misting upwards, drifting into deeper blue. In the south the bare cones of hills would be forming black above the curl of willows along the creek and before him gradually the naked river shone through its mist, green within moving white; the edge of the sun came levelling the round worn land, discovered Big Bear before his lodge, naked with grey clay stroked over his body. Waiting to pray as the first light touched him.

>   the sun helps me to stand
>   the sun helps me to walk

And he was praying on, as he had the night before. That he have strength to complete his vow in the dance, that all the prayers of the People might be answered; especially that water be given. That his prayer be answered. The river filled its bed now like burnished green stone. His Crier came out of the lodge door and stood beside him but facing south to the camp and the bare hills, and the ridge far and low up the creek valley now outlined completely in light. Where once the Sarcee Cutknife on such a morning had sung his death song to the People. The night before the Crier had shouted to the Thunder Spirits in the four directions:

>   come, have a smoke
>   come, and smoke

and then the oldest men had come slowly, followed Big Bear into his lodge where a white buffalo skull lay on a bed of sweetgrass. The old ones had laid three small sweetgrass fires about it, and a fourth in the centre of the circle they made and, singing, beating a drum with willow sticks, had cut tobacco, and dedicated the pipestems, then made their offerings with their heads bent steadily to the ground. Again and again, from each in turn had risen the prayer that there might be strength to complete the Thirst Dance, for the blessing of all men.

Now as the sun bulged orange and massive into the dead-blue sky the Crier shouted again:

> come, hunt out the Centre Tree
> the tree to hold Thunderbird's nest

Slowly Crier walked the great camp, shouting, all men emerged and then young warriors also from behind the tents on their horses, painted and armed by the hundreds. The horses wheeled, whirling the brilliant war-yellow faces and bodies and arms in and out of the sunlight; children and girls and women gathered in the camp circle, laughed with happiness and anticipation. The Crier returned from his round of the camp through the dancing horses; he called out eight names, the first Wandering Spirit.

The eight men dismounted, entered the lodge and sat down. Big Bear rose, almost white in his clay in the lodge's darkness, placed his hand on Wandering Spirit's curly black head and sang softly,

"Help me complete this, this vow I have made."

He repeated it to every man, as the pipe followed him to each, and each in turn smoked. The ashes were emptied on a sweetgrass smudge, all arose and went into the sunlight. Big Bear began walking across the open flat, the eight scouts around him with all the People trailing; singing the Thirst Dance Song that had been revealed to him, which he alone could sing:

> the sun helps me to stand
> the sun helps me to walk

On a small rise he stopped; within the wide loops of the river across its wide valley stood thick, dark spruce, and birch and poplar yellow-green in fresh, glistening leaves. The eight scouts left their horses and advanced on foot, stealthily, as though stalking a Blackfeet camp, and vanished among the trees. Big Bear stood erect in the gathering heat; behind him the old men and the young on their horses, children, dogs, girls, boys, women, settled on the ground as silent as only the People could be when the very life of the band depended on it, but all dressed in the brightest clothes like painted flowers over the flat, all motionless in the strange silence of two thousand people waiting, a silence that hesitates on the tip of bursting.

Suddenly, from the trees below, a long wolf-howl. Immediately it was echoed by another there and the ridge swirled alive in laughter and running. Big Bear led the men down the slope into the trees, unerringly towards the sound across dry creeks and spongy ox-bows and deadfall to the scouts surrounding a tall, straight poplar, four sweetgrass smudges already smouldering about its base. The sounds of mounted warriors crashing through the brush and bending willows surround him as he prays before the chosen perfect tree facing east, north, west and south in turn, then the scouts' rifles fire one by one and the old men are there with their axes, chopping each a stroke until the tree crashes south to their cry answered from the ridge. The young men charge through the brush past the fallen tree, screaming their high, thin warcries, each counting coup on the long branches, now a slashed and ribboned enemy. Then chopping echoes everywhere, trees splinter down among rifle fire and the sounds roll over valley and river and across the prairie hills while dogs run crazy circles between women and children and down into the brush about the chopping old men and young riders throw their ropes around fallen trees; ducks from the river marshes leap up, squawking in the brilliant air, and little boys shriek down slopes and banks to plunder their nests. The world spins dancing happiness.

The young men emerge from the woods on their foaming horses; the trees snake behind them up the slope, the centre tree ahead, and everyone follows to the camp circle, shouting, singing,

> when the wolves return
> spirit power
> will make joy

Kingbird, his black stallion switched by a sinewy branch jerking past, had to drop his rope and race away like a prairie fire flaming across hills and coulees before a western wind; when he returned, the black spraying foam, girls surrounded him in laughter and he was almost run away again. But Sits Green On The Earth stood her ground, wagging at him the end of the rope he had dropped and with a lunge he swung her up behind, now controlling stallion and rope and beautiful girl through the wild cheers bursting about them; immediately other young men charged fleeing girls and so the chosen tree was dragged into camp. The young men spiralled away and every warrior who had slain an enemy in battle galloped past and fired a bullet into it. Last of all came Big Bear, on foot, and he fired into it also as it lay, its butt end by the hole dug for it, its leafy top to the north, almost ready for the Thunderbird's nest.

But first came the re-enactment of what had been acted secretly in the woods. The branches already slashed from the tree were flung over its butt and the People eddied back until they were only faces held again in that strange silence, tiered in a half-ring toward the river bank. Suddenly above the bank a painted face appeared. It was Wandering Spirit, face yellow in

huge strokes between his shouldered, curly hair, eyes searching, listening. He beckoned behind him and the other scouts
appeared, their faces as vivid, their eyes intent on the brush
pile. For an instant they vanished, then lifted again as if out of
the very ground in a depression nearer the pile. Four Sky
Thunder crept forward alone, at the brush he listened with his
ear against the hide of an invisible lodge, then swiftly his knife
slit a hole in it, moved in and plunged into that sleeping Blackfoot's heart; his other hand was in, he had sliced away the
Blackfoot topknot and was crawling back, his hand aloft as
with the scalp. Immediately all eight leaped to meet him,
screaming, and hurled themselves on that sleeping Blackfoot
village of branches, hacking and stabbing. Guns exploded,
women and warriors and children shrieked as the entire
assembly flooded over the branches, everyone trying to
capture one twig, one leaf, one scrap of bark as trophy of the
great conquest.

Big Bear came forward and tied his gun and a piece of buffalo leather to the few branches left above the great fork in the
Centre Tree. These were his offering to the Thunderbird, and
others followed him. Lucky Man with a long streamer of red
cloth, Poundmaker with a braid cut from his hair; a long procession bearing gifts. All the men were working in a kind of
confused willingness. Some trimmed branches from tree
stems to set up as walls for the Thirst Lodge; others dug holes
to set them in; still others were dismantling the lodges of those
who had said they wished to help Big Bear in this way, opening
the skins so they could be laid over a part of the rafters when
the framework was complete. Into this working bustle as
women laughed, watching their men sweat for once and the
sun rose hot to midday in the dazzling sky, something was
breathed. Like the faintest of scents straying across the valley

so that as each turned to his neighbour the beginning excitement of it already stood there, naked in the other's eye. But then it was no breath, certainly; it seemed to explode out of the air that everyone knew had been burning livid with it all morning: the farm instructor is killed. Blood jerked in the heart and everyone stopped to stare, rigid with amazement. Who had done it? How? Which instructor? Killed? And suddenly it was obvious the farming instructor was not dead, only terribly injured. Perhaps not even injured, only slightly drummed: the greatest coup. The immense swirl of Thirst Lodge building had floundered into tiny tangles of silence, and then men were working steadily on. Hope, happiness, fear, excitement swallowed again like the memory of warm raw liver dipped in gall.

Centre Tree was rising. Pulled by a spray of ropes, its butt held and guided into its base by many hands, its top washed in gift-cloths drooping to the motionless air, guided by four crossed lodge poles. Big Bear stood between Little Pine and Poundmaker, facing the tree as it rose, chanting over and over:

> Tree wake up, wake up
> spirit power
> will make joy

When it stood erect, set tight in the earth, he murmured to Little Pine,

"He Speaks Our Tongue has found an axe handle for your farm instructor."

"Ahhh," Little Pine agreed, his grizzled head hooked forward as if he were peering into a darkness. "That Craig is a poor thing."

"Young men are always young men."

Little Pine answered nothing.

"The police will have to wait."

"Yes," said Little Pine. He seemed unbelievably old in the hot sunlight; as if he were bereft and now tired from his long travel to find where he must make his last camp beside Pound-maker's reserve. As though he would now wait for all the words anyone had yet to say to him and answer all with the last word he would say; and that word would have to be, "Yes."

So the poles for the walls were set upright in circle around the Centre Tree and other half-trimmed poles were brought as rafters for the roof; the sun heated the cool green ground under their feet and the understanding that the police must wait became as clear to all as the details of what had happened. He Speaks Our Tongue was somewhere among the younger men, talking, and so was his brother The Clothing, telling more detail than perhaps could happen to two men in several days, but everyone saw the police astride their horses on a nipple of the south hills; everyone knew when the officer, who with his men had been camped beside the Little Pine and Poundmaker Reserve departmental supplies for ten days now and allowing them nothing because none of their visitors had the permission of their farming instructors to leave their reserves, so that they were all now living on fish trapped in weirs they had built across the river, everyone knew when that Stripe Arm rode down and sat on his horse at the edge of the camp, looking. No one said a word to him there in his brilliant dress uniform. After a time he turned his beautiful horse, shin-ing almost like his boots and saddle, and rode down slowly back toward the long slope.

Big Bear did not see that; he was watching the last of the twenty-four rafters being placed in position on the great fork below the Thunderbird's nest; he was hearing, not the iron-plated hoofs of the police horses drum away or the People shivering in nervous laughter around him; rather he heard the lodge-hides being dragged over the ground to be thrown across the rafters where the dancers would rest, heard the leafy-green poplar flicker being woven between the uprights. He stood facing north and the entrance of the Thirst Lodge; he had not drunk anything since that morning and now for an instant he looked directly up to Sun in the naked sky. He felt Lone Man beside him, handing him the bleached buffalo skull for the altar and when its weight hung in his hands he walked forward. The lodge was complete, Sun was almost on the western hills, it was time to build the altar and begin the dance. Wailing, he entered the lodge and passed the skull through the smoke rising from four sweetgrass fires there.

The square hole for the altar had been dug before the Centre Tree; Little Pine, Red Pheasant, Mosquito and Big Bear placed a small peeled stick at each corner for the Four Thunders, then Red Bone placed the largest stick in the centre for The Only One. Big Bear took the pipe, pointed it to each stick east, north, west, south, praying

> to you who have
> given all
> we have today

then he lit the pipe, pointed it again, praying, and passed it to the men. When it had gone their complete round, the drum began to beat in the north-east part of the circle. The pipe stem was broken over the altar.

Big Bear was dancing. Many men were dancing their own particular vows with him, and women on their side of the Lodge, but he kept his eyes on Centre Tree so that nothing but the spirits could live in his emptiness. When he was younger he had to fight that at the beginning, the distraction of beautiful dancers beside him, across the circle, the nag of thirst and hunger already digging steadily toward a promise of pain, but now the drum beat carried him very easily over that. Perhaps it was the look into the sun, so overpoweringly Sun that during the altar building he was physically blind but in the ceremony he felt lit by light so sheer it was nothing outside himself, purely and completely himself. He danced now with that round black sun centred in his eyes on the Tree, a corona of light licking around its edge with sweetgrass burning. Some far edge of himself knew the air was cooling, that mosquitoes were whining as Sun pulled himself reluctantly down from the long summer day, but he was simply dancing on drum and song sound, to fulfill his vow, his sacrifice of thirst and hunger for the great council all the River People together must now hold, the gaunt People who must now, finally, speak with one voice. The drum rhythm changed, again and again, the sounds chanting high and thin changed with it, but he danced on intent.

Big Bear was dancing. He had slept twice, briefly, though the drums had not stopped nor the dance. Daylight entered the Lodge with grey dew that cooled his face, that he could lick an instant from his hard lips. He was concentrating on Thunderbird now, praying that his dance had already pleased him and his body hammering toward one long desire of the water only Thunderbird could give to continue his dance. In the hotter sun he comprehended he had not touched water since the previous morning and he was very happy for that; his concentration on Thunderbird did not shift when in the growing warmth under the leafy rafters young Little Bear began to dance his warrior-making vow. The drum beat quickened, the voice of the singers out-shrilled again and again by piercing bird-bone whistles, but he danced focused upon the lovely white bark of the Tree, listening to it. The ropes circling above him snapped taut again and again in the screaming rhythm of drums and whistles and prayer as Little Bear threw himself against them, anchored on the tree and on bones dug through the muscles of his chest, trying to tear them out of himself. The bones had been well set, as they must be, but Big Bear did not even hear the cry of Iron Body who finally hurled himself forward and with his added weight tore Little Bear from his vow into manhood. He danced on, intent.

Big Bear was dancing. Sun shafted fire through the wilted leaves, driving through him. He saw himself seated, almost tipped against, the Tree. His body a brittle husk, as hard transparent as snake-skin discarded on sand. There was no movement anywhere, nor sound, as if the hundreds of People he knew around him were each clamped within themselves upon silence, a vision given everyone gigantically, and abruptly the light spilled out like a match flame before night wind and above him Thunderbird spoke. His body lay, waiting, and rain rushed the valley and camp over white, sunlight hesitated on a leaf turning there, then rain falling through like ribboned, flaring streamers. He saw his tongue against the Tree, his throat swallowing, water moving a little farther and then a little farther into his mouth, but he saw only Thunderbird's wild colours smeared broken and flickering in the cloths of the rain and he ran his last cow, floating through rainbows of pink water chuckling under bluish ululating ground and the cow ran above him in the blood and white of her streaming hide through gold and violet sunshine flaming to poplar green. He drank; Running Second stood there with a leaf funnelling water into him and smiled, her round face streaming shiny, and she merged and doubled, double into not eight but six shapes as indistinguishable blackness hung there distorted in a glazed bulging eye under a black hat rim, blackness strung aloft like heads and bodies, ahh, hung under a pole bobbing to tear themselves loose and coming away suddenly in spouts of black words and words where their bloodswollen souls might have smiled from their faces, one giant flowering upward between his clawing fingers now, folded back, chuckling, a horrible spring of clotted black blood laughter.

Sunlight rested quietly cool, damp and cool with warriors riding four abreast to the Lodge entrance. Big Bear saw them dismount there, and coming in, and he himself was standing. Walking to sit beside the drummers. The drums talked gently to the glistening earth and dancers blessed by Thunderbird, and the warriors advanced dancing encouragement to the dancers; to tell of their exploits. When they found their place they were led in singing by Wandering Spirit and Fine Day; it was Fine Day, head of the Rattler Lodge in Poundmaker's band who stood by the Tree to begin with one of his great deeds as the drum beat and the People gathered close in the calm, mosquito-ridden air. And after him Wandering Spirit, white clay and red signs for thirteen enemies killed covering his chest and back.

"I am very young then," Wandering Spirit orated in a high carrying voice, "and I go with Bare Earth of the West People. It is in the Eagle Moon and I run a lot over the snow, ahead scouting. I am thin and hard from running all the time. Day Bow is also with us, we scout two together and find the Bloods camping on the Piegan River. Smoke comes from a big bluff and we know where they are. Buffalo herds are there too. We run back to camp and start for those Bloods at night; the day is very warm and we wait for night. Bare Earth says, 'We'll go along the creek where it is thawing and get closer.' We do that.

All at once there is a Blood rider, and then a bunch of them. We throw ourselves to the ground. Many Bloods are chasing buffalo close to where we lie, killing them close to our track. We see one coming from the camp on foot and we say, 'We are all killed anyway, we may as well shoot this one.' We couldn't dig any pits because the ground was frozen but we tie up our battle clothes lying down there. The Blood doesn't even see us but went over the hill. We head him off. I outrun the others, two are a little behind me. I stop on a little hill and call to him, 'Where are you going, my friend?' He makes a noise and pulls his gun. I shoot him. He turns around and sits down facing us. I run up to him. He turns to face me. I throw away my gun and draw my knife. It had belonged to a dead man and it was dangerous to use. As soon as I grab that knife I am afraid. My heart goes tum-tum-tumtumtum. All my partners fall back but I don't stop. I know he is waiting to shoot me in the face when I come close. I come up to him. He sits in the snow and aims right at me. I duck and he misses. He is loading his gun again and I catch him by the hair. He was shot in the hip and can't get up. I take his hair with an eagle feather stuck in it. He is not dead yet. The other men come up and take what they can. When they finish stripping him he was hardly dead yet. We start off, there is no place to hide and we keep on. They don't chase us right away, and we reach a place where there was shelter. One of our men was killed. We get away from them. When we get home with the scalps, girls are dressed up and ready to dance. A row of girls face the row of old men who drummed and sang. I was in the middle and the girls danced around me, always looking at me. That is when I became a Worthy Young Man. Hi-yah!"

The applause muttering here and there throughout the story now caught Wandering Spirit up in a great shout. An

Assiniboine arose in his place, but through the leafy walls of the Lodge Big Bear had seen riders on the flat east of the creek. Three horsemen. And a buggy, turning down into the valley, the horsemen flashed like steel in the sunlight under the black ragged clouds, and he was standing again and moving forward as if the warrior had also risen to dance; exploits would have to wait. Now was needed dance.

Big Bear was dancing. The blessing of Thunderbird could have meant the acceptance of his suffering but what had come upon him with the blessed rain sent fear like a hound deep into him and he had to continue. The council must be held, it must be held and nothing could be allowed to stop it. What might stop it he did not dare consider; the People were everywhere about him intense in contemplation and worship and he would dance. He danced. He had not eaten buffalo for a long time and he could not rest too long for perhaps he might not be able to begin again, though the fear of that was nothing compared to the other he would not consider, and he was praying over and over as he danced, swaying only a little now, barely raising his feet to the rhythm of the ground:

> Thunder you know I promised
> but bacon and flour with a few sweet fish
> empty a man
> thunder giver
> give
> give

The drum continued, and the singers. Sun blazed up the given moisture. Superintendent Leif Crozier sat above the People on his rain- and sweat-washed gelding, staring over them, his white helmet low over his eyes and buckled with a gleaming strap under his chin. There was no way he could get near the Lodge where Big Bear was, naked, motionlessly, dancing.

III

Robert Jefferson: It is certain that a stand must be made somewhere, but it seems incredible to be forced into making it on Craig's dignity, who has never had any. Indians cannot be allowed to take axe-handles to their farming instructors whenever they may wish — I am one myself — but they would never dream they could do it to a man of sense; they are by nature the most calm and deliberate of people, willing to endure things that would drive even an Englishman to raving mania and though they do wild, violent things impulsively when their blood is up, they are as quickly shamed by such actions. A man who cannot exercise patience and forbearance in full measure should never have dealings with them.

Not that Kahweechet-waymot — "Man-that-speaks-our-language," or "He-speaks-our-tongue," it is simplest just calling him "Tongue" — is a good Indian-Affairs Indian; far from it. I have only seen him twice, the first time last Friday when I went to Little Pine's and he was trying to chop rails in Craig's yard. From the way he wrestled the axe, the way he answered, he is what I imagine Fine Day or Wandering Spirit were ten years ago: moody, leanly strong, little interested in women or children and no one would ever think them suitable as chiefs; they are warriors, and by Indian definition great ones. But all the Sioux are gone, the Blackfeet on reserves, so a warrior like Tongue earns salt bacon trimming rails to fence in John Craig's garden. Who can wonder?

And John Craig has that infuriating demeanour of a Scot who has lived in the United States long enough to become

convinced he is everyone's equal, though in the crunch he
knows he will undoubtedly prove more. The problem is he has
never been crunched; like the yapping dog so small no large
dog has ever found it necessary to teach him his true size.
Physically he is big enough to throw Tongue and his brother
right out the door, as he did, but that is out-walshing Walsh
with a vengeance: he provides the heroics but it is Corporal
Sleigh and his nine men who face a few thousand acting out
remembered glory in their annual sacred celebration.

"Well you know, Bob," Craig said, I remember the very
first time we met. "I got this job because I know someone," as if
that was the only way to get one, though there is only one
person in the Territories to know if you are going to use it. He
has not bothered to learn a word of Cree on the strength of it.

So to preserve unblemished the dignity of Whiteskins, as
the Cree have it, represented in the person of our "Mr. Craig,"
which is all I've ever called him audibly, we are making a stand:
Kahweechet-waymot must be arrested and tried for hitting
Craig three times, though Sergeant Mackay could only find
two bruises, one not worth treating. It was perfectly inevitable
once Craig made himself intelligible enough that he would get
drubbed: he report to Sleigh, Sleigh report to Crozier, Crozier
would have to come and arrest Tongue. The police bluff
Indians, all the time, but cannot ever allow themselves to be
bluffed; if Crozier cannot manage his bluff as he did at
Blackfoot Crossing the Saskatchewan country blows up. I can
feel that hanging in the night air; that was in Crozier's furious
Irish eyes when Craig reported.

Singing for the Thirst Dance began Monday evening June
16, and lasted well into the night. We could hear it here, as I
can hear drums now, though they are on the river bank almost
at Little Pine's reserve three miles up the valley. Tuesday they

built the Lodge and if Craig — again the pattern of inevitability is so clear in hindsight — if Craig had any actual interest in his Indians he would have been with me watching them, nowhere near his Agency so Tongue and his brother could "annoy" him asking for grub just because they are hungry. I have never seen their sacred Lodge built in such a panorama as the Battle River Valley and was up on a good ridge watching them at their old-time fun now actually forbidden, when I heard bridles clinking. Corporal Sleigh and his men rode up behind the ridge, he with the usual lop-sided grin above the pipe in his lean face.

"I've got to arrest me a Indian boy that's took a club to our Mr. Craig."

"Good!" I exclaimed before I thought, and then we laughed together. Sleigh dresses like a dandy but he is a warrior in the Fine Day tradition; nobody needs to explain Craig to him. "He'll be down there by now, bragging about it. He won't want to come, I should think."

"I guess I'll have a look anyways, he just might."

"With nine men?"

"Na, just me." I must have stared at him, almost laughing, though I realized in an instant he was right. One man might bring it off where ten are worse than useless. So he rode down with Interpreter Laronde and they came back the same way. "He won't come and the chiefs say, 'If you take him you'll have to take us too,'" was all he said and twenty-four hours later Wednesday afternoon he was there grinning over Crozier's shoulder, on a different horse and dust washed in runnels from the cloudburst that had just passed over.

"I told him to take a bag of flour," Craig reported to Crozier. "If I hadn't got my arm up he'da killed me, he's a powerful brute for all he claims he's —"

"You told him that?" Crozier exclaimed. "When?"

"After he hit me."

"Good sweet hell!" Crozier turned so hard on his heel that his horse, hanging its head and blowing, almost got his elbow in its eye. "Don't ever learn to talk Indian or they'll really find out what a shit you are. Jefferson."

"Yes sir?" I could barely say a word; Sleigh had his head down, scratching himself as if he had suddenly discovered fleas.

"Where's the best place to set up camp? What are those old buildings?"

"The old agency storehouses, but our garden —"

"Good. Inspector Antrobus, get the men over there, there's water in the slough, and grass around too. I'm going to see Big Bear."

Only five of us went on to the Thirst Camp: Crozier and Sleigh and a constable riding, Indian Agent Rae and I in his buckboard. Crozier had changed to his parade uniform.

"I'm writing to Macdonald direct about this," Rae swore steadily while the wheels jolted over a buffalo trail worn a foot deep to the creek, "it's that goddam Vankoughnet leaving his Ottawa desk once after rotting there since before Year One and one night he hears a wolf howl, in passing insults Big Bear who doesn't bother answering, and then he knows everything. One trip expert. The only guy he listened to out here was Wadsworth from Winnipeg, pen-pushing penny-pincher just like him, still mad at Dewdney for naming Reed assistant commissioner. And we're the ones'll get shot for twelve hundred a year!"

I did not bother to insert that I get exactly half that.

"You know they cut the Department budget a hundred thousand? They send me a thousand bags of flour and that's supposed to last a whole goddam year! Last year *before* all the

Cree come up from Cypress that lasted exactly four months! I've got to get written authority, I — the storehouse at Pitt hasn't had a padlock for two months, Quinn has to write to me and I write to Regina and I don't know where the hell *they* write to, I haven't got it yet. A padlock! Written authority to wipe my goddam ass!"

"Quinn's lucky he has wild Indians at Pitt, they don't steal."

"Don't worry, they're learning. I'm writing that old cuss in Ottawa personal and confidential. Right now I should be working nights, they've cut my clerk, on the annual report due July 1st — it's tabled in the House next March! — about every penny and where every goddam Indian is right now in the whole goddam district. I oughta tell them two thousand three hundred and eighty-one of them, plus stragglers, are dancing on the Battle River."

"I would estimate there are no more than two thousand here."

"Quinn reports Big Bear alone is over five hundred, and at least that many stragglers roaming around deciding god knows what. We'll get our heads blown off because Craig follows my orders to the letter because I follow *my* stupid orders to the letter, well my god I've got orders winging from Ottawa on high that...."

Rae is strange, the way many persons born in the Canadian provinces are. He broods on wrongs. In silence, probably for years concerning his job or the inevitable government, and when the two coincide, as they do with an Indian Agent who always feels himself on the spot while Ottawa officialdom as it seems without thought decides the rules of the game he has to not play but live, the brooding suddenly breaks out and spills like water. Ordinarily he is most deliberate and calm: one of the better agents. The hot bumpy miles from Battleford obviously helped compose whole paragraphs for Sir John if only

Tongue will give himself up. If. Poundmaker is like I have never seen him, as though he knows no white man, even me, his brother-in-law. Pushing to get to his lodge, among all the screaming I could not even ask about my wife, where she might be with our son. When Craig came Tuesday evening because he insisted they would attack him alone at Little Pine's, she told me she wanted to go to her parents who are at the Thirst Dance; she took Robby and went. Red Pheasant's band is camped beside Poundmaker's but I could recognize no one even to ask among all the paint and noise and pushing before we finally got into the chief's lodge. Little Pine and Lucky Man and Bear's Head sat there with Poundmaker. But they would not speak; Poundmaker kept saying without bothering to look up at me,

"Big Bear is head chief here. He is dancing."

As if he would have gladly shot us all. That does not make sense, he has been trying to farm so hard for four years and this spring they worked superbly for me — for Indians. I have never seen a camp with so much war-paint. There was no way of identifying Tongue, the braves were riding wildly beyond the lodges, waving guns; even the ones pushing back and yelling insults as Crozier marched through had their breech-cloths tied up — and that was not for comfort in the heat — but the drums and shrieking whistles and singing seemed only to increase from the Thirst Lodge. I had never seen them in such near frenzy, then, though no one touched us. A boy no more than ten was snapping bits of gravel, stinging me through my shirt from behind and I saw him stoop for another bit as I turned just before entering the lodge. It looked almost like Horsechild whom I saw with Big Bear at Poundmaker's when they first arrived, but I could not be sure; his face was smeared with mud too.

"The chiefs won't exercise any control," Crozier said under his breath to me; outwardly he did not appear at all perturbed.

"I don't think they can," I said. "The people are too excited."

"When's it over?"

"Tomorrow evening, about sundown."

"Good. All right. Ask the chiefs to bring the prisoner to the old agency buildings on Friday morning. I'm not coming here with the men, there's too many women and children here."

The chiefs would only agree to talk with Big Bear, who might be through dancing soon; they could not say; yes, it would be better to meet away from the camp. They could not say who would come. Crozier and Sleigh marched back side by side through that yelling to where the constable held their horses, trailing Rae and me. That little devil Horsechild apparently could not get through for I felt no more stones; after six years at a reserve school I know his kind only too well.

Why not admit it, I'm tired and depressed. I just had an hour's sleep Wednesday night, and I can't seem to sleep at all after going to the camp again today — yesterday now, Thursday afternoon. My wife and Robby are perfectly safe with Red Pheasant but there are eighty-six police and mobilized civilians — armed like pirates — bivouacked here. Their horses have trampled my demonstration garden out of sight. The women are terrified of what will happen, for Tongue is getting too much young warrior attention to ever surrender, they say, and though many older men don't want to fight, they certainly will because this doesn't now have much to do with axe handles and bruised arms any longer. Robby was chuckling in his moss bag and I could feel the bump on his gum. Toothless little devil, mercifully unconscious of pride and old wild freedom and face. Poundmaker and his people laboured this spring, put in two hundred acres of grain and eight of potatoes, seven of turnips, three of carrots and two of mixed gardens though nothing is up yet, it's so dreadfully dry — Big Bear's dance helped on Wednesday! — but in a way no Indian can see me different from Craig lying there, snoring on our bed. Big Bear's terrible eyes looked that right through me as soon as he arrived at Poundmaker's — you have a beautiful wife, and son from the People but what more are you than a dog sitting guard at the door of Government? You keep numbers of every hoe and seed, you dole out food that is ours by treaty a pound at a time, exactly measured to how little a man can get and still survive to work as you say, eat your one pound today and work exactly as I say and tomorrow you get one more pound —

Food! My god it's always food! Bull Elk wants to eat the guts at treaty butchering; Tongue wants flour but he can't get any unless he works and he can't work because a rail snapped up and bruised his side while he was clumsily chopping so he could get food! And then Craig shoves him out, hitting exactly that painful spot. So finally, at midnight on Wednesday night we harness the six oxen on Little Pine's reserve, over-load three carts with every scrap of bacon and flour stored there and with all twenty-five policemen riding escort drag all that food past their camp towards our bivouac at the Poundmaker Agency. The only possible trail goes through the Thirst camp, we can't get very far around it because of a marsh and the valley hills to the south, none of us can believe why we aren't wiped out in the hellish drive for there must be several hundred unrecognizable warriors shrieking their circles around us in the dark, screaming the Cree warcry, shooting till the night seemed lit by bullets whistling above our heads. At Cutknife Creek I was certain we were finished. It's impossible to imagine a better place of ambush, thick willows all around the muddy crossing, the streambed muck. And the carts mired there, horses screaming as they floundered in quicksand; Craig was driving one of the ox-teams by then, the Indian drivers simply disappeared at the first shots, but even his beating and double-teaming couldn't force the loaded carts through, we had to get in there and pack every sack through the creek on our backs and reload. And while we were slogging around up to our hips, the warriors also, simply, disappeared. When we got to the old agency we worked what was left of the night piling all that food up as strengthening for the barricades. The bloody food, and they're hungry and to the best of our ability we'll shoot them from behind it today, my god.

Crozier told me that at Blackfoot Crossing last fall he had nothing except bags of flour and salt bacon slabs to build a barricade right in Crowfoot's camp, and it worked perfectly well. Perhaps, since no shot was fired. Our barricade, backed by a marsh to protect us from warriors while guaranteeing mosquitoes, has dense creek willows to the south and is easily commanded from the top of the ridge no hundred yards away, but Crozier seems satisfied. He has, he says, no doubt of the outcome. In the Territories for ten years, he seems willing to walk the tightest possible line as long as Big Bear does not achieve his great council; Indian talk, he says, may not forever be cheap. The Battleford volunteers are very serious, though some, like my young brother freshly ignorant from England, jubilant for possible adventure; the police quite content that action should come. Even happy. They have that monolithic soldier attitude in situations moving towards inevitable violence: they have been trained to provide exactly that kind of ultimate solution and they know they are proud and will stand firm together; sell their lives dearly. That expression sounds to me excessively mercenary, and so stupid.

There have been no drums for a long time. If my shack had
a larger window I think I could see light coming over the Eagle
Hills. Friday, June 20, 1884. Pray God no Canadian schoolboy
ever has to memorize that date. Our bruised Craig snores on.
This game is not worth my candle, nor anyone's.

IV

South-east, down the valley through the gap where the lodges
of Young Sweetgrass had stood, Big Bear could see the dust
lift from the trail where the last of that band's travois had
dragged over a ridge. Blue day, to see forever. The Thirst
Lodge silently withered in the rising sunlight, the Thunderbird's nest spangled with brilliant cloths above the busy morning of grass already faintly brown and of River People and
dogs and horses and fires breathing upward like thin trees in
the ring of lodges. A squall of boys broke up from the trail,
dragging shrieks and pandemonium after them among the
animals as they spread, and Horsechild dropped at his feet,
hair streaming in sweat already, eyes on the fish speared across
the fire.

"We ambushed them, where the trail turns, below by those
rocks," he said.

"They would have expected it at the creek," said Big Bear.

"Sakamo-tana wasn't awake, I had to wake him and we
thought we couldn't get beyond that."

"Ambush is harder where it's expected," said Big Bear. He
felt cleaned out, the muscles in his legs shifting easily as water
over rocks when he squatted; Running Second was smiling,
turning the goldeyes. Bear grease and your hands are a great
blessing, he thought to her, these sacred days.

"At that place where he was all winter they said Sakamo-tana had a new name, something the end is 'Poundmaker,'" said Horsechild. "What does that mean?"

"Did he tell you his name?"

"We had to wait so long anyway, it took them so long to move," said Horsechild, ashamed.

"Warriors in ambush concentrate on what's coming," said Big Bear gently, "though saying that name means nothing. Whiteskins like to say their own names, and each other's too."

"This is one like that?"

"Yes. Jean-Marie-Lestanc-Poundmaker, but it's good you and he don't remember it. It's the priest's name, in that school."

Horsechild's glance turned from the fish hissing fat into the fire. "He couldn't remember, how could he forget if that's his name?"

"He'll remember, soon enough," Big Bear said. When he has eaten there enough winters, Running Second returned his thought as she handed him a stick of almost tasteless fish.

"Can I come too?" asked Horsechild suddenly through his full mouth, not daring to look at his father.

"My hands will be empty, I won't wear anything around my neck."

Little Bad Man was coming towards them and Big Bear spoke loudly for him to hear; he greeted them, sat, and accepted tea as they ate in silence. He was wearing leather leggings but his face was already painted.

"Did He Speaks Our Tongue sleep in the warrior lodge?" Big Bear asked finally, unnecessarily.

"We all sleep there," said his older son. His mother Root Grubbing Woman had been the largest, most peaceful, softest woman Big Bear had ever kneaded, though Running Second would soon be there; not at all like fierce The Wallowing One dying so young, his first woman when he himself had been so shot through with all kinds of young fires. Yet Root Grubbing Woman had such a son, made so like himself but hacked out as it seemed in a kind of unending fierceness twisting blacker each spring, when he saw him he often thought he was looking into the clear Battle River: himself thirty years ago, but without the voice.

"I have something to say," Little Bad Man said now, so formally Big Bear would have wished never to hear it if he had not known already, but for an instant happily it was delayed by a rider cutting through the scatter of the circle to them: Kingbird on his black, run hard. Little boys surrounded the horse; Kingbird slid off but Horsechild did not move.

"We watched them since the sun rose," Kingbird ran up to their fire, too excited to sit down. "They've made two barricades around the agency building, like this," he stooped and drew lines on the dust, "each side, here and here, logs and flour sacks piled up. Here's the slough and the willows here and the little ravine comes at it here, all along the flat just below the trail."

Little Bad Man grunted. "At the bottom of that nice hill."

"Yeh!" Kingbird exclaimed, but Big Bear seemed to be looking north past the Thirst Lodge to the river.

"What did Wandering Spirit say?" asked Little Bad Man.

"He and Iron Body and Fine Day just laughed. There are sixty police there and fourteen others from Battleford, and Jefferson and Craig too."

"Stupid police." Little Bad Man was laughing, laughter shaking his big belly as he leaned back. "At the bottom of that nice, long, hill!"

"And I saw Coward Antrobus there, hiiii!" Kingbird crouched down as if he were on a galloping horse; arm crooked holding a lance, he circled the fire charging Little Bad Man, up now as if also mounted, his painted face set in a disdainful police glance down his patrician nose. Kingbird jerked to a stop under that very nose, his arms flew up like an umbrella exploding, and the disdain on his half-brother's face broke into consternation when his body scrambled away with him as it were, still fighting vainly to control itself and his face. The tableau of what his two sons had done to the inspector below the old Government House in Battleford was so perfectly acted that Big Bear added his roar of laughter to that of his sons and his wife and the little rapt boys gathering. The Magpie, appearing at that moment around the lodge, stopped in startled amazement.

"He's got that same grey horse," Kingbird gasped finally. "All we need for him is one of those things, fancy for rain, to snap open."

"Too bad they both broke, there," said Little Bad Man, sitting again.

The Magpie emptied her skirt of turnip roots beside the fire; she sat and began to peel them with her knife. Running Second poured more tea as Big Bear said, loudly in his heavy formal voice again because Twin Wolverine was walking through the centre of the camp, wearing leggings and a leather vest and his face unmarked under the hot sun,

"This was to be a time for council. I won't wear anything around my neck."

Twin Wolverine sat down where Little Bad Man moved aside to make place for him. He said, "Poundmaker will take his club, he said he will have to take it."

"It's that Antrobus," Big Bear said. "Poundmaker is still too young to forget until necessary."

"Who may be old enough to forget insult?" said Little Bad Man blackly. He did not lift his painted face as he said this and Horsechild, glancing from his father to his three brothers, suddenly liked the middle one a little; with him there flickered at least a little hope for fight.

"One remembers insult clearly," said Big Bear, "only when there are not five hundred friends there too."

"He has eighty-five."

"It doesn't matter what the other one has, as you know," said Big Bear. "Poundmaker is young, but he's a good chief. His club wants to go with him only if something starts. I danced for a council; I want to ask each of you: you do not start, anything, until someone has begun it."

There was a long silence, though horses galloped to the river in a flurry to drink and the circle was filled with the loud River People and the animals, living.

"Yes," said Kingbird, too young still to say what he might have wished. He saw the swing of a skirt between lodgeskins and the memory of Sits Green On The Earth jerked his manhood up in him. But there was nothing else he could say, yet.

Twin Wolverine waited for Little Bad Man in turn, but the silence lasted so long the oldest living son said, finally,

"I am taking a green poplar branch, with leaves."

Big Bear had once seen him kill two Bloods. When he had to, shooting one dead on his horse charging him and then the other slit with the knife from his belt; on the Belly River the year of the White Sickness in the coulee where his first son had died, that coulee and his first fighting son there mutilated like a fallen warrior as he could never forget. Also of The Wallowing One, but how different from his full-brother; almost hard like Little Big Man, yes, but not black, and with a voice too. A voice. Such a voice, that first son of his manhood.

"I have something to say." said Little Bad Man again ceremonially.

"I am hearing," Big Bear answered; there was no way to slip this aside.

"I have two horses and a saddle with red blankets which I wish to give my father. And some clothes, to my younger brother," Little Bad Man added, lip twisted up slightly at Kingbird needing new clothes, now.

He gave a shout and his oldest son, almost the age of Horsechild, emerged from behind the lodge with the horses, the pad-saddle on one and blankets piled there in a great heap. The space to the Thirst Lodge, crossed by People intent on their morning doings, was dense with them suddenly standing before him and his sons, with more and more still pushing through until even The Magpie's busy hands stopped peeling roots and Running Second put down her fire stick and knelt, watching. Little Bad Man, the warrior, was giving away his personal possessions for he expected to die today. He had no further use for horses or blankets or clothes, and it was clear to all that his father had only one gift worthy to give such a son in return. The sacred bundle Chief's Son's Hand, hanging on His tripod behind the lodge. Big Bear could see every layer of cloth in Him, every deed they represented unfolding into legend, feathers studied on the passing river, to the last bright red added at the Thirst Dance and he received again the inhuman exaltation of vision he first felt as a young warrior on Bull's Forehead Hill above The Forks so weak from fasting he could not lift his arm, when his voice had first learned His terrifying song

> my teeth are my knives
> my claws are my knives

That first time he had seen his own face streaked with mud

mauled by The Great Bear of his vision, had made the pipe offering of his thanks first alone in the rapture of his hunger and thirst, then again and again when necessary with these People, their joy in His given power rising with his like the flaming sun and the terrifying shaggy form towering there, maw agape and reaching up, stars glistening from those giant claws. Bear was warrior Spirit, the greatest the River People had even in legend, and now his warrior son longed for the power, longed to be renamed into Him as he himself had been perhaps led by The Spirit to suggest, he thought that now with a shudder, on the plains before his last buffalo. Or was it Coyote? The desire of his son, the desire of the People facing the danger of this new day pushed him: Little Bad Man was the son, now it was right, here were the proper gifts, now it was right to pass Him on with a prayer. Bear? He was praying, Bear? He could not feel Him, no warmth on his chest, no good weight of Him on his soul against the back of his neck. All he suddenly felt as Thunderbird spoke down to him from blue sky was a slow inevitable tightening around his neck, he was gasping openmouthed for breath though he could not so much as lift his hand and blackness passed before him like shapes, moving, and then, then he knew again what he had known as certainly when he awoke that morning as he had known he would be asked for Him. He would wear nothing. No one must wear Him. Today. His breath stood in his chest like power and he was in the perfect life of his vision and of his exploits guided surely by the sacred bundle, the exploits hideous to every enemy of the River People for they knew him and could only shiver when the Northwind blew like the Great Parent of Bear growling across the plains; lived that vision and saw himself standing on the ground before his lodge, his living sons seated there, speaking aloud to the

People. He was thanking his warrior son for the gifts. Praising him for the magnanimity and sacrifice of his spirit. Speaking on and on, his voice like rolling Thunderbird over them and they listened motionless while he recalled the great sons of the people and how they had fought at Belly River and the Ochre Hills and Ribstone Hill and then the greatest of all, Broken Arm, the terror of the Blackfeet until he was given the vision of peace for all men like a giant bird rising as fire crowns a spruce and had never fought again, though at last the cowardly Blackfeet cut him down when he walked unarmed and alone into their war camp to speak for his sickened People. Big Bear saw himself talking until he knew Wandering Spirit and Little Pine and Poundmaker and Fine Day and Four Sky Thunder and Lucky Man had come through the press and had listened for some time; then vision broke, and his voice stopped. Wandering Spirit and Fine Day and Four Sky Thunder faced him in war paint; Poundmaker held his club with the four knives set into its knob. Big Bear looked around at his people, at the six men facing him across the dead breakfast fire, at his wives, his four sons seated by his feet. Then he gestured and the crowd moved; dust from warriors circling drifted up beyond the southern lodges.

Little Bad Man said quietly, "When I hear a shot, Crozier is dead," and walked away.

"Can I come?" pleaded Horsechild.

"I don't want to see you," said Big Bear. Turning, beginning to lift the red blankets off the white mare his grandson offered, which his warrior son had forced him to accept.

When they rode over the rise on Poundmaker's reserve they knew the police were on the flat just below them. They were facing north towards the river and all they could see at first was a log shack between two flanking barriers of grey logs torn from the other shacks that had stood there; the wagons between the barriers and the slough blue in the noon sunlight. Horses lifted their heads inside the wagons, almost to the willows on the east where a creek in spring fed the slough. But certainly bits of red moved there, everywhere, and Big Bear studied the trail to Battleford cutting across the bottom of the slope. It would have been so easy to just charge, down, but he still could not lift his hand. He turned from that, finally. Around and behind him curving west in the curl he had ridden, the rolls of the valley seemed covered with men on horses and on foot. Higher on the level of the prairie lay the dark outline of Young Sweetgrass and his band; watching. And under the bare west hills, indistinguishable in the distance moved the dark straggle of women and children coming closer to see; the boys would soon be crawling ahead up the willowed gullies. He could hear his heart beat in excitement, but he felt a little sick. His body clean and strong, he was sick looking at why they gathered here on the beautiful world. No joy, no joy.

The one man needed here he saw easily, no more than two horses from him on the ridge; but he could not turn his eye. He Speaks Our Tongue was only staring into himself, harden-ing himself. Warrior.

Wandering Spirit angled his horse in close. "It's enough, they won't come further."

There was a heavy snuffle of horses. Big Bear pulled his mare completely around to face them all, and shouted in his gigantic voice:

"I am going to talk with the police. Does anyone wish to come along?"

No one looked at He Speaks Our Tongue; no one moved. Far away, over the motionless heads of the Rattlers, Cutknife

Hill rippled in the heat. Suddenly Poundmaker raised his arm.

"Hai!" He handed his club to Fine Day; he and Big Bear dismounted and walked down the sloping plain side by side. The air shimmered with quiet, their shadows puddled about their feet crunching the soft dry grass, here and there a tuft touched the green against the ground. The door of the centre building opened as they approached, they disappeared into it and in a few moments emerged again. They were walking together, Big Bear short and broad, Poundmaker tall and slender, on the sloped earth.

"They won't get us that easily again," said Big Bear. "For a few handfuls of flour. Crozier is smart."

"The police are so stupid, they'll bloody this whole land," Poundmaker's face glistened fury.

"It would be good to smoke now," said Big Bear, and he sat down. After several strides Poundmaker stopped, looked back in astonishment at him sitting in the wide, empty plain.

"Did you bring a pipe?" he asked finally.

"It was stupid of me to forget, and tobacco too," said Big Bear, gesturing. "But Little Bearskin McKay will have both."

And clearly that was the Hudson's Bay trader dusting a small cloud towards them in his rig on the Battleford trail. Poundmaker sat down reluctantly.

"It isn't for just a bit of flour," said Big Bear, "as Crozier knows very well. He doesn't want us to hold council, but he wants neither of us in jail either, to shame anyone into giving himself up and we return strong from jail. That would be worse."

Poundmaker was studying him carefully as the sound of the horses and wagon came bumping over the prairie.

"If he can make us shoot first," said Big Bear, "the council is nothing because then we've nicked a grizzly."

"Soldiers?"

"They'll shoot like Bluecoats. Sitting Bull said too, talking to soldiers and police is never anything. You heard Crozier there; he does only orders, like that poor thing Craig."

"But he gets rubbed out."

"That may be. But the soldiers will come and we don't get even what they let us have now."

"I sometimes hear a thought," said Poundmaker slowly, "though I was never a warrior like you and my father Crowfoot, that fighting toward death is better than being dragged there by hunger. Yesterday I heard Louis Riel passed the Cypress Hills."

"We must get to the highest chief and talk," said Big Bear fiercely, his mind running red in his visions, the hat by the Tramping Lakes blacker and bigger over him than ever. "We danced for a council."

"If it's possible," said Poundmaker. "Yes."

McKay's wagon was there, pulling around to shade them a bit where they sat. The trader spoke his greeting, hoisted himself down and squatted, his stubby pipe already in his hands. As it began its second round Big Bear spoke for the first time.

"The gophers play nicely on their mounds in the sunlight."

McKay grunted, waiting.

"How can young men, their children crying for hunger, sit behind doors in the dark? An old man, perhaps for a time. But the police will not accept old men."

"That's not the way," McKay said. "They must have that one who did it."

"He doesn't come."

"He has to."

The horses above them streamed sweat after their forty miles of sand in the hot morning. McKay got up, lifted nose bags from the wagon and went forward to tie them in place.

"This is our sacred time. After so much talk," said Big Bear, "the Young Men will not be humiliated, before all the People."

"Ahh, the young men," said McKay, knowing very well that no Indian would physically force a friend to anything, least of all surrender to whites; that when the two chiefs offered themselves they were doing the last they could do. "It's only a day's worth of flour, the man will not be hurt. Do you all want to fight for such a little bit?"

"Perhaps. Many would not want to, but they will if they get to feel like it." Big Bear was standing up as he spoke, looking to the police barriers. "They are saddling," he said.

Poundmaker handed the pipe to McKay, wordlessly gestured thanks, stood up and walked fast towards the warriors spread along the skyline. The trader stared up the slope, then stood and faced Big Bear. They were the same height. In the bright sunlight the old man seemed suddenly shivering.

"Tell the police again," Big Bear said rapidly, "I danced, I do not want to fight, there are many women and children here, the chiefs don't want to fight for this thing but Young Men do what they feel strongly. That is the way they must be. Tell the police again."

He walked away, towards his people. McKay was swearing silently but the heavy Scottish oaths churning in his head gave him no relief because he was concentrating on that stocky figure striding to the ridge. The line of police was issuing smartly, in order, from behind the barriers, folding into a double file with banners and gleaming full-dress uniforms, and when he turned and saw that he started to curse out loud even as he leaped into his wagon.

The short police column trotted forward steadily until it reached the centre of the plain. There it halted and the shorter column on foot came marching from behind the barriers to join it. Finally, Crozier rode out. He shouted a last order to the civilians stationing themselves behind the barriers with their rifles, and galloped to the head of his police. Commands rang distantly, the columns regrouped into ranks of mounted and un-mounted men facing up the slope. Sixty men outside, all so exactly alike they looked churned from one mould.

Big Bear began to see what was shaping itself before him as through a greyish mist. It was all perfectly bright, but strangely colourlessly grey, and precise where his physical eye could not possibly have seen anything. He saw the tiny straight lines of police who all looked exactly alike as a bird would see, a hawk soaring in grey, and the dark spread of five hundred indi-vidual warriors and three times as many women and children like a variegated lake folded over the hills, levelling the valley; he saw behind the left barrier, no more than a tiny line scratched on the lodge of the world as seen from the hill where he felt the white horse breathing between his legs, saw a young man who looked like Farm Instructor Jefferson blowing his nose with his fingers in excitement and the clot fly and splatter the barrel of the new repeater rifle he held, polished nicely but fired no more than ten times; he saw Craig beside Crozier riding up the hill, saw his heart shaking like an autumn poplar leaf in wind; he saw McKay whipping his horses around the thin police line and the wheels spiralling dust up the slope after Crozier, and he closed his eyes and heard the long unin-telligible curses running from Little Bearskin's lips though the air hung perfectly silent over everyone, waiting, until the sad-dle leather of the four horses began to creak, their walking hooves, and then McKay's wagon dancing and spinning in air over gopher mounds, against unused buffalo trails converging like spokes towards the creek and the river, that sound came bumping up also. Yells and riding and shrieks had greeted the police filing from the fort, but all that had evaporated into the brilliant summer air over the valley. Big Bear opened his eyes; he saw Crozier gesture to McKay, wheel his horse back towards them so tightly it reared, and come riding up the last little stretch of the slope. Craig and the interpreter Laronde and Antrobus were behind him. They were standing there before them, facing them, Crozier and Laronde dismounting.

"You agreed to bring He Speaks Our Tongue here to be tried." Laronde called into the silence. "In the name of Her Majesty the Queen, he is asked to step forward."

Nothing moved. Crozier spoke to Laronde again, who said loudly, "He Speaks Our Tongue, you must explain what you have done. Come forward, and tell us."

Still no one moved. Suddenly Big Bear saw Crozier stare at Poundmaker and he understood what the police chief was saying before Laronde could shape words, "Poundmaker, I came to your reserve for this man and I will take him if I have to arrest you all!" for Antrobus, still on his horse, a dark one however, was raising a signal with his arm and police commands drifted up the slope and immediately those look-alikes began to come forward again. In his complete greyness Big Bear saw Rattlers all over the hill exploding in screams and war-cries that echoed to terrified shrieks of women far away, and warriors on horses at the wings were racing down to circle, warriors on foot heaving forward toward those few approaching men and horses until the hill seemed one huge bristle of clubs and rifles and knives jamming tighter, piling up like ice in the bleak Saskatchewan and held for what could be only an instant by the high tiny centre of chiefs, of Crozier; and he saw a light flash of leaves gesturing here and there, Fine Day watch Poundmaker intensely while screaming "Wait, wait!" his rifle swinging above his horse hoofing air and screaming also, Little Pine on his old stallion shout for peace, peace, saw himself as the bodies and mounts of warriors jostled his pale mare roaring towards Little Bad Man alone on a small rise to the west with his rifle steady as a rock, "No, no, wait, we must talk, no, stop!" And then again there seemed to emerge as it were a small quiet; no shot exploded; Lucky Man stood before Crozier now with He Speaks Our Tongue beside him and McKay appeared out of somewhere translating swiftly and though rifles now pointed everywhere, some space remained still between the line of police drawn up and the warriors; there was even some small space around Crozier and Craig and McKay and the dis-mounted chiefs and the Young Man on the hill.

"Craig wouldn't give me food!" He Speaks Our Tongue was shouting at McKay, who scrambled to translate, "He's got all the food and my baby was sick and I told him if a dog came he would rather give him food than me working till I was sick but he wouldn't do it, he grabbed the chain and I jumped behind my brother, I was scared he'd hit me with that chain on the door and he was talking something I don't know and I said I'd bust the door with the stick I had to get food and he came running and pushed me where I was sore and I hit him, I was scared —"

Craig was shouting something, denying though there was so much sound over the hill again that Big Bear riding between the rigid line of small repeated holes that were the drawn rifles of the repeated police and the shifting, boiling line of his people almost dancing in tension, their weapons swooping about like gulls, even Big Bear riding silently there in the impervious cloak of his greyness could barely comprehend what was happening now, though he saw Crozier fling his arms wide to McKay, This is impossible! and move a step forward; raise his white gauntlet over He Speaks Our Tongue. Who screamed,

"Don't touch me!"

"I won't touch you if you come. But you must come with me!" McKay was shouting Crozier's words. "You have been accused of striking an official. You must be tried! If you are innocent you will go free. On my word. But you must come from here, now!"

"I will die here!"

"No dying! No! You will not be hung, look at what you are doing to your friends!"

Big Bear then understood that between this grass and this bright sky something was disintegrating in a noise so indistinguishable and terrible that what happened stood before him in pure and absolute silence: Wandering Spirit faced Corporal Sleigh frozen on a polished horse; sweat had burst through the streaks of his face and chest and his muscles bulged trying to heave his rifle up to that chest bristling bright buttons, gasping to lift that small rifle seemingly heavier than any stone; Crozier's gloved fists clamped to the belt of cartridges across He Speaks Our Tongue's chest and four huge dismounted police were wrestling themselves towards them, rifles barred across their chests; Poundmaker faced Antrobus, had ripped his rifle from his grasp and swung it up in triumph with that glittering club; Little Pine and Twin Wolverine flickered poplar branches, shouting; the middle rank of mounted police heaved forward around the wrestling centre on the hill; he knew himself screaming, WAIT STOP WAIT soundlessly while trying to kick and batter the helpless white mare between black heads and white helmets and grey bodies floundering around him so tightly none could sink, hammer through to where Little Bad Man sat on his giant warhorse, an immoveable grey rock breaking aside any flood, smiling a little, his rifle following steadily that staggering centre. But out of his soundless cry that could only wait for the rifle to kick, Big Bear came to hear like a gentle wind from Thunderbird touching through the flaming air that in the whirling, strange and beautiful silence granted him nothing but a rifle shot could break the power that held them all. He sat motionless then, seeing everything, for the shot would not come.

And it did not. The police horses and men had battered themselves to surround the centre, it was moving slowly down the slope into colour, staggering as warriors whirled and whirled around it, shrieking, and the other police pushed themselves towards it, using crossed rifles and their horses to wedge back the crush. Bits of scarlet tunic flew, horses shrilled with terror as knives nicked them, and the little boys came leaping out of the ravines onto the plateau dancing a frenzy dust on the naked ground. But He Speaks Our Tongue was silent somewhere in that broadening clot of red with white helmets moving now in ever more certain inevitability towards the barriers. It seemed to Big Bear, motionless on the hill, that he had just blinked his eyes to confirm they were open when there was no solid scarlet left on the plain; only the tangled colours of warriors riding out their screaming tension at last, through and out the clusters of them running everywhere; still brandishing the rifles not one of them had been able to fire.

Behind him on the hill was scuffle. Iron Body and The Clothing, He Speaks Our Tongue's brother, and Miserable Man were beating Interpreter Laronde. The police, strangely, had left the Metis behind. Little Bad Man galloped up, face bulging with fury and rifle lifted to crush Laronde's head as he reeled from clubbed rifles and knives and clubs, but the trader McKay was whipping his team near, shouting as he leaped from his wagon,

"Let him go! Let him go!"

"He grabbed Tongue first, he pointed him out," yelled The Clothing.

"Don't blame him, that's his job. He has to do that." McKay had thrust himself between them and they paused as if curious in their frustrated rage. "You don't kill a man just doing his job," McKay said, and Laronde slid through their circle under his arm, scrambling up on the wagon.

Poundmaker rode up. "Crozier said he would give out food," he shouted.

McKay turned in his seat, "When?"

"Here on the hill."

"Then come on, I'll go right down with you and remind him," said McKay, then stopped lifting his whip, looking at the rifle in Poundmaker's hand.

"You are a brave man, to take that. But you must give it back."

"No! I took it away before he could use it on me."

"The gun isn't his. It belongs to the Grandmother. You've humiliated him completely, you can give it back," McKay sat a moment, looking the round of them, then touched the whip to his team. "Come, I'll remind Crozier of the food," he shouted, rattling away.

Poundmaker, with a jerk, levered cartridges out of the rifle so fast they made a bronze arc falling in the sunlight. He said, "Crozier had on an iron shirt made of chains, under his coat."

"I wasn't aiming there," Little Bad Man said, and rode south towards Cutknife Hill.

"Hai!" cried Miserable Man, "if you're giving back a gun, take my old flint-lock, I'll keep that. Here!"

Even Poundmaker had to laugh then, looking with the others at the battered old piece Miserable Man presented formally as a trader crossing a stack of buffalo robes; their laughter grew easily in the air, greeting the women and children coming up toward the plain.

"My son," Big Bear said as Poundmaker came past him, "you have been cut."

"That was," Poundmaker paused; two long cuts in his thigh ran blood into his moccasins. "It was my club. When that Antrobus was in front of me those knives wanted blood so much I had to push them in there." He rode after McKay.

Later Big Bear became aware of Little Pine sitting silently on his old stallion beside him. They could just distinguish Jefferson and McKay dealing food to the warriors who filed by the door of the building; the long straggle of women and girls carrying flour and bacon on their backs, tying them to the backs of the dogs, already led shouting happily out of sight west toward the line of the river.

"Just like treaty day," said Little Pine heavily.

"I don't know," said Big Bear. "I've only had one. Maybe my old women will even get me some tobacco."

They both chuckled a little then, not from happiness.

"The Clothing should have stayed away," said Little Pine, "I think they got him there now too."

"That was what it was, a day's worth of flour." They almost laughed out loud, at all the food passing north of them. They looked back again to the barriers, saw the red police harnessing their horses to the wagons; and also the knots of riders which had not gone near that door wheel suddenly away, stringing out, pounding hard south towards the Hill. The Rattlers would not eat white food tonight; perhaps none at all, but certainly not white, tonight.

"But to get beef," he added after a moment, "someone may have to get killed."

"Your power was too strong today," said Little Pine. "They could not stop a council."

"It was strong enough," said Big Bear, "today, to save police." He looked a moment steadily into the watery, brown-streaked eyes of his old friend, and it seemed to him that very soon now they would not talk again. "Ah my brother. We will have to pray about today. Is there a council here? You saw them, you know them."

Little Pine knew that there were no more buffalo or Bloods to ride against.

"The power given you can hold them," Little Pine said.

For what? He almost said that, for it seemed to him momentarily that he did not know anything which he had just an instant before known so certainly he would never have to think about it. What he had known as certainly all his long life. There had been prayer and power and now between the long green earth and sky something more was gone, gone.

They sat on their horses side by side as the brilliant day cooled a little, and neither thought of eating.

v

The council voice of Big Bear had wandered into the August afternoon and the directions of its sound were growing discernible. Forming from a barely apprehended, shapeless mass darkening out of mists, like allegories drawing a spare outline from bits scattered about the fly-buzzed afternoon under the council tent with its lower skins rolled up for air to move and the ears of all men to hear. Presently the voice sought particularly Big Child, Star Blanket, One Arrow, Beardy, Shadow On The Water, James Smith and the Saulteau John Smith, all seated in the front ring of the circle, all chiefs with a memory of the Carlton Treaty hardening on their sun-black faces. " .... stay in the land The First One gave me, I wish all that is to make my claims good by this evil. I know a chief and perhaps two chiefs of this land. I have never spoiled a handful of it; I have never for myself wanted the Earth; he takes more from me than I can ever take from him.

"I see clearly the one who cheats me. I wait for the day when we are together, when I can tell him straight.

"It is good in one way I am cheated, for now I begin to understand what great good The Only One had given me. Now I can truly worship the kindness of That One. They play too much on me when they say, 'You don't know anything.' There may be some things that can be known, now, in this very place after two passings of four years with the Start to Fly moon shining here again. This is the place where it was done, here."

There was no accusation in his tone but the chiefs were staring above him into nothing, as if they could not face the ground.

"Though I wasn't here with you when it was done, I have seen it all. We have talked long, here and at Duck Lake and before that many talked at Cutknife Hill, though a few went home from there early and some others would not talk, all chiefs and we have said how we look at things and how our people understand our life now. But we know that it will not amount to anything; it is all among ourselves. What we say will not reach the whites of the world because there is no one among us to speak to them for us. We tell the agents a part of our thoughts, what they understand of that, but we know they will not speak to the world for us. They will only tell certain things to Government.

"What I see is this: I speak out to one white man, and there is always one higher. I speak for my band as a chief speaks for his people when they have decided, but the Whiteskin I speak to isn't like that. Even the Governor, or the one who came talking so loud and fast from Ottawa and left before the first snow would freeze his shining skin, there is always one higher whom I never see. This is the thought that has come to me: who wastes a bullet on a tail when he knows that sticking out at some other end there could be a head with bear's teeth? It is time to see that one Whiteskin *than whom there is none higher!* It is time to see that one. It is time to say some things to that one. I see that when my children's bellies hang big under their ribs, when my wives lick sores on their lips from stinking meat, when my young men can't run over a hill without spitting their sweet blood against the bushes. It is time, now.

"Though I was not here that time when it was done, I have seen it. Every man of us was blind when making the treaty. He did not understand what use he had for it. He was rich, his food and clothing were in his hand; he could do what he liked with it. The land was wherever he wanted to go, what are iron posts driven into the ground? He was full with it all. While he was enjoying such living there came a man, a Government to him, without invitation. This Government talks and talks that he will be given much to live even better, but if that was all the Government had done we would not have been persuaded. For we have been given Earth and Buffalo, who needs more to breathe than air?"

Big Bear paused to drink from the buffalo horn Lone Man lifted up to him. The men facing him, under the warm shade of the lodge and beyond in the rippling sunlight, remembered as he recreated what he had refused to see there eight years before because, as he had told their messengers blandly and with no apparent foresight, he was a hunter and *mus-toos-wuk* was coming north just then.

"Such talk could never have persuaded People, and Government knew it. So first the Governor that came here and stood on this hill above Fort Carlton called upon The Great Spirit to witness the treaty. Then he invoked the name of the Queen, and finally he mentioned himself, the Governor Morris. After mentioning these three names, the Governor made a treaty not for the sake of his Government but on account of The First One, The Almighty Spirit, and the Grandmother. This was hard to understand and we talked for one or two days only, a little, of why it should be necessary in the name of these to make treaty when we were willing to share as we have always done under one Sun and one Moon, the rain that gives any skin to drink, but the Governor Morris said that the Grandmother's white children were sometimes very different from us and he wanted to have us all live together like brothers. He said, 'I want first to help you stand on the same place with my white children, to live together like two brothers, and after you get to that place my Government will not need to help you any more.' He said, 'We are not coming to buy your land. It is a big thing, it is impossible for a man to buy the whole country, we came here to make certain it is kept for you.'

"We therefore understand that the land is only borrowed, not bought."

A massive sound of approbation moved the People listening.

"Yes," said Big Bear, "I am willing to speak. The Governor Morris told me what no one had said to me before. He said, 'You don't know anything,' and he was not the last Whiteskin to tell me that much of what I might not want to know and so would never have asked him to tell me." He was smiling while the laughter, led by Lone Man's guffaw, grew around him. "So, since I came north again and during the winter and since the leaves began to come, I've been walking certain places, trying to understand something. The Thunderbird gave me to make a Thirst Dance, he gave me friends to help me make it and answered with rain, that is why I came to Cutknife Hill and then to Duck Lake, and why I have now come to Carlton. Talking to you I have been trying to understand and make myself understood that I am trying to get hold of the promises which they made to me. I see my hand closing again and again, but nothing seems to be in it. I cannot find it. I walk the Earth; I walk from the Cypress Hills to Frog Lake to Edmonton and Saddle Lake, from Whitefish Lake to Cutknife Hill and Duck Lake and here to the crossing on the Great River, I dance with my friends beside the Battle River, and all that was promised, I can't see the half of it. All I see is the little piece of land I must choose and then never leave unless some Farm Instructor says I can go. What is that, when I must have the mark of such a thing on paper to walk on the land they have borrowed? I feel as if I choked. I love The One Above, I ask That One whom we love to help me. If we respect and honour the Queen because of her great work on the Earth, how much more must we honour the Earth? Is this queen more to us than the Earth? The proper way to live with the Earth is to give each one the right The First One gave every one man. Let every man walk where his feet can walk.

"I know how it was done. While Governor Morris was speaking a man was writing words on a paper beside him. When the Governor had finished the People said what we wanted and the man wrote down those words too. After we had done speaking they placed a paper before us to make our names on, but we refused until they had given us a copy of the words which we could send around among our people to hear what they said, for words written down always say the same thing. But they would not let that; it was not necessary they said, we could trust them, so then we made our names. They went to Battleford and sent back a copy which they left with us, and after they went to Ottawa they sent another copy. And then we found that the words no longer said the same thing; then we found that half the sweet things were taken out and all the sour left in, and we knew we would never stand on the same place with the white man on our land. But to this day we wait for the white man, that he will fulfill his first promise. That is what we know about the treaty.

"My brothers!" Big Bear's deep voice lifted to a great shout that shivered the lodgeskins and rolled out into the afternoon heat, "The Whiteskins have brought all this evil on us, but we trust them. Who does not have a white friend? Who has not received good things from them? What Person was ever shot by police? The buffalo has been taken from us. On this Earth he was our life, and how can he return except The One who took him from us return him again? I see his track in the deep paths he wore to sweet water, and at river crossings where wind moans through his wool hung on the low bushes, I see his shape in the wallows, the print of his tongue where salt gleams like frost in the Scattering Moon, I hear the thunder of his running under the Tramping Lakes, and at Sounding where The Giver Of All runs the great herds still and they graze the soft spring grass and lick their little calves. Eiya-eiya-a-a, where have we gone, where, where.

"We must stand together under The Only One. We must work toward that good work every day without stopping, as long as Earth is. We have The Spirit. The sun works every day, why? To enlighten the world. We must do the same, our spirit must work constantly to enlighten every one for there is a large meaning in every word we say. Why keep it here, among ourselves? Why do we keep turning the same word over and over among ourselves and then swallowing it again? Only a sick dog eats again what he has once spit out. Our word is for all, especially for the white man who never hears us speak as one voice with power. We speak too many words here and there, to too many low Whiteskins; there is always one of them higher who hears nothing. I say we must choose one of us from all the bands to speak our words. To speak to no one but the one Whiteskin than whom there is none higher, whether that is in Ottawa or across the Stinking Water. To speak to the Grandmother like I speak here. I do not believe she wants us to starve the way we are."

Flies buzzed overhead on the hot worn hides.

"I only have a few words left," Big Bear said, "and I am happy you are listening. Last year when the River People came north we saw some things Whiteskins do. There is no way to go north and south now but to cross those two iron rails they have bolted down into the land, split it open like a thong jerked too tight. It is an iron thong. On it runs that Iron Horse that moves of its own fire, that pulls long carts faster than a running prairie fire and when these carts fall off the track their hard edges will cut open heads. We also saw in one place People who had pulled ploughs like an ox through the ground because there was no Government ox to do that, and People sitting empty beside full sacks of grain that can't be sold because the Government says so and can't be eaten because the Government hasn't given them the grist mill it promised. At Whitefish Lake in winter we saw Seenum who can't live on the big reserve Governor Morris promised him eight years ago at Pitt because they say now the Governor did not say it. When

I come here I see you don't have enough seed for all the land you have broken. Where is the seed? It is sitting somewhere on its promise. I see all this, having come north from the last buffalo. And I also see my young man He Speaks Our Tongue, who did wrong to beat an instructor though he had a just complaint as Little Pine and I heard Crozier say from behind his table in Battleford when he had heard the witnesses, I see him sitting since the eggs were hatching in a dark jail waiting for a trial, and he is sitting there still. He will have the justice of the Queen's law, when? Just wait till the white judge comes, wait. These are only a few things I see, now that I am trying to live with the treaty, promises in it that I can't find between my fingers. All I find there is the Iron Horse on its track choking the Earth, throwing sparks to set the prairie burning and it of course has no concern since it can outrun any fire.

"I see clearly the one who cheats me. I wait for the day when we are united for then I will speak to him straight. I was happy when your messengers said, 'Come, talk to us.' I turned around immediately. I am very happy to speak to the chiefs and councillors and everyone here. My band has accepted no reserve. We have thought to take it at Wolfdung Hill on the Battle River and we have thought of Dog Rump on the Saskatchewan, and there are four other places, and four more where it may be, for the thought has come to me: we are too scattered. It has come to Seenum at Whitefish Lake also. We are small here, we are smaller there, and who hears us? Who stirs in his sleep when a single buffalo runs? But when a herd moves, ahhh — we too must shake the ground, we must speak with one thundering voice, we must have one huge reserve for us all, for our hunting, for our life where we will live as the treaty says we can: as we always have but also with grain and food growing as the Government will help us. Then when we move every Whiteskin will lay his ear to the ground so he won't get trampled.

"I have said what I was willing to say when I turned on the Fort Pitt trail to come to Duck Lake, and what I was willing to say here at Carlton too. There are white listeners sitting here; very good. Let them hear that in every lodge in the Saskatchewan Valley from Edmonton to Fort a la Corne the People are saying the same thing! And Piapot at Qu'Appelle, though they would not give him supplies so that he could come here to say it. Crowfoot at Blackfoot Crossing is working for the same thing; Poundmaker has told me.

"There is one more thing to say on this hill. Eight years ago, here, when the People first stood before Governor Morris we did not forget our brothers the Metis. When we under-stood that we were going to get some sweet things we wanted our brother to have a share, but the Governor stopped us. He said, 'The Metis are my children too. It is my business to look after them, we will make all contented.' That is another promise no one has got his fingers on, and our brothers have gone over the Line to get one who can speak for them. He is now closer to Duck Lake than we are, and perhaps the head-men here think he can better help the Whiteskins understand us because Americans like land too and he knows them. Our brothers suffer but this must be talked through. I have known some Americans and they talk faster and wear nicer clothes, but they are still Whiteskins and not like People. If one of them has many things it's not because of the number of his friends, it's because he has grabbed more. Just to trade the whites we know for those we don't — this has to be talked through. But it is true, when I see so often the ones we have now are dishonest, I feel something around my neck and I tell my People I am afraid to take a reserve. I feel very sad to leave my large liberty for such choked little places where little iron pegs stick in the ground and where little instructors have nothing to do but watch me live. About the papers they must sign before we can go visit our friends? There is nothing in any treaty about such papers. Did you ever sign one? I will never ask anyone if I can go somewhere, will you, chiefs of the People? But there cannot be any point in getting angry with instructors, who wants blood to stain our grass? We want our land clean and pure so that when we are together on one reserve large enough for our life, all together, we will find only peace there. When will you have a big meeting? When will you speak each for your people: this is what we will do, together?

"It has come to me as through the bushes that you are not united. That you cannot speak for your people because they do not know what can be done, because the advice they have heard has not been good. Let us become united, and I will speak. Otherwise the Government sends us nothing but these things as think themselves men. They bring everything crooked, they take our lands and sell them and clap their hands on their hips and call themselves men. Men! Years before the treaty we heard that the Hudson's Bay Company had sold the land to the Government. When, from whom had they ever received it? I know that they sold what was not theirs for more money than all the People have received after eight years of treaty, and besides that the Company still has more land than all of our reserves together. The railroad that strangles the land has even more than that! At Where The Bones Lie the Governor Dewdney has built his new house, he told me, and the land there was sold for so much money that, if we could touch it, we and our children and all their children after would eat beef twice a day as long as we live. What are these crooked things that we see around us while we dig for gophers with sticks so we have a few bits to put in our children's mouths? While we go begging, one by one, alone to an instructor for a handful of flour? While we sit with salt pork growling in our bellies and can talk about nothing more than how to beg some poor white to give us a cup of tea? No wonder the buffalo have gone away! They would die of shame to be run by hunters whose arms hang slack as pig's fat!

"Whose chiefs and councillors see no more wisdom blazing before them, whose words for their people are only complaint and whine!

"What has become of the First People?"

The chiefs and councillors of the one thousand six hundred and seventy-eight Indians listed by John Rae as being in Carlton District sat like motionless rocks before Big Bear. Sweat ran down their faces, their bodies.

"It sometimes comes to me," Big Bear said dreamily as if his clear sharp voice stood in a whisper at each ear and every man alone could hear it, "that we have been breathed over; like the trance that falls over us when the windigo is coming. Our power songs call helplessly into the night, our wisdom cries through the trees and among wolf willow for us but we cannot find it. Ice forms in our bodies, hair pushes out of our faces and arms and legs; we feel growing in us the craving to devour the human being that sits beside us. And we are terrified. Eiya, eiya-a-a-a.

"The drum was talking last night. I could see the burning feet of ghost dancers come up the sky and at last my spirit began to walk. This is a very good place for me, I was born only half a morning's ride up the valley. That was so long ago it might take longer to ride now. There were fewer trees in the valley as my spirit walked for I saw my grandmother a young women in a winter lodge among the bushes in the valley and that was before any white had come here, it was when our fathers were coming out to the plains for buffalo and fought the Siksikas and the Bloods and the Gros Ventre here on foot with the first guns from the traders. I saw that, and I saw my mother pounding pemmican, and I saw myself one winter being born under a spruce tree. She carried me back to the warm lodge though by then a Company building was already standing behind a wall where there are so many now, and those police are there now too. Under that spruce tree a bear had been sleeping and I was so eager to get out my mother had no time to spread the clean hide she had brought for me and I fell with my nose in something the bear had left behind. Since then I have always had something big with bears. Everyone knows how the Great Parent of Bear gave me my name and a song when I was young, and it came to me that last night He was giving me to scout through my dreams. I was wearing His Hand, I know, and this is what I saw.

"I saw everything grey. I saw the valley of the Great River empty, with very few trees; and then I saw Fort Carlton as anyone can see it right now if he stands on the coulee hill above the valley; all the buildings and high wall, and I could see nothing there at all but black scattered around, wide, with a little smoke going straight up as of wood resting after burning too fast. I don't know when that will be. I tried to see better and I think there were places where snow lay on the ground. But it was all grey, there weren't any leaves, and smoke was all I could see where there should have been Fort Carlton. I saw that, and I am telling you. These are my words."

After a moment Big Bear added,

"Don't allow any man to poison my words. Speak to your people and we will all together make one great council. Then I will speak again. Even when there is snow on the ground, no one likes that big a fire. And I think only words can stop it."

FOUR

Frog Lake,
April 1 and 2, 1885

I

All that summer, 1884, the telegraph wires of the North West Territories sang daily with information for Lieutenant-Governor and Indian Commissioner Dewdney. On August 2 Agent Rae reported from Carlton that "Big Bear is to have a big council at Duck Lake next week"; on August 5 Sub-agent J. Ansdell Macrae reported from Prince Albert that at "a meeting between Big Bear, Lucky Man, other chiefs and Riel which took place a few days ago, nothing of more importance than a pledge of mutual support transpired (so far as can be ascertained)"; on August 14 Superintendent Crozier reported from Battleford that Riel "has not had a meeting with Big Bear but I am afraid he has some private way of communicating with him" and that Big Bear and the Carlton chiefs "are now in council there"; on August 21 Sergeant W.A. Brooks reported from Prince Albert that Big Bear and Riel had arrived in town on the 16th and 17th, and that "Riel stayed at Jackson the Druggist and before he left he and Lepine held a conference with Big Bear the result of which I have not been able to learn.... I have heard on pretty good authority that Riel has given up the idea of going back to Montana." On August 22 Dewdney himself reported to Sir John A. Macdonald: "Reed wired me that he thought the Carlton Indians were a little unsettled by the presence of Big Bear who had promised to obtain all sorts of things for them."

Two months earlier, on June 14, Dewdney had begun a long private letter to the Prime Minister with the paragraph: "I have returned the day before yesterday from my trip north. You will have gathered from my telegrams that Indian matters were on the whole satisfactory, and instead of finding our Indians malcontented I never saw them more contented, taken as a whole."

Nothing that summer would make the Governor change his opinion. Rae wrote to him and directly to the Prime Minister: "The Indians who are *very* badly off must either be treated rationally, if not generously, or as I said before we must be prepared to fight them." In addition to regular police reports and a long special on the Cutknife expenses, Crozier wrote him and N.W.M.P. Commissioner Irvine: "It does not seem to me reasonable to expect a lot of pure savages to settle down and become steady farmers all at once.... Government policy should be, as it has been in the past, one of conciliation. There is only one other, and that is to fight them. In my opinion, it will be difficult to prevent an actual outbreak with all its attendant horrors for the settlers, if matters go on as they are going. Indians when at war do not fight openly." But Dewdney was involved with his first North West Territories Council meeting in his newly christened capital of Regina (he informed Sir John on August 5: "In council Irvine is worse than nobody for he can't understand what is going on & half the time he doesn't know which way to vote."); he was tangled in a Department of Indian Affairs power struggle between himself, Vankoughnet in Ottawa and Indian Inspector Wadsworth in Winnipeg; besides, his Assistant Indian Commissioner Hayter Reed had a much more reassuring opinion on what was happening.

In July Major (ret.) Reed laughed in the public newspapers at the very idea of any danger; he had himself been in similar situations with Indians many times ("This is perfect non-sense!" responded a furious John Rae in Battleford); he was thereupon ordered to investigate the Indian grievances as dutifully reported from the Carlton Council by Macrae on August 25. Reed reported in length to Ottawa on January 25, 1885. The Indians, he found, had a few justifiable grievances (the working stock given them was sometimes wild), but the basic problem was "Big Bear is an agitator... only too glad to have an opportunity of inciting the Indians to make fresh and exorbitant demands... Riel's movement has a great deal to do with the demands of the Indians." And, since halfbreed claims were going to be investigated "soon," Vankoughnet instructed Dewdney to keep reminding the Indians "that they have really received much more than the Government was, under the Treaty, bound to give them." That in a letter dated Ottawa, February 4, 1885.

Meanwhile, the Department wanted Big Bear to choose a reserve in Fort Pitt district and the Wood Cree band of Ohnee-pahao was persuaded to allow the Plains Cree to camp near them on their reserve at the southern end of Frog Lake for that winter. By the middle of October Big Bear's band, now numbering seven hundred and fifty, was moving to Fort Pitt for the annual treaty payments; at the same time his nephew Little Poplar arrived with his personal following (which included a new, sixth wife) from Montana to visit them. Learn-ing from a trail encounter with Wadsworth that the govern-ment had inspectors to check Government accounts, Little Poplar appointed himself Inspector for Indian accounts. He found them only fair with Inspector Francis Dickens of the North West Mounted Police, very good with newly arrived

Trader W.J. McLean of the Hudson's Bay Company, and extremely bad with Sub-Indian Agent Thomas Quinn. The band was insisting it had a right to fresh beef during treaty payments and Little Poplar soon discovered Quinn was no more than "the man Government sent up here to say NO! to everything we ask." After the River People had refused to accept payment and danced for two days, McLean finally slaughtered some Company beef; payments of about five thousand dollars were then made, and during the trading that followed at Fort Pitt Big Bear agreed to see himself in a photograph for a first time.

It is morning inside the fort, and in the right half of the picture cluster fifteen men with very white faces and a small black and white dog; six watch, arms folded, from the background of mudded Company walls; the nine in the foreground with the dog are half turned left towards the five Indians but obviously very aware of being watched themselves. Stanley Simpson faces directly left, his profile sharp under his black hat, his eyes on the giant ledger he holds ready in his hands. Corporal R.B. Sleigh lounges thoughtfully in ascot and fur-trimmed jacket between the high wheels of a cart, his hands in his pockets. In the left half of the picture Matoose is seated on a bearskin and Four Sky Thunder, Kingbird, Iron Body and Big Bear stand behind him. All are draped in striped ceremonial trading blankets and display fancy top hats; in the centre Big Bear's three ostrich plumes blur against the crooked Company stovepipe in the background. A manufactured eagle headdress has been placed on his folded arms and his face seems hunched up, swollen black; as if so early in the morning he were already tired of staring into something.

Little Poplar decided on Battleford for the winter with ninety followers; Twin Wolverine went west to Buffalo Lake with one hundred and fifty others. Big Bear and the remaining six hundred trailed thirty-five miles north to Frog Lake. It was a gentle, beautiful winter that came to wooded valleys and round low hills; the lake fed countless fish but there was no large game and the River People knew nothing about hunting it anyway; the Rattlers danced often in their great lodge of a long winter evening, talking and talking; the father of The Magpie drew his knife when he could not get provisions and was trapped inside the Government storehouse until police galloped up to arrest him; before noon on March 16, 1885 an almost total eclipse blotted the sun upon the snow-bright sky; the Rattlers crouched behind bushes and fired their guns until it reappeared. The whites at Frog Lake were debating village names; they anticipated the telegraph within that year, and the railroad within three.

For along Frog Creek, which drained the lake into the North Saskatchewan, straggled a settlement that boasted it received more mail than Fort Pitt. On April Fool's Day, 1885, there lived along Frog Creek

— Sub-agent Thomas Trueman Quinn, 38, from Minnesota, and his wife, Lone Man's niece; his blacksmith nephew Henry Quinn; his carpenter, Charles Gouin, 40;

— lived Farming Instructor John Delaney, 39, from Ottawa, and his wife Teresa of three years; his interpreter John Pritchard, a Scots half-blood, and his family;

— lived Hudson's Bay trader James Simpson and his Cree wife he called Catherine; his clerk William Bleasdell Cameron;

— lived Father Leon Fafard, o.m.i., 36, from St. Cuthbert, Quebec, and his Onion Lake assistant Father Felix Marchand, o.m.i., 26;

— lived George Dill, 38, from Muskoka, Ontario, speculator and trader;

— lived saw and gristmill operator John A. Gowanlock, 28, from Parkdale, Ontario, with Teresa, his wife of six months; his clerk William Gilchrist, 21, and his mechanic John Williscraft, 65.

— lived also Corporal R.B. Sleigh and six constables. All seven, however, left for Dickens' headquarters at Fort Pitt before sunrise on March 31: when he received news of the Battle of Duck Lake, Quinn consulted all whites and they decided the police should leave immediately so as not to unnecessarily arouse the Plains Cree. The River People had moved in along the creek between the mill dam and the rest of the white settlement.

James Simpson was in Fort Pitt on Company business, but he was expected back for Good Friday, April 3.

II

"That brown with the blaze there you gave Red Bone," said Big Bear, "he always winters good."

Kingbird stopped, leaned on his rifle butted in the snow. The gelding pawed steadily at the opening it had worked around on the marsh grass, head down; other shaggy shapes were scattered beyond, near the grey willows at the edge of the still blank-white lake.

"That first raid," Kingbird said, "was the best. Later at Cypress Hills when we kept after the Bloods it wasn't much good."

"He's so strong in spring it's too bad there's always the limp he got when Bad Arrow borrowed him to run buffalo," said Big Bear. "It was a badger hole, I think."

"The stupid Bloods just kept running to the agent and he kept running to the police," said Kingbird.

"Though he could have slipped running by that small water hole."

"Bone only rode him four days."

"Well the buffalo came then and Bad Arrow borrowed him to run and after that he always needed him. It's too bad," said Big Bear, watching the brown move, starting to lift his own foot again in its soaked rag wrapping, "all those years Arrow had to ride that limping horse and Bone could never lend him a better one."

Momentarily they forgot about sinking through the thin clean snow into the sodden layer sinking beneath; they thought of the old man now dead as they slogged up the slope from the marsh. The air pressed moist and warm down under the leaden clouds.

"After a few times like that," Big Bear said, "those Bloods came to the Hills. Piapot hacked up their tobacco and threw it in the fire, before Big Buffalobull Irvine came too."

"Their horses were all wind-broken and saddle sores anyway," said Kingbird. "From running pork!"

Snow was gone over the rounded hill and down its southwest exposure to the frozen lake. Directly across west were the lodges of Ohnee-pahao and his Wood People, and below the point of the lake smoke from the Whiteskin chimneys stood in the grey sky. Out of the tall wooden houses where they slept high under the roofs as if they couldn't stand to sleep where they lived. The marshy line of the creek, black from water, disappeared into the dark trees beyond that, southwest, where the lodges of the River People must be though their smoke was not visible. Water ran everywhere, living in the soil it softened on the slope, from under the greyish banks rotting against hillsides, near the furry blue flowers unbending against the ground from roots the horses had not pawed out. Son and father said nothing more, nor did any of the men following them as they trudged along the high ground and floundered through hollows; their dogs too exhausted to bark when the camp dogs charged them, howling. Not even that drew children from the tied-up lodges.

"A few rabbits, enough for us to eat sometimes every day," said Big Bear. He was rubbing his feet, watching Running Second fry bannock; the smell of bacon fat churned his stomach a little. "Thunder shot a coyote, and a moose left tracks that went away between the bare ground and the new snow. I could dream nothing, no bears, all bear brothers are snoring for spring."

"There are some bands," said The Magpie suddenly, very loudly, "who have lots of food. On their reserves. Even clothing for children when it gets cold."

Running Second looked up, open-mouthed; Big Bear contemplated his youngest wife near the door, gutting her fish violently. Her leggings were black with water and she was thin still, he had in six years worked nothing of her to softness. He said thoughtfully, as though he were actually answering her, and now Running Second glanced to him in astonishment,

"Yes, I have heard that such reserves could be, somewhere. Though no one is living on them at the moment except perhaps a white man, looking. There could be one like that, I think, between the Red Deer and Battle Rivers, around Sounding Lake or perhaps, Buffalo Lake," he said, still looking thoughtfully at The Magpie and in the darkening lodge he saw her flush as her knife flickered through the silvery fish, for she knew he had seen her standing long, looking after the People that had followed Twin Wolverine to Buffalo Lake. "I think when Little Pine went to buy horses at Blackfoot Crossing in the Frozen-over Moon he wanted to tell Crowfoot there would be room even for Blackfeet on such a reserve. Beautiful, all the wide grass and water for *mus-toos-wuk* when he comes back. But they've given Crowfoot a paper for that Iron Horse and he was gone to Calgary. That's a white place."

Running Second said softly, not raising her head, "Someone came yesterday from Battle River. Little Pine has gone to the Sand Hills."

After some time Big Bear said, "That isn't why Matoose was sent for us." His elder wife looked at him, but of course she knew only rumour. He said, almost to himself, "He left before that, he could not know," and he was going to say something to Horsechild who had lain all the while against his thigh, motionlessly gazing up to him, but he stopped.

He had been about to ask his youngest son to run for Lone Man, but Horsechild had no clothing. Having thought of asking his son to do something as painful as running naked across camp in the cold evening, he felt ashamed and he had nothing to give him to ask his silent forgiveness; therefore he could do nothing but accept a gift from the boy. Big Bear lifted the navel cord bag Horsechild wore around his neck, opened it, took out some of the tobacco kept there, stuffed his pipe and offered it to the spirits before he accepted the coal Running Second held for him, praying silently to them for his son. The boy lay, smiling up in happiness.

The Magpie flung the fish guts through the lodge opening and immediately dogs snarled and slavered outside. She was still thin, Big Bear thought, but not gently so like Sits Green On The Earth across the fire, tending the teakettle carefully with Kingbird's sleeping head in her lap. That was a good place to lie, head held by the child obviously growing in there. Trader James Simpson had once told him Sits Green had the shape and face, especially the eyes, white men would murder for; since she was his daughter-in-law he had never looked directly at her of course, nor had she ever spoken aloud in his presence but he could see enough of it from the line of her thigh, the black hanging sheen of hair. On the last night, Little Pine, spread out one like that for warmth.

Lone Man came in, and helped them eat the bannock and bacon. Big Bear murmured, "No one said Little Pine was sick."

"No," said Lone Man heavily. "Some say there he was poisoned."

"Ahhhh." Big Bear chewed steadily for a time, "I remember him waving green branches, on that hill last summer."

"We all saw that, and heard him too. And others."

"Ahhhhh," Big Bear stared into his small fire. In the circle of his daughter-in-law, his two wives, his son-in-law, his two, youngest, sons; mounds in the dark lodge.

"The Young Men," said Lone Man, "the Rattlers sit in council all day, in the Greatlodge."

"I haven't called a council, or heard of one."

Lone Man said nothing.

Big Bear said at last, "Tell me what they have heard. What they keep talking."

"Dumont and Riel have fought with the Carlton police. And killed them."

"What the holy he — excuse me, ladies —" George Dill bowed slightly over the table, laughing unself-consciously, "what difference does it make, what that Little Bad Man — little! — says, there aren't any breeds around here to do nothing."

"Oh but Mr. Delaney just said there are quite a number among the Wood Crees," Terry Gowanlock began in her pretty voice, still smiling, but Dill interrupted,

"Look, it doesn't matter then, any mixed bloods, and there's any number of them around you don't have to look far for reasons, ha, living with a tribe they're no better than Indians.

They won't do nothing with Riel. The closest real breeds are St. Albert and that's two hundred miles the wrong way."

"Well, they might go through. If they move toward Batoche," said John Gowanlock, "they could come past here."

"There's Edmonton and Victoria and places like that make a lot better picking than your mill, Johnny my lad, and they'd have to pass Pitt right after. There's shorter trails to Batoche."

"Then what about their logging camp," Gowanlock persisted, "at Moose Creek. That's only twenty miles —"

"Okay, maybe ten there, no more 'n fifteen even, and they still have to drag their squaws and little half-Hiawathas along. With their horses like now in spring? Naw, there's nothing."

"That's the way it'll be, George," said young Gilchrist, laughing into his teacup. "You've been out here so long, you know it like it is."

"Before ye were bo-orn Billy-o, with a bit of time off, so don't forget it," Dill drew thumb and middle finger down his fringe of mustache.

"But John," Gowanlock turned to the fireplace again where the farming instructor had sat silently sucking an unlit pipe since rising from the supper table, "isn't it really the Indians? Isn't that why Quinn — all of us really — sent the police away, and them saying they'll protect us from the halfbreeds, well, maybe that's their idea of a joke. They were all over the mill too, worse than ever, 'It's Big-lie Day!' prancing around."

"Oh that one with the warbonnet, you said it was, Mr. Delaney, the lynx skin and eagle feathers, he had such a wicked look in his eye," cried Terry Gowanlock. "What was his name?"

"Travelling, or Wandering Spirit," George Dill said, watching her slender hands gesture just beyond the candle, the light glint from her wet, bowed lips.

"The Wandering Spirit!" she shuddered deliciously.

"Aren't those shoulder ringlets of his something?"

"The envy of any woman," she laughed. "How can an Indian have such —"

"Would he joke about his warbonnet, John?" Gowanlock asked again.

"They're nothing but kids," said John Delaney heavily, not moving in his chair. "Anything to get dressed up, strut around, and he hasn't had an excuse since New Year's. If Quinn knew —"

"I've just had the most marvellous idea!" Terry Gowanlock exclaimed, "When you said New Yea —"

But she was again interrupted, by a knock at the door and for an instant all six sat immobilized, as if that very ordinary sound was suddenly so strange they remembered they were surrounded by almost a thousand Indians whose faces all looked more or less the same, blank to them. But immediately the door opened, and they knew that round white, face.

"Oh, come in Cameron," said John Delaney.

"Everything still standing at ol' Horse Blanket Company?" said Dill, but William Cameron did not glance at his erstwhile partner; he stretched his hands shaking a little, to the bright fire.

"Your chief back yet?" John Gowanlock asked.

"No."

"Maybe Straggle-beard Simpson," said Dill to see Terry Gowanlock's mouth open again in laughter but he was disappointed, "maybe he heard what happened to Crozier at Duck Lake, and there's all them police with guns in Fort Pitt.... " Gilchrist's laughter drowned his voice but Cameron swung around towards the table so hard his hand hit Teresa Delaney upon her stool by the fire, knitting.

"Oh — I'm so sorry Mrs. Delaney, I — please excuse me," he said, and turned. "That's not funny George. Nine good men dead isn't funny a bit. And James Simpson is the last man here that needs to worry. He's traded with Big Bear for twenty-five years and he's a good friend —"

"Twenty-five maybe but more like forty," said Dill, "and he's got a couple of mostly red stepsons with the Wood Crees and there's always his woman to —"

"That's enough," said Delaney abruptly, as if aware for the first time he was there. Tight silence, the only sound the click of knitting needles.

"I just stopped to tell you he isn't back yet," said young Cameron. "I was going by to Quinn's. Goodnight, Mrs. Delaney," and he vanished out the door.

"Goodnight," she called after him.

Fire and candle shadows wavered hugely across each other over the room. John Delaney was leaning forward in his wide chair. "You know Dill," he said, anger turning into his voice as though he were grating it out, carefully, while he spoke, "that I don't have much use for the Hudson's Bay Company. They've been here two hundred years and it's their profit to keep Indians wild. The Government has hired me to teach Indians how to farm and every one I and the priest civilize and Christianize takes fur money out of their pocket, *but* at least that company's *responsible*. They don't skip from band to band trying to steal them blind and then run for Ontario with two hundred percent profit!"

"Just one —" Dill hesitated, his tone dropping hard and thin, "you're damn crazy, two hundred percent with three traders, Gowanlock too —"

"Now really, really," John Gowanlock's arm waved before his boyish face, "we're all together here, remember, there's only twelve or thirteen of us in the whole bush so come on now, eh. We're all really working for the same thing."

"Terry, the cards are on the shelf," said Teresa Delaney from her stool, gesturing without losing a stitch. "Why don't you show everyone more of the five-handed game."

"Oh of course! And my idea, let me tell you my idea when you mentioned New Year's, Mr. Delaney. The dance at Fort Pitt on New Year's was so absolutely marvellous, we must have one here now! We must get Mr. Carral and his string band and of course invite everyone from Pitt who was there with all —"

"That means little Chickenstalker Dickens and all his twenty-five men!" interrupted Dill with mock grief.

"Of course, and it will be held on Victoria Day. The Queen's Birthday," said Terry, "that leaves us almost two months to plan."

"Perhaps a bee-utiful reading from the sweetest novels of Father Charles?"

"The warehouse might be cleared," said Teresa Delaney. "It's almost empty now with the police...." She was alone beside the fire as the others grouped around the table.

Dill spoke casually, "I see Big Bear come in from the Moose Hills, this afternoon," between Terry's card explanations.

"How was hunting?" asked Gowanlock.

"I didn't see nothing." Dill, watching Delaney shuffle the cards, said very deliberately, "Kingbird come in too," but the farm instructor did not lose his rhythm.

"Is that the one that has the lovely wife you pointed out to Teresa and me?" asked Terry, depend on her.

"The one and only. Yes sir! Present company excepted of course, she's the most beautiful woman west of Ontario."

"You're wicked," said Terry.

"She's just a red squaw," said Gilchrist but studying Dill; the trader seemed to be tugging his jowls while staring at Delaney's huge greyish mutton-chops sticking over the table as he dealt cards, and suddenly the clerk remembered the trader's epithet for him: Hopeful Edgar Dewdney of the North.

"You're wicked," Terry Gowanlock said to Dill again; she obviously had heard it too.

"Experienced," said Dill calmly, arranging his cards. "I keep my eyes open. You're much too young Billy-o to know about such things, but you give Sits Green On The Earth a nice warm bath and you wouldn't so much as be able to tell the difference. You wouldn't want to."

"Now really," said John Gowanlock, embarrassed.

"I'm really worried, George," William Gilchrist laughed, "I'm so young and inexperienced with Indians, if something happens I won't even know enough when to start running."

"Don't worry about it!" said John Delaney very loudly. "Isadore Mondion the Wood Cree councillor said he'd warn me in plenty of time."

The faces gleaming about the table all stared at him momentarily; John Gowanlock cleared his throat.

"Just keep your eye on me, all the time," George Dill smoothly passed off three cards. "When I start picking 'em up and laying 'em down, that's the time you *run*."

Teresa Delaney was knitting steadily, beside the fire.

In the Greatlodge the Rattlers were eating. Though not even a Worthy Young Man, Thunder had gladly presented his lone coyote for their pot; he squatted just inside the door, staring about happily with eyes large in the flickering light, empty stomach almost forgotten. Kingbird sat in the outer circle of Worthy Young Men before him; inside that was the Warrior round, Wandering Spirit and Four Sky Thunder at its far turn across from the fire. The two old servers only moved about, pouring broth from the pots, stirring the fire, spearing tidbits on their red sticks and placing them between warriors' lips. Kingbird did not feel like eating. It all seemed heavy to him; like muscling through rotting sodden snow.

"Where's Little Bad Man?" Round The Sky beside him leaned over.

"With my father, at Quinn's."

Round The Sky laughed silently, nothing more than a slight movement of air as if they were lying in wait again, somewhere; but Kingbird could not recall such happiness clearly; he was looking past Matoose on his left, down the circle. Oska-task chewed steadily beside Miserable Man, not quite as big as he but nearly as ugly from the White Sickness. Neither would get into the next circle, no matter what happened, for Man would always be too poor and Oska-task too stupid. Beyond them Little Bear, scars healed on his chest: he would certainly, young though he was, and He Speaks Our Tongue beyond doubt; he ate as if he was tearing someone between his teeth, his eyes glittering through the smoke. Round The Sky was still laughing mirthlessly beside him,

"Whiteskins," he said, "they really want it, the police go and it's Big Lie Day too."

Kingbird thrust his coyote rib behind him, ungnawed, and felt Thunder's fingers take it. The lodge flap slapped, Little Bad Man's powerful shape brushed by in a rush of air between warriors and past the fire so hard it leaned away. He sat between Wandering Spirit and Four Sky Thunder. The servers moved quickly to him but he gestured them aside, muttering to the war chief on his right, his hair pulled down, tied on either side of his wide face with its high eyebrowless forehead, pendulous nose, thick drooping mouth. He glared under the hoods of his eyes about the men eating or leaning back in morose silence, and suddenly he waved to a server, drawing his fingers as in a loop around his neck several times. The old man started to poke at the fire with his red stick, beginning a high shrill chant; in a moment he was pulling the roasted large intestine of an ox upwards, tugging it higher into the air until the apex of his stick was gone in the smoke, the intestine dangling like a blotchy snake, turning a little. A warrior, Bare Neck, stepped beside it, held it aloft in his dark hands, chugging it up and down to the rhythm building in the lodge slowly around the circle. It dangled there, shaking, before his shaking breechclout, and the inner loop of the intestine, doubled within itself, began to emerge out, down like a pale rod. Laughter and hoots erupted; as Bare Neck chugged by Little Bad Man his naked arm thrust out, seized the intestine, a knife flashed and the short length of it waved in a brown fist. Shouts now: "Good length!" "Too short, too short!" "Is that all you have?" while the warrior danced on past Bad Arrow, past The Pigmy and paused before Iron Body still seated, twitching in the dance. Imperceptibly the tip of the inner fold of the intestine again crept down into view against his naked leg lifting and falling, and again a knife sliced out and Iron Body was standing too, the tiny circle of severed intestine caught aloft on his knife tip; he grunted clumsily, the knife thrusting upwards in jerks. The lodge was uproar.

Thunder shrieked behind them, "What is it? What is it?" and Round The Sky leaned back to him, laughing openmouthed,

"Body's foreskin is too short. It's peeking out, don't you know that?"

Kingbird abruptly put his hand on Matoose's shoulder and pushed himself up. He grunted, "I'm going to just sleep."

"Yeh, give her more than that!" Round The Sky and Matoose grinned around at him, but he was already gone.

Little Bad Man glared motionless through the ribaldry of hacking up and eating the intestine; he had thrown aside his blanket and sat naked except for his breechclout and moccasins, his wide shape glistening hugely red between the taller warriors. He leaned toward Wandering Spirit.

"The pipe now, and you are war chief. Remember, Quinn gave you nothing to go visit your relatives. That was sign."

Wandering Spirit stared into the fire as the other lifted the Rattler pipe up in two hands. His rifle lay before him, its bronze breech polished and the thick soft curls of hair framing his face seemed to focus a fierce light into his sunken eyes. The drum began to beat. Wandering Spirit's body grew hard and rigid, lean; drawn like wire through the blazing fire of his eyes. His power song started in his throat. One by one the Rattlers rose to their feet, were held dancing in their tight place by the drum beat beating and the war chief's song working them beat upon beat toward its swaying scream.

When Cameron opened the door of Quinn's house, light from the agency office across the dark hall lay in a rectangle on the floor. There were Indians there, he could see moccasins, and smell it too coming out of the cool moist air, stronger than what was already soaked into the logs of the new building; he walked across the light into the doorway.

"Evening Cameron," said Quinn. He was tilted in his wicker chair against the table built to the wall; his huge length in a crumpled slant as it seemed the width of the small room, his green tam pushed back on his hair.

"Hai!" Little Bad Man rose immediately and offered his chair, mouth open as if he was laughing, "Here, sit, so your poor bow legs won't bend any more from standing."

The joke common in camp seemed ponderous between those long teeth, but Lone Man and John Pritchard and Quinn laughed and so did young Cameron, who heard it often enough to understand. But Charlie Gouin, seated in a corner on the floor did not laugh, nor did Big Bear on his chair. The old chief's face appeared blotched from sun on snow, the skin around his eyes in thick folds. His deep voice went on as if nothing had interrupted it.

Pritchard whispered to Cameron, "Uneeyen', that's Riel, he talks of that Riel."

"....he told me then already the Americans wanted more land, everything they can get, they have lots of money and everything south of the Line and they'll pay, plenty. He told me that. It has started now, and then he wanted the People to help him. He was trading on the Missouri River and talking all over, 'Blood will run,' he said, 'lots of blood will run, they pour us out like water.'"

"What have you heard, what has started?" asked Quinn sharply. He looked up at Little Bad Man filling the door-width, massively, yet delicately too as if balanced there, the twitch of his lip swaying him ever so lightly.

"I'll tell you this now. When I ran my last buffalo cow there," Big Bear said, "I saw something. I saw a spring shoot out of the ground as if it was water and I covered it with my hand to stop it, but it spurted up between my fingers and ran over the back of my hands, I could not stop it. That was red blood, Sioux Speaker."

Quinn was staring at the doorway where Little Bad Man had disappeared.

"I thought," said Big Bear, "I would have to see it on my hands last summer, but I didn't see it. My power was still good, then." He stood up. A short man, eyes brooding against the peeled log wall.

"I have two pretty good horses," said Lone Man, standing also, "they could get to Fort Pitt before morning." Quinn did not move, his left hand still inside his white-striped vest; Lone Man's voice pleaded, "There is also a different trail I know."

"My good friend," Quinn said, smiling, "you are the uncle of my wife, *nimusum* of my little girl. How could I look into your face again, and take your hand? I'll give you plenty of food for the whole band, there's no need to go anywhere. On these cold hunts. Just keep the young men quiet, and keep them here."

Big Bear continued his thoughtful rumble as if he had heard nothing of what transpired in the room, "No Young Men can talk and dance forever, just listening to what others did. That is not strange, for it is in the nature of Young Men to do dangerous things. It is strange, unless we shoot some-one nobody hears us. Whenever somewhere there is killing, suddenly doors with food behind them open and open. That is strange."

Slowly Quinn's left hand pulled out of his vest as if it were drawing up his knees, and he stood erect. He was over a foot taller than the old chief gazing steadily up into his face.

"Goodnight Sioux Speaker," Big Bear raised his hand. His voice was deep and soft as moss. "Goodnight." And the two River Men went out.

Cameron said, after a moment, "I thought *nimusum* meant 'grandfather.'"

Quinn was sitting again, but he obviously had not heard.

Pritchard said quietly, "Yes, but she's the daughter of Lone Man's brother, to a Cree that means his own daughter, so he called Lone Man 'grandfather.' Anyway," the interpreter added, slowly as Cameron thought that through, "grandparents are very important for teaching kids, and if something happens to a father."

"Oh."

"They seem friendly enough," said Quinn leaning back. "It should be all right."

"I think we should have left like you said right after you heard about Duck Lake," said Cameron. "Coming across from Delaney's I just about stepped on an Indian. They're guarding you."

Quinn laughed. "It's pretty dark out there, you sure it wasn't a dog taking a squat?"

"Yeah, and dogs need rifles for that."

Quinn grinned, slumping on his chair. "Father Fafard was right there. We all agreed. If you go run the first time you hear the bush rustle...."

"But Rae said the whole country's in rebellion. Crozier's been attacked!"

"We all agreed."

"Well, I've been thinking about —"

"Who hasn't? That's over two hundred miles away, Duck Lake. And these are the hottest Indians, don't I know it? But if I feed them enough, they'll keep quiet. Otherwise they'll head for Poundmaker's again, or Batoche, for sure."

"Isn't that for the police," said Pritchard hesitantly, "and soldiers, keeping Riel and Indians apart?"

"Haa!" Quinn roared so loud Charlie Gouin's head jerked erect in the corner. "What soldiers? You know any around here? There is no Canadian army like we had in the States after the Confederate war to fight them, and anyway, how'd they get here from Ontario? The railroad isn't finished around the lakes and the States won't let them come armed that way, so how'll they get here? Walk over the ice?"

"Wolseley did it in '70," said Cameron.

"Wolseley! He took three months from Superior to Red River, in the summer. Today is April 1, eh? There's just the police, and once the Indians start shooting like they mean it, the police are finished. I scouted four years for the U.S. Cavalry, you can't tell me anything about fighting Indians."

Pritchard began, "That Dickens at Fort —"

"Dickens is a nice deaf little man and has a famous father that writes nice story books and twenty-five men. He can't stop Wandering Spirit and Little Big Man blowing their nose if they want to."

Trader and interpreter were staring at him as if they could not believe their ears.

Quinn leaned forward his gaunt, battered face with its heavy mustache. "I said it to you, Cam, right away when Anderson come with the message, everybody pull out before daylight. But Fafard is right. My first idea was just get out, and I think maybe some men better leave with the women first thing in the morning, yeah, they should, but if I go and Delaney goes and the Father, who's to show trust in their word? That they won't shoot even if the breeds have started it? Like Wandering Spirit said today, they'll protect us from the breeds, okay, let them talk like that and I don't believe a word that bugger ever said, but I act as if I believed everything."

"You said yourself," said Cameron, "nobody has to wait for orders to save his life. If Rae —"

"Nobody's scared Tom Quinn yet, and sure no goddam Indian will."

Pritchard stood up, a short sturdy man, "I better go to my house."

"Check the horses once more, eh?"

"Yeah. My Sal said he'd sleep in the stable there."

"Well-l-l," Quinn thought a moment, "I don't like that much. He's got to stay behind the hay with Henry then, and no guns."

"Oh no, not with a gun."

"Okay then. Hey Charlie!" Quinn's voice suddenly crashed in the small room. "Finished your tea?"

The dark face in the corner lifted, opened bleary eyes.

"For god's sake, it's only the evening before Maunday Thursday!" Quinn took two strides, leaned over and hoisted the carpenter erect, the empty mug dropping with a clang at his feet. "Perry Davis Painkiller. Here, haul him to bed."

"I'm w-working for you," said Gouin, clamped to Pritchard's arm, "you've gotta pro-pro —" he could not find the end of the word.

"You're always safe at night, you know that, just make it to confession Friday," said Quinn, pushing him out. The outside door scraped behind them, Gouin still sliding past the word he wanted and Pritchard murmuring quietly.

"It's very handy, all right," said Cameron.

"So where'd he get the painkiller?"

"Confession," Cameron persisted.

"Nothing like it," Quinn said, mustache lifted in grin and as deliberately as Cameron refusing to understand tone. "The only practical religion for the sinful working man."

There was a whisper of moccasins and Mrs. Quinn entered with a teapot; perhaps she had heard her husband bellow at Gouin. While she was pouring, Father Fafard and John Williscraft came in for a moment. The priest and the agent spoke Cree, the only language they had fluently in common, while Williscraft slowly turned the worn peak of his cap back and forth in his knobbly hands, standing in the doorway with his white hair bristling around his head as if sprayed against the darkness. The priest turned to go, then said in his slow English to Cameron:

"Maunday Thursday tomorrow. Church, perhaps?"

Quinn grinned as the young trader shifted a little. "I — I don't, well, I don't know."

"Of course, Easter we all ... have it." Fafard's heavy lips smiled, he turned with a swirl of skirts; Williscraft followed.

In the silence after the door closed, they heard the drum. Quinn leaned forward, cocking his head, listening, and after a time the song came too. He sat back, his left hand crept into his vest, his right occasionally lifted the tea mug; he began to talk. Of his half-Sioux mother in Minnesota and his Irish-French father killed there in ambush by the Sioux while scouting for Major Brown during the massacre in 1862; of himself fighting through the Carolinas with the Wisconsin Regiment of what was now called the Grand Army of the Republic; of himself with the cavalry scouting against the Cheyenne and Arapaho (before they got smart and signed on as scouts themselves) and Sioux; of Dewdney saying they definitely needed a man like him to handle the Plains Cree. He was talking about his escape during the Minnesota Massacre just fifteen and six-two already when his three-year-old daughter came in a long nightgown, knuckles to her eyes and crawling onto his lap. The tiny girl was classic in her ugliness, the bulbous nose and ears of her father protruding against his black vest as he wound his long arm about her, and yet the receding chin which under the mustache gave him a perpetual beak-like expression seemed in her a brush of softness, almost of beauty as she curled there and slept. He was talking of the Sioux raid where he had been trading, how he folded himself into an empty barrel and worked it under the counter with his fingers and the bloody bastards missed him when they sacked the store though they damn near fried him after. He talked until Cameron put his hand to his pink mouth, yawning, and stood up. By then it was almost eleven o'clock.

"Listen," John Delaney said, though the girl could not understand even that word of English. He was not listening to anything himself; the throb of the drum on the moist air less in his ear than the thud of his heart. An extraordinary feeling broke up in him: to say to her "Listen!" and then talk, endlessly, as long as he dared, knowing she did not comprehend a syllable of the fly-blown obscenity he was laying over her; feeling the bones of her hand fold under his, of her beautiful shoulders, saying anything, everything, letting pour out the words he refused to know coiled and squirmed deep inside him to the give of her skull under his fingers, which he had not even recognized all the three years they were ramming up in his throat before anyone who would have understood them, plugged much of him speechless, the silken slip of hair and then the soft mould of her face in the moist cool darkness. The first words to emerge after "Listen!" were always the same, and when he began to understand that he had a flicker of concern sometimes that she might eventually begin to recognize them, repeat them somewhere meaningless to her though they were, but that could not be more than a flicker; he never knew them himself, exactly, in order. They were no hail mary or agnus dei overlearned thoughtless slaver but a slimed thoughtless unyoking of "unbridled liberty" — YES — "unbridled liberty" from nails and knobs and slivers of the cross, of clenched lips

and clenched legs propriety, of god's beard and fundament
aylmer ontario, of pawing through the wounds and private
pricks of jesus shrivelled against wood, exploding breasts lank
as needles clickety clack knitting a parched tight childless sack
of a desert belly, wordless features folded sterile and boiled in
suffering sacrifice god offered under him in the public dust of
the ottawa aylmer road he was riding in his ignorant almighty
lord so stupid happiness to marry her to the stare of long-
jowled neighbours tiered around him, the words he had
arranged for them to hear while reading again and again all the
three years of her sail mary full of grease the letters with thee
into their rotten gapes like curses grinding teeth,

> Ah, once more I'll go to my beautiful West,
>   Where nature is loveliest, fairest and best:
> And lonely and long do the days to me seem,
>   Since I wandered away from Saskatchewan stream.
>
> Ontario, home of my boyhood farewell,
>   I leave thy dear land in a fairer to dwell,
> Though fondly I love thee, I only can rest,
>   'Mid the flower strewn prairie I found in the

most absolute pure frozen christ shit.

Sits Green On The Earth moaned a little. Her moan
shaped her, a soft blot in the bowl under the spruce that
could swallow him into eternal resting oblivion, he could
release anything and it vanished, it had never been, he was
nailed the harder down in paradise; beautiful beautiful annihi-
lation he had to nevermore control, clamp down. Feed it to
her, feed her. Her hands eased his gently from her small-
swollen belly and the bend of her hip and back jolted him. It

seemed to him he could feel Kingbird's hand there on her yielding skin, smelled him, and something moved, drove him down into a red molten core and he was spreading out limitlessly, limitlessly....

"Listen," he hissed "listen!" Words poured from his open throat like spring lava.

Running Second lay against Big Bear. There was a long pain through her stomach and into her spine and now working to slice itself to the toes of her left leg, but she held the chief tightly, holding him warm while he shivered sometimes as if, exhausted though he was, he could not quite release himself to it. He had always had sleep completely, like a child, and now like a child he was shivering. She could hear The Magpie and Horsechild and Kingbird too, breathing, and she breathed like them, long and easy asleep; and Sits Green On The Earth stood inside the lodge flap. Waiting to hear anything. She was getting very careless, Running Second thought, breathing carefully, not to wipe all that white off herself with snow. Big Bear shivered.

Long before dawn one by one the leaders left the greatlodge for their places. Little Bear, and then Little Bad Man and finally Iron Body went, and the Rattlers who had decided to follow each went with them. Thunder remained by the door, still watching from behind Round The Sky and Matoose who did not go. Though no one danced now, the drum beat on. Wandering Spirit sat with arms folded, his rifle lying between him and the fire, his eyes fixed as if he were in prayer.

.   .   .

III

Teresa (Mrs. John) Delaney: Thus we parted on the night of the first of April, and all retired to bed, to rest, to dream. Little did some amongst us imagine that it was to be their last sleep, their last rest upon earth, and that before another sun would set, they would be 'sleeping the sleep that knows no waking' — resting the great eternal perfect rest from which they will not be disturbed until the trumpet summons the countless millions from the tomb. Secure as we felt ourselves, we did not dream of the deep treachery and wicked guile that prompted those men to deceive their victims. The soldier may lie down calmly to sleep before the day of battle, but I doubt if we could have reposed in such tranquillity if the vision of the morrow's tragedy had flashed across our dreams. It is indeed better that we know not the hour, nor the place! And again, it is not well that we should ever be prepared, so that no matter how or when the angel of death may strike, we are ready to meet the inevitable and learn "the great Secret of Life and Death!"

George Stanley (Mesunek-wepan): I brought the oxen up and put the yoke on them to try the plough. I hitched the oxen to the chain on the plough, went down to the field and put the plough in the ground but found that the frost was not yet out. While stopping in the middle of the field I saw a man riding quickly towards my father Ohnee-pahao who was sitting on a hill nearby. As soon as I saw this man I immediately unhitched as I could not plough anyway and I wanted to hear what this man was going to talk about. This man was Chaqua-pocase — one of Big Bear's men. He had the farm instructor's horse and carried a rifle on his side. When I got to the hill where they were talking, I looked up at the sun to see if it was dinner time. It was nearly midday.

IV

Isadore Mondion, the Wood Cree councillor, did not hear his dogs snarl outside his cabin; he awoke as his door scraped. Four men were coming in, he could tell from the moccasins slurring a little, and were settling themselves down by the door. He stood up from under his blanket, walked across to the mud fireplace and blew the coals glowing there into a blaze. He laid on two sticks of birch, pushed the copper kettle over it, and turned.

"The night is dark," he said.

A short grunt of agreement. Mondion could make out something of the four men now, he knew Little Bear at the head of them, his rifle erect, butted on the ground, its barrel taller than he sitting. His leather vest hung open and his chest gleamed in streaks, as if he had just finished sweating, or was still.

"It's warm outside." Again agreement, but no motion in that dark except the small circular gesture of rifle barrels. Doubled inside his door. There was a scurry of his wife and children among the blankets in the farther corner where he had risen. "This is a late visit."

"Who are you with?" That was Bad Arrow, sitting behind Little Bear, "You are not of the People. With the People or the police?"

"My mother was of the Wood People, but you are right," said Mondion sarcastically, "that may not be enough for some. My father came from beyond the lakes, he was a fearless Iroquois."

"He paddled canoes for the Company."

"Yes, and some I know have hauled wood for the Company!"

Little Bear gestured with his free hand, brushing something aside. "Wandering Spirit knows what you said to Delaney. The police have left, and he wants no more whites to leave."

"Wise, brave men," said Mondion, balancing easily on his feet before the fire flaring now so that the room leaped with shadows. "To send four brave men to guard one."

Little Bear swung down his rifle as he surged to his feet, but Mondion knocked the barrel aside and clamped him around the waist, lifting. For an instant he swayed and held him off the ground, as if in the firelight he would crush Little Bear into himself while in the corner his wife and children shrieked, but the rifle was free and it clubbed into his back and someone broke wind like a guttering explosion and the thick column of them against the fire toppled. Mondion was on top in an instant, but then the others were upon him.

"....ohn...John. John!"

Delaney's eyes were open but he was certain he had not moved; as though still asleep. A thick bar of shadow, angled across the small square of the window's grey: outside if the sky was still overcast it must be nearly dawn and the darkness of the low peaked roof hung over the two small triangles of lightness cut from the window by his wife's arm, her hand clutching his shoulder.

"John!"

"Keep quiet," he said. He thrust arm and blankets aside in one motion and was upon his feet on the floor when he finished it. "You'll wake the Gowanlocks too. I heard it."

Though he could not have heard the first knock below and he was chagrined that she had. If she suddenly heard so well, what could she smell? He was lifting his trousers, feet worming for his cold boots, but he stood erect, forgetting, and his head knocked against a round rafter. He was chewing oaths in silence.

"Do you have the gun?" The whiteness of her, topped by the huge tuft of white sleeping cap, sat up against the darkness shivering and he shivered with her, not for what she would feel but the jagged spurt of a possible hope that if there was only some shooting maybe, maybe....

"Holy dripping hell," he swore aloud, hand about the rafter with his feet finding the first stair step. They would certainly knock politely three and four times when they came to cut throats, Indians knocking! His legs felt strong, incredibly strong muscles shifting against his cold trousers as he lowered himself down the ladder-like stairs, his hands sliding from rafter to floorbeam, his loins in a sweet singing rest, and he seized the beam framing the stair-hole and swung out into the darkness of the lower room, dropping lightly to the invisible floor that met his feet exactly where he expected it. Three stupid years stumbling around in a haze of remembered white Ontario, why hadn't he met her then when he was laughing at Quinn no more than a Sioux halfbreed anyway but Jefferson too and all the others gone nice lazily red woman while he laboured and dreamed of pale legs who could have imagined needed an axe handle at least to pry apart and jaws more than that? Embers in the fireplace blinked at him and he almost smiled knitting needles as he opened the door. A shape against grey, John Pritchard, yes, and fully dressed as if he had not even been to bed.

"There's trouble," the interpreter said.

"W-What?"

"Here. Our horses are gone, from the barn there."

A short heavy shape moved beyond Pritchard, coming forward around him out of the morning dark that was lighter than Delaney had expected. It was Little Bad Man, his strange, shallow, voice already speaking white puffs into the air; when he stopped Pritchard said,

"He says it was halfbreeds from Edmonton, or maybe Moose Creek, they sneaked in and got the horses, he's very sorry but they danced last night and they —"

"I heard that, they were still drumming when I got to bed."

"Yeah, they danced so long and then they fall asleep he says and forget to guard the horses and then the Edmonton breeds or something got them, but I say my son sleeping in the barn there thinks some of those of this man I am interpreting right now took them. These guys."

Little Bad Man was speaking again, at length; behind him the bare sky was already streaking red as for the sun rising. The stairs creaked; perhaps it was Gowanlock coming but Delaney was trying to sort apart what Pritchard had told him under cover of the translation as he tried to distinguish the broad heavy-nosed face before him, a mounded silhouette merely against the growing red light. If they wanted to get someone it would be Quinn: if young Salomon Pritchard was right and Big Bear's band had really taken the horses it was to prevent Quinn from leaving; he had run them so stupidly hard and close to Ottawa regulations too long. Always daring them to the letter of his orders so they had to starve their pride out before they got it. John Delaney was almost smiling again, thinking of the supplies he had given at his own expense, of Big Bear and Kingbird so pathetically grateful to him and Dewdney's angry letter: "this is impossible and *must* stop. The effect is to show up other officials who obey.... " Pritchard was again translating:

"He's really sorry he says, just he and his men are to blame. The halfbreeds must of been watching and when they sleep they steal those horses. He says they'll protect you now for sure, all the time here, if —"

"Where's Sioux Speaker?" Delaney said Quinn's Cree name very clearly, so Little Bad Man would know exactly.

"In his house...." Pritchard glanced sideways, frowning. He translated: "He says Quinn is protected now by Wandering Spirit but I say that his wife's uncle is in that house there too and that big man is his big protection. Yeah!"

"How many are over there now, before sunrise 'protecting' him?" Delaney asked, Gowanlock walking in the dark house just behind him, and a white figure also that could only be Terry, but before Pritchard could say anything Indians appeared at both corners of the house. There were so many of them, so suddenly and without a sound that Pritchard's mouth hung open, speechless, for a moment, his head flicking from one side to the other, then he stepped up beside Delaney, nudging him, voice sharp and quick,

"The one thing I think is do what they say," as the River People with Little Bad Man at their head, moved in.

Teresa Delaney was standing somewhat higher, on the stair-steps with her feet like blocks of ice on the wood and both her arms stretched up beyond her face, her hands hooked to the beam above her sleeping cap. It always seemed to her it was Pritchard who broke the great dam that was her husband's shape across the doorway and let the stench and blackness flood into her small neat house until it slapped around her walls, clawed over her furniture she could not see now in the darkness though she could hear that scraping aside, breathing and snuffling even against herself, she could feel it, yes, that must be, there, at the hem of her thick cotton nightdress that

protruded o goodness some inches below her mantle, beside
and to her very toes almost like claws, plucking. Her toes
strained to curl, her leg muscles hunched to lift themselves up,
up into clean pure air, and for an instant she saw the open, free
glades bent over hills about Frog Lake, the lake itself one
white teardrop pointed south but she remained frozen to this
cold wood, her arms hung as if they were nothing but hooks
inert in — slippers, why hadn't she — her boots she would
always wear her high boots tightly laced to the very in bed she
would never again take off her high boots with thick woollen
socks again never — afterwards she remembered that it was all
swimming about below her in the darkness with amazing
quiet, only Pritchard's calm voice and then her husband's
ghostly face rising up before her out of the bog, his giant
whiskers so black that for an instant she knew they had already
axed unevenly away both his cheeks and jaw, slashed a wide
crooked crescent between his nose and his full, thick lips moving over her and she was shivering even more, straining in
some terrified place to shrink into purity beyond that violent
soft wet touch, his whiskers so much blacker she wondered
why he did not light a lamp at least and then she could report
exactly what or who was forcing this unbelievable rudeness
upon her, touching her as she stood above it all on her very
hem and toes, though if she had her long steel needles there
would soon have been a sound or two to identify it. Then. His
pale hand gestured there and his voice was repeating at her
words which came eventually, later, as she remained there suspended and, waiting for something, perhaps "...all to
Quinn's, the halfbreeds...plan...they'll protect...." and
everything black and stinking flowed out the door again like
Ottawa mud inevitable in spring really Teresa dear it is so
difficult. Lightness seemed coming in about her then; she

gradually became aware of her body shrunken to certain wrinkles inside a sheath of cold cotton suspended from her arms and touching her nipples only, of a pattern of the table squeezed out of shape against a wall and fireplace, and chairs thrust close to it but fortunately there was no fire in the hearth now, with the tips of her breasts burning. And some cloth, and hair, perhaps it was Terry Gowanlock, that Terry, washed up on the step under her feet and the empty room angling into crookedness as light came. And she saw with great precision the delicate white flounces of her nightgown about her feet not noticeably dirty, and felt axe marks on the beams under her hands, felt her body stretched with the burning spots of her breasts searching out with fire all the tubes and channels and tiniest passageways of her body between wood and wood. The last cluster of his words she found were "...worry, we'll be right back...." and so she stood for some time as a red shaft of sunlight suddenly cut across her pale blue mantle so that it too seemed to burn, richly, thinking about that.

Little Bad Man was walking from the farm instructor's house so fast the men following almost ran to keep astride. Over the eastern hills the sun heaved its red shoulder.

"Ho-o-o!" cried Little Bad Man into the perfect morning, lifting his great bare arms wide and high to it, carbine and fist clenched aloft. "That's good for People when the sun comes up, red like blood, Hai!"

They all cried out with him, faces gleaming, the cluster of dark men between small scattered houses dripping momentarily crimson, arms and fists high.

"And four bloody livers to chew!" yelled Miserable Man into the sky above his swinging flintlock. They were laughing as they moved up the incline, already hearing the creek run.

"Oska-task," said Little Bad Man to the scar-faced man beside him, "you go to Mondion's and tell Little Bear there that Mondion can run now."

"The Company —" Oska-task began heavily, but the other interrupted him,

"Little Bear will go to Dill, in his store." A grin slowly formed on the ravaged face as he concluded, "There are four of them, with you it will only be five."

Oska-task was gone with a long whoop that carried him down the slope and through the creek thigh-deep, laughing. Young Cameron had been warned just in time to come out and meet the rest of them on James Simpson's small porch.

"You have ammunition," said Little Bad Man, his feet planted solidly, his body swaying a little again.

"Yes," Cameron said, "some."

They were each speaking in their own language, very exactly though each knew the other could recognize only an isolated word, and face to face squarely with the silent surround of men slightly below and the curtain twitching where Mrs. Simpson peered at a window, they understood each other's meanings very clearly indeed.

"We want it all."

"You know the regulations as well as I, where's the paper from Sioux Speaker?"

"We want it all, every grain and bullet!"

Cameron looked past him, as if at the valleys and creek now washed in a delicate rose, then shrugged, moving already. "I can't stop you, that's certain. And I don't want the door or lock broken." The dark men opened as he stepped off the porch, surrounded him as he walked across to the shop. Little Bad Man looked momentarily down the creek, watching the horses and men that had appeared there just beyond Delaney's warehouses where the police had quartered, coming up towards Quinn's. He turned quickly north, to the church and priest buildings towards the shore of the frozen lake, and the red sunlight hooked in his eye. He was smiling as he strode after the others.

In the Hudson's Bay Company shop a momentary hesitation had dampened the men; the orderly shelves, the smell of cloth and tobacco, the long counter held them suddenly in the quiet shared rituals of trade. Cameron, after a quick sideglance, said very loudly in English, "The barrel's behind the counter, you know where, but I won't touch it."

They all looked at him, his hands in his baggy trouser pockets, motionless; the thump of Little Bad Man on the porch and Four Sky Thunder shouldered between them, lifted the counter board and went behind to hoist up the powder barrel. They were all pushing then, dividing the little at the bottom.

"There's not much in that," said Four Sky Thunder, "maybe three pounds."

"Is that all?" Little Bad Man demanded. Now Miserable Man had leaped the counter; knives and axes and files, even muskrat spears were spraying through the air into hands reaching everywhere.

"That's all. You can look, but there isn't any more."

"You had two barrels at least before the police left, and bull —" but he did not finish what he had begun for a deep voice spoke behind them at the door, suddenly,

"Morning is beautiful. Red and beautiful our father the Sun, beautiful to sing."

It was Big Bear, with the sunlight spraying around him so brilliantly they could only see his blanketed outline set in the black lines of the doorway, his right arm bare and half-lifted as if he were about to begin an inappropriate oration. Strangely, on his head was the top hat McLean had given him at the trading in Fort Pitt during annuity payments the previous fall; he had never worn it since, and the single remaining ostrich feather glistened through the light like hoar-frost, swaying slightly and broken in a right angle, against the doorframe. Tall black hat.

"Of course trading is good too," he continued almost dreamily, his arm rising no higher, his voice a quiet sweetness at their ears. "I have often traded so early in the morning just when the sun stands up. All my life I have traded with the Company and their traders are good." He seemed to be looking at Cameron backed into an angle of the counter but his voice murmured on as if he were musing to himself, "Though they need a little help, white memories always need a little help so they always write everything in their big book when trading is done. A man of the River People of course always remembers, exactly, his debt with the Company. From year to year. It is very hard and sometimes impossible to hunt today without ammunition, and there are still many muskrats. The Wood People could teach us how to trap, or even spear them, if we would ask them. Morning is," he was turning to the red-orange light and they could distinguish the worn blanket he wore, going, "beautiful, to sing."

Four Sky Thunder and Miserable Man came out from behind the counter, and abruptly Little Bad Man roared, "Muskrats! Singing the muskrats!" He was laughing so loud the windows in the little shop shivered and all their answering laughter spilled out as they leaped into the sunlight. Dancing and pushing. And Thunder was coming up through them, panting, his skinny arms waving around Little Bad Man for Cameron still somewhere inside the shop,

"Wandering Spirit says young Cameron has to come, come to Quinn's too."

So they all stood about laughing a little, showing each other what they had; waited while Cameron came out slowly and pulled the door shut and thrust the heavy brass key into the lock, twisted it, pulled it out and put it in his pocket. They were all around him.

"Who are you with," said Little Bad Man, walking beside him, "the halfbreeds or the police?"

Cameron gestured quickly, and perhaps he did not understand. He was not wearing a coat, only a shirt bright with blue and red squares and he seemed to be shivering in the fresh morning.

"That's real nice," Thunder was saying, handing back to Miserable Man a long butcher knife with a pale wood grip, "he's a good trader, he sure has nice stuff."

"It's too dull," said Miserable Man. "But I think Kingbird got a file, otherwise I couldn't even get it through your thin hide!" They laughed together, walking very fast to keep up with the others.

Wandering Spirit was speaking, his left arm folded into his blanket and his right bare and gesturing, pacing so hard in the small centre of the Indian agent's hall his ringlets tossed. Hemming him around in the tight room were the Rattlers of the River People and the white men in clusters: the two priests Fafard and Marchand with old Williscraft, Gouin by himself, Gilchrist beside Dill, and at the far end blocking the doorway to the agent's smaller office sat Quinn in the huge chair he had pulled out of there, with Pritchard on the floor beside him and Delaney and Gowanlock in chairs also. As Little Bad Man thrust Cameron before him into the crowd by Henry Quinn at the door, Wandering Spirit's glances flickered at them, but his ringing voice did not stop,

" . . . . the head of the Whiteskins? Is it the police, or Big Whitebeard, or the Hudson's. . . . "

" . . . . it was that one over there, that big slab-face, Iron Chest, what's his name," Gilchrist was whispering furiously in Dill's ear, "and that one with them scars on the chest, there, they musta come in the window the bastards and had me by the shoulder before I was even awake, Gowanlock and she stayed at Delaney's for night and I was all alone in the whole damn mill miles away and this halfbreed they was dragging along kept translating what they asked. 'Are you for the half-breeds or the police?' and I just about laughed, such a stupid question the breeds or the police for god's sake and I said sure as —"

"You better shut up," said Dill heavily, gesturing to the war chief pacing by them, "Curley's talking."

"I can't understand nothing any —"

"All the more you should shut up, you fool."

" . . . . say nothing but 'No! No!', always No! to the People. Has any Person ever heard him say yes? We want fresh meat!"

Quinn was leaning back in his chair, perhaps laughing though it sounded more as if he was rasping his throat. He said to Delaney, "You got a old ox that's wore out, with the Wood Crees."

"There's more than one, the broken-horned blue one in Mondion's corral or. . . . "

"Well," Quinn gestured and shifted to Cree; immediately three men left, with Henry Quinn going suddenly with them too. Delaney stood up; he was almost as tall as Quinn, towering above Wandering Spirit before him, his head and shoulders huge, almost bearish.

"It's time for breakfast," he said.

Wandering Spirit looked to Pritchard, listened to him.

"Yes," he said to Delaney very softly, "my men would eat some food for the morning too."

The farm instructor stared at him as Pritchard translated, abruptly shrugged. "Bring your big men," he said, his thick lips twitching under his mustache, "sure, bring all of them."

"I eat my food the Government owes me here," stated Wandering Spirit.

"Hey Tom!" Gouin said into the silence, "my rifle's gone, one a them —"

"So join me for breakfast, they're protecting me from the halfbreeds," Quinn said, not getting up.

Teresa Delaney and the fat Wood People woman in the house for instruction that week were at the stove frying bacon, the huge kettle singing on its hook over the hearth fire. Terry Gowanlock sat behind the table and looked wide-eyed at Delaney and her husband coming in the door, followed by Pritchard, Gilchrist, Dill, the priests Fafard and Marchand in their long black vestments and white-haired old Williscraft, fumbling last and finally getting the door shut behind him.

"We'll all eat breakfast here," said John Delaney.

"There are only two loaves of bread left," said his wife, pointing to the gaping cupboard. "Two of them came in and took everything, I could just get these two away."

"Make bannock then, enough."

"They didn't go in the cellar though," said Terry Gowanlock very brightly. "When they opened the trapdoor it seemed to be a great deal too dark down there for them, they wouldn't go down!"

John Gowanlock slid behind the table on the bench beside her. "That's all right, my dearest, it's all right," he murmured but she did not look at him, staring at all the white men standing about as though she could not remember something else very important demanding to be said.

They were seated and had begun to eat when the door opened again and the Rattlers started to come in. Little Bear came first, then He Speaks Our Tongue; they wore only leggings and breechclouts, their chests were smeared fantastically. They and the endless men following them spun in glistening circles of ochre and orange out of the light at the doorway, circles and stars and jagged flexing streaks, shifting waved lines. Only their expressionless faces were unmarked; they held their weapons in their right hands and reached over the shoulders of the seated whites for bread and bannock and bacon with their left. The room was thrust full with them too tight to breathe.

"Cook everything there is," said Delaney quietly across to his wife. "Let them eat everything."

Dill was the only seated man chewing now; his jaws worked, and he spit gristle between legs onto the floor. "By god I'd rather shoot it out than sit on my ass with a table fork in my hand!"

"Watch your language," Delaney said. Big Bear stood at his chair back, without paint, his lined old face staring down the table at the sunlight laying patterns of dishes, cups and knives about. The farming instructor doubled a slab of bread over bacon and placed it in his lean hand; his fingers closed, sunlight on the moons of his nails, lifted. "Just keep your mouth shut and sit still. They're just eating yet."

Father Fafard held a piece of dry bread motionless in his hand. He glanced up to Round The Sky, unpainted also and standing behind him. "Do you remember," he said softly in Cree, "the winter you lived with me when you were a boy on Ribstone Creek?"

"No buffalo come north that winter," Sky replied as quietly, "but the rabbits were fat then."

"And you a good hunter," said the priest, smiling.

The sounds of men chewing, tearing food surrounded the silent table. Pritchard translated loudly: "He Speaks Our Tongue says, 'When we have eaten we send men after the half-breeds who steal your horses. We have seen the trail, very good. After we eat, one gets hungry on the trail. We'll protect you from the ones making war.'"

"We must prepare, Holy Thursday Mass," Father Fafard said in Cree and then English. He stood up slowly, nodding to the pale Father Marchand across the table from him.

Some River men went out the door, others stepped back. The priests bowed their thanks silently to Mrs. Delaney silent beside the bare stove and went, Little Bear and Round The Sky exactly behind them. On the path outside Little Bear confronted Father Fafard suddenly, shouting in his face, "Who are you with, our halfbrothers or the police?"

Fafard looked at him, not saying a word, and abruptly Little Bear swung his gun barrel.

"Ohhh!" gasped the Wood People woman at the window, "Little Bear hits the priest on the eye with his gun. But Round The Sky...."

"What?" Pritchard demanded.

"He has stopped him, they," she seemed to whimper, almost crying, "they are going again, now."

He Speaks Our Tongue swung his arm up at the men in the room and one by one they went out, though Big Bear did not move. Then Tongue said, "When the bell rings, you will all go to the church. Wandering Spirit says that word."

Wandering Spirit stood in the doorway of the Hudson's Bay

shop and young Cameron suddenly with a shudder aware of it, could only stare blankly. The war chief wore his lynx hat again with its five eagle feathers, and his shoulder-length hair framed yellow smears laid so thick around eyes and over lips that he appeared to have no mouth at all, his face one hideous gouge of ridged, yellow, mud.

"You write the debt, there," he gestured with the Winchester in his right hand at the account book Cameron was leaning over, "but I want no tea today."

Recognizing trade words, the young clerk turned but Wandering Spirit said, "No! Today the sun didn't rise for that. Today you go to the priest's house with your friends. The priest, there."

What he demanded was clear enough from his gestures and, though he was no Roman Catholic, Cameron closed the book, shoved it under the counter and came out into the sunlight. Up the slope directly opposite gaped the smashed windows and door of George Dill's store; Cameron closed the Hudson's Bay door carefully. Dark figures hurried everywhere between the buildings and somewhere down the creek valley a horse whinnied piercingly into the warm indifferent spring, but there was no sound of dogs.

> *Glory... God on high, and on earth peace to men of goodwill ...we adore thee, we bless... O only-begotten Son... who takest away the sins of the world, have mercy upon... who sittest at the right hand... most high in the glory... God the Father... have....*

Salomon Pritchard, oldest boy of John Pritchard, was pulling the bell-rope to the known swing of Fafard's unintelligible Latin ringing from the altar, leaning into it easily, the little bell swinging he knew, shining in the sunlight as he had often lain on the grass and watched it gleam and vanish up there before he was allowed to pull that sound himself, rejoicing and happy as the light it swung back and forth. The sung Latin seemed beautiful to him now, far more than his father's English, as the tune sang in his head sometimes all day or at night when he repeated the prayer that mostly became no meaning but simply one long ululating sound flowing over his lips like last night in the hay where the small barn seemed to be cracking out of its buried frost, the horses snuffling a little, breathing against each other as though through fur. He was thought-lessly rocking in the rhythm when a shoulder jolted him, at the open door feet shuffled around him and Miserable Man blundered in; his flintlock thrust ahead muzzle-up and his huge flat face a gruesome yellow shifting of eroded and ridged pocks. And directly behind him came Big Bear, pushing hard as if he would trample on the big warrior's heels, his blanket still folded around him and head bare and right hand empty, his eyes gleaming like bright obsidian pierced in the unpainted folds of his face. They were almost leaning against Salomon, stopped inside the door side by side, and the boy missed a swing; the bell stuttered above; but he caught the tug then again correctly and four beats later when young Cameron slid by and clattered into the pews crowded with all the white people and half-Indians in the settlement — all except Quinn and his father who had sent him on to his duty with one yell such as he had never heard him make before — he managed to hold beat almost steadily, could hear the approaching *Dei Patris* when with another bend he must stop and the bell could not be rung again until Easter morning, lifting his head in the rhythm to concentrate on the motions of the priests at the altar and laying the white vestment of his shoulder into the

rope's pull, when Wandering Spirit was suddenly in the doorway. And through the men there, into the aisle. Soundlessly
there, his half-naked body past and up the aisle so fast the eagle
feathers leaned back over the yellow gash of his face, the
Winchester swinging as if part of his arm, grown into his hand
swinging closer to the rounded cloth-white shapes facing the
altar. " .... en - n - n," sang Father Fafard, and turned as if on a
swivel to the congregation in the tiny church; so faced the war
chief coming. The gun-barrel mark a black ridge across his left
eye. Salomon saw the stare frozen between them one instant,
jerking on the rope and the bell stuttering again, but Fafard
lifted his hands and the people sank in a long creaking rustle to
their knees for prayer. Wandering Spirit stood; then lowered
to one knee in the centre of the aisle before the priest, his gun
butted on the ground, head high. The grey feathers on his
bonnet twitched a little against the white vestments.

*.... from whom Judas received ... the thief the reward of his
confession ... grant. ...*

Salomon realized at last he was still jerking the rope. The bell
clattered crazily as Fafard led the prayer and Father Marchand
was waving his arms again and again in a kind of frantic
stasis; stop! stop! and come forward to serve in the next
procedure, and though he understood all this immediately, his
eyes set open upon the younger priest's face above the heads of
the kneeling congregation so white now it seemed to dull his
vestment, and opened his hand to the rope so that the bell bur-
bled out, he could not quite straighten himself, much less
move. Miserable Man was a wall beside him, flintlock erect
taller than he, and Big Bear rasped breath there as though trying to heave up some gigantic weight and his nose broken.

Wandering Spirit was on one knee under the closed eyes of Father Fafard in prayer and Salomon knew that of himself he could never move past that gun barrel gleaming a blue slow circle in the sunlight above the congregation, he was swaying in the great terror space of the confessional it seemed, scrape his soul clean kneeling and clenching himself to squeeze at least a tear into his necessary agony at not even feeling any sorrow for anything as the Father so prayed for him and he could remember nothing anyway and Wandering Spirit's eyes, he saw them suddenly now, he was in front of them somehow, yes, they were just a little to the side glaring up against Father Fafard's broken profile and Mrs. Gowanlock's beautiful blanched face rounded in the black shawl was rising out of heads on her slim neck and her eyes crossed his with terror circling around the tiny church...yeah, her black boots waving little circles out of the white and red layered petticoats tumbled in snow, webbed with black lacing out of sight against the blue sheen of snow, wallowing about to face him laughing where he had leaped up unconsciously from the brush unable to believe his eyes, her red lips stuck over with dry snow and laughing past him down to Quinn's child sitting erectly motionless on the tin lid at the bottom of the hill, waiting inert for another pull up and slide down, not believing his eyes — did white women like River men laughed actually wear black leather laced all the — her white arms he had seem them once in the house — that couldn't, some white flash there — he unlaced that in the hay, unlacing and unlacing two black unending columns rising above him and he frantically climbing unlacing to at last white and red

This is my body....

Something had happened and not happened, Salomon could not understand which. The sounds and the motions at the altar were all wrong; he himself could not be standing at the side altar with the violet vestments clutched in his hands. He was. The two priests were dropping to their knees to adore the Host suddenly blessed and made into Jesus Christ as he knew and had been taught perfectly on the centre altar but he could not understand how it had been done, so quickly, there was no time, the congregation still apparently kneeling for the prayer, but Wandering Spirit on his feet in the aisle facing kneeling priests and altar and crucifix,

"That's enough! Stop now, you priest stop!"

Both the priests leaped erect. Father Fafard was stuffing white Host into his mouth; his cheeks bulged, his eyes glazed in watering but he flapped his hand at Marchand who was muttering desperately at the chalice, scooping it up, throwing his head back to drink and Wandering Spirit screamed, leaped beside them, and Marchand's body folded suddenly like a missal flipping half-shut, his head snapped up, then forward and down or his cough would have exploded in the war chief's livid yellow face, splattering him purple with wine from the chalice. The dark, holy blood.

"Go out! Now!"

Father Fafard put his arm around Marchand, drew him back between himself and the altar, and faced Wandering Spirit, half his face in complete calm.

"We will stop now if we must, and go out," he said almost steadily in Cree. "It is not good that you do not let us finish our worship. You did not let us hold confession this morning, as we should have, but we will go with you out of the church, now. You must not," he raised his voice with his haggard face as if speaking to people far beyond the walls of the little building, "you must not make disturbances here, for these are our holy days and our —"

"That's enough!" Wandering Spirit swung around from the altar, his rifle coming up, "I talk here now! Take off that white, and you too," he jerked toward Salomon, "take that off, now. Everybody goes out now."

Fafard walked very slowly down the aisle, right hand crossing himself and the other half-lifted with a crucifix to the congregation, lips mouthing in silent repetition *Kyrie eleison . . . Kyrie eleison* and Marchand followed, face still blotching with suppressed coughing. Then everyone else, as Wandering Spirit swung his rifle impatiently at them: the half-Indian women and few men, the two white women, the white men. Some crossed themselves at the font by the door but they could not turn to the altar while doing so.

Down the sunlit valley shouts of the River People rang where a boil of them was turning near the agent's house: the logs of the Government buildings where the police had lived were leaping apart. Kingbird ran up to Wandering Spirit,

"I want my little brother Cameron to give me the Company flag, for dancing."

"He stays with them all, there," Wandering Spirit said, gesturing down the valley and hurrying to outflank the men surrounding the whites.

"I'll bring him right away, just get out the flag."

"Take him, but bring him back fast."

To the moment of his death sixty-six years later William Bleasdell Cameron remembered with terrible clarity four happenings that then followed one after the other, though he was never certain in exactly what order, nor how long they lasted. He did know for certain that when he walked north toward the ringing church bell and tugged out his watch, for already he was a meticulous man, having of necessity to walk very fast in order to keep ahead and slightly to the right of Wandering Spirit, that his watch said nine thirty-eight; later, when he was already across the creek, he saw Father Fafard's gold watch swinging on its chain from Round The Sky's hand and he thought then it indicated three minutes to eleven and when he groped for his own he found it gone; he never recovered it. He was convinced that the priest's watch must have been slow to begin with because it was clearly impossible that all that happened in only seventy-nine minutes; and certainly the sun was higher too, he thought, later. And he also decided that the four events must have taken place in this order, though of that he was never so certain on earth:

.... he was in the shop again, with Kingbird whom he had always considered his friend, who had now somehow gotten him away from all the other whites back to the isolated reassurance of the big Company ledger on the counter and was dancing a gentle circle beyond the counter with the Hudson's Bay flag draped around him like a blanket and Salomon Pritchard was translating his song, which seemed very silly and also unnecessary at the time,

> I'm cold
> Don't stay around here
> I'm cold

a red corner of the flag almost dragging and young Pritchard translating, with many stumbles, a question which he himself was stumbling to answer, "Who are you for, our half-brothers or the police?" with "Those halfbrothers, that war is far away, let's —" but he never remembered how he managed to finish that though it seemed a careful enough beginning at very least;

.... Big Bear was standing in the kitchen of his superior James Simpson's house and talking to Mrs. Simpson (how he could possibly have seen this he could never explain though he stated once, under oath, that the front door stood ajar and he had seen the two short dark figures inside, recognized them bent earnestly toward each other though he had no memory of walking past the house any more than walking from the church while a long procession wound away from him toward Quinn's, whooped about by riders);

.... a huge, brutal shape leaned against the counter before him, scarred limbs like trees and yellow, ravaged head, while on the warped boards already blackening lay a torn piece of foolscap,

> Dear Cameron
>   Please give Miserable
> Man one Blanket.
>   *T.T.Q.*

with Salomon Pritchard, who for some reason still seemed to be there, explaining that the young Cameron had no blankets, they had even taken the ones off his very bed in the house (though how Salomon could know this, whether he was there or not, he never had to explain, though he thought it must certainly be true even much later);

.... and tea — tea pouring out of a round hole in the square tin he held against himself, black granules of it stretching down into a spotted-orange shawl, a growing black cone over a carrot of tobacco already on that shawl on that warped counter when the first shot exploded outside.

And then, very quickly, two more.

Thomas Trueman Quinn was shot first, as he had to be. By Wandering Spirit. The war chief had started all the whites moving away from the agency house toward the camp of the River People, which the women that morning had moved up out of the valley onto the bare slopes across the creek, almost surrounding the Wood People camp and in clear view of the settlement; John Delaney, with his wife on his arm and both still dressed as for mass, led the others out of the agent's house. Quinn, emerging last of all, and following a few steps in their slow procession, suddenly stooped by a bank of rotten snow against the hillside before the looted police barracks. Just beyond, John Pritchard had opened the door of his cabin and stepped out; he saw the two by the snow, and stopped. His son Salomon ran from somewhere, panting, up beside him.

"You have a hard head that can't be changed," said Wandering Spirit in Quinn's ear, "and a mouth that says only 'no!' But today you'll do as I say. Go to the camp." He gestured with his rifle after the others straggling in a black line towards the creek.

"Why?"

"Go!"

"Here is my place," said Quinn without any emphasis whatever. He stood there above the war chief, almost gigantic, his feet wide on the soft sloping ground and his left hand coming up to insert itself in his vest, his right brushing the tam back on his wide forehead. As though he would take for himself the widest possible view of the brown warm hills and the lake's blinding ice. "Big Bear has not asked me to visit him. He told me I could stay here. At my place."

"Go!" The rifle came up.

"No."

He said his last word and the rifle exploded against his chest. He staggered, it fired twice more, and the long body collapsed into snow already bloody.

Down the slope, walking towards the creek, Delaney lifted his head at the shots but did not look around. "They're shooting into the air," he said to his wife, feeling her fingers clench on his arm. "They haven't had so much fun for quite a while."

Williscraft was running past the Gowanlocks towards the Delaneys. A rifle fired, his cap leaped from his head but he ran only faster, his grey hair streaming in the air, screaming in English, "Don't shoot! O don't shoot!" He Speaks Our Tongue took him then, very neatly with two fast shots as he ran and his body hit the ground so hard it bounced, still screaming, into the brush.

Big Bear burst from James Simpson's house, down the knoll straight into the dust and smoke and cries and shooting. He roared,

"Tesqua, tesqua! Stop! STOP!"

but his great voice was lost in the immense lake and creek valley and the far hills, nothing among the Rattler warcries of River People. Miserable Man passed him, screaming. Big Bear's movement slowed gradually, finally he was standing still. He was not quite at the place where they were shooting, facing the cloudless sky and his hands were working as if trying to squash down something boiling in front of him. But after a little while he stopped that, too.

Charles Gouin wheeled in time to see Quinn fall. Wandering Spirit was not even looking at the agent; he was on one knee,

aiming his Winchester and Gouin felt the bullet pass him
before he heard the shot. He ran, down the slope towards
Pritchard's house and he heard the war chief yelling "Bad
Arrow! Bad Arrow, that one!" clear and high above the rising
noise between single, staccato cries and shots. He had smashed
his face then into the worn path just in front of Pritchard's
door, but he heaved himself again to his knees, his feet, saw
Bad Arrow up the slope waving his smoking flintlock, dancing
about, and heard Little Bad Man scream somewhere, "Shoot!
Shoot!" He was at the door, his fingers in the catch but somehow he could not seem to get any strength into them to give
one little tug, there wasn't any way he could make them move,
then it seemed to open by itself and in the same instant
Miserable Man's terrible flintlock swung out of the sky and
exploded a sheet of flame against his chest. He fell backwards,
across the doorsill to the feet of John Pritchard and his wife
and son, fire blazing where his chest had been.

As Williscraft rushed by bareheaded, Teresa Delaney
looked back over her husband's shoulder to see why he
ran, and she saw John Gowanlock already beginning to sink.
Terry Gowanlock held his arm, trying to hold him, draw him
up but he was inevitably bending her; he jerked both his arms
up to her suddenly, as if they were on strings, then fell, and she
with him. His face was blurred below her, she seized it in her
hands to get its shape precise again, but it seemed to be melting and she got her face down to his, against his where a
slipperiness slid it suddenly aside as if he would escape her
completely clutched tight now against her face, red blisters
growing at the corners of his lips filling her left eye, a sound
popping like bubbles, "... be brave... be... br..." and she was
devouring his hair with her mouth, his ear and skull in a frenzy
of teeth and lips, sliding her face through saltiness, tearing her

face up to the sky as she felt him stretch and shudder and something at her shoulder was inevitably shaking her loose. So Terry Gowanlock had to see Delaney fall then, not very far from her, his big body blurring down to earth somewhere beyond the toes of her husband's boots.

John Delaney said, "I'm shot, good God, I'm...." his arm fell away and Father Fafard was running by, and Father Marchand also screaming French, but Delaney staggered some steps ahead spun, as one leg crossed over yet keeping his balance doubled up, "The bastards, out of my own...the goddam red...." coming back to where his wife stood and Bare Neck got another shot away, a clear one this time and the farming instructor sank at her feet. Her rigidity crumpled then. Teresa Delaney was down beside him, his head was in her lap "...those goddam fil...." she was cradling him against the knitted shawl that had always protected her. Across him Fafard was kneeling, lifting the cross, craning his face forward with its gigantic bruise down, hissing, "*Confiteor*, say *confiteor!*" and Delaney's voice strong as his broad perfectly powerful looking hand, so cleanly veined and working perfectly still, every finger with its trimmed nail lifted and curling perfectly to clutch the cross, "Yes! yes, I have sinned, I confess to Almighty God, to blessed Mary...to you...that I have sinned exceedingly, in.... O I have sinned...through my fault, through my most grie...vous faul...ray fo...." His white beautiful teeth seemed to slick over brown, then wash away completely in red and over his thick lips between his whiskers ran nothing but living red glistening in the sunlight. She was being jerked away, wrist circled by steel and her arm stretched back, endlessly, and finally when she was completely torn loose she found a sound within her for her husband at last. It was heard everywhere across the valley, above guns and warcries.

Father Fafard lay two strides from Delaney with his face in the dirt, blood working a worm at his nose and mouth. His hands were folded under his forehead and the back of his neck had been ripped away. Bad Arrow stood looking down at him.

"That Wandering Spirit," he muttered to the others around, "always right through the soul. Fantastic!"

"He's still breathing," said Round The Sky.

"That Whiteskin woman there," cried Thunder running up in tremendous excitement, thrusting between them to look, "she can really scream, eh? I never heard her scream like that. Can she scream!"

"One could almost think she was young and full of juice," said Four Sky Thunder and almost everyone laughed, a little.

"He's still breathing," said Round The Sky again.

"Well then shoot!" shouted Bad Arrow. "Anyone can see that, I can see it, I can even hear it. Shoot!"

Round The Sky placed the muzzle of his rifle at the rim of the little black cap and pulled the trigger. Bad Arrow was dragging the screaming woman down towards the creek.

Young Father Marchand ran beyond Williscraft; just over a knoll and its shoulder might hide him, but The Pigmy's bullet slammed through his throat and he slid suddenly down against the slope. That was where George Stanley, the teenage son of Chief Ohnee-pahao found him when he panted up from the creek, soaked to the chest and streaming water. He knelt down and looked. "I'm very sorry," he said. "It must be God's will." He tore up dead grass and tried to wipe the blood away, even to stuff the hole with it, but he couldn't. The priest lay in his black women's skirts, eyes following him, eyes so dilated they seemed only black holes into the long mystery behind the sheet of his face. The boy pulled out his silk handkerchief and tied it as gently as he could over the wound above the red and white collar. There wasn't much blood coming then, and after a few moments he stood up and looked around. There were some shots, yells in the brush but most of the noise was coming from the direction of the lake, shouts and shrieks where the church and school and Hudson's Bay Company were. People swirled there, far away tiny dots in the immensity of the silent world and suddenly he sprinted down the slope, that way.

George Dill and William Gilchrist ran best of all. They passed Williscraft before he fell and Marchand and Fafard before they started, Gilchrist's small spotted dog around and between them in wild loops from one to the other, barking in a slaver of excitement at firing guns and singing bullets and the long carrying cries of the warriors above which rang the voices of Wandering Spirit and Little Bad Man everywhere screaming orders, screaming warcries. Neither man, of course, understood any Cree nor could have recognized any particular sound the River People might make, leave alone a voice; even if their lurching muscles and chests burning for air had not been propelling them through brush and marsh water and over sandy knolls that appeared mountainous hiding ridges of rotten snow and squitchy floundering sucking mud, towards the far green hills so quiet and peacefully rolled out in a solitude of April sun and perfect, fluffy, clouds on their deepest horizon. There were millions of square miles out there, just over there where a bird dipped in a wave and was over in an instant swallowed like a hand closing it away, lost where no man had ever even walked they knew, uncountable millions of bushes and creek beds and banks and caves of shelter, or even just deadfall, even beaver dams, anything, for no man ever went there, it was the great lone land they knew that while their chests flamed and breath roared and rasped through the chambers of their heads and their feet sank silently into sand and if they could only have annihilated one the other, that other crashing alone so terrifically, so close and not able somehow to separate as if they were bound ultimately by some ignorance, some absolute pure hatred of the other very like death while that cursed black and white cur gambolled circles about them, leaping up at each in turn on its hind legs, tongue lolling at the unprecedented participation of this morning romp. Gilchrist ruined a stride to kick and the dog swung aside and back again for more, laughing aloud, and Dill passed as he lost his balance and rolled, tumbled over his head and over on his feet again and running still; almost passing Dill up a small slope again with that deadly dog barking along easily beside him. So Little Bear and Iron Body and Bare Neck and The Pigmy and He Speaks Our Tongue had a good, respectable run on the agency horses after them; even Chaqua-pocase who, because he had the farming instructor's horse (by far the fastest), made the mistake of riding to tell Ohnee-pahao because he did not think anything would start so fast — the sun wasn't halfway up the sky yet — and galloped back when he heard the first shots and through the creek and passed the younger one with his dog half lying over his bloody head and got in on some of the run too, why, he had Dill under his very gun barrel. The trader was staggering about then, still standing more or less, facing the riders who circled, firing, and Chaqua-pocase let out his cry and pulled the trigger but nothing happened in his flintlock. He stared at it in horror as his horse passed the crumpling trader; it was so long since he had made a run that in the excitement of his fast ride he must have dropped the barrel; shot and powder had run out. He kicked his exhausted mount on, into the silent hills, too mortified to answer the last shrieks of his companions.

"Two, two," sang Tongue. "The oldest and the youngest, I got two."

"You had the fastest horse," said The Pigmy. "But I got that young black-skirt, he's just over there, lying there."

"That big Delaney," shouted Bare Neck, "sticking himself into places, any kind of places, that's the one I got!"

"No white will touch me!" roared Tongue. "Where are the women to slash them up!"

The horses were frantic, almost uncontrollable at the stench of blood. The men slid off and held them straining at rope length, looking down on what had been Dill. Thunder came dashing through the mud and stood, panting, in their circle.

"I fired at this one twice," said Little Bear, "but I missed both, such a stupid horse!"

After a time, one by one, they glanced at Iron Body. Who said suddenly, almost thoughtfully,

"I hit only one black and white dog."

Thunder stared round at each one in turn, completely amazed, then down again. "I saw that one a few times today," he said at last. "I don't think he was sick before this."

All the Rattlers, except Iron Body, roared with laughter.

Towards evening James Simpson returned to Frog Lake. Where the Fort Pitt trail turned across the bare face of a hill between clusters of poplar he could look down, across a flat, to where Frog Creek wound by the mill. There was no movement there, no work; the windows seemed black, almost gaping when he would have expected them glazed like the water in the setting sun, and for a moment he thought the door of the house hung open. But he did not stop his team, nor urge it any faster in its weary trot. When two River men with rifles stepped out of the bush where the trail bent out into the settlement, he pulled the horses up and sat in the buckboard, silent.

"Wandering Spirit says you come to the camp," said one of them.

"Wandering Spirit?"

"He does the talking now."

"Since when?"

"Today, after this," the rifle gestured to where the settlement must be, around the turn.

"Get up," said Simpson to them, and they clambered up behind him on the loaded buckboard. Standing there awkwardly, feet thrust between bags and boxes, one hand on the seat and the other holding their rifles. Simpson drove his team with one hand; ponderously rubbing his grey beard with the other as they moved steadily forward, he saw the smashed doors, windows and the furniture and clothing, sacks ripped about, saw white bodies gleaming in several places, naked and scalped but otherwise perhaps unmutilated. The blinkered horses shied at nothing; there was obviously no smell now. By the church he could see two smashed wine barrels with a small stain lying on the ground around them. He stopped before his shop and the man said behind him,

"Our camp is over the creek now, you go —"

"I am looking in what was my house," said Simpson, and very deliberately wound the reins about the buggy pole, got down and went up over the broken door. The kitchen was smashed, the stairs leading to the bedrooms torn down from their moorings as if they had collapsed under some terrific weight. The papers in his small office were trampled on the floor, the chair and desk hammered to splinters. There was no blood in the house, nor in the debris of the shop next door over which he glanced momentarily. He said to the men still standing in the wagon,

"What is all this? What is it?"

"You have eyes."

Simpson climbed up and unwrapped the reins. He had to beat the tired horses before they would move from where they knew they belonged and down to the creek. Across it, on the edge of the setting sun that cut its light under a bank of cloud, were massed the points and poles of lodges. He let the horses drink before he forced them through the fast water, and in the creek he was becoming aware of camp sounds.

"The Wood People," said the one who spoke behind him, "are camped with us now. In the centre, till they join us."

Simpson said nothing. Children and dogs, finally men came out towards them and when they surrounded him he stopped, got off and left the team and its load. With his right hand he gestured his way through toward the centre of the camp, between lodges and past fires where women looked up an instant and then away, quickly, though he looked at no one, walking on with his face set, still pulling at his thin grey beard. In front of Big Bear's lodge a big fire burned; around it sat a circle of men. Big Bear was sitting there, drinking tea. Bareheaded as always.

"Hello," Simpson said. He stood and said his one word half across the circle of silent men. Then, "You are here."

"Yes," said Big Bear without looking up.

"When did you get back from hunting?"

"Yesterday noon I came back," Big Bear said. "They sent for me."

"Did you have a good hunt?"

"No."

The sun was gone, suddenly, and it seemed colder even near the fire. The trader stood under the stubby round tower and flat saucer of his black hat, watch chain drooping from his left vest pocket, the tops of his fingers thrust into the pockets of his baggy dun trousers that the wind ruffled against his legs. Not far away a drum began to beat again, and quickly a singer's voice lifted in a fast, happy rhythm. Women's voices, cackling in a scalp dance.

"If you wish to come into my lodge," said Big Bear, "you can come in and stay, in my lodge."

"My wife...." Simpson began, but stopped.

"She is with her sons here with the Wood People. In their lodge."

"Thank you," said Simpson, "but I would like to stay with them."

Big Bear nodded, his head still down. "Your young man with the bow legs," he said abruptly, "he's here too. Your wife led him wrapped in her blanket and shawl."

"Are there other white men?"

"No. I invite you to drink my tea."

Lone Man shifted the circle over and Simpson went forward, sat down at Big Bear's right. The chief gave him his own cup and reached for the black kettle.

"All these years we lived together on this land," Simpson said after a time. "Long ago when you taught me about the buffalo. We are grey now, both of us, and I never thought I would live to see this."

"I saw this long ago, but not those six black ones, not yet."

"What?"

"It is not my doing, this thing of my young men."

"Ah, I know. But it will all be yours. You will carry it all on your own back."

"My friend, I am very sorry for what has been done." Big Bear sat before the fire, its light picking over his worn blanket, the face of his massive head no face at all, seeming no more than red shale crushed. "I have prayed about this for years, and cried for it today. There was a time when young men sat around me to listen; I was the greatest chief of the First People. But now they laugh at me. For some time they have been trying to take away the good name I have lived so long, and now they have done that very well. It will do them no good, but they have thrown away my name. It is gone, and I am old. That is the way things are."

The cries of the scalp dancers rang from the Rattler lodge, through the camp.

FIVE

From Fort Pitt
to Fort Carlton,
May and June, 1885

I

Friday, April 3. Fine weather. Mr. Mann, Farming Instructor, wife and family arrived from Onion Lake at 1 a.m., reports Indians at Frog Lake have massacred all whites. Fatigue all night barricading Pitt. Extra guards posted etc. Henry Quinn arrived from Frog Lake having escaped just before the massacre, confirms reports of Indians risen and all whites shot. Rev. Quinney and wife arrived from Onion Lake escorted by Chief Saskatchewan. Guide Josie Alexander left for Battleford with despatch.

Saturday, April 4. Fine weather. Extra precautions taken to protect Fort. Johnny Saskatchewan arrived from Battleford with despatch, reports general rising throughout the country, left same morning for B'frd with despatch. Le Cotau (Little Poplar's brother) arrived from Onion Lake confirms report of massacre; reports H.B. Co'y employees safe, also women. False alarm at 11:30, another at 4.

Sunday, April 5. Easter. Indian Necotan arrived from Onion Lake with families. Reports Big Bear due at Bighills today, also that some of the Indians inclined to leave him. Short divine service in barracks. Stables levelled in afternoon. False alarm during night.

Monday, April 6. Severe snowstorm during night and morning. General systems adopted for general use. Henry Quinn sworn in Special Constable. Flying sentries taken off and sentries posted in each post through portholes. Nothing unusual today.

Tuesday, April 7. Fine weather. Everything quiet last night. Magazine torn down. Little Poplar and 9 tepees arrived from B'frd; he asked for beef and provisions, proposed talking it over in morning. All civilians, including the three Misses McLean, sworn in and armed. Sentries in every house, four hours on duty each. Everything quiet during night.

Wednesday, April 8. Fine weather. Grub taken over bad ice to Little Poplar. Stockade and bastion built during day (bastion to command the back of Fort). Little Poplar reports that Indians have burnt houses at Onion Lake. Nothing unusual during last night.

Thursday, April 9. Fine weather. Rev. Chas. Quinney left to scout across the river, returning in morning. Indian Necotan persuaded Little Poplar to bring his camp to the bank of the river. Extra bastion build behind orderly room. Everything quiet during night.

Friday, April 10. Fine weather. H.B. Co'y Dufresne and Indian Necotan left to scout; went as far as Onion Lake and report no Indians there. Indians burnt down farmhouse and priest's house before leaving, taking all provisions with exception of some 50 bags of flour. Mr. Quinney scouted across the river, reports 3 tepees of Little Poplar's band missing. Nothing unusual during night.

Saturday, April 11. Fine weather. Sentries posted outside during day. Started to build scow. Horses exercised. Everything quiet last night.

Sunday, April 12. Fine weather but windy. Large quantity ice drifted down river. Divine service in morning. Horses exercised in morning. Dogs very uneasy during night. Fire signals supposed to have been seen by No. 1 sentry (behind Mission House) during night.

Monday, April 13. Fine weather. Const. Loasby, Cowan and Quinn left for a scouting expedition to Frog Lake. A number of Indians arrived from Frog Lake, at top of hill 800 yards behind Fort. Sent a letter signed by Big Bear demanding that police lay down their arms and leave the place, they report all prisoners safe. H.B. Co'y Mr. Halpin from Cold Lake a prisoner, acting as secretary. Double sentries and doors barricaded. Mr. McLean went out and parleyed with them and gave them grub. By contents of letter it appears 250 armed men are around Fort to our 38, plus the three Misses McLean. Chief Little Poplar crossed over to help McLean in pacifying Indians. Everything quiet during night.

Tuesday, April 14. Very windy weather. Mr. McLean still parleying with Indians at noon. During parley the three scouts out yesterday galloped through the camp towards Pitt.

Const. Cowan was shot dead and Loasby wounded in two places before hauled over barrier. Horse killed and Quinn got away, but missing. Indians fired upon by all. McLean and Dufresne taken prisoner. Indians threatened to burn Fort tonight with coal oil brought from Frog Lake unless police left. After a great deal of danger got to the other side of river in scow with colours. Ice running very strong. All white civilians and halfbreeds in Pitt went to Indian Camp as prisoners.

Wednesday, April 15. Very cold weather, snow. Travelled.
Francis J. Dickens, Inspector, N.W.M.P.

II

Kitty McLean: The first four weeks of our captivity weren't uncomfortable. Nothing moved; the Indians just ate and danced and though my sister Amelia said the ground at Frog Lake had little similarity with the beds in the Young Ladies Academy on Red River, Papa had made certain we had several hundred pounds of flour and some bacon and beans and tea, and when they shot the Company cattle the Indians guarding us naturally gave us a share. The boys ran them with bows and arrows as their fathers explained they used to run buffalo, but cows don't run straight and the horses were no longer trained for anything so if it hadn't been for the sharp shooters picking them off one by one while the others laughed at tumbling boys, the herd might have lasted forever, once they included what the Government had given them at Frog Lake and Onion Lake, when Ohnee-pahao and Cut Arm consented to kill theirs also. But over eleven hundred Indians living like that, killing meat every day, devour a fantastic amount Papa says and by the middle of May the work cattle were nearly gone and the whole camp, prisoners, everybody, had been dragged back to Fort Pitt to see what they hadn't ruined the first time. Mama had made certain of one good blanket for us each when we first left Pitt, when we drove with the buggy full and still thought it would only be a matter of a few days. She had Liza pile ten of the double 5-point blankets new from the storeroom on the wagon, and of course Duncan had his Grandmother Murray quilt, so we had a blanket each for the servants too, Angus and William James missing it all at school in Winnipeg.

Papa said an Indian captive had to supply himself, though I never noticed that in the books I read. Food usually appeared there without the least worry by the heroine, though she could rarely eat any and was always perfectly clean and disdainful and aloof about the fate worse than death suspended over her head and any instant about to fall if the hero continued not arriving; though in her heart of hearts she was dreadfully afraid in a way that only showed as brilliant courage outwardly. Corporal Sleigh said once he never read a book because people in them never walked in the mud, and I said of course they did, in some books it rained rather often, but he said even if it did the mud was always *arranged* properly. You never got the sense of anyone being downright dirty the way Territories' mud stuck to you in globs you could barely walk. And I laughed, wondering why you needed or should want that in a book when you had it at your doorstep every day, even in Winnipeg.

"*Robinson Crusoe* isn't like that," said Amelia. "There's plenty of mud."

"That's why I don't like it," said Liza. She now always lay between Amelia and me; we would spread two of the huge double blankets on the ground and one over us as we squeezed close together for it was the ground that was most cold. Liza was soft, almost like her voice. Amelia said I was the most cornered, bony thing to try and get warm against, and she was certainly no whit better, but Liza said we were a good deal warmer than blankets, one of us on either side. "Why couldn't you find something nicer, Kitty, when you were digging in what was left of the drawing room?"

"Nicer like *The Old Curiosity Shop*?" I said into the tent's darkness.

"Yes, that or —"

"I couldn't find it in the ruins. Perhaps some Indian has it and he'll use it for a charm, all full of magic word signs."

"Or maybe Inspector Francis J. smuggled it out on the scow!" Amelia hissed and I laughed aloud, seeing his face again purple under his straggly beard so unlike Papa's full bushy one when Amelia at a Fort Pitt Literary Evening made the mistake of reading aloud, with great dramatic effect, the death of Little Nell. Though perhaps it had been no mistake; Amelia refused to admit anything when Papa scolded her after, the men of the barracks sitting there with some wiping their eyes openly and Corporal Sleigh and Sergeant Martin almost bursting with suppressed laughter while Inspector Dickens stared ahead, small and stiffly purplish among his big men as his famous father's most famous story crawled sweetly on towards its doom.

"Kitty! You'll wake Duncan," Liza said at my ear.

"Or worse, Hodson," said Amelia, behind her. We were laid tightly into each other like three spoons, with me facing out against the canvas. I listened, but there was nothing from Duncan at our feet, though the cook was audible enough just beyond him at the door; obviously in sleep also.

"I don't know why Papa insists Hodson sleep there," I said, "without a weapon anyway. The Indians just stare at him, so tiny and pockmarked with his thick glasses and black hat, they think he's a grub or something. We protect *him*. Little Poplar looked at him like he'd squish him between —"

"Don't mention that beast," Amelia muttered.

"He's rather handsome, in a big-stomached way."

"Kitty," said Liza softly; her bosom against my back, warm and soft.

But I couldn't keep quiet, I felt like arguing with Amelia, always so superior and all-knowing, Mama telling her things I never heard though I loved her of course, completely, she was always so brave whereas I simply did before I thought, "And with eight wives already and only heaven knows how —"

"If you're going to tell your stories," Amelia interrupted, "stick to some facts even you can't deny. He has only six wives."

"Eight," I said, triumphant. "Six here and Mr. James Simpson says he had two more at Little Pine's Reserve, the two oldest sisters of the six he has here. He's put them away with their eight girls and five boys, total, because the boys are old enough to care for —"

Amelia snorted. "If he's starting another sequence of sisters, you're third in line yourself."

"Oh Liza's as good as engaged to Henry Quinn and I'll probably...." I could see it happening again as plainly as if the darkness had been simply the evening light when we began getting the tents up side by side: Little Poplar standing there big and fat with his ugly men facing Papa; Amelia and Liza trying to straighten Mama crumpled to the ground. "Do you agree?" and I translated.

"Of course not!" Papa burst out and I didn't have to translate that, Little Poplar understood and had already taken out his big American revolver and Mama, who was reviving, collapsed again as a hammer clicked; but it wasn't Little Poplar's Colt; if Mama had remembered her guns she would have heard that. It was Kingbird's Winchester cocking, at Little Poplar's ear.

"What's this to you, my son," Little Poplar said standing perfectly still. But Kingbird wouldn't acknowledge they were any relation, or that he was younger; he was not looking at me, or smiling. Just sort of studying the sight near the muzzle of the gun he held.

"It's my affair," he said to the back of Little Poplar's head. "Shoot him and you're dead."

And then an old man put his hand on Little Poplar's arm and gently tugged him away. I could see in the darkness the evening sun pouring red over the trees and our dirty tents on the flat below Frenchman's Butte, the birches white as if they were dipped candles, but Liza clutched me, sobbing against my back and I was crying too and so was Amelia, we all hugged together in one folded bundle with our feet tucked up and our heads bent down, crying. Of course, lying as we were I had nothing to bend my head into but my left arm under the blanket, but I had my right arm back across Liza, I could feel the warmth of Amelia's stomach, tight against us.

"It was that stupid Francis J.," Amelia whispered, sniffing, "sending those scouts out when Papa warned him again and again they'd find nothing, only get captured and that would make it worse. He's supposed to be so intelligent and an inspector eleven years and never promoted he's so stupid!"

"Henry Quinn was sent, he knows the country," I said.

"Well...." Amelia grudgingly thought of Liza also, apparently. "I suppose, yes, he got away from the massacre to warn us and then he escaped that shoot-out in front of Fort Pitt and he even survived their dance in it thanks to Isadore Mondion, three-time survivor that's something of course, but those silly policemen wouldn't listen to him riding right through the camp they stumble on by accident and almost get Papa shot when he's about persuaded the Indians to let us all leave without fighting, after all why should they listen to Henry, just a lucky American halfbreed is all he —"

"Oh Amelia," sighed Liza between us.

"It's not what *I* think, Liza, it's them, that's what they always think, whether they ever say it or not."

"Not all of them," I said; Liza was sobbing silently against me, I could feel her.

"You have to admit, Kitty, Corporal Sleigh is exceptional."

Which of course left me nothing to respond. If I could only have seen him face it out with that constable — Liza couldn't even remember his name but it must have been that loon-face Robertson — when bloody Constable Loasby had been hauled up over the log-and-flour-bag barrier and Corporal Cowan stretched out on the slope, mutilated just beyond our rifle range, and we were all so terrified of what must have happened meanwhile to Papa in the Indian camp beyond the hill when those returning scouts galloped blindly in and got run down as if they were buffalo — they behaved as stupidly, dashing one straight line for our indefensible pile of logs four hundred yards from the river — and with all the shooting and smoke and shouting with Mama in the house hugging the crying children — I heard her through the log chinks where I was firing over the barrier against the corner of the house — wailing that Papa had certainly been killed when the scouts tried to charge through, the Indians would never believe him now that the police were to be trusted not to attack, while Julia tried to control the babies, wailing herself — and I threw my rifle away and jumped over the barrier shouting, "I'm going to see about Papa!," Corporal Sleigh's face a white streak cut by his black mustache and beret behind me, and Amelia scrambling over after me knowing exactly what I wanted to do, "Everybody stay here, I'm going too!" and then, Liza explained later, after all the men at the barrier had gotten over their frozen astonishment Mr. Sleigh knocked down the constable clattering up the barrier with his rifle in his hands, standing over him and glaring around at the other men staring at him (where was Francis J. then? Writing his little diary?), saying just loud enough for everyone in the enclosure to hear, "Keep down you fool! You want the young ladies killed, running after them with your little rifle!" The beautiful brave young ladies. Oh how I wish I could have.... There are flowers gliding under our feet as we move, hand in hand, purple crocuses sprayed golden at the centre and we lift them high in our hands in the wild, fresh air, Amelia in her right and I in my left up the slopes and benches of the treaty hill above the little grey prison barricade of Pitt and its flag painted against the grinding streak of river, the warriors standing above us with rifles in their left hands, their right slowly lifting till we are among them feathered and slashed orange and yellow and red (the Hudson's Bay Company sells that brilliant paint; Papa is very explicit in his orders to get the very best which won't run when you're sweaty or in rain) and tall Lone Man throws the rifle with which he has shot Constable Loasby off his horse aside and takes Amelia's hand; and Kingbird, there, he touches with fingertips and mine rest on his, saying in beautiful Cree, "The beautiful brave Princess of the Yellow Hair!" their shouts about us an immense escort, guns firing into the air as horses stream by and we float over the hill and there is Papa. Standing to receive us beside Big Bear, his brown beard twitching at the corners as though he were about to cry.

And Big Bear already understands more than anyone will ever think to ask him. Amelia knows this like I know it at one glimpse of his massive head, but Papa does not for he understands only single words of Cree and the sound of Big Bear's voice can't be understood in the exact words he says, which are sometimes silly Amelia insists. He simply says, "Princess of the Yellow Hair" to me, a man barely as tall as I with his almost black bare right arm outside the worn blanket, looking at me. He dictated the letter we received at the Fort:

> .... I remember your inspector well for since the Canadian Government have had me to starve in this country he sometimes gave me food and I don't forget the blankets ... we had a talk, I and my men, before we left camp and we thought ... so try and get away before the afternoon as the young men are wild and hard....

but the translation, I know immediately on hearing him, is nothing, it is wind rubbing willow branches of a winter night where his voice is the sun now, all golden. Papa is explaining and explaining to him, the interpreter who is a prisoner from Cold Lake getting tangled and I straighten the translation about getting the police to go, letting them go and they will leave the horses and all their equipment and Fort Pitt open there without a shot or a man lost, I will persuade all the civilians to surrender as your prisoners and we will speak for you if you do us no harm, kindly, let the police go without shooting the Fort is yours without a shot they will go but Papa cannot see beyond the hill where Big Bear already sees the police leaving, as he has always known they will, their few horses still in the stables and dragging the giant scow built at Papa's orders and not hidden from Big Bear either to the river running with its spring ice now, grinding and running. And only after a time

the enraged screams of the young men who finally comprehend they won't be able to wipe out a retreat on the scow
as they would have on foot which Big Bear knows too, since
before the police agreed: Papa goes on explaining to him
while we are leading the straggle of civilians out, squealing
wheels through the soft mud barely pushing forward long
deep welts across the flats behind the gaunt straining haunches
of horses, Mama coming last with Baby Larry clutched in
her arms and the warriors wheeling from their screams
and shooting at the river's bank through the green-haloed
poplars swirling towards the fort now tilted open everywhere
like Hodson's face slumped asleep in his chair and Papa's
explanations, which do not — Papa, why don't you stop talking, I have never seen you so — Big Bear gives his opinion that
Pitt will not be touched until morning when all will be divided
equally among everyone but the young men are flaming
through the horse stalls and bolts of calico cloth and sugar barrels and horsehair of our sofa and Henry Quinn crawls out of
friendly bush into what he thinks safety and is instantaneously
leaping about as if dancing too, streaking his face with soot and
trying to get inconspicuously beyond the barrier into the bush
once more, but in the sunlight Amelia treads mightily at the
organ — "It's the last time, I know," she winks at me holding
Robinson Crusoe in one hand and the Bible, where the family
tree branches from Scotland and Grandfather Murray building the stone gates of Fort Garry to lodges across a lake far
away, in the other and my feet among the sharded sky-blue
dishes while Papa yells at goggling Hodson, "All that doesn't
matter, who cares what you'll hang up to cook, it's the flour, the
flour!" — and she tramps out an ompha march on the organ
and the warriors return from scattering in terror and realize
the Machie Manitou lives in that box with white depressible

teeth and they shoot it full of holes after Lone Man pulls
Amelia away, throw ropes around it and there it is dragged in
the yard and mashed carefully with long-handled Company
axes that lie across its rubble after one swing. Fire leaps out,
terrifyingly, as if it had been poised, lurking there forever
between Amelia's legs and mine pumping steadily, every day, is
that what is flaming between me, a pillar roaring up me like ice
fingers dancing in noon sunlight and the house corner behind
which I hear Mama sob, almost screaming now, catches light
but Papa beats it into blackness with his coat still beat explaining to Big — Papa there isn't that much left to burn on this hill
or the world when will you close your — having begun to
actually scream explana....

Duncan. It was Duncan. Liza was sitting up between us,
holding him in her arms and I clamped around the edge of the
blanket, against the night air working fingers down my back.
Her voice soothing Duncan is so soft I'm not awake, even
when she begins to pull me over.

"Time to turn," she whispers, "come on, all together."

"My back...."

".... tuck you in, but it's too hard, we have to, Kitty...." her
hands on my hip and shoulder, but the aching relief to my stiff
side, the feel of her hands pushing the blanket solid and warm
under me, turned, swims into the length of her legs against
mine through the tied layers of cotton and when she eases
down back to me my arm is in the hollow of her waist pulling
the long roundness of her tight and warm and good between
my thighs, the other hand over her almost hard nippled breast
with all that silly wool and cotton — on this ground the only
warmth must be Indian naked — my arm and hand one splin-
tering ache laid along the blanket of the ground holding her
hard and this time she does not push me away, nor reach for

Amelia breathing and warm just there beyond the cup and curve of my hands, my face in her sweet hair and her arm coming up to me, covering, drenching me over in spongy black sleep, weightless.

The shadows of trees, branches; certainly leaves over the grey canvas. Morning stood there and the voice of the camp crier coming nearer, singing, "... come, come, council meeting, Big Bear calls to the council...." and then out of some lightness again above me, straight up along the knobbly poplar holding up canvas in the short crotch of another I heard my father answer a few English words of agreement to Cree. And Little Poplar somewhere far away laughed aloud, the crier's voice moving on. We had not turned again, all night, but my right side was hardly stiff, especially when I moved fast. It was after all from the night of April 14 to — yes, tomorrow is the Queen's Birthday Papa said at supper — today, after our thirty-ninth night on the ground.

"There's a bit of warm here," said Amelia bent to Liza pouring water over her hands; who would not look at me. "If you never wash properly you'll always have more red spots, and yellow too."

If you held a blanket close enough there was no way to tell you weren't an Indian except by staring in your face; which was impolite. The sun was already high in the long spring day, at the green rim of Frenchman Butte above the lodges standing among the trees of its shoulders, the smoke blue as the sky reaching up between them. Lone Man's wife, Nowah-keetch, suckled her four-year-old boy, he standing beside her while she knelt stirring bannock batter and Mr. Stanley Simpson, their prisoner, tended the pan already cooking with it. The little boy's black eyes stared at me going by across the slack brown he was kneading slowly with his thin fists, at the blanket point hanging half over my face; Mr. William Bleasdell Cameron sat on his heels beside Mr. Simpson at the fire, fingering a huge black bruise along his jaw.

"…. Louis's pinto's front legs were hobbled, but that crazy stallion can move backwards like a crab and when his hind legs get in range, by…. "

Louis Patenaude, Mrs. Simpson's Wood Cree son in whose lodge Mr. Cameron was technically prisoner but more protected than anything else, as we all were protected by Wood Crees. Immaculate Mr. Stanley Simpson not so immaculate now, not so completely the sharp thin nose knowing everything a proper girl should not do, or even think, not so impeccable frying bannock at a smelly fire mixed between the brown fingers of a suckled woman. Let Amelia like him, sticky one-eyed fop who could only hunt like someone trotting a curried hunter to hounds. And Mr. Cameron played the violin, beautifully, but couldn't keep out of range of that creamy stallion's hoofs with his bow legs as the little boys shouted. Beyond Little Bad Man's lodge and dogs swirling two and three-legged to mount each other like dominoes stood the council lodge with men gathering, in the small flat above the creek. Papa was there at the outer edge, his tan hat brushed but his beard uncombed; spraying out, as if he had lain all night with his chin square on the ground, staring under something.

And they must have done the pipe ceremony very quickly for Wandering Spirit, not Big Bear, was already talking. His Winchester, the bronze of it polished almost to gold, as always in his left hand. Talking war, his eagle-lynx bonnet on his head.

"…. no more messages come from Poundmaker? Days ago we heard the soldiers had attacked him but the messengers from the Battle River did not agree, who could say what they meant when one said this and one that. I say the messengers saw no fighting; the soldiers did nothing at Cutknife Hill; I do not think Poundmaker is there. He has gone to Batoche to Riel and our horses are strong now, the grass is good, we should go there to join him and eat the cattle he said long ago he has waiting for us. There is nothing left at Fort Pitt, and there is nothing between here and Batoche that can stop us, now."

It was so funny! When Wandering Spirit's high, clear voice waved his arm around it looked as if the next instant his head would vanish into Quinn's huge striped coat hanging in the air and only his curly hair spreading like a flange over the collar kept him from sinking; his fierce head bobbing on curls! No one, of course, except I saw that. The inside circle of Plains Cree was rumbling agreement and the others around us made no sound at all. Papa said to Pritchard, translating beside him in a whisper,

"Do you think the Wood Cree can argue him out of it again?"

"He'll say more," said Pritchard quickly, "harder, I think."

For Wandering Spirit was staring out of his funny brown collared jacket, blackly at my father. Turned slightly, away from Big Bear seated at the centre of the council ring. It was beastly how they treated him, his own son Little Bad Man sitting beside him in council and laughing when he walked through camp wearing nothing but the one blanket, so shabby now, Papa had persuaded him to accept as a gift while the others were looting Fort Pitt. That ugly bull of a Bad Man not so little, sneering in council. The war chief was beginning to ring:

"There is another thing I will say here. When I began this war, over there," he swung his rifle north-west, "I made a vow. For a long time I had been looking around, on every side and between the sun and the earth I saw too much white poking around. Everywhere my ear heard talk I did not understand, laughing as if I knew nothing, Whiteskins who walked onto my land sticking their smooth bellies out over it full of food against mine growling weak and empty. The food the Government said was mine was in piles behind walls and locks I was told not to touch. After this long time I got tired of thinking about that food and listening to my belly, and at last I made a vow. I said: I will never again look at a Whiteskin except along the barrel of this gun! Spirit Help Me! Now I look around in this camp and what is there to see? White faces, everywhere! I hear their voices, talking together. There are some People who listen to them in the darkness and say aloud what they have heard here in the light. They keep us apart, River People and Wood People. White faces! I am not talking about the halfbreeds who are my brothers. It's those Whiteskins there, sitting as if they belonged in this council! As if they spoke, here!"

His rifle had swung to Mr. James Simpson sitting beside his stepsons, then found Papa in front of me. John Pritchard was not translating anything; he seemed to be leaning away under the war chief's glare, that small round hole facing us, but Papa understood quite enough without translation and sat perfectly still. I could not dare lift my hand to pull the blanket corner tighter over my hair; it did cover one eye.

"And there is the Company chief," Wandering Spirit went on, "whose girls are brave but he has never learned to talk to us. When we wanted to get him out of the fort to save his family he would not come, but when we had killed some police that attacked us he soon got those out of the way using his family for a trick with the flat canoe, where he knew we could not kill them out on the river. Now we will have to kill them some other time! And he has powder, bullets for my gun, hidden somewhere and he will not tell me where it is, even when we burn the Company house."

Wandering Spirit raised his clenched fist and gun high into the air; far down the North Saskatchewan valley smoke lay like blue mist beyond the hills where Fort Pitt still smouldered.

"My blood roars," he cried up into the sky, "every time I see Sun again: I have not kept my vow!"

Cut Arm, the big Wood Cree chief who had vowed to protect us, sat in the inner circle directly opposite Wandering Spirit, in front of us; my stomach growled. Of course I hadn't eaten anything yet, and the war chief was far too noisy and excited for so early in the morning. Let him talk. A woman with a baby on her back was walking beyond the council circle, through the feathered-green trees; it looked like the red-striped blanket of The Black Stone, Wandering Spirit's wife.

Ah, Big Bear stood now, between Little Bad Man and Wandering Spirit the glassy-eyed yeller, who had seated himself. The old man (he's shaped like a white man, Papa said once, short and heavy, not slim like an Indian. He's one to watch.) held a worn stone pipe before him in both hands.

"This pipe," he began slowly, and I could feel myself turn limp at the sound. My legs were just water; fortunately I was squatting. "It is very dear to me, this pipe. All the great men who have come to see me have smoked it...there were so many...." his mind seemed to wander, his voice fading like the organ when you forget to pedal. "And my wives. All of them smoked it in turn, all of them smoked it and there is only one left. One by one they have gone to the Sand Hills and this is all I have left to remember them."

His wrinkled face suddenly lifted; looked around the People, then turned half from them down the valley towards the smoke.

"I pity every Whiteskin we have saved!" he cried out. "Instead of speaking bad about them, give them back some of the things you have taken. Look at them: they are suddenly poor. Naked. They have never before, like us, been often hungry; they haven't known until now how the teeth of cold bite. Look at them, and have pity!"

And at that strange contradiction of the war chief there was a long silence. Enough guns lay everywhere but no one stirred. Little Bad Man was flicking his eyes around as if to see whether he dared laugh, and suddenly Little Poplar stood there. Gunless. His arms folded over his chest and bending, smiling towards Papa. As if he would protect him!

"I look upon the children of the Company's chief as my own. I would not want to do them harm."

A conversion! He sat down and John Pritchard said nothing. I couldn't see his face: his position was tricky enough, once Government translator and now protecting the two widowed white women in his tent. I edged forward and whispered into Papa's ear,

"That fat swine, he said —"

And his whiskers jerked, almost turning to me before he caught himself. "Kitty! What are you...."

But I interrupted him, finished quickly what Little Poplar had said. Anyway, everyone there looking would recognize my blanket.

"He talks about 'children,' after last night," Papa said; he sounded rigid with fury. "And Big Bear?"

I told him about the pipe, the wives, and his pity; Papa barely nodded, his eyes on the old man talking again.

" .... some here were in a hurry to start trouble," came his voice, low now but rising hugely. "Vows are dangerous for they can lead a long hard way, sometimes. When the messengers came from Poundmaker telling us that the Government's soldiers were marching to fight there, who wasn't frightened? Those are big Whiteskins, and they come from the east on the

Iron Road we have seen enough of and they travel without women or children when they go to fight. Perhaps no one was thinking of that when the smoke left his gun muzzle, when fire ate the church at Frog Lake. 'We will talk only to the Grandmother, we will talk to the Company, to get the police and the Government away from here. We want nothing of the Government putting our names in lists and the police giving orders, just saying "No."' These were words I heard then...."

"He doesn't understand either," Papa muttered into my translation, "Not even he gets it straight that the Queen and the police and —"

"Papa, he knows — but those others don't — he knows — listen...."

But there was no way I could get it through to him; even Papa would never understand Big Bear's comprehension, and I had to try and keep up,

"....when I said I was going to find the one and speak to that one than whom there is none higher. This had been given me to see, at last, and I said that last year to every chief at Battle River and Duck Lake and Carlton and to every white I met. You heard it many times. But who will listen? What River chief ever started a war before the grass was green, before horses could carry warriors? There is someone you all know as well as I started this too fast at Duck Lake and it has come to me that he won't know how to finish what he has begun. It comes to me that something has already happened at Batoche and the messenger you sent two days ago is almost back already, for he won't have to go all the way to Batoche to see something. As for my son Poundmaker, I say no white soldiers will take his people captive. I don't care what some messengers said about soldiers with guns that were shooting them twice, I know that under the shadow of Cutknife Hill it is not given that whites will do great things. I think they will have been very happy to get away from there — wait till you hear the end of that. Since some began this at Frog Lake and carried it further to Fort Pitt you have done little but eat and wait. Now, waiting has been with me all my life, but if I started something like this I would finish it fast. It comes to me that our horses can travel now, but they will not go to Batoche, I think, which is many days from here. I will not meet Poundmaker anywhere that I want to go. This is a good place, under that flat hill where a trader was once wiped out for not trading straight. This is a good place to wait some more. Here. And our waiting is almost over. It will not be long now."

Absolute silence among the seated warriors; Little Bad Man and Wandering Spirit stared up on either side of the old man. His voice seemed to be coming from high up, as if it might be only wind turning the leaves on Frenchman Butte so gently that there was no sound whatever of them touching, only the hush of air brushing my ears, reading down to me what already hung there in the air as happened and what with Big Bear's vision had now inevitably touched the earth. I could feel that, like light spiralling back and forth through my hollow head but I could not...where did those Cree words come from, I had never heard...were they words, they were, sounds...as if the high oration had melted into chant, or dirge...the old man stood with a wide black hole in the middle of his face and the sound coming out of there.

"What's he saying?" Papa's elbow prodded my knee.

"What's that? Kitty!"

But there was only that sound turning in my head. Translate what? And words emerging, spinning over me after a time too, though my mouth could say nothing.

"....comes to me from long ago when we fought the Siksikas before many of you were born and the Bloods, not one man among River People could do what I did. The buffalo tongues I gave away, the enemies I sent singing to the Sand Hills — and never made certain they had no weapons before I faced them, either. All those South People heard of Big Bear: he was head chief of the River People and the sacred Chief's Son's Hand hung behind his lodge and the sound of his name breathing down the wind stretched their hearts on the ground like dried meat. When I said anything, the People listened; when I would not take treaty there up the valley, you were happy. But now, I say one thing and you do another. You remember my vision, but you turn your backs. You have thrown my name away and I will have to lift what you did at Frog Lake; my back will have to carry what you did at Fort Pitt. I called this council, though I will not call another. I said wait, we must talk with them, but you were very busy. Where you think you are going I have already been four times; I felt the rope around my neck long ago. If there had been any good in shooting Whiteskins I would have done it six years ago when Sitting Bull and his two thousand Sioux wanted to, when we had warriors full of buffalo meat and there was no Iron Road to haul in soldiers. When you," he bent over suddenly and swept his long right arm under Wandering Spirit's chin, "were still saying sweet little things to the Governor at Carlton, and you," he wheeled as startlingly to Little Bad Man glowering on the other side, "had no more on your mind than to find another woman alone in the bush bending over to pick up firewood.

"Why have I never taken a reserve! The Little Men, and Coyote, I saw what they had to show. One more summer, but you would not wait!

"Your waiting is almost over, one man alone can return from Battleford in two days. And before I finish I'll tell you why you see so many white faces here. They are prisoners. And you have to ask them for advice because you know nothing about how the white man fights, you know nothing about what he can drag into this country with his Iron Horses. They don't, and never will, fight like People; they leave their women and children far away and you need these Whiteskins because you have very little powder left after shooting all the cattle and you are going to want these to say perhaps some good word when the long, long columns of white soldiers come through the trees. The horses are ready to travel, though we have little meat left and some of you will remember that spring is a bad time for food if you haven't saved pemmican from the buffalo pound hunts when the snow was flying. I haven't seen much pemmican around here, though I'm old and my eyes aren't what they once were. Also, it has come to me that there is perhaps no place for us to travel, that perhaps Riel is finished waiting at Batoche. It may be he is already waiting in another way, in another place. Over the hills I see that messenger coming, so I'll go now. You won't have to tell me when he comes, but tell me four days from now if you don't see the soldiers of the Grandmother's Government somewhere around here. Though I, maybe I won't need to be told that either. My ears are still almost as good as my teeth. You were too busy to listen when I shouted 'Stop,' and I have called council for the last time. That's all I will say."

He laid the pipe on the ground and turned and walked away; past the council lodge and into the willows where the creek ran. No one moved or lifted his head. I may have been the only one there who could look up and watch him go.

.   .   .

Feel willows where the blanket must have slid away from my face, silly green willows snicking at my face like a high sound Weesa-kayjac himself had shaped into tunnel for me to run and my legs running me with my skin stinging — Big Bear stood half-turned against a bush, an arch of golden water curving from him in the sunlight, joining him to the creek.

"Your father is a good man," he said without looking back. "I've known him only since the last treaty payment. It was good you translated for him."

It wasn't necessary to try and say words, his tone told me everything. He finished what he was doing and turned and came towards me.

"That feels good," he said, not smiling; "to embrace the whole earth in one flowing stream."

We walked through the willows back to camp, though he had not touched me. The leaves shimmered as if they were heat over the plains. "What will happen?" I said, no one but I to hear his voice.

"Tomorrow Little Bad Man will give the Thirst Dance."

"What?" Because he had made me see the columns of soldiers coming. They must come eventually, Papa said and we McLeans talked of little else every evening but in this bright green and blue world they seemed only, overpoweringly, unnecessary.

"A new chief sometimes does that, if he can. If there's enough food." He stopped and looked at me, and then he walked on. "A good life should be told in four parts, like everything is four in the life of a Person. The first is to be a child, the second a man proving himself, the third to be known to your band as a good man. And the fourth, if The Only One gives it, is to be known to all the People, everywhere; and honoured. But I have known men who have seen another part coming, and another after that, and it's too long, too long."

He seemed to be walking very fast, his voice so distant it sounded oddly weak, almost unsure of himself and my mind was stunned blank, empty and blank but my voice was talking after him, I must have been thinking it somewhere to reach after him with that,

"Today it's the Grandmother's birthday.... "

"Ahhh," and his feet stopped. "Then a celebration is needed. Of course something good to eat and an old story for all of these," for children had appeared as if growing out of the earth, everywhere, wearing bits of rag and their brown skin laughing faces, shouting and running among the grey cones and smoke of the camp under the Butte. Big Bear's hand touched mine. "There is an old story I will tell you soon, that my mother's father once told me very long ago. About Weesa-kayjac and the inexperienced women." It seemed to me I saw Duncan's dirty face streaked with poplar sap there, certainly beside Horsechild, as the children swam him away. His broad shoulders above them.

Between our two rectangular tents burned many small fires with as many small pots and kettles set on stones over them. Mama was boiling underclothing; and Henry Quinn came around a corner with an armful of wood.

"Kitty," Mama glanced back at Henry poking a branch under a pot, "you should have changed — you know."

"He's looking into the pots anyway," I said loud enough so Henry would hear it, "why else would he do squaw work."

Julia shrieked, Helen's small head between her knees, her fingers busy in hair,

"'Ere's another un, m'am, there's no keepin' 'em off the poor dears, such a awful leggy things!" She flipped the louse towards the fire, but the heat seemed to blow it aside.

"You didn't kill it, Julia," I said. "The only sure way is do like the Indians."

"Uh?"

"Between your teeth," said Henry behind me before I could say it.

"Why don't you try to run off again?" I said to him.

"Kitty!" Mama exclaimed. "You will go into the tent and — you know what you have to do."

"He almost got us all scalped, the sneaky rat," but I was muttering it under my breath, for Liza mostly who would be in the hot tent waiting for her clothes; but only Amelia was there, her strong, pale legs sticking out under her blanket.

"Isn't it your turn to wear the extra clothes?"

She grimaced, squinting around to her fingers exploring the skin on her shoulder. "Liza said she'd try once more to get Mrs. D. to let Mama wash her things. Liza can do it if anyone can."

"I should think. I can't see why having your husband die in your arms should keep you ever after in the same pair of laced boots and bloomers. She could stay in the tent, like us. How can she do it? Do you think she even pulls them down, ever?" I was pulling down my own.

"That may be a mystery you won't know till you're old enough not to run around in barely a blanket when Mama doesn't see you."

"I don't know why you sit in this heat, you've got no more to cover than I."

"You could hardly understand," Amelia said in the tone only a sister four years older can produce. "And leave Henry alone. Papa told Liza she is not to go on with it now."

"Praise God from Whom —"

"Don't blaspheme. It'll be damp for a bit so try and find some discretion, somewhere, until —"

"Who stuck her foot in it last night? I'm just asking."

"She'll forget him the minute we're out of this bush."

"Big Bear said soldiers will be here in four days."

"He did!" Amelia stared at me, her beautiful green eyes shining. She did not waste a word on how he could know. I was on my knees and we were hugging each other, her bare arms cool around my back in the sun-heated tent.

"You're so lovely. If you were an Indian you'd be —" she broke off. "Put your things outside and get on your blanket, I'll comb out your hair."

I did that and settled myself in front of her. "Make sure about the lice. And they're having a Thirst Dance tomorrow too."

"But if the soldiers...."

"That Little Bad Man is the chief now, and he certainly doesn't believe it."

"He makes me shiver, that animal; more than Little Poplar."

"Wouldn't it be beautiful to ride up behind one of the warriors, when they gallop around for the lodge rafters!"

"Oh Kitty you goose. He's married, and his beautiful wife will soon have —"

"Shut up!"

And it was Amelia, of course, who noticed the Hudson's Bay flag next day flying at the tip of the Thirst Lodge being built on the naked crown of Frenchman Butte. It was in memory of "The good days of the past, before the Government and the police," Four Sky Thunder said in his quiet kindly way, smiling exactly as he was smiling, Mr. Cameron said, when he set fire to the Frog Lake church after the priests' bodies had been thrown into it.

And then Amelia told him the flag was flying upside down. As fast as shouts could carry over the hill a young man was up the centre pole, tearing the red flag loose and tying it right but with that something final and black dropped over the new chief's celebration. Old people muttered more than ever about the messenger who had come back late at night, not from Batoche but from Battleford as Big Bear had said he would, saying the earth between the rivers there trembled with horses and soldiers. The Wood Crees would not dance and the dancing that did begin, very loudly, did not even continue past midnight. There was no one at all in the Thirst Lodge when the sun rose May 26 and suddenly the lookout on the Butte sent down a long, wailing cry. He had seen something white far down the North Saskatchewan valley: the tents of soldiers above the smoking ruins of Fort Pitt. Papa said Company losses there would be not much under $70,000.00, including the buildings.

III

Men ran from lodges and caught up the stake ropes of their horses; dogs howled, women left unlit morning fires and began to strip their lodges while boys erupted into circles about the bushes and over girls. Wandering Spirit rode singing through the swirl on the tall grey mare which had been Quinn's, plumed and painted with his Winchester in his hand and leather cartridge belts crossed on his naked chest. He herded the forty white prisoners together up the butte to the Thirst Lodge. It was empty, its covers and flag jerked off and poplar leaves steamy in the sunlight. The prisoners huddled there while warriors galloped circles around them for some time screaming warcries. Abruptly Wandering Spirit ordered everyone down to the camp again, to pack for immediate moving. The straggling cavalcade flanked by mounted warriors, Red River carts squealing, dog and horse travois bumping over tree roots, a red and blue trimmed bobsled stolen from Fort Pitt dragging over the ground and cutting into muskeg along the creek while two men smoked serenely on its back seat, one holding a pink parasol over the other as the sun grew hot over the narrow glades. Noise animal, human, mechanical, and screams where a colt bucked through the procession scattering it with feathers from a quilt that had slid, belted, under its belly. At the rear the war chief marshalled his scouts. Three miles this uproar wound through the brush, north, and by mid-afternoon of May 26 settled to camp again in a valley of a creek flowing into the Little Red Deer River.

Eighteen miles away Major-General T. Bland Strange was having fatigue parties of his Alberta Field Force clean the two buildings left partially unburned at Fort Pitt. He had ordered the heart of Constable Cowan, found on an adjacent stake, placed inside the bloated body for full military burial. Scouts led by the Reverend John McDougall and four Stoneys found what they believed fresh Indian trails across the North Saskatchewan leading south; a steel cable was stretched over and a small force crossed. The trail was followed for three days, by which time they were in Battleford and it became clear the massacring Cree had gone elsewhere. They had in fact discovered themselves to Major Steele's North West Mounted Police scouts who all day followed a trail north of the river that eventually circled east; after thirty miles of rugged riding, the seventy scouts were charged by twenty screaming warriors less than three miles east of Pitt. Finally, shooting at last! The police blazed heartily away into the midnight darkness until the warriors galloped off leaving one dead: Meeminook from Saddle Lake, Athabaska Territory, riding a black Hudson's Bay Company stallion. The kill was credited to Constable Thomas McClennan, N.W.M.P. who cut off an ear, looped a rope around the head and, with it tied to the saddle of the terrified black, whooping dragged the body back and forth on the rocky moonlit prairie along Pipestone Creek until someone caught up with him and hacked his rope through.

About the same time Wandering Spirit was facing Straight Tongue McLean and Greybeard Simpson. An old man had seen the two traders talking earnestly with some Wood People behind a bush, crept nearer and heard enough to suspect Wandering Spirit would like to know of this conversation. The war chief demanded whether they had been trying to send a message to the soldiers. Promptly Straight Tongue said "No." At the same moment Simpson's two Wood People step-sons entered the lodge, jumped across the fire and placed themselves on either side of the Company men. Their rifles were cocked and aimed at the old accuser. He became con-fused facing those steady muzzles, and could not seemingly explain what he had heard of Straight Tongue behind the bushes offering a reward of five hundred dollars to the man who would get in touch with the Master of the Soldiers. After prolonged shouting and fury between Plains and Wood People the old man slunk away, disgraced, and the prisoners were sent back to their lodges under Little Bad Man's guard this time. Near dawn the scouts returned and reported Meeminook killed; amid the wailing Wandering Spirit moved the camp again. They traversed the valley and struggled up a narrow wooded ravine cutting into the open face of the north ridge above the stream. Here the war chief ordered halt, and pits dug: shelter pits further up the ravine for women and children and prisoners, and rifle pits lower in the ravine and all along the wooded rim of the bare ridge overlooking their trail through the valley. The warriors sang and chose their places; they adjusted their rifle sights by shooting at selected points across the valley. Old men and children and women and prisoners dug into the red earth with sticks and pans, and towards evening of May 27 the pits were ready. Snug and camouflaged as rain sifted through the poplars.

That same afternoon General Strange advanced to join Steele's mounted scouts with 197 infantry and 27 cavalry and one nine-pounder field gun. He had only three days of supplies left in his march from Edmonton and few carts so he transported most of that in scows along the river parallel to his advance. After a few miles the trail bent north however, where the river turned south; the scouts discovered a campsite with 187 lodge circles at the foot of Frenchman Butte and when Strange arrived warriors were seen high on open ridges there and fired upon by the gun, for practice, as night fell. It was cold under the thin spring rain, with tents and greatcoats and most of the food in the scows hiding behind an island on the river three miles away. At daybreak on Thursday, May 28, the force advanced north through the wet bush along the obvious trail. Between its ridges and hoofprints some of the soldiers noticed purple woodviolets blooming.

The warriors, behind branches stuck in the breastworks of their pits, looked down the bare face of the glacis before them and over the mist hiding the creek to the strip of prairie along the edge of the glistening trees. Everywhere only silence. The sun rose higher on their left, slowly lifting the mist; between the trees suddenly a flash of red, a clink of bridles: police scouts. On foot and leading their horses, very slowly, along either side of the muddy trail. Five hundred yards across the valley those whites entered the clearing and at a signal stopped. Several redcoated men came forward to stand talking well within Sharps rifle range, then obviously a halfbreed rode among them and pointing across the creek to the ravine and

the ridge. A bearded man in blue wearing a cocked and feathered hat more beautiful than they had ever seen rode out of the
trees on a dapple horse. He listened to the halfbreed; he put a
short glass to his eye and moved it so that for an instant sunlight winked at each warrior staring between the leaves along
the ridge, then he put that away and with the scout rode down
to the creek, light flashing on the gold braid of his coat. Such a
careless approach to muskeg startled the hidden warriors into
grins; the scout's horse suddenly sank to its belly. Promptly
both wheeled back and out with some difficulty, and the beautiful man waved to the trees as he rode back up. More blocks of
soldiers emerged there, immense numbers of them walking
and spreading out among the trees, who could say how many,
and horses pulled a wagon loaded with one gigantic shining
gun out to the edge of the clearing. No one approached the
creek; there were more soldiers moving sideways through the
trees when the gun suddenly burst smoke. The ball tore high
through the trees over one rifle pit and the warriors in it jerked
erect to see shattered leaves and branches spraying as thunder
rumbled along the valley. Far behind them women and horses
screamed as the sound faded but none of the warriors heard
that; they were firing wildly all along the front of the rifle pits,
their ambush and the hopeless range for Winchesters and
muzzle-loaders forgotten.

The gun continued to fire high, sending its shots screaming
over the ridge to rip apart the dense silent poplars somewhere
far beyond the women and children and prisoners terrified in
their pits. Wandering Spirit ran between the pits on the ridge,
yelling the useless rifles to silence and grouping the Sharps buffalo guns in two pits opposite the gunners. Soon their bullets
pinged and sang about the gun and the crews had to lie down,
the chief gunner kneeling to fire. He Speaks Our Tongue

shrieked with delight when a gunner dived behind a wheel of the rocking wagon. In a wide red swath soldiers on foot were dashing forward along the creek, gaining shelter among the willows and firing up the slope where they could see nothing but blue, dazzling sky. Then the muzzle-loaders and Winchesters above them began again, with good effect now for the warriors heard a scream here and there, saw a frocked priest running among the willows where rifles spat. Three mud-covered soldiers emerged on their bellies from the willows but then nothing faced them except the naked glacis hissing bullets. Others crawled out and they lay behind grass and willow clumps, firing steadily up into the sky.

Suddenly, Little Poplar was dancing upon the skyline. On the immense bow of the naked ridge he seemed tiny as an ant twitching to the astonished soldiers, who until that instant had not seen so much as a feather, anywhere, but he was precise in every tiny detail, screaming and waving a Winchester in one hand and a long-barrelled American Colt in the other. He wore a beaver hat stuck through with a feather and a black velveteen waistcoat buttoned very tight across his paunch but just then he turned his back and it was obvious he wore nothing else. He bent over, slapped his naked twitching rear to them and so danced gracefully out of sight as bullets snickered longingly around him.

"You almost got that extra hole!" Miserable Man roared.

Wandering Spirit ran up behind the double pits to Little Poplar, shouting in admiration. "The police are riding that way," he yelled then and pointed west, "to cross the valley there if they can. Take some men along the ridge and stay opposite them."

Little Poplar tore off the coat and was gone with a whoop. The war chief turned and ran east behind the pits; Charlebois who understood some English waved at him out of the ground opposite the gun.

"The man with the gold, on the horse," he yelled above the firing, "that's the Master of them. He's showing that gun how to shoot I think, and they'll have our range pretty quick."

Wandering Spirit looked down at the men working furiously over the gun gleaming in the sunlight. They fought wearing all their best clothes; as if they were dancing for their women; as if for them war itself was indistinguishable from a war dance.

"That gold one under the hat should be dead by now," he shouted to the two pits with the buffalo guns. "And spread out now, away from here. They're not coming up the ravine so I'll take some men from there and move around," he gestured east. "We'll get their horses and kill those making the gun spit, if you don't soon."

He vanished among the trees down into the ravine; the warriors began to crawl out of the pit when a shrill cutting sound ran out of the sky towards them and a black ball fell, almost gently, with a PLOP on the pit's rim; hissing half-buried as it lay. He Speaks Our Tongue stared at it, motionless, and burst out laughing, but Charlebois jerked back, scrabbling on all fours back between the trees while still oddly trying to flatten himself against the soggy earth when it burst before his bulging eyes with a sound so close he did not hear it. He raised his face out of the ground at last, into silence and the slightly dusty hole with white poplar roots seemingly unravelled, sprayed over tiny blue men rubbing again far away down there on that black gun. After a time he tried to push his head forward to the edge of that hole he had not noticed before and could smell now, clean earth and gunpowder, and suddenly he knew that part of his face must be gone.

None of the non-combatants remained in the shelter pits after the first four shells had gone over. Leaving food and belongings in the ravine, the women and children scattered in various large groups northward, old men armed only with clubs following behind them. Several groups of Wood People took the opportunity to escape their half-brothers and half-captors; they struck east while all the Chipewyans fled north toward their country beyond the Beaver River. William Cameron and Henry Quinn got away with a friendly group but McLean and Simpson with their families were too closely guarded by River men; they had to remain with the largest group of the River People that retreated north six miles until Big Bear came and said they all could stop now and they clustered to wait, fearfully, and listen to messengers galloping back from the front and as quickly returning to it again. An old woman wailed over and over into the air,

"O Sun, remember our children today, and I will show you a looking glass."

Steele reported to Strange from the left that he was still being fired upon a mile and a half down the creek; enemy strength must be at least six hundred combatants and there seemed no way he could turn their position. Strange ordered him to return as Major Hatton reported that enemy were circling in from the right and firing into the horse corrals loosely held at their rear and the men there had little cover. The general ordered some troops back to the corrals and then walked forward and personally helped carry the third of his wounded men up from the creek (the officer whom he had originally ordered to do so retorted: "I've been shot at quite enough today and I'm damned if I'll go down there again") and the police scouts arrived back just in time to cover an orderly retreat. The gun fired until the last moment, retiring at 10:30 a.m.

with no more than twenty-two shells remaining. The men of the 65th Mount Royal Rifles grumbled loudly on the six-mile retreat to the river; they had eaten the last of their rations at 3:30 that morning and had not been allowed a bayonet charge up that slope: they had come two thousand miles and walked five hundred from Calgary to fire into air and trees for three hours and then see exactly one savage, and mostly his ass at that? On the banks of the river Strange discovered that the supply scows, still behind the island, had no power to cross to their bank against the current. After two hours' rest the entire expedition retreated the final fifteen miles to Fort Pitt to await supplies from Edmonton and perhaps Major-General Frederick D. Middleton from whom nothing had been heard since May 1. The scows eventually drifted by three packed Middleton steamers and his advancing cavalry en route and arrived at Battleford to the cheers of the entire populace though the few men on board could not explain if there had been a rescue or a victory somewhere up north, yet. It was clear however that, true to his word, General Strange had not "committed a Custer."

In fact, the gun fired its last shot and retired when only a few warriors were left scattered here and there along the line of pits above it. These warriors were there more as scouts than combatants; the unnatural gun that spoke twice, once when it fired below and then again when its shot landed on the ridge, was obviously unfair; it was ridiculous to stay and shoot against such a fiendish machine. When Wandering Spirit returned from his foray against horses too well guarded to stampede, he found almost all the men already moving north on the cluttered trail left by the women. Abandoned lodgepoles and skins had been made into a travois on which lay He Speaks Our Tongue, his mouth open, singing. Sweat gleamed on his chest but below that he seemed only earth and he had no legs at all, his trunk simply ended in black clotted earth through which shining ooze worked itself as the poles dragged over stones and bumped into trees. Further ahead, Kingbird was leading the stallion he had not had to humiliate with a travois: Matoose hung dead across his back. Kingbird tried to show Wandering Spirit the spot where a bit of shrapnel had exploded one of Matoose's own cartridges up into his chest, but the hole was so tiny and the stallion almost uncontrollable, seeming at times to throw himself deliberately against the poplars that twisted the trail.

"It's the trees," Kingbird said, "he doesn't like all these trees."

Wandering Spirit said, "They can't pull that gun between them."

Random firing behind them faded but He Speaks Our Tongue sang on powerfully in his death song until the women met them and raised the wailing. All moved on together slowly, and it was near evening before the rear scouts caught up to report that the soldiers had run away before midday. Camp was made then and riders and women returned the miles to the ravine to carry back what food they could on the trail too narrow for carts and assist the few wounded who had not been able to keep up. The Chipewyans and half the Wood People were gone: Little Poplar declared himself war chief and was already explaining his plans. He had made some big police jump, he declaimed, and after a few days rest it would be time to kill all the Whiteskins: first in Battleford and then Prince Albert. At that place he knew there were big boats to go down the river and across the lake to Winnipeg and when every white there was killed they would go on the Iron Road to the east and kill every one there too, especially the man who was the Master of the Government. After that no white from anywhere, even the Grandmother, would want to come and take land away from the People; if anyone did, he would easily be killed as well. For himself, he had never thought very highly of the old fat Grandmother anyway; he declared the Americans laughed at her and they had more to eat than anyone.

Horsechild awoke into darkness. This in itself was so unusual that for some time it seemed he must be having a vision before he was old enough to starve and pray for it, but then he knew the sound was the women's death wail at the edge of the camp — perhaps his father would take one of the widows, but they both looked thin and cold and hard, no better than The Magpie — it was the breathing, he thought then. All the breathing again in his father's tattered lodge, there was no more Running Second but he could hear Kingbird again and his bulging Sits Green On The Earth and of course The Magpie and his father, just at his back but the hardest to hear nevertheless, and his friend Duncan against his knees in front of him and the three McLean girls and their women slave and the young Company Simpson who could take one eye out of his head, round and hard as a stone. Horsechild hunched together and shuddered with happiness. He would stay awake and just before dawn get up and squeeze that out of his face and run away where he could hold it in his hand, warm, round as stone all blue inside. He would put it in his eye; how would a green hill look through a blue eye? He lay with his ear on the earth and he could feel the roots of grass nudging forward there like worms. He was asleep.

IV

Kitty found they could only stay one night in Big Bear's tent. Chaqua-pocase had declared that a Big Whiteskin must die as atonement for the great slain warrior who had once beaten a farm instructor and then killed two at Frog Lake and was usually credited with part of Redcoat Cowan at Fort Pitt as well. Late the evening of the battle when He Speaks Our Tongue's singing ended Chaqua-pocase went shouting to McLean's tent, but Big Bear suddenly stepped in front of him and wrenched his rifle away before he could close his mouth. The following morning the warrior had his rifle back again and, though he stood glowering beside the shallow grave at McLean standing with Wandering Spirit, he did nothing more than that; as for others, McLean's respect in coming to the funeral seemed to satisfy them. When the camp got in motion slowly north again McLean told his children there might be some who would make trouble with Big Bear for his action, especially if they saw too many McLeans about, so Cut Arm the Wood Cree chief had offered them room in his tent.

They were slogging on over the thin, spongy soil of the bush, everyone from Kitty up taking turns carrying smaller children. McLean had only one tent now and he and the stumpy cook Hodson packed it alternately on their backs; Louis Patenaude, bringing two tents up from the ravine after the battle, gave them one. Wandering Spirit had moved in with them. Balls of rain rolled down his curly hair as he carried tiny Larry between the dripping trees.

In the wet camp that evening the McLeans had nothing to eat until Amelia came with some flour and a bit of bacon fat given her by Wood Cree women; then they had to borrow a pan to fry it. Most of the Pitt plunder, food, furs, carts, blankets, had been left scattered about the brush in that scramble from the Little Red Deer valley. While they ate McLean told Kitty to ask Wandering Spirit what he thought they might now live on, since there seemed to be no game but rabbits and no camp their size could live on that. After a moment Wandering Spirit said, not lifting his head, that he wasn't hungry.

"Why did you leave all the food, Papa?" Duncan asked then.

"Hush," said Mrs. McLean.

"No, he's right to ask," said McLean. "We couldn't get carts through the trees, and cutting a trail would take too long. And if the Indians did that, the troops would know exactly where —"

"*If* they follow," said Kitty. "After running off just when they —"

"Kitty," said Mrs. McLean, her voice rising.

The sun rose clear and for two beautiful days the camp remained on the ridge between the Horse Lakes. Many warriors rode back again on the trail to Frenchman Butte while the girls helped Mrs. McLean boil clothes and the women fished and the children set snares for rabbits and chased ducklings into the shallows and pulled off their heads, though they were no more than balls of fluff and barely one mouthful. Duncan and Horsechild brought in eleven duck eggs very nearly hatched, which Horsechild enjoyed all the more for that, and a duck mostly bristles from her brooding. To Kitty the ridge seemed a park, clumps of birch scattered about bright grass on the hillsides. From where she and Amelia and Liza sat in the warmth with nothing to shade their faces except bandana handkerchiefs they could see Stanley Simpson's black head, a dot among the short rushes of the lake, and the gun he was holding above the water while he waited for a fat duck to come closer. Amelia said, "He's been absolutely motionless up to his neck in there for half an hour. He'll catch his death."

Liza said nothing. Kitty, though she could not avoid thinking of rescue sometimes, had at that moment decided again she absolutely didn't care if she never heard another gunshot in her life. The clouds were piled up white as if they'd scraped themselves flat blue against the hills. Toward evening of the second day the warriors returned waving rifles and bayonets they had picked up at the battlefield and laughing about the soldiers they had chased away. On the day of battle those cowards had run all the way to Fort Pitt, maybe further. They were herding some oxen as well, and drove carts piled with flour and blankets and lodge coverings. Little Poplar led a dance far into the night but an alarm near dawn roused everyone, fast, into a cold drizzle. All day they hacked their way north in a longer straggle than ever, though now McLean had an old ox to carry the tent and their few blankets and even Larry and Helen, held up on its back and crying when branches slapped water at their faces. Evening camp revealed that five halfbreed families, including John Pritchard's with Mrs. Delaney and Mrs. Gowanlock, had disappeared.

"James Simpson and I are the only bargaining power they have left, when the soldiers catch them," McLean told his family. "That's why they watch us so closely. It's too risky."

"Catch them!" Amelia snorted. "We'll walk out of here like we walked in, on our own. All the soldiers have done is make it more miserable, that's all."

McLean was trying to warm Larry in his arms. "Cut Arm hasn't done anything criminal, and he's had about enough. Just you keep telling him he'll get a big reward, we'll see to that."

They slept in their wet clothes and were ordered out again before sunrise. A haze rose around them in the rain and for some time each plodded on enveloped by his own personal mist as of loneliness. The creeks were swollen, the marshes abruptly bottomless of frost. Then in mid-afternoon the sky suddenly cleared; they came upon the blue ford at Loon Lake in sunshine. Only a few Plains People crossed; the rest set up against a ridge on a bit of prairie sloping to the lake. In that slightly dryer camp Kitty thought for a moment at sunset that she was happy. Some Indians were eating their dogs now but Stanley Simpson had killed two grouse and the boys a porcupine with sticks. She was almost alone for a moment when she went to dip water and a loon called far out on the lake so that it came to her clear and softly ululating on the glittering water before it lost itself in camp noise and she lay down in Cut Arm's crowded lodge unaware of the wet blanket or Liza shivering. But then she was startled into dawn by shouts growing louder, by Cut Arm leaping from his blanket and saw his brown body jerk and collapse just beyond the flap. Dead before either of his wives could shriek.

"Redcoats! Redcoats!" women and warriors were screaming.

"Dear God!" Amelia sobbed, and that was bursting in Kitty too but there was no space left to her mind for rational thought. She was whirling, flung and flinging herself about in a wash of excitement and terror that was the Indian camp under organized attack and individualistic defence. Her mind was insisting in a kind of calm frenzy that Cut Arm's private bullet must surely have been a stray one, that no police would possibly shoot into camp, and in fact no other bullet seemed to come so low again; most of them thudded into the lodgepoles or splattered tiny rips upon skins and canvas high above their heads and when the women had stripped the lodges down, sang off between bare poles and into the surrounding trees quite harmlessly. By then warriors were above them on the rocky tree-lined ridge to the west, their rifles spitting and muzzle-loaders puffing smoke over the disintegrating camp towards the police seen now as tattered flashes among the south trees, and Little Poplar galloped screaming across the camp, a little late and having mislaid his velveteen coat somewhere though his Winchester glinted as he swung it beautifully in the rising sun and quickly more warriors and boys and even old men streamed through the women and children dragging lodges and blankets and pots and babies down to the ford, the two movements of bodies threading each other like skaters passing, tangling into momentary snarls but arms and legs separating furiously while bullets yowled on and the war whoops of the approaching police sometimes outshrilled all else, even the dogs. Warriors held the swamp to the left, against the lake, very briefly but were slowly, steadily driven back towards the human and animal tangle at the ford. By then the small clearing lay washed bare by litter and rags and skins among the naked lodge cones and the police charged the ridge held by the warriors. Little Poplar was shouting there, rallying his men, the firing steady and about thirty police rushed the slope; in minutes they had gained the crest from which a torn scarlet body rolled, bounding down against rocks. The others pushed on, outshouting the warriors now, and soon Little Poplar and his men were sprinting between trees and willows towards the wide blue waters of the ford. Across it, tight to the water, lay another wooded ridge.

At that moment Kitty was in the ford. She had been safely across once, alternately pushing Liza who was trying to balance their one blanket upon her head while struggling through the chest-deep water, and shouting at Horsechild and Duncan who were, amazingly, clutched together astride Kingbird's black stallion and drumming its sides with their heels, beating and flapping while it whirled like a dancer about rocks and rushes. Suddenly the horse leaped, as it seemed to Kitty, over the head of The Black Stone with her child on her back and lodge-skin in tow, not into the ford but the lake where there was no footing whatever. It bobbed up, swimming, its narrow head thrust out like a submerged log while the two boys

sputtered up screaming with delight, their heads and still flapping arms above water. Kitty and Liza were across then,
Amelia jerking them up to the trampled brush under the ridge
and they stood gasping, looking across at the police uniforms
flash along the ridge.

"If they'd only, stop shooting," Liza sobbed, "the warriors,
surely give up!"

"Why don't we —" Kitty began, and then she saw Lone Man's
wife dart to the ford with Quinn's little girl clutching her back
and her own small son running at her hand. "It's four feet deep —
there she can't —" and she was in the water again, plunging
ahead as if she would swim in her water-sodden clothes before
Amelia or Liza could scream.

"Kit — te-e-e!"

There was nothing cold about the water this time. But
moving in it was very like a dream, stretch, stretch in despera-
tion but never quite touch, though she seemed instantly there
and already had the boy in her arms, Nowah-keetch crying
and shouting something, pushing him at her with the huge
dark eyes of the little girl staring across her shoulder. She
could not have believed how heavy the boy was; it wasn't at all
the boy she had packed for miles through mud, his weight
seemed to sink her at the very edge of the ford into slime
beyond its bottom and she had barely strength to turn, his
streaked face glaring into hers, leave alone stagger forward the
two steps that sank her in water, heaving her feet up though
abruptly the weight lessened and she could begin to move,
almost float it seemed. The boy moaned, his mouth clenched
and his expression unchanged but she could hear it welling
inside him with the bubble forming on the point of his nose.
He seemed to be trying to climb her, onto her head, so she
pulled him in down to his neck, against his muscles turning

rigid in the cold water and murmuring "Shu-shu-shu-shu" into his face but bodies hurtled about her then, the ford boiling with them as though they would splatter it dry while at the same time its water tore at her more violently than ever, startled into a current more fierce than the warriors, yes, it was warriors hurling themselves in everywhere about her. Two men gasped by with something on their shoulders like a log laid between them and red dripping on the white boiling water as they churned past, and watching those red plops instantly dissolve she was aware too of pockmarks all around her, popping on the surface of the water as if someone were showering her with pebbles. But these, she decided, hissed; as if the water tore and protested. She was, she had been moving her legs, the backwards boy parting water so close in front of her she could hardly focus on that white mucousy bubble growing larger and larger at his nose and with a terrifying suddenness like a scream the bubble itself vanished, flicked away by a hiss her staring eyes could not see and her head jerked back, her bandana flying from her blonde hair, the corner of her eye caught on a patch of scarlet behind her among the willows above the ford. She was motionless in the water, rigid, she and the child staring through each other, and she heard English:

"Good God stop! That's a white girl! Stop! Stop firing!"

She was aware then of noise because it sputtered down, into nothing. Kingbird was at her shoulder, pushing her up the incline of the ford to hands stretched for her through the speared rushes and then they were away from the treachery of brilliant water under gloomy, quiet trees. The boy was gone and Kingbird was still there running beside her. Running her in silence.

Between the lake and the wooded hills however, they were held. For three days she barely thought of it. The trees grew thick to the edge of the water, white palisades against green; the only way through for the few ruined carts was laboured cutting. Kitty wondered a little why they continued, warriors now chopping doggedly on until their soft hands blistered and they finally gained the protection of a peninsula guarded by swamp. On its rocky point she had found a short spit of blackish sand among rushes, away from camp where Wandering Spirit sat motionlessly gaunt by their fire, speaking to no one but her mother. Here the wind brushed away mosquitoes and she found she was contemplating all about her the far edge of Loon Lake, a crescent that heaved slightly and fell as if breathing, the shining three miles of water to the ford where the police had disappeared south again without crossing. She wished not to think about anything; and in that she was successful until it came to her she wanted to be warm again. Truly and completely warm; soaked with it. She opened her eyes to the sound of wind clattering the rushes and saw Big Bear standing there.

"Will you tell me the story now?"

"No," he said. She was startled at one of the People, especially him, speaking so categorically. "This is land like my grandfather came from, all trees and water. Far in the sunrise, not so long ago."

"Why not make canoes?" she asked, the water like sheet steel in the sun and her legs aching again from the suck of muskeg. He was looking out also, as if pondering the lake's polished flatness, the wrinkles of his face pinched together at the slits of his eyes.

"The River People are now horse People. Water is for getting over and a horse does that better than a canoe because it has a tail to hold onto."

"You get all wet with horse."

"Yes, but there's always the sun. Once I wanted to cross the river at Fort Pitt when I had no horse and someone dead now gave me a canoe. But that turned itself over, very fast. Too fast, and I had to walk out of the shallow water where it did that and back to all of them on the shore. A horse will take you far enough so you won't get laughed at."

Kitty thought a moment, weighing tone and words and for a moment her mind did not seem to be quite awake, there was something — and then she turned quickly away or she would have laughed. But behind her he laughed aloud, and then she could also.

"Your mother is a good woman and you are so much like a Person," he said, "but it is the nature of People to listen to everyone, even whites. And it is the nature of whites, I think, to laugh at a Person who accepts from a horse what he won't from a canoe someone has made."

"I wanted to — but I didn't want to," Kitty said. "You laughed first."

"Blackbirds build nests on rushes, why shouldn't you laugh."

She looked up at him, and he said it as an abstraction:

"With living things, they do what they do, and you laugh. With made things, you are humiliated."

She smiled her gratitude, then remembered what else he had said. "I want to be more like you. A Person," she added after a moment because he did not say anything looking over the water that a wind rumpled slightly, suddenly a wedge widening.

"Does that little man with the black hat ever laugh?"

He had never asked her anything before and for a startled moment she did not understand he referred to Hodson. Who even liked to wear his hat in the heat of the kitchen. "Yes," she said then, "he's been with us two years and he laughs, yes."

He seemed to be studying the lake, the muscles of his naked arm beside her like smooth tinted rocks. He smelled of smoke and sweat, sharply sweet; she felt her legs, arms, outer and inner parts of her whole body loosening as if they were clothes being unhooked. He was speaking then, saying a thing she heard his voice say several days later as if he were speaking aloud to her, then: "Blackbirds live by water and leave diving to the ducks." But here, where this water barely frothed against these rocks and sand she could not have said she heard it. All he said to her was,

"The Sun will warm you."

So she took off her clothing. Every piece that she had not removed the six days since they fled the Horse Lakes in rain, laying each aside and Big Bear picked it up and spread it over the rushes as though he were a woman drying clothes she had just washed. The blackish sand on her skin was cold, so horrifyingly cold she felt her stretched legs and body shrink to tiny, shivering worms but the sun bulged over her stark in the livid sky and heat began weaving loops of warmth about her. She felt herself becoming again, the farthest tips of her moving out towards fire until she knew herself too complete to comprehend, too enormous, each unknown part of her vastness she could not yet quite feel but which would certainly surround the whole earth bending back under her. And there was the heat, it rounded her head and he was passing over in his dance between the long green rushes, the curves of his massive chest ablaze above her, chant reaming the hollows of her head up through the sand that held her body and gradually arching her distended and enormous as if she were poised by planets rocking, singing her suspended while Sun devoured her warmer and warmer until she was suffused. Herself; completely; open and radiant. Held in his chant, rocked in his radiance.

"Words are not just sound," the old man said. "Now I will tell you the story of Bitter Spirit." And he did.

She never remembered a word of it, nor a situation. And he told her further of a certain man who, fasting, decided he must make a journey toward morning and who took with him three friends, each seeking a gift. They travelled east very far on a difficult trail before they arrived at a beautiful lodge on the top of a hill where the sun shone from morning till night and were invited in by one who looked like themselves, though he asked them neither where they came from nor where they were going. They rested there and ate his food, and then each made his request. One wanted success in love, and it was granted; one wanted success in hunting and war, and it was granted; one wanted wisdom in medicine and that was granted also. But the fourth, the one who had fasted, asked for nothing less than to live forever. At that their host looked at him for a long time, but he asked again and so his request too was granted. He was transformed into rock. Rock gives us the pipe by which we pray to The First One, for rock is the grandfather of all, the first of all being as well as the last.

She was beside him in fiery warm clothes, listening intently, her hair blonder then and not frizzed as it was later but very long and loosened as though incandescent about her shoulders and down her back; he squatting on his heels, she almost thought pulled together under that worn blanket. Two tiny figures on sand and surrounded by light.

"Remember," he said, and she had forgotten those words too.

A month later she saw him again; in Prince Albert when he was led out for his daily exercise. And she nearly heard his voice once more, his incredible voice. Friday, September 11, 1885 at Where The Bones Lie, though for over two years the place had been known officially as "Regina."

V

A Canadian Volunteer: Major-General Bland T. Strange with his Alberta Field Force had attacked Big Bear at a small creek near Frenchman's Butte and, as the Indian held the position while the general retired, the creek and valley were promptly named "Stand Up Coulee." I have seen the official report as I have seen the place and I daresay General Strange defeated Big Bear — the enemy is always licked — but why then did the general retire eighteen miles to Fort Pitt? Tactics, no doubt. He sends word to his commander (from whom he has not heard so much as a war whoop in four weeks of campaign) that he has run the enemy aground; several days thereafter he decides it advisable to find out, again, where the Indian is and discovers that the degraded and undisciplined savage, you know, has disregarded the most common courtesies of war, cut a road north and decamped; he may be on his way to the North Pole for all our general knows. That whole manoeuvre, like the tactics of the military generally in the North West Rebellion, requires an education rare in Canada to appreciate.

Howsoever, General Strange is camped at the coulee with Steele's Mounted Scouts out, Big Bear *et al* has vanished, and here is Commander-in-Chief Fred Middleton himself arrived at Fort Pitt with three steamboats by river and assorted cavalry by land early on the morning of Tuesday, June 2; to take personal charge of the campaign against the last rebel left in the field.

One might suppose that an immediate march to General S.'s camp would be in order, but no. We must pitch tents and a number of the infantry are forthwith ordered to manufacture packsaddles, although an excellent wagon trail exists. While the infantry is thus gainfully employed and we putter about horses and saddles, the Commander-in-Chief takes the day to compose a letter:

Fort Pitt June 2 1885

Big Bear:

I have utterly defeated Riel at Batoche with great loss, and have made prisoners of Riel, Poundmaker...[etc. etc.]. I expect that you will come in with all your prisoners (whom I am glad to hear that you have treated very well), your principal chiefs and give up the men who have committed the murders at Frog Lake. If you do not, I shall pursue and destroy you, and your band...[etc. etc.].

I believe Big Bear never received this fearsome missive; that may be due to the lack of general amenities, such as mailboxes for one.

About sixty packsaddles, so-called, are turned out and next day loaded on the wagons that follow cavalry and infantry out to meet the encamped general. The commander is heard to declare, "Not a man, not a man! Who is this Major Steele, it should not have been done!" even before he disappears into the tent and by noon Strange has struck camp and is marching his infantry north-west, towards Onion Lake it is rumoured, where no Indian has been reported in well over a month. At midnight a courier arrives: Steele has met and fought Big Bear at a lake some fifty miles north-east. By four a.m. June 4th we are on the trail, mounted men, infantry. Howard with his Gatling gun and of course, not to be forgotten, the packsaddles still carefully stowed in the wagon.

The noble red man, you must be aware, seems to have sadly degenerated since the days of Fenimore Cooper. The trail left by Big Bear is no moccasin track discernible only by the bruised leaf: it is a road cut through the woods much better than many a Canadian road, beaten by the feet of hundreds of horses and oxen and carts; over it horsemen could easily travel six miles an hour.

Not we of course. Three miles out we uncover a relic of the coulee exchange: the half-buried body of an Indian killed by the fragments of a shell. The only apparent casualty. Two miles further we strike an old cart trail from Fort Pitt leading north-east which the Indians have obviously followed. Such an extraordinary thing must be considered, by Jove. The boys unsaddle and rub down, anticipating another forty miles before camp, when lo the infantry tents go up and we are ordered to follow suit. And we're nailed to the spot till Saturday morning, two days later!

We have precise reports that within one good day's ride Steele with forty-six men has driven the Indians from their camp and is waiting our reinforcements; three wounded have come in, there is a cut trail along which supplies could be rushed while we ride ahead with three to five days' provisions to complete the enemy's demoralization, rescue prisoners and bring murderers to justice. But what are we ordered to do? The idiocy of packsaddles is not enough; we camp on that wide trail and two hundred men equipped as for battle are turned into a factory of "travails"!

A travail may be a mystery to many so I will attempt to describe one. Suppose two long poles between which a horse is harnessed as between cart shafts, the rear ends of the pole drag on the ground and the load is carried on cross-bars just clear of the horse's tail; that is simple enough, but to suppose how small a load can be so transported or what the antics of a horse accustomed to civilized saddle or harness will be, is another matter. All Thursday and Friday we cavort about with what

Indians themselves gave up as soon as ever they beheld a wheel, diverting ourselves by collecting again and once again our supplies from out of the willow bushes. By Friday evening the infantry has been sent back and on Saturday morning we rush forth to continue our forced march. The travails? They are packed on top the packsaddles on the wagons.

Our sudden speed may in fact be due to the news, received via courier from the rear, that except for the Hudson's Bay traders and their families, all prisoners have escaped the Indians, including the poor ladies Mrs. Delaney and Mrs. Gowanlock whose husbands were murdered at Frog Lake; all have arrived at Pitt without military benefit. Our commander, having neatly disposed of General Strange, may nevertheless yet discover there is no one left to hail his conquering approach. We give a cheer for the escaped prisoners and ride, otherwise seething.

Before we can halt for the day, that is within five miles, we come upon a little open patch and see, drawn up and waiting for us, Major Steele's Scouts. Bronzed by sun and wind, unencumbered by red tape, they have pursued and fought till down to their last bullet and are now returned to show us the way. We glance at our commander, of the build of Falstaff albeit somewhat brighter in complexion, and are again impressed by the vast advantage education confers on one. Here is Steele, poor ignorant devil of a big-shouldered Canadian with his sixty-five men away up in this blawsted, howling wilderness, you know, and no wagons, no tents, no military procedures, positively nothing. With us everything is done with dignity, a sense of the eternal fitness of things. Travails, packsaddles, wagons, Gatlings, surgeons, hospital and marmalade comforts; orders every night with unfailing exactness and "Mount!" in the morning never more than two hours behind.

Couriers carry despatches and special war correspondents from every major newspaper chronicle our advance, describe the terrible nature of our hardships so that all Canada must marvel, daily, at the indefatigable determination of our commander. After we meet Steele we ride another twenty-five miles.

Next day, Sunday June 7, the trail has fewer mudholes. It leads through dense poplar averaging the thickness of a man's arm, over rolling country with occasional ponds and marshes. There is hardly a mosquito or fly; clearer weather is seldom seen. We halt for noon near the Horse Lakes and, the wagons overtaking us, have the privilege of looking past our hard tack to the general tucking into fresh bread and jam.

Whenever we pass an abandoned Indian camp there is a general rush for loot and trophies. Until now none of this comes near to what Strange's boys told us they found at the coulee (one said the fur alone would average more than two hundred dollars each — if anyone had an average, haha), but early on June 7 the order comes down no one is to go ahead of the advance guard or leave camp after halting; we are getting close, obviously. That night we camp on the hill above Loon Lake ford where Steele fought and his generalship and aides proceed down into the Indian camp on a tour of inspection, the Mogul flattering himself that at last he is once again first man in. Steele of course had no transport, or time, for trophies. Visions of furs richer than his load at Batoche dance in his head when he sees something. A figure, moving among the bare tepee poles and he begins to wish for body guard, and Gatlings — what a prize the chief of soldiers would make for Big Bear. And the Army, lost without all that skill to manoeuvre it! The figure saunters into full view, and instead of the dirty blanket expected it wears a neat blue jacket with brass buttons, riding breeches into the pockets of which its hands are thrust, immense boots, and a forage cap tipped carelessly on the back of its head. Doubt and dismay! Nearer it comes, whistling, unarmed save for a pistol in its right boot, toes neatly turning over abandoned stores for examination. The general is deprived of all save offended dignity for the tune is "Yankee Doodle" and the man the very target of his orders: Lieutenant A.L. "Gatling" Howard, commander of our "patent murdering machine."

Who can forget a moonlit evening round the campfire. Firelight glints on polished rifles. "Gatling" Howard, whatever his countrymen may say of an American fighting against men supposedly struggling for their rights, has more than enough stories to turn the curls of an Ontario boy. A few of us have roughed it a bit before now, however, and one by one we venture our one moose again, stalk our bear if available, and some may even be hesitating on the brink of a Parolles analogy, out loud, but there are weathered faces all about under the wild, noisy spruce. We swallow literary thoughts with cribbage, drown them with the endless tea.

O Tea, thou sublime infusion of sloe leaves, brown paper, rags and general refuse, what is life without thee! How often hast thou revived our bodies when mercury shrivelled, or on summer plain hid the nauseous alkali under thy all-veiling scum. Who givest zest to the unfailing pork and beans of our native land, gladly for thee do we suffer and swear in impenetrable forests. Though the commissariat be manned by idiots, as it is, and we deprived of our dried apples, our bacon and sugar, our molasses and flour, but with thee, as we dissect the dark and bloody mystery that bears the name of Armour, as we break our last tooth on the so-called biscuits of Portage la Prairie, with thee in our bellies we can forget the imported old women that lead us, and manfully suffer. For we bloody well will.

The sight of Steele's battlefield has revived us and we lay our heads on our saddles this Sunday night with the hopeful prayer our commander at last will test our energy. And indeed, next morning the wagons are left behind, guarded by the Gatlings and French's scouts; even the general's spring mattress is to remain. We have three days' provisions and are in the saddle at six a.m. It is our turn to take the lead but in an instant the captain catches us up: new information has arrived. No one knows from where; perhaps via medium, but by nine-thirty we are already a hundred yards down the slope and almost at the ford. Before we reach it we notice a long bundle on a rack and one of us rides over. He cuts open the bundle but it is a warrior, not a prisoner as we feared. His friends must have returned for a hasty funeral. He is a disgusting object, our friend of the filthy slit blanket and little feathers, and we think of the Frog Lake settlers and are glad; he is a good Indian now. Our commander, passing, is forced to remember Steele's success and vents his jealousy with a muttered, "Some men are worse than savages," but issues no orders for proper burial of the dear departed. Nor did he ever at Batoche, I may add. We ford the narrow arm of the lake where Steele was stopped and ride into dense trees.

Abandoned carts lie everywhere along the trail between lake and hillside that is really impossible for them now. Within three miles we turn almost directly north, along a ridge between Loon Lake and another, un-named, where at another campsite we unearth three more bodies, none of them white. One is certainly a chief. As in all camps, here too are bits of boxes or wool tied to bushes that indicate prisoners were held here. The outlet of Loon Lake faces us, a river forty yards wide with a small wooded peninsula looking almost like an island beyond it. What with consultations and conferences, by the time we are over there is just enough daylight left to camp. We bivouac under the trees while the police scout around.

Revelations again. They find we are within fifty yards of the next Indian camp and from the warmth of some ashes deduce it could not have been abandoned earlier than that very morning! (I have seen the official report: "Evident traces and signs of Big Bear's having camped in the same place within 48 hours." Perfectly true; one could also as truthfully say he had camped there within 48 years.) We count 73 fire circles, which means some 560 Indians and therefore no more than 140 fighting braves. A swamp cuts off the peninsula west and north and where the trail enters it we find the huge body of an Indian woman. The poor creature lies in a sort of kneeling position facing the swamp, her body tilted forward so as to throw its weight on the raw-hide tied to a sapling by means of which, with horrifying determination, she has strangled herself. A dog stands as if guard over her and the faithful little brute snaps pathetically as we approach. It has the name "John Delaney" on its collar. Was she Delaney's servant, or perhaps the killed scout's wife? A policeman says she was just too fat to cross the marsh and the tribe deserted her when they heard us across the lake, approaching; she hanged herself in terror. Of us! We go back and lay our heads in our saddles under the spruce trees.

Orders for June 8: three days' provisions, early start. In earnest at last. And suddenly the night is shattered by a rifle shot! And another! Everyone has his rifle in hand now, waiting; hearts pound. But if anyone was green enough to expect a night attack he is disappointed: the shots were cartridges falling out of a belt into the fire over which it was drying.

Perhaps the sound of a shot, so long unheard, recalls our commander to a remembrance of the many lives in his charge. Who may say for certain, but certain it is that after turning out at an unholy hour, we ready and our wretched horses kept saddled under the spruce where, as everyone knows, there is excellent forage, after three hours we are informed, never having advanced a foot, that the marsh is impassable for us. We explode a number of imaginative expressions among the mosquitoes, turn our ponies out to feed along the swamp and are at leisure to explore. The terrain ahead actually does look bad; about a mile of that ugly muskeg between us and the high ground north, but there are scattered willows, in places even frost several feet below the surface. Obviously Big Bear has gotten his entire camp through, are we less than children, women? We have sufficient leisure to decide about that, and also that no such swamp would stop a Canadian but in Ottawa's sublime wisdom our disposer is none such. We walk south, along the shore to the rocky point of the peninsula. Glasses here show the entire shore-line we have followed, the ford where Steele was stopped, the heavy woods on the steep east shore, the river outlet to the point where we now are, and a bit of the swamp: a trail clearly meant to distress any old woman. Even more important, from this spit of blackish sand covered with moccasin tracks the west shore is easily studied. It shows itself high ground with scattered timber and we are certain wagons, Gatlings and all could traverse that side to pick up the trail again north of the swamp. We return to camp, send a delegate to the Mogul's tent, and discover a few of the boys have gone fishing.

While we chew fish and ravage mosquitoes, in the camp's only tent a solemn conclave gathers. A brilliant lot: a major-general, a captain of Royal Engineers, an infant lieutenant, an

Indian Department assistant commissioner and a major of the militia. Each knows less than the other; our delegate is heard and dismissed; Steele and Herchmer are not asked for opinions as our disposer does not admire the Mounted Police. It is at last decided that tomorrow we will continue pursuit straight north in the troop order Boulton, Steele, Dennis, Herchmer. This every man can translate for himself: Boulton is Steele's senior and therefore in command; Steele must wait for Boulton, who supports his pants with red-tape and never stirs until he has signed orders in his pocket. Dennis simply fills in with bodies, but Herchmer, well, Herchmer is Boulton's senior, and he must be placed last or else he is in command and that means he will have his mounted men across that swamp before our Mogul has completed arrangements about jam for dinner.

June 9 sunlight through the spruce finds us mounted again and waiting. At length our general emerges, mounts his grey charger, paces to the head of the columns. A long very erect consult with Boulton and aide; finally two of Steele's halfbreed scouts are ordered forward and they ride into the muskeg. We watch as they struggle, fight from willow to willow, man and horse labouring together, and they get through! We cheer them till the branches shiver. But the general raises his arm for silence and himself rides forward; his personal bravery is beyond question — as a captain in the Hindu Mutiny of 1858 he was recommended for the Victoria Cross — but his wisdom in riding there before all his paraded troops is not. The horse is gigantic, as it must be to transport him, and no more acquainted with swamp than its rider. In a moment he is in to his stirrups and a couple of Steele's Bow River cowboys are unlimbering their lariats, all agrin at the prospect of snaking that eminence out of there and the rest of us ready to curse them into immobility, but the horse is too strong anyway. He flounders back out, heaving, all amuck and that is the last of that. Shortly after noon the two scouts struggle back with the report that the trail divides north and east; the Royal Engineer is busy constructing a footbridge over the outlet river and next morning, June 10, we swim our horses back and walk over the bridge with our saddles. Our progress thereafter is a feat unexcelled in the annals of Canadian military retreats: our trail literally smokes behind us with burned bridges, carts stolen by Indians (in perfect usable condition but which "in accordance with military usage" must be destroyed, you know), flour, blankets, travails and, of course, packsaddles so-called, all smoking. We are at Fort Pitt in time for supper on June 11.

O infantry, thrice blessed in being twice ignored! After a day of reading mail we poor devils of mounted men must carry out one more daring stroke. The Chipewyans in the north have come in to Strange and surrendered at Beaver River; since Otter has moved north from Battleford and Irvine from Prince Albert, Big Bear may now be caught in a pincer movement between them and forced out, south, so of course we ride into the unmapped wilderness after General Strange, north! The most we discover is a cache of thirty bags of flour, already guarded by Strange's men be it said, and a week later two Indian couriers catch up with us and interrupt a small fishing expedition our commander has organized on Cold Lake with the information that the McLeans, Simpsons, and all other white prisoners have been released by the Wood Crees; they have no supplies and are trying to reach Fort Pitt. The transport officer, Bedson, is sent to meet them and we ordered an immediate return to Pitt; our peerless leader is himself before us in a high-speed buckboard to make certain he will be on hand to receive their thanks.

As it is, all the troops are at Pitt by June 20 and the prisoners come in two days later. The entire plateau around the half-rebuilt houses, where Morris and Sweetgrass once performed the ceremony of Treaty Six, is covered with men and infantry tents, supplies, horses, and two steamers are still tied up against the bank of the river where Dickens fled. Middleton has his spring mattress etc. aboard the *Marquis* and there Factor William McLean, 62 days a captive with his pregnant wife and seven small children, and two servants, presents him with an ancient peace pipe from the Wood Cree. They were most reluctant participants in rebellion, their great chief is dead, but they have protected the whites from the savage Plains Cree of Big Bear. And our terrifying Mogul of the Mustaches accepts the pipe! By June 24 the Wood Cree are coming in, bringing with them some Plains ringleaders that include Wandering Spirit of the curly black locks who murdered Quinn and out-generaled Strange at Stand Up Coulee. The first night at Pitt this killer begins to moan in what is called a death chant; after a time he stabs himself. He is messily inaccurate about where his heart is however and since he did it properly in the full circle of braves, these rush for the surgeons. They push Curley's lung back into his chest and sew him up neatly; he will doubtless live to hang.

"Gatling" insists this is the first Indian war in the western hemisphere ever fought without liquor; perhaps the first war of any kind, ever anywhere on earth. He says he hasn't been so dry since he learned to switch bottles on his mother. An oldster tells him no Canadian army drinks; when they marched with Wolseley against Riel at Fort Garry in 1870 the column was so dry they called Wolseley, thin as he was, General Teapot. That strikes a roar; certainly our elephantine eminence deserves such title on silhouette alone. The campfire brightens. The lack of women is again bewailed in detail; the cleaner squaws seem generally petrified, with fear that is (roars), the few whites married except for the three McLean girls — pretty enough though so bronzed one begins to wonder, and — well, I confess to lewd guffaws that I had manoeuvred Miss Kitty around into the partial shadow of a steamer smokestack and the only thing she had to offer was that the Indians had been hungry enough to eat 428 of their dogs!

The laughter about our fire draws others and songs, dances are rolling out under the moonlight on the river hills. "Gatling" carols again the praises of his machine working the Indians of Montana: when wolf willow and sage is mowed level, you know there's no more than grasshoppers left breathing there, and mighty few of them. A breed come in with the Wood Crees is half-dancing a jig, rolling his eyes and laughing exploits. He speaks good English, wears a fine belted coat and starts to tell us we were so close behind them one night they heard two gunshots from our camp. We howl at each other, remembering June 8 and our diddling before the swamp. We crowd around and he, nothing loath, rattles on about their crossing when suddenly an English halfbreed pushes through, grabs him by the shoulder and spins him around.

"Pierre Blondin! Where'd you get that coat?"

From the fast white roll of his eyes I know Blondin's guilty. The newcomer yells this is the beast that bought Mrs. Gowanlock from the Indian who killed her husband but when John Pritchard made him put her in with his family and the other woman, protected, he tried for two months to get at her and one night almost dragged her out under the tent before Pritchard shot at him — look, that's John Gowanlock's coat — and he tears it open. In the firelight I see something like "JAG," maybe, embroidered on the inside pocket. I glance around once and we're on him. His clothes are flying in shreds and when he breaks out, screaming, he's mother naked. He's fast but he hasn't a chance, we've got him headed for the river, the boys coming with a shout from everywhere and the first of us beside him stride for stride between the tents and wagons and over duffle and my riding quirt takes some solid bits out of his tan ass as he runs and some on the other side and behind with willow switches that work him damn near as good. Towards the river he stops sounding off, suddenly, just runs bloody and his moccasins are too much for my boots so I dive at him, feet legs belly I've got him and the boys working his head and some his legs while I'm peeling him apart in the middle wherever my fingers can get in, then I've really got him where he'll never forget it and a sound comes out of him high this time, and thin like a gopher just before he's hit by a weasel; he's jerking like he's made of cut string, down the bank jerk jerk and a steamer wall faces us, dropped there, and out of a hole in it rises a huge red face surmounted by a woollen nightcap.

"What's that?" the face bellows. "Men?" It's the Mogul!

So the surgeons got Blondin too. We found out next day. As a matter of fact, in three months of war I don't think the military all told actually finished more than thirty maybe thirty-five of the bastards, breeds and Indians put together. The official report says eighty-four, but you know what you can do with that.

VI

West above the centre of Turtle Lake the clouds were heaped in bright flounces, foam streaked with dirt, but below that they seemed supported by a horizontal wedge faintly brownish-yellow like a long polished stone anchored at its tapered end in a thin spit of trees on the curve of beach to the north and at its broader end by the opposite, even thinner, shore. Between this stone and the fading shore rose stubby blackish and purple columns, sheathed in changing grey on their inner curves, interlaced bars and beams like an immense neglected scaffold hurled over the water and sometimes lightning split through those beams into the lake; then they could hear the sound of it too, as of gigantic construction going on there which would never be completed in time.

Horsechild said, "I have a little stone."

"This is good land to get away from someone," Big Bear said without looking at the boy beside him on the sand, "but it's always too close in front of you to see. Even at the edge of lakes trees look over your shoulder."

"Here it is," Horsechild said, and placed the stone in his father's hand. It was an almost perfect half of a globe, the edge of its flat side softened around as if carved and polished. Over its roundness curled a blue line. Big Bear turned it between his fingers slowly as if it were an eye and he were trying to peer through it into the head only momentarily missing. Horsechild continued,

"It was by her foot, by that swamp where The One Who Fills Her Seat choked herself."

Big Bear had to lift his head back in order to see white clouds trundling above him. "That's the way," he said. "For women sometimes everything is given so easily."

"She was still moving a little and the dog wanted to bite Duncan, but he kicked it. Then it stayed away and we could watch her, and this was by her foot."

Big Bear continued to stare into the sky moving up like water.

"I've held it every night," said Horsechild. "In my last sleep somebody came to me in a dream and invited me to come along. I was walking along behind him and the willows got too thick, and muskeg, and when I got out into a clearing, on the north side of it, he was far ahead on the south but I couldn't get there before he was gone." He kicked at the sand. "I couldn't trail him, he didn't have tracks."

His father fondled the stone and the boy waited, grooving circles into the stark-white sand about his feet and then lines radiating until he seemed to squat in interlacing suns, but shivering a little for the heat had gone from the long day; and the sand too. He did not like the lake hoisting that blackness up out of the west. He did not like lakes at all, and they had been camped forever by this one. Open space impossible to walk, that swallowed you bent. More than a day he had stood in the sunlight of the rocky point with a fish spear but he hit nothing; the treacherous water bent his point aside the instant they touched.

"It's hardly half a moon yet since we crossed that swamp," said Big Bear thoughtfully.

"Is it fast?"

"He'll come again. It's the land, it's so close around we're walking in it and can't see. We aren't Wood People, we are the River People of the plains and that's where he wants to show you something. Have you started to dream power before?"

"No, and not fasted either."

Big Bear laughed, rising as though his old body were unfolding itself from the sand. "Fish and little ducks are no fast, truly. Nor the porcupine that came with Kingbird today."

"Wah!" the boy exclaimed jumping up, reaching for the stone.

"He'll come again," Big Bear said, "but perhaps you can follow him far enough only on the plains." He stood a moment, staring across the water stippled by wind and then up to the clouds, their brownish-yellow blanched to white and grey and re-arranged now into one sagging belly that contained the sky, about to burst over them. "Come on," as the lake was suddenly wiped away in a rush.

They trotted up the sand but as they sprang to the ledge of black soil above it the hail ran up, over them; ahead through the poplars like a herd of horses into brush. They crouched under a spruce, Horsechild sitting between his father's knees as though he was not yet as tall as he, and when the ice had passed they ran on in the rain. The Magpie and Nowah-keetch were bent under a blanket trying to protect the fire a little in the open glade; in the bark shelter half torn away and rattling Kingbird and All And A Half still knelt for gambling as if the blanket had not been pulled out between them. "Even his water is icy, the Blue Thunder's whipping us," shouted Big Bear, backing under the bark, shaking rain from his grizzled hair. Horsechild dug into the blankets and hides where Quinn's girl and Lone Man's smallest son cowered. No one said anything.

The rain moved over the glade like slate falling, slabs over slabs; the two women staggered a little, the smoke of the fire churned up gradually darker despite The Magpie's efforts with splintered sticks she sheltered against her body. Water fairly bounced as if shot out of the ground speckled in ice, and then suddenly sunlight cut level under the trees washing all over in blazing red and the rain stampeded east through the poplars. Thunder rolled and crumbled.

"There's nothing to eat yet," The Magpie declared, dropping the blanket. "Half a fire and no roots." A dog emerged from under the dripping trees, edging towards Nowah-keetch who had the smoky fire breaking into flames again, but The

Magpie shrieked, "Just come, just you come and I'll throw you into the pot too! Shaking your water, there's enough here!" The dog hesitated, slunk away before she hurled the stick.

After a moment into the glistening sunshine of the clearing Quinn's wife appeared; Lone Man's oldest child, Born Upside Down, followed her and they went to the fire to empty the roots out of their skirts into the pot. As the women squatted, watching the fire struggle up, Lone Man and his son Muttered came out of the bushes from the north. The strange evening light blazed the wetness of their faces and chests, gilding them between black hair and blacker leggings as they walked. They went directly to the fire; Nowah-keetch thrust a stick into the pot and fished out a bone partly covered with meat. At Lone Man's gesture she passed it to her son. Muttered was looking past her to the shelter but when Horsechild, sitting there now beside Big Bear, continued to stare motionlessly ahead the boy took the meat, accepted the Winchester Lone Man held out to him and walked back the way they had come. The bone steamed faintly, wisps breathing between fingers and teeth.

"There's plenty of grass in that slough for four horses," said Lone Man.

"My black like the white mare yet?" asked Kingbird.

"Enough so he won't hop very far. She's on the long rope."

"A hobble has never held him; he can hop half a day's running in a night when he smells something he likes."

Big Bear said suddenly, "He was strong enough for any four mares when Sweetgrass gave him to me. Ah yes."

"Winters don't bother him, but bush and slough grass — he needs that big mare here."

"She's still got all the iron Henry Quinn put on her hoofs, he'll feel it."

"Nine winters since then," said Big Bear. "Nine winters since Sweetgrass was so happy for the treaty, and nine since he left for the Hills."

Mrs. Quinn had dug her tiny Sarah, and also Lone Man's Wolfboy out of the blankets under the birch shelter. Sits Green On The Earth came dragging a bundle of wood she had somehow kept partially dry under the bush. Kingbird watched her carry her stomach across the clearing; she tilted back against it, legs apart and feet turned outward as if she could now barely walk, the child so low and heavy in her.

"Wandering Spirit won't need that mare any more," said Lone Man. "So I took it, it should be hers now." Looking at his niece, Quinn's wife, who with Nowah-keetch was shaking out the few blankets. Drops sprayed in the sunlight, dusting colours. "At Fort Pitt he was singing, 'All who wish to look on me once more, come now!' And then he stabbed himself but couldn't finish it, such a big warrior."

"Did you go to see him then?" asked All And A Half.

"That big killer, vows and everything, always stuffed more in his mouth than he could chew, what was he to see?"

"He sent to Seenum at —"

"Seenum! We needed Americans more than Seenum. If you want to fight, fight to wipe out, with everything you can find."

"He almost sent tobacco to them," All And A Half murmured and Lone Man grinned at him sardonically.

"Yeh, and they'd sure smoke our willow stuff."

"Nine winters, at Fort Pitt," said Big Bear. "That's the place where Sweetgrass made the first treaty marks for River People. Do you remember that, those hills of Fort Pitt?"

"No," said Horsechild. He was gazing into his father's face as if he would plant himself there if only he could.

"You were very little then and ran to Red Bone when he called children to come see Sun go to sleep. The leaves were turning yellow, and the buffalo had started to come north."

"The earth," Lone Man said, "was covered there with soldiers' tents now, and those smoking boats on the river. I listened to everything and some Wood People told me more but didn't show my face, not where I could see the place where the policeman Loasby pretended to be dead. I took his gun and bullet-belt away from him, lying there shivering like a poor little fawn when you've killed its mother, that big policeman! Hey-Hey-Hey-Hey!" Lone Man screamed suddenly. "The police and the McLean girls all shooting from the fort and bullets spitting and my heart was shivering but not one dared touch me, and I took his gun away. Unfortunately I had already killed his horse He-e-e-e-e-ey — Hey!"

Distantly from the east thunder echoed him.

"Get more wood," said The Magpie and Born Upside Down moved.

"Wuh, that was a fight!" All And A Half roared. "Big Bear and Little Poplar keeping Straight Tongue McLean away from Wandering Spirit and those crazy police trying to ride through there. Not far from where you took that gun there were three young men standing by that Cowan with bloody hands eating heart, just then! I saw them."

Big Bear said in half-chant, "Truly truly, on the hills of Fort Pitt is the place to eat heart."

Even the women shaking the last blanket stopped to stare at him.

The happiness was suddenly wiped off Lone Man's craggy face. "Yes," he said quietly. "But it was good The First One let me feel that one more time. A warrior of the River People."

"Sing," said Big Bear. "Sing."

Lone Man's face changed and he sang the song of his last and greatest coup. Of riding under the very guns of his enemies, of taking a man's weapons from him while he was alive, a man wearing police decorations; sang so loudly that when he ended he was answered by his twelve-year-old son guarding the horses beyond trees; answered by happy cries of the ten River People in the camp, down to the very children and Big Bear's voice leading them all in acclamation. And then The Magpie had words to complete their laughter.

"There's food to eat now," she said.

Eating meat even when it was mixed with half-raw roots to thicken its soup was too rare a pleasure to spoil with talk. The lone dog lay at the edge of the clearing, head along its front paws, waiting. Women and children ate when the men had been served; the girl returned with brush and scraped out the last bits and coating in the pot. The Magpie brought to Big Bear his worn pipe.

The old chief stroked bowl and pipestem, rock and wood, the grooves and grains and smell of it. There was nothing but willow bark in his pouch and he was preparing that when Lone Man handed him a short twist of black tobacco. He carefully shredded tobacco and bark together into the bowl; Kingbird laid a coal in it and Big Bear lifted himself erect. Standing in their small circle he offered the bowl to the four cardinal directions.

"You First One, Spirit of All, you have given food and tobacco once more, we thank you. Only One, have pity on every human being who is poor like we are."

He sucked the coal to glowing, held the smoke in his mouth while he faced round the circle again, and then sat down. Lone Man accepted the pipe.

"Have all our people that went north gone in to Fort Pitt?" Big Bear asked.

"When the fat soldier that rubbed out Riel accepted the pipe of the Wood People from Straight Tongue, they were across Beaver River and they heard that and many came in too. But not Miserable Man and Four Sky Thunder." Lone Man inhaled deeply and passed the pipe to Kingbird.

"Those two," said All And A Half, "are in the east now. I met them and told them where Little Bad Man and Little Poplar were going south. But I don't know if they'll meet them. They had only one travois horse."

Kingbird snorted. "Miserable Man won't walk to the border, not carrying his belly."

"The evening I left," Lone Man said, "the soldiers called out names. That bow-leg Cameron told them to them."

All And A Half accepted the pipe. "Wandering Spirit always said he saw too many white faces in camp."

There was a momentary silence, Big Bear alone looking at his former councillor. Suddenly he said in the dreamy tone Horsechild knew he used when it was necessary to say something he did not like, "A warrior of the River People sings it to the whole world when he has killed with honour. Whom did they call out?"

"They already had Wandering Spirit, in his blanket on that big boat," said Lone Man. "He came with the Wood People and when our people came in the soldiers lined up and called out Bad Arrow, Little Bear, Round The Sky, Iron Body, Charlebois, Dressy Man and Thunder."

"Thunder?" asked Kingbird, startled.

Lone Man shrugged, looking at Big Bear, who said,

"Thunder was running around, he was seeing everything."

"Cameron didn't see anything," said Kingbird. "He was

walking away towards the camp very slowly with a lot of woman's clothing over his head."

"He saw it start," said Big Bear, "and he heard the warriors singing. He knows no Person will deny what he has done, it was done where anyone could see it and almost every man there was jumping to get into it and the women sang them in the scalp dance that evening. White law is the way it is because Whiteskins are liars; Little Pine and I saw that with He Speaks Our Tongue last summer. Whiteskins say they haven't done something even when they have and so their chiefs have to get everyone who saw something to talk so they can at last find who actually did something. That's why they want Thunder, and others, because they know some River People have finally learned to be liars too."

The slow dreamy darkness of the northern summer was seeping under the trees from the glazed sheet of lake, half-darkness as of eyes drooping to the song of mosquitoes delighted in the damp air. Sits Green On The Earth had brought a grey bit of bear fat to Kingbird and he was rubbing it hard over his face and shoulders. Where he sat, All And A Half shifted a little while Big Bear talked, as if he was uncomfortable. Momentarily the tips of trees, cloud bottoms racing across the sky were overlaid with planes of colour as if the last edge of the sun was hacking them open.

"Big Buffalobull Irvine is two days north-east of here," All And A Half changed the direction of talk. "At Green Lake, with over a hundred men through the bush but he won't smell anything. And the soldier who attacked Poundmaker, from Battleford, camps by Birch Lake. He must have more than three hundred, the big meadow is covered with their wagons."

"And horses?" asked Kingbird.

"You should see them, big and fat, they carry those thick Whiteskins all day almost without sweating."

Kingbird laughed, "Little Poplar will dream about them."

"I don't know," said All And A Half, "there's so many soldiers —"

"The Master there is called Otter," said Lone Man. "I heard that."

"Birch Lake is a good camp," said Big Bear. "His men came here and rode and walked up this side of the lake and some were on the other side too. We saw them signalling across. I thought perhaps they would find us but they were looking for more than one lodge. And that muskeg would have made their nice clothes dirty."

"Muttered and I were in a spruce tree," exclaimed Horsechild, "just across the slough and they rode under us, so many wagons and guns too we almost got tired sitting there."

Lone Man said, "If one of them had looked up he would have seen only a squirrel."

"A spruce grouse," Big Bear said. "Flying away." Everybody laughed at the soldiers, except Lone Man and The Magpie. She was rubbing her gaunt arms with the bear fat.

"Even after rain around the buffalo," she muttered to herself while staring at Big Bear, "there were never mosquitoes."

"If those soldiers poked around on the other side of the lake," Lone Man said, "maybe they met Chaqua-pocase and Oska-task, somewhere, with the horses I sent."

"Oska-task?" asked All And A Half.

"They left with five horses, three had flour and beef we helped the soldiers at Pitt with, they had too much to watch carefully and far too much to carry anywhere. They were bringing that here while I stayed at Fort Pitt, but where are they?"

"Bare Neck said the soldiers have Oska-task at Birch Lake. He heard that once, listening by their camp."

"Then those soldiers are eating the beef," said Kingbird heavily. "I don't think they got Chaqua-pocase on Delaney's horse."

"No," said All And A Half. "They only had one of them, and maybe he'll catch up to Little Bad Man and those going to Milk River."

"They'll try to get that far," asked Lone Man, "over the Line?"

"They were starting the morning I said I was coming here, two days ago this morning."

"Who was starting?"

"Little Bad Man and all those, everybody, Little Poplar, Bare Neck, The Pigmy, Lucky Man, you know, all of them."

"I think," said Big Bear, "tomorrow morning it will be time to start to think about visiting Twin Wolverine in the Peace Hills."

"How often have the trees heard me say that?" The Magpie exploded suddenly. "How often? But I just talk to trees!"

Lone Man did not look up with the others; he was looking down ino the darkness at what he perhaps held in his hands. Dusk had risen from the ground and his gaunt face emaciated by days of pursuit and bush riding seemed to float up bodilessly in it. He said, "There is the last thing I have to tell you, of what I heard at Fort Pitt."

Even The Magpie stared at his tone.

"Twin Wolverine has been dead since before we fought the soldiers at Frenchman Butte."

"Tell us," Big Bear said, after a time.

"Seeming Glad came to Fort Pitt with that, though he was ordered to stay with Bobtail on his reserve because they had taken something from the Hudson's Bay Company there when they heard what Wandering Spirit started. Twin Wolverine didn't take anything; he was coughing at home then, and he went to the Sand Hills coughing."

After a much longer time Big Bear said, "It would seem many trees now grow between Buffalo Lake and the Peace Hills."

He would remain silent now, Twin Wolverine his second elder son to die before him, and his last wife began to keen. The Magpie's voice rose to a high, thin, wail that held itself, shivering slightly; Nowah-keetch, full sister, followed; then Sits Green On The Earth, wife of the half-brother, and Quinn's wife who had no son to mourn. Their sorrow burrowed into the darkness about them, tunnelling through, and over the vacant lake; and then Born Upside Down also in the far bushes, feeling her woman's blood stir for the uncle who might have cared for her until a man would want her. Horsechild looked pleadingly across his father's knees to Lone Man, but he signalled "stay" as he stood up; Kingbird made no move. All And A Half rose; he and Lone Man walked across the firelight towards Muttered with the horses. Watching them go Horsechild saw the sky had been driven clean of clouds and between the innumerable stars it glowed with the pale wolverinish shimmer of early summer that told him the ghost dancers must be lurking just below the black wall of trees, flexing themselves gently, ready to leap up, over them. He shuddered, moving his thigh to touch his father's; the darkness pounded him with mourning. He clutched his little stone more tightly.

".... the Red Ochre Hills, riding towards the mountains where the sun sleeps. It was late in the Moon of Falling Leaves but Sun was warm and the dry grass happy at so many ponies of the People and Young Dogs and Assiniboines riding together in a wider, longer line than the land had ever seen. We crossed the Red Deer above the Forks but Chief's Son's Hand had no message for me, though I prayed there and the buffalo came to us and the others ate fresh hump and liver until their bellies hung so full they couldn't have lifted an arm if the Blackfoot had charged screaming, and then we rode towards the falling sun, Little Pine and Piapot, and Star Blanket of the House People, were on those horses, and Little Mountain and Foremost Man and Grizzly Bear's Head and Little Horn and Red Pheasant and Lean Man, and all their strong young men dancing every night while they sharpened knives and braided ropes, and the two with yellow hair from the Sutherlands of Parkland People rode and danced there too, Yellow Hair and Curly Hair with their young men. These two laughed more than anyone and could break any arm just by twisting it, they were so strong, and riding with me too was Bear Son, already a Rattler, and Twin Wolverine and Little Bad Man, on his first war trail. And Wandering Spirit too, so young then he had never lifted a scalp and barely dropped a buffalo...."

Horsechild could feel the blue line in the stone he rubbed; it lay under his fingers as if it were a ridge, a groove wrought by his father's voice singing. The men and horses, blacker clumps of darkness, had formed out of the dripping trees at the rim of the clearing; he could hear their snuffle. Big Bear's voice rose steadily towards the brightening sky. Lone Man was there, beyond the fire, and Muttered too, reddish bits of them leaping an instant.

"....always war dance and the night after we rode through the Bow River where it joins the Belly so small over its rocks it begged us to cross without getting our horses' hocks wet, there the Great Parent of Bear came to me though I had unwrapped nothing, had not sung the song he once gave me or scratched my face with fresh clay. He came to me as he never had come before, and showed something I had to think about two days. The warriors hunted in the long coulees, and danced, until I could talk to them. 'My children, I have seen a buffalo bull with iron horns goring, stamping a warrior who wore the feathers of the People; we charged it but could not kill it. It ran us with its iron horns leaving something like one slice of blood there. This is the Great Parent of Bear who gave me Chief's Son's Hand telling us we should go back, now where we come from. There is something too big ahead.' And some believed that and picked up their guns. . . . "

Sits Green On The Earth tilted her head a moment to rest on Kingbird's shoulder; the other women wailed their thin weaving of sound around Big Bear's lament. "This one in here," she whispered, "is bumping like he wants to get out tonight." The fire ran its tiny tongues against the darkness, and suddenly Kingbird lifted his hand, drew his finger down the middle of her forehead, nose, mouth, chin, throat, between her breasts and over the globe of her stomach and across her hand on it and down into the hollow between her thighs; she felt him there like a knife-point, the edge of his nail down her face and hand as if he had split her, completely. His voice at her ear,

"If that one is white, bring him here anyway."

" . . . . 'never like this before,' that chief said whose name I will never repeat for The First One has given me to forget it, 'they are flowery red and rotting from the White Sickness, there is hardly anything left in a Blood camp but hungry children and whatever is left we'll stretch on the ground, hairless, forever. Don't believe this dream, my children. We'll finish them forever, we'll ride their horses after the buffalo wherever we please when we finish this.' So only a few went back, and I went forward with Bear Son singing for happiness and Little Bad Man smiling too but Twin Wolverine beside me said nothing, just looked into my face but I rode forward with my bundle, with them, against what the Great Parent of Bear had shown me. Some thing was in me from The Evil One, bigger than any in my long life, or ever after. And when we camped at the Little Bow Crossing, barely enough water in it for all our horses to drink in the evening we sent scouts ahead in yellow paint. It was getting dark and Little Pine started to sing about his dreams; we all listened, and suddenly a coyote yelled on the plain behind us. It was so flat, there was no place to hide up there and when he stopped singing I handed the pipe to Little Pine. He held it, and suddenly he said to Twin Wolverine, 'What did that coyote say?' Twin Wolverine said, 'There's a hard time coming, you better go home.' Bear Son said he had come to find Bloods and Siksikas, and Little Bad Man said nothing; he wasn't even a Worthy Young Man yet. Little Pine looked at me and said, 'You know, you can't always believe Coyote. Wait till the scouts come back.' So we did not listen, but every man told his friends what bad he had done so that if he did not return and his deeds were sung in memory, no one could say there was something secret, something hidden left to blacken the glory of his going, his war cry and his own name the last sound he uttered. And early in the morning before the sun awoke the scouts found some Bloods camped in their favourite valley on the Belly River, where it bends south a little at the place they now have to call Many Ghosts. They saw only a few tents, the sun wasn't up when they looked into the mist along the river so they stole a few good horses and came back. We saw them riding back and forth, wildly, as they do when the enemy is close, on a long ridge between the south and north bends of the river waving to us as the sun came up red on the straight land and we saw them circling and the tops of far mountains lay white with winter under their horses' bellies. An easy camp, asleep. So when we looked at each other we heard our hearts talking with happiness...."

Kingbird's hand remained there and Sits Green On The Earth could not breathe. Big Bear's voice rumbled on; she could feel the baby straining inside her as if it were no longer the boned body she had felt growing; rather a wave, beating, again and again, and she longed to collapse under its power, fall back and spread herself open and groan, let it wash from her clean; but she couldn't move. His words more than his finger nailing her down there. And he was talking, in a hollow slowness as if pulling the words one after the other out of a gigantic hole inside himself and having to stretch in further and further, barely able to reach them,

"Bare Neck shot him first, Bad Arrow dragged his wife away...sold her to Pritchard for two horses, who would want such a dry thing...I wouldn't have shot him."

"I thought you never knew. He came again and —"

"I love you too much," he said so slowly, "you're too much woman, to let go and I thought if nobody knows I can share her, he such a miserable big man full of blood and that dry stick between his blankets, but some men started to laugh at me, there was only one way I could get over it. It was a hard thing. I would have sent you to him then, if my brother and Wandering Spirit hadn't started that."

" .... forty lodges no more than prairie grass to a running fire. Above them we yelled in Blackfoot 'We are here!' and galloped down those coulees clean and came out bloody on the river bank, around and around like a devilwind and only a few of the women and children got below the river bank, trying to hide there because the water was too low to hide a pebble and one big woman on the bank killed three warriors with her axe and her right arm was shot away and she picked up the bloody axe in the hand she had left and killed Blackstone too, in the middle of his song, before Little Bad Man opened her with his knife from behind and let her great spirit go. There was a worthy scalp from each side of her head; none of us had ever seen such a Blood woman that could send four warriors to the Hills. I knew it was better than a dream just to hear her last cry. A-a ha he ha, a-a ha he ha. There were only a few men left there and we were busy with them when some started shouting and pointing north where a long ridge bent down tight to the river: Blood warriors, and Piegans with them. A long line boiling up there against the blue sky, more and more, and we stopped jerking off those last scalps and watched them, circle, guns spitting into the air with the quick sharp bark of American Winchesters and more all the time and then I saw the man lying in front of me had one of those shiny new guns too and I only had a flintlock in my left hand and a short knife in my right. A song began up there, we could just hear it and a warrior with a shield started down for us. It was the song of his shield he was singing and making new words for it as he came. We learned that day his name was Mountain Chief, and there are enough families of the People that know his name and the words he sang to this day. Bear Son yelled, 'There's too many of them, the scouts didn't see those!' and we took the last scalps quick and the rest of the guns and rode up the coulees and hard over the prairie straight into the morning sun, to find some place where...."

While his father's voice sang Kingbird felt his wife shuddering; long and hard, until he knew for certain it had nothing to do with the child that wanted to get out. He said then, "I would have sent you, but not chopped off your nose. You are too much for me. I would have given you to him, there is nothing else, except kill him...."

His voice stopped; her body quietened finally against his.

"I ate his sweet sugar too," he said.

"This one won't be white," she whispered. "No! It will not be!"

"....fighting all across the bare prairie with not even a clump of wolf willow for shelter or a mound high enough to hide a gopher. Beyond the ridge where the scouts had not seen it was a bigger camp of Bloods and their friends than any of us had ever seen in one place. They had those American guns and could hit us long before we could touch them, so some of us sang our death song behind dead horses and slowed them a little and we got across to the ravines above where the river has turned north again. Bear Son stayed behind his horse and killed a Piegan and smashed his empty gun into a Blood's face, breaking it Hey-Hey-Hey-Hey, and jumped on his grey horse and rode after us, he was so fast they couldn't catch him and he slid into the long ravine where we had ridden our horses into the bare brush before and some of us were behind rocks and shooting. Those Bloods and Piegans ran into the ravine opposite and there was a long shooting back and forth and throwing rocks over the ridge but when Mountain Chief and a half white called Bear Child who rides now with the police as scout came riding out of the dust, they didn't stop. Mountain Chief was singing the new words of his shield, 'My body will be lying on the plains,' and he rode right into us. We were shooting him behind and in front but he was too powerful. He took a musket away from Leave Him and killed him with it; there were seven balls in that gun, Leave Him was so excited, and when that Blood fired it at us it kicked him so hard we thought it had killed him when we couldn't, but he jumped up onto his horse again still singing and he had too much power that day; we crawled for the river. There was nothing to be seen but smoke and at first they didn't follow, but that Bear Child now called Potts could see better than a mousing hawk and soon they charged so hard some of us had to go back against a ridge which broke straight off into the river below. Here our few horses started breaking their legs, the river was deeper against the banks and sucked warriors under when they fell into it. Bear Son was screaming as the grey horse he had taken snapped both its front legs trying to stick to that sheered-off cliff, 'The river's all blood! blood! . . .'"

Lone Man heard Nowah-keetch say, "It's her time now"; she stood up and the darkness swallowed her also beyond the fire. Wolfboy had crawled into his lap. He could feel the tiny boy squirm down, peering out under his arm at the ghost dancers spiralling pinkish-orange and lavender over the sky as though they were huge fluffy geese, wing-shot and yet somehow keeping themselves aloft, half-flimmering upon each other but sinking steadily, relentlessly lower. Lone Man pulled his son tight.

" . . . . Sutherland brothers screaming in a white language no one understood on the ridge and when their legs were finished they lay on them and tore Bloods apart with their teeth and knives but their yellow hair came free at last and they had to be left there, above the river for the Blood women to finish cutting what was left of them. We were back through the river by then, some of us, and the warriors with Unborn Calf had followed us axing horses in the river and the Piegans and Bear Child firing everywhere so we were on the little prairie across the river trying to get to the trees with always less of us to get there. Mountain Chief had stabbed Rabbit Head between the shoulders while he was crossing the river and took his spear from him and Bear Son swung a Winchester he had taken up with one hand to shoot Mountain Chief and he jerked his horse's head around to take the bullet, but there was no bullet left in that gun; I heard it click but was too busy to do anything there I yo ho, I yo ho, I am here now! Bear Son threw him over his horse by his foot and they were rolling over, together, both their knives held so I got my work finished faster and went back there, almost to the river bank but Bear Son had him by the hair then and drove his knife into his back; but Mountain Child was still singing and his war bonnet had worked down on his neck and the knife stuck in that. That Blood saw the handle sticking out behind himself and grabbed it and that knife drank blood, deep, and Mountain Chief pulled the knife out of him again, still singing and holding the knife up to the sun, and there was nothing for me but shoot before he would lift his hair also. I knew I would miss, his power was too strong that day, but he ran without scalping when I shot and then I had to get back if I could, there were too many of them coming up out of the river, there was nothing to see there but horses' teeth foaming. Stones and bullets screaming in the smoke. In that moon Sun is supposed to go to bed soon but He was up there, high, looking to see what would happen to us; He seemed too interested ever to go till He saw us wiped out, but we held them at the trees till Sun finally got tired of it and started for his blankets. Little Bad Man danced with happiness, his face sliced open two ways but three scalps dripping at his belt and I said to my sons, 'Bear Son lies by the river.' We had nothing but some arrows left, and stones. We were throwing the black rock that burns in showers at the horses as they kept charging at us under the big trees.

"Little Bad Man stared, but Twin Wolverine, suddenly, started to walk. He still held his musket and hadn't fired it once that day; he hadn't opened his mouth and his knife was stuck in his belt with not a drop on it. But now he sang, loud. The song he sang was Coyote's, that we had heard the night before at Little Bow crossing and he walked out into the clearing toward the river where shadows already reached out black from the cliffs. He was walking into those warriors hot with our weapons and blood and it seemed to me that I had dreamed this somewhere, before, and might dream it again someday when I was very weak. A Piegan wheeled, charged him and I saw him kneel and aim and pull the trigger and that warrior flew up arms and legs, splattered to the ground and the horse galloped on; another rode at him. He had left the musket where he shot with it and as the Blood came on a beautiful sweating black horse Twin Wolverine ducked aside, the warrior was looping over and there he lay, knife through his throat. All the time he was singing the new song Coyote had lent him, and all those warriors stopped then, not riding at him and holding their guns in front of them as they watched him walk without a weapon in his hands to the river and lift the body of his brother Bear Son upon his shoulder and turn his back to the sun and come between them to us still singing and the whole valley there quiet at last, hearing that."

There was silence in the clearing, even the women now making no sound. Only the ghost dancers high above them seemed to groan.

"Twin Wolverine came to us under the trees and laid his brother down on the earth there. He was running with blood for Bear Son had been cut everywhere in the fighting and had taken three bullets but his hair wasn't touched. We covered him with the earth, the black rocks and stones took him by Belly River and no women's knife cut him open. The Bloods and Piegans turned away then so there would be someone to tell our story; they had killed almost three hundred of us and as they rode back across the river and up the ravines where our warriors lay piled and their women laughing at their work there, we could hear them singing. But Mountain Chief sang louder than them all,

> My body will be lying on the plains,
> The guns, the knives they hear
> Me.

Twin Wolverine, my son, would never take his name, 'Coyote Song.' We gave many others back to the earth on our way for Northwind howled down on us too before we found our lodges again, and no woman ever sang him in the scalp dance. They sang the fallen warriors and wailed those dead too young ever to find glory. He would never tell of it, my second son, or sing it in the Thirst Dance. But no chief who was there ever walked between him and the fire; they would look at him and go around. And now he has choked out his breath; my son has ridden to the Sand Hills without breath. Without breath, without breath."

The Magpie screamed into the sky, and the three women echoed her.

Over the clearing wind ran, from trees leaping to trees. Horsechild heard and the stone answered nothing to his hand. The ghost dancers were gone, there were only hard bright stars above him and a black mass of cloud bulging up from over the lake. Big Bear stood up and walked away; then he was returning from behind the bark lodge. First in the low firelight Horsechild saw his father's hands holding the sacred bundle, and finally above him his voice came, higher, more piercing than the women.

"My River People are wandering, they have no place now. One sacred pipe stem is with Little Bad Man, and perhaps it will get over the line, to the Missouri River or the Bearpaw Mountains. But one must remain here, with the River People where they once were great and rode wherever their eyes touched land. You must take the stem you have," he spoke, and Lone Man stood up, "to the People left at Little Pine's on the Battle River. And I have nothing but this, kept in a clean place: Chief's Son's Hand. I will unwrap it once more, now, so I can teach you the songs and the proper unwrapping that Bear Spirit first taught me when he gave it to me, at The Forks."

"I have seen you many times, my father," Kingbird managed finally, standing also.

"You must know it exactly," Big Bear insisted, "to teach it to your son. There will be an old man at Little Pine's to name him."

It was early afternoon the next day when they separated. At the southern tip of Turtle Lake Kingbird and Lone Man with the women and children went south-west, Sits Green On The Earth and her first son riding the travois behind one of the three horses. All And A Half would not leave Big Bear, and no one asked Horsechild about it. For four days they walked and took turns riding their gaunt horse more east than south, easily avoiding the noisy soldiers, and (though a date never meant anything to him) it was in the long bright evening of July 1, 1885 that they three came out on the wooded bank of the North Saskatchewan River. Directly before him, between the grey water churning below and the straight line of prairie above, protruded the burned timbers of Fort Carlton; but a little south of that Big Bear saw the still green tops of the spruce under which he had been born. It was the place.

SIX

The Trail to the Sand Hills, September, 1885; January 17, 1888

I

Canada: North West Territories: The information and complaint of Richard Burton Deane, of the town of Regina in the North West Territories, superintendent of the North West Mounted Police, taken the third day of September in the year of Our Lord one thousand one hundred and eighty-five, before the undersigned; one of Her Majesty's stipendiary magistrates in and for the said North West Territories, who saith: —

1. That Mis-ta-hah-mus-qua, otherwise called Big Bear, not regarding the duty of his allegiance, but wholly withdrawing the love, obedience, fidelity and allegiance which every true and faithful subject to our Lady the Queen does, and of right ought to bear towards our said Lady the Queen, on the second day of April in the year of our Lord one thousand eight hundred and eighty-five, and on divers other days, as well before as after that date, together with divers other evil disposed persons to the said Richard Burton Deane unknown, did, within the Dominion of Canada, compass, imagine, invent, devise and intend to levy war against our said Lady the Queen, within Canada, in order, by force and constraint, to compel her to change her

measures and counsels, and the said felonious compassing, imagination, invention, device and intention, then feloniously and wickedly did express, utter and declare, by divers overt acts and deeds hereinafter mentioned, that is to say: — In order to fulfill, perfect and bring into effect his felonious, compassing, imagination, invention, device and intention, he, the said Mis-ta-hah-mis-qua, otherwise called Big Bear, afterwards, to wit, on the second day of April in the year aforesaid, and on divers other days and times, as well before as after that day, at and near the locality called Frog Lake, in the North West Territories of Canada, did conspire, consult, confederate, assemble and meet together with divers other evil disposed persons to the said Richard Burton Deane unknown, to raise, make and levy insurrection and rebellion against our said Lady the Queen, within this realm.

And further (etc.)...to wit, on the 17th day of April in the year aforesaid and on divers other days and times, as well before as after that day, at or near the locality known as Fort Pitt (etc.)....

And further, to fulfill (etc.)....

And further to fulfill, perfect and bring to effect (etc. etc.)...at or near the locality known as Frenchman Butte (etc.)...did conspire (etc.)...with divers other (etc.)...in contempt of our said Lady the Queen and her laws, to the evil example of all others in like case offending against the form of the statute in such case made and provided, and against the peace of our Lady the Queen, her Crown and dignity.

Sworn before me, the day and year first above
mentioned, at the town of Regina,
in the North West Territories
of Canada   *R. BURTON DEANE*
    HUGH RICHARDSON
    Stipendiary Magistrate.

And take notice, that you have the option of being tried before
a stipendiary magistrate and a justice of the peace with the
intervention of a jury of six, or before a stipendiary magistrate
in a summary way without the intervention of a jury. Which do
you elect?

II

Magistrate Hugh Richardson, the Court: "Do you recollect,
prisoner, being charged by me with committing crime?"

Big Bear: "Yes."

Court: "Do you recollect the nature of the charge, what the
charge was?"

They were in a small, closed room and it stank. Of whites,
he could see nothing for a time except whites crowded tall like
black trees around him, the burn of the soap and powder they
used to make themselves more white, even the browner ones
whom the sun must have seen a little that summer, standing in
his nostrils as if he had taken a warclub over his face. In the
tiny box where he had to stand or sit on a chair as they gestured, to see them moving their papers where Riel had to sit in
the hot Moulting Moon, and Poundmaker a little later, sweating too. It must have been worse for his long legs, and a wob-
bly chair, layers and layers of wood laid between him and the
earth. There was only one good face here that he could see at

first: Peter Houri's dark and wind-hammered trying to tell him exactly what the two white Bosses said across their papers. Watching Peter listen, ponder how to say all that, Big Bear saw momentarily the camp by the lake where he had last heard the old wives chuckling their endless laughter as they did under each new moon for the right listener, those years ago, the day before the iron road had squealed and come crawling along there and he and the People had to see it. A good quiet face, folded brown together like land in a long autumn.

"My friend, I have seen his Whitehair and I remember him," and he told him at length, gently; Peter's head tilted a little, his right hand on his heart the way he always stood, struggling to fight clear some meaning between them. Big Bear concluded, "I understand what he wants to tell me, and you understand, but we haven't been given words or signs for it, so just let him say his white things." Houri stared gloomily at him, and translated finally:

Prisoner: "No, I don't recollect it, nor did I understand what was the charge laid against me. I do not understand that."

Court: "Then you are charged this Friday, the eleventh day of September, 1885, that you, not regarding the duty of your allegiance which you owe to the Queen, with other evil-disposed persons, compassed to levy war against the Queen in Canada, against her Crown and dignity, and on the 2nd April you did so at Frog Lake, on the 17th April you did so at Fort Pitt, and subsequently, on the 28th at Loon Creek; and take notice, that you have the op —"

There was an interruption, a fumble of more papers under bent heads, and then the Court continued,

"Uhh — that is, on the 28th of *May*, and that at *Frenchman Butte*, and take notice you have the option of stipendiary magistrate alone, or by stipendiary magistrate with a justice of the peace and a jury of six; being tried, that is. Which do you elect?"

F. Beverly Robertson, for the prisoner: "A judge and jury."

A short, very dry little man was reading loudly from a paper; he read on and on, his thin lips barely moving in one long snore running together in Big Bear's head; if he could have felt wind fondle him and his legs been folded under, not dangling over such a cut edge of chair, he might have fallen asleep to that wavering mosquito. Then Peter had to try again to put words to what he had done wrong, why they kept him in jail over two months though they allowed Horsechild to share his black hole and let him walk once in the sun every day and he listened to the few words which said as much of that long snore as the language of the People could formulate; and as Peter Houri finished Big Bear laughed out loud. His hands rose and over them silently talking, his deep laughter rumbled through the startled courtroom, over the astounded judge and Justice of the Peace Henry Fisher, the two Crown lawyers and the thin, hairy man named to "protect" and "speak for" him, over the rows of faces staring moonishly at him over other low walls, nothing but heads, and when his hands stopped his vivid explication Big Bear heard his laughter faintly answered among faces he saw rising behind the Big Bosses' heads; then he recognized one face there, and another he had not expected to see again.

Houri glanced swiftly about the official court but uncomprehending amazement faced him there; Richardson seemed so thunderstruck at the response to the charge his hand could not make a gesture toward the gavel. Houri's shoulders sagged in relief and he said very fast,

Prisoner: "Not guilty!"

Clerk Watson: "Are you ready for your trial?"

Mr. Robertson: "Quite — ready."

Clerk: "These good men you shall now hear called are those that are to pass between our Sovereign Lady the Queen and you; if, therefore, you challenge them or any of them you must challenge them when they come to the book to be sworn, before they are sworn, and they shall be heard. I call Albert Smith, Henry Grove, William Hunt, Robert Martin, John Morrison, J.W. Smith."

Big Bear, still smiling towards the two faces, said to Peter Houri, "Like the Grandmother, I've never seen any of those before."

The six were sworn, and Mr. D.L. Scott rose for the Crown: "May it please your Honours, gentlemen of the jury.

"The charge you have just heard read is known as a charge of treason-felony. In substance it alleges that the prisoner, along with certain other persons, designed and intended to levy war against her Majesty, which means the lawfully constituted government of the country, and that he expressed that desire, showed it conclusively by certain overt acts which are set forth in the charge. The difference between treason-felony and the higher crime of treason is this: that in treason it is necessary to show that the prisoner actually levied war; in treason-felony it is not necessary to show that he actually levied war, but that he merely *intended to do so*. You will see by the evidence given in the case that we go further than actually necessary. We show that he not only designed to levy war, but that he actually did it, and that is the best evidence of intention — the fact that he actually did levy war. There is a difference, too, in the punishment. For the charge of treason upon conviction there must necessarily follow a sentence of death. Upon a charge of treason-felony the punishment may be imprisonment from a day up to imprisonment for life, any term the court may think proper to inflict.

"Before describing the four charges that are set out, the four overt acts, it may be necessary to say something about the rebellion in the north. It is not necessary for me to mention any of the circumstances connected with that rebellion, because the whole matter from beginning to end is now almost a matter of history. The circumstances are just as well known to you, in fact better known to you, than you will hear from evidence today. It will be necessary to give formal proof that about the 18th of March rebellion did break out in the north, that until the 12th of May following the whole country in the neighbourhood of Duck Lake and Batoche on the South Saskatchewan was a blaze of rebellion. Though it may not be possible for us to show a connection between that rebellion and what we allege was carried on by the prisoner and others in the neighbourhood of Frog Lake, the fact that rebellion actually existed a very short distance from Frog Lake and Fort Pitt may convey to your minds the conclusion that there *was* a connection between the rebellion at Duck Lake and the rebellion carried on by the prisoner and the party with whom he is connected.

"The prisoner is a chief of a band of Cree Indians who occupy a reserve near Frog Lake. He is one of three parties whose names stand out prominently in the history of the late rebellion as being the leader of it, in the different parts of the country. It is possible we will show that this man was chief of a band who was in rebellion; it is possible that we may not be able to show that he was the leader of the movement in that particular part of the country. It is possible, in speaking of the outrage at Frog Lake, of the massacre there, that the defence may make it appear to you from the evidence that he did not go so far in committing those outrages as some members of his band; that he possibly may not have intended that that massacre at Frog Lake on April 2, which is one of the charges against him, should be committed on that day. It is possible that this may be shown. It is possible further that it may be shown that at least to a certain extent to his efforts on behalf of the prisoners, the prisoners owe their lives; but gentlemen, though that may be shown, it is not a question for you to consider. That is a question to be considered in mitigation of the punishment, if convicted. You must understand that if he was acting with those parties at that time in open rebellion against the Government, and he continued to act afterwards with them, it is nothing, as far as this offence is concerned, whether he wanted to go the length some of them went; even if he wanted to save the lives of the prisoners, it is then nonetheless the fact that he was in open rebellion against the Government of the country, and ought to be punished for that offence.

"Now, gentlemen, the four overt acts I have alluded to are these:

1) At the massacre of Frog Lake, 2nd April. You have all heard the particulars of that brutal outrage.

2) After committing the outrage at Frog Lake, they appeared before Fort Pitt and on April 17th, the police having withdrawn down the river that day, they entered the fort, and sacked the fort and the buildings in connection with it.

3) Upon the 21st of April, somewhere in the neighbourhood of Frog Lake, to which they had returned after sacking Fort Pitt, a letter was dictated by the prisoner and a halfbreed named Montour, then in camp with them. We will be able to give you a pretty good idea what the intention of the prisoner and the others then present was in writing that letter.

4) On the 28th May the last overt act was committed. The prisoner and those with him met the troops at the neighbourhood of a place called Frenchman Butte, and there engaged with the volunteers of the Dominion under the command of General Strange and were, in fact, in open war, on that occasion, against the Government.

"These are the four acts we charge against the prisoner, and I and my colleague, Mr. W.C. Hamilton, will now bring forward evidence to establish them."

Did you see any of the murders committed?

John Pritchard: No, I have not seen one. I have seen one that fell alongside me.

Scott: What caused him to fall?

Pritchard: It was the shot, Charlie Gouin had a shot from behind and he fell. That was all I seen.

Scott: You did not see who committed it?

Pritchard: No, there were too many all around us — too many Indians.

Scott: Where were you taken to after you were made prisoner?

Pritchard: We were taken to the Indian camp — to the prisoner's camp.

Scott: Were there any others in the camp besides the prisoners taken by this man and his band?

Pritchard: At that time? No, I don't know any.

Scott: Were there any others joined him afterwards?

Pritchard: Yes, there were some Indians, from Long Lake, the whole Cut Arm band that was at Long Lake.

Scott: Were you in Wandering Spirit's tepee on the 21st of April?

Pritchard: Yes.

Scott: What occurred there?

Pritchard: It was about that letter.

Scott: What letter?

Pritchard: The letter they got Montour to write to send to Lac la Biche.

Scott: How did you happen to be there?

Pritchard: It was Wandering Spirit came for me.

Scott: Who was there?

Pritchard: He and Big Bear and Montour.

Scott: Then tell us what was said, after you were all four there.

Pritchard: It was Montour asked how they would write the letter.

Scott: Montour asked Big Bear how they would write the letter?

Pritchard: Yes, he asked him, the first thing when I got in that I recollect now was that Big Bear said he had — he wanted to send an Indian to Whitefish Lake to invite the Seenum Indians to come. He was about sending an Indian. He enticed those Indians to come in and join him, and then he said to Montour, I want you to write, to do the same, to send a letter to your friends at Lac la Biche, and then he says, for my part, I send word to Seenum if he did not want to come to join me let him buy a fast horse and clear the country. The chief at Whitefish Lake was to do this.

Robertson: That he *had* sent?

Pritchard: Yes, he was about to, he was ready to send the Indian.

Scott: And then he asked Montour to write to his friends at Lac la Biche?

Pritchard: Yes.

Scott: Then what did Montour say?

Pritchard: He commenced to write the letter.

Robertson: I suppose the writing should be produced.

Scott: Did you see what was put down in the writing?

Pritchard: I heard the words and saw the man write it. I know a few words.

Scott: How do you know them?

Pritchard: After he read it to Wandering Spirit; he wanted to know the contents of the letter.

Scott: I submit, your Honour, that I am entitled to show the conversation that occurred, that even if the letter was read afterwards, what occurred beforehand in conversation in the tepee during the time the prisoner was there is evidence in the case.

Court: If reduced into writing, without accounting for the letter?

Robertson: I ask that this evidence be interpreted to the prisoner.

Court: I think it is quite open to you, Mr. Scott, to show the purpose for which they came there, but going further than that, I think you will have to produce the letter. A man says something in another's presence, that will be evidence. We don't know whether that went into the letter or not, so when you speak of the contents of the letter, it is improper.

Robertson: I quite agree any conversation would be admissible so long as it is not giving what was put into the letter. There the line must be drawn.

Scott: What was said after the prisoner asked Montour to do this?

Pritchard: Montour asked him, shall I write them to tell Alexander Solomon so and so.

Court: Shall I tell Alexander what?

Pritchard: To rob him and deliver up his guns and the ammunition he had, as the Indians would rob him anyway.

Court: Him?

Pritchard: The Company there, yes.

Court: And what did the prisoner say then?

Pritchard: He told him, yes.

Court: Then did he ask him any other questions?

Pritchard: He told him, shall we tell the news about this place, about this what was done here, and Big Bear said yes. That is all I remember.

Court: Was that all the prisoner said?

Pritchard: Yes, that was all he said.

Court: That is not the statement that you gave me, Mr. Pritchard. I am going to tell you what you said — I have a perfect right to make that remark. I want to refresh —

Robertson: I don't think you have the right. Unless you can prove it according to the rules of evidence, you have no right to make a statement to the jury that he once told you something different.

Scott: Are those the only questions you remember Montour asking the prisoner?

Pritchard: Yes, that is the only questions I remember now.

Scott: Did Montour at any time put a sentence to Big Bear as to what he was going to put in the letter by way of a question?

Pritchard: That is all the sentences that I am perfectly sure that was pronounced, now.

Court: Mr. Robertson, before you ask him any questions, I propose to ask the interpreter to interpret to the prisoner what I have taken down.

(Peter Houri translates.)

Robertson: Mr. Pritchard, who were the leading spirits in the band that took you prisoner?

Pritchard: Big Bear's son, Little Bad Man.

Robertson: Is Big Bear's son a good son to his father?

Pritchard: No, I don't think so, because when the father said anything the son bucks against it.

Robertson: Who wanted to take Fort Pitt?

Pritchard: Little Bad Man and Wandering Spirit, they wanted to take the headmen there that was leading the Indians.

Robertson: What did Big Bear say about that?

Pritchard: He tried to save the families that were in the fort. He said if he could get the police to leave the fort it would be good, that is what he said.

Robertson: You said earlier Big Bear came in to Frog Lake on 1st of April and told the agent he was going to be loyal and show the Government something — my learned friend interrupted. I would like you to finish that.

Pritchard: He said he was going to be loyal, and not rise. They say Big Bear is going to rise to war, and I am going to let them see that I and my band are not going to rise.

Scott: How did you happen to hear the prisoner try to persuade the Indians to let the police at Fort Pitt go? Was it a council?

Pritchard: No, it was a whole body of men standing together on the hill that was just going to rush into the fort, and then he called out and told them to try and save the families that were there, and the police that were there, let them go. That was all he said.

.... his young men would not listen to him? How did this come to your notice?

James Simpson: Because I was into the camp often trading with them, summer and winter, the same as if I was living with them altogether, and I found out that if he had anything to say, the others would not hear it.

Scott: Then how does it come that, if he had counselled the Indians to kill the prisoners, they would have done so? He must have had some influence, to turn the balance?

James Simpson: If you get into a camp of Indians, and they speak to you and you said, do this bad, they will do it; and say do this good, and they would not do it perhaps. It would depend, whether they wanted to do it.

Scott: That is what you think?

James Simpson: Yes.

Robertson: How long have you known Big Bear?

James Simpson: Nearly forty years.

Robertson: How old is he, do you know?

James Simpson: He ought to be upwards of sixty.

. . . . mostly feasting and killing cattle. Having dances.

Scott: What kind of dances?

Stanley Simpson: They have a tent erected.

Scott: What do you call that dance?

Stanley Simpson: I think they call it the grass dance, I'm not sure. They have music and grub. They generally kill a dog or so and have something to eat.

Scott: Did you hear the prisoner speak at any of the dances?

Stanley Simpson: Yes, I heard him speak at the thirst dance at Frenchman's Butte. He was speaking to several Indians, some of his band and Wood Crees and he cut up a piece of tobacco, and he said he wanted his men to cut the head of the white people off the same as he cut this piece of tobacco off. He wanted the head of the "master who is over the soldiers," he said.

Robertson: You are a very young man. Do you understand Cree?

Stanley Simpson: I don't understand it clearly. I understand a good deal more than I can speak.

Scott: And he said he wanted to cut off the head of all the others?

Stanley Simpson: Of white people that were in the country that were on land that they had not paid him for, he used principally the head of the officer in charge. He did not say they were to cut off the heads of the white people, only the officer, but they were to kill all the white people.

Scott: What did you hear of the intentions of the other members of the band?

Stanley Simpson: They intended to take the country for the Americans, they said, they would pay them well for having taken it.

Scott: Can you name one who said that?

Stanley Simpson: The Lone Man is one, I could not name them all.

Scott: Is Lone Man the one who took you prisoner?

Stanley Simpson: Yes.

Scott: How were you treated as a prisoner?

Stanley Simpson: I was badly treated. At first I was treated pretty well, they gave me a horse which was to be mine all through and at first we had lots to eat, but the next morning Lone Man told me — it was his horse — told me there was no horse for me, that I had to get to work and load his carts with bacon and flour and later I had to cut roads and dig rifle pits, make breastworks, any other work.

Scott: How did you happen to go with the Wood Crees when you were Lone Man's prisoner?

Stanley Simpson: We were told the Plains Crees would kill us.

Robertson: You were free to go with whichever you liked?

Stanley Simpson: No, Lone Man wanted to take me across the Line with him.

Scott: Then how is it you went with the Wood Crees?

Stanley Simpson: He made me work too much and I wanted to get to the same place where Mr. McLean was, and I ran away from him.

"Mr. Tompkins, you are an interpreter in the Indian Department?"
"Yes."
"You were taken prisoner by a number of armed rebels under Louis Riel on 18th March?"
"Yes."
"What was the state of the country around Batoche between the 18th March and the 12th of May?"
"It was all in armed insurrection...."
"That is a long way from Frog Lake and Fort Pitt, Batoche?"
"Yes."
"How far?"
"I don't know the miles."
"How many days?"
"I should say about six days."

(Stanley Simpson recalled.)

Robertson: Just tell us in Cree what it was that Big Bear said, at Frenchman's Butte.
Stanley Simpson: I can't say it, I can't pronounce the words properly, only a word here and there.
Robertson: And after all it was mostly a guess of yours?
Stanley Simpson: No, I could understand that he said this.
Scott: I would ask my learned friend to give a question to Mr. Houri to put to the witness in Cree. That is all he says he knows about it.
Stanley Simpson: You don't want to put a very hard question to me, or perhaps I can't answer it. Big Bear spoke very

slowly, as he always does. I am asked by Mr. Houri — if he had given me some tobacco, or something of that sort — I don't understand enough of it.

Scott: What is the word for cutting a man's head off?

Stanley Simpson: I can say "man's head" all right enough, and he had his knife, and he —

Robertson: Give us the words.

Court: They use a great many signs as words?

Stanley Simpson: I would not be here and say I understood it, if I didn't!

Scott: You have traded with Cree Indians nearly four years —

Robertson: I can talk to an Indian to a certain extent without any words at all. The words that were read to the witness were: "If the captain of the soldiers does not give us tobacco, we will cut off the tops of the trees." I wish to submit that the evidence of that conversation should be struck out.

Court: I may later have something to say to the jury about that.

"What were you doing when you were captured, Mr. Fontaine?"

"I was jumping off my horse."

"Had they been chasing you?"

"Yes."

"Did they do anything when they were chasing you?"

"I think they were shooting."

"You think?"

"Nothing hit me."

"And then these men took you to Poundmaker's camp?"

"They said so."

"Was Poundmaker there?"

"I don't know."

"Didn't you see him during the time you were in camp?"

"No, because I didn't know him. I might have seen him."

"When did you first see him to know him?"

"The first time was right in here, when he was sitting there."

"But they said they were taking you to Poundmaker's camp."

"Yes, they said that."

"Did you see any others armed there besides, at the time they took you prisoner?"

"Yes, I saw some Indians, with guns."

(The case for the Crown is here closed.)

Robertson: Does your Honour think there is a case?

Court: Mr. Robertson, I cannot stop a case.

Robertson: Your Honour has the power of a judge at *nisi prius.*

Court: I can only tell the jury what I think of it.

Robertson: Unless the constitution of the court is a little different from the Court of Assize.

Court: That is strictly the power of a Court of Assize.

Robertson: Then I will call.

Big Bear was at your house that morning, what did he do there?

Mrs. Catharine Simpson: He did nothing there, only what he told me.

Scott: I object to what the prisoner said.

Robertson: It is really part of his conduct in connection with what was occurring there; it is something he came and said to her.

Court: But that would not be evidence.

Robertson: I think it would be in that view. Supposing he came to the wife of his old friend and warned her he was afraid his young men were going to make trouble, and that he wanted to make her safe, that would clearly be conduct.

Court: Wouldn't that be almost parallel to the horse case, where it is not allowed to show that the prisoner told the owner's brother that he would not steal the horse, and afterwards he is charged with theft?

Robertson: Here he comes and actually warns her she'll be protected. Tell me, what did he do then?

Mrs. Simpson: He said pack up your things, I think there is going to be trouble.

Robertson: For what purpose would he tell her that?

Scott: There must be a stop to this somewhere, really, this is too far.

Robertson: He clearly went there to give her a warning, and what he said is really part of his conduct at the time, surely.

Scott: I object to anything further than the warning being given.

Robertson: Well, what did he do after that, or what did you do?

Mrs. Simpson: He said gather up your things, I can't be everywhere to look over my young men. I think there is going to be trouble.

Robertson: And what more did he do?

Mrs. Simpson: He ate pea soup.

Robertson: Pea soup!

Mrs. Simpson: He likes that.

Robertson: Did, did you give it to him?

Mrs. Simpson: Yes. While Big Bear was eating I was packing up my little things. I heard a shot outside, and I ran out to the door and I saw the man fall, so then I went into my house again.

Robertson: And what did Big Bear do?

Mrs. Simpson: He got up and went out, and I heard him say, don't do so, leave it alone, stopping it.

Robertson: You heard him crying that out?

Mrs. Simpson: Yes.

Scott: Before that what had Pritchard and Mr. Quinn said to the prisoner in your house?

Mrs. Simpson: Pritchard did not say anything, but Tom Quinn said, Big Bear, could I remain at my own house, and Pritchard, and this woman also? Oh, I suppose you could, Big Bear said. When they went out I quickly got hold of my things and I wanted to go after them. They were already a piece from me, and when they were getting on to their house I heard a shot and saw the man drop. They were quite a bit ahead of me already and I was going to follow them, and when I looked I saw the man drop, Tom Quinn.

Scott: Did the prisoner tell you what to do yourself, to be safe?

Mrs. Simpson: Yes, Big Bear said don't be afraid and told me to go to the camp so I went to his camp. That is all, what I have said.

William McLean: Personally I have known Big Bear since the 29th of last October, by reputation probably seven or eight years before.

Robertson: Was he a good Indian or a bad Indian?

McLean: Well, some say that the dead Indians are the good ones, but in his life I considered him a good Indian.

Robertson: You were a prisoner how long?

McLean: Sixty-two days.

Robertson: During all that time you saw Big Bear's conduct?

McLean: Yes, I may say almost daily, if not daily.

Robertson: And you still remain of the opinion Big Bear is a good Indian, though a live one?

McLean: Yes, I do as far as the Hudson's Bay Com —

Robertson: Can you tell me whether Big Bear took any part himself in pillaging Fort Pitt?

McLean: None to my knowledge. I am sure he had some tea given him, but I was with the Indians when the pillaging was taking place, but he was taking no part.

Robertson: How did his son, Little Bad Man, treat Big Bear during your imprisonment?

McLean: With utter contempt.

Robertson: You remember the letter coming to Johnny Pritchard from Norbert Delorme, who was then in Poundmaker's camp?

McLean: Yes, I was sent for to read that letter.

Robertson: Did you do anything in consequence of having read that letter?

McLean: In my estimation I think I did a good deal. I tried to prevent the Indians from being influenced by the contents, to prevent them uniting themselves with Poundmaker at all.

Robertson: Did Big Bear, in that attempt, side with you or against you?

McLean: He sided with me always. He never went against me.

Robertson: Does Stanley Simpson, the clerk under you, understand Cree at all well?

McLean: Well, I don't suppose he could understand any conversation being carried on. He might understand short sentences.

Scott: I understood you to say the prisoner was a good Indian as far as the Hudson's Bay Company was concerned. Wasn't he the cause of some trouble to the Indian Department, occasionally?

McLean: I don't know, I'm sure. In our dealings, he was a good Indian.

Scott: Wasn't he in the habit of grumbling about the way he was treated by the Government?

McLean: No more than anybody else. A characteristic of all Indians is grumbling.

Court: I understood this man was the Frog Lake chief?

McLean: No, that was Ohnee-pahao; this one had taken no reserve yet.

Court: What was he grumbling about?

McLean: I don't know, I'm sure. Actually, I think it was the Government that was grumbling, because he wouldn't go on a reserve.

Court: What occurred when you went out to the Indians, out of Fort Pitt?

McLean: I had a talk with their leading men for some considerable time, with a view of getting them to desist from whatever intentions they might have when they came there, and go back peacefully to their reserves. The prisoner in the dock, that one was listening, and the Long Lake chief Cut Arm was there, and the Frog Lake chief. I was prepared to give them very liberal presents if they left, and I have been very successful with the Indians during my twenty-three years experience amongst them. However, I failed. The police scouts surprised them, riding towards the fort and Wandering Spirit, one of the leading men, jumped in front of me and caught me. There was shooting over the hill towards the fort. Now, he says you have spoken enough, we don't hear any more, we are in a hurry and you have to stay here with us, we don't want to hurt you or your family. That is what he said, Wandering Spirit. If we wanted to hurt you we might have done so.

Court: Did Big Bear say anything to this?

McLean: He was perfectly mute, as well as the other chiefs. Wandering Spirit was war leader.

Court: The police, as a matter of fact, did leave the fort?

McLean: The prisoner in the dock advised them strongly to leave, and they were allowed to leave that same day, in the evening.

Court: How did he advise them?

McLean: Henry Halpin wrote letters for him, to them. Several letters.

Court: How do you know?

McLean: I saw the letters, I had them in my hand, and two of them I know wore into atoms in my pocket during those sixty-two days.

Court: Were you there at the time they were dictated by the prisoner?

McLean: No. It is impossible for me to be five or six hundred yards away from the fort and in the fort at the same time. These letters were written on the 14th, when I was in the fort. I met them in their camp on the 15th, about eleven o'clock and the scouts rode in shortly after noon and the police left that evening.

Court: I understood the fort was taken, and they left on the 17th.

McLean: I would have understood so myself from some of the witnesses that spoke in the box where I am myself just now, and the charge read, but such, however, is not the case. The fort was vacated and taken on the evening of April 15.

Court: Whom were the letters addressed to?

McLean: One was to me, I'm not sure but there might have been one addressed to Inspector Dickens commanding the Mounted Police, and I am certain one was for Sergeant Martin, an old personal friend of the prisoner in the dock.

Court: As to the pillaged goods, you are certain you saw the prisoner with none?

McLean: I am perfectly sure he had none because I was very frequently in his camp. I gave him one or two blankets myself but there was no one in the Indian camp so wretchedly poor looking as him.

. . . . On the 19th of March I was going back from Frog Lake to my post as Hudson's Bay clerk at Cold Lake and I met Big Bear camped there on the road, hunting. And I talked to him then.

Scott: I object to any statement made by Mr. Henry R. Halpin.

Robertson: I wish to show that certain intelligence was given by Halpin to Big Bear, and I wish to show as a fact, and as a matter of conduct, how he received it. What information did you give him?

Scott: I don't think that is evidence.

Court: I think the question may be asked.

Robertson: And then, how the prisoner looked? That is a matter of conduct.

Scott: Also whether his jaw fell?

Robertson: Yes, and to bring it out if it did fall! It goes to show the state of the prisoner's mind at the time he received that information, and where it is a question of intent, it is perfectly proper evidence. What did you tell him?

Halpin: I told him I had seen in the Battleford *Herald* that there was trouble in Batoche, and that Riel had stopped the mails there. I told him I thought there was likely to be lots of trouble.

Robertson: What did his conduct indicate then?

Court: No. Mr. Scott, I will tell you what I will do, though it is not strictly proper: I will let in his reply.

Scott: Of course, I don't object to that.

Halpin: His reply was: I think it is very strange. He said it in Cree, he was surprised to hear it.

Court: That is parallel to the horse case. You can have your opinion somewhere else, Mr. Robertson, but not here.

Robertson: The cases are not parallel. Your Honour rules out what his appearance and demeanour indicated upon receipt of that?

Court: Yes. You have got the prisoner's answer, that he expressed surprise.

Robertson: You parted then?

Halpin: Not right away. I had dinner with him and invited him to come to my house at Cold Lake and he came then, the 21st of March he had dinner in my house. He left the evening of the 22nd, before a heavy wind started, to see if he could get a moose.

Robertson: He was still hunting then, even two days after you told him Riel had already started something?

Halpin: Yes.

Robertson: When did you see him next?

Halpin: On the 7th of April. I was taken prisoner by Lone Man at Cold Lake and brought to Frog Lake, and I saw him in Lone Man's tent at Frog Lake. He shook hands with me and said he was glad to see me and told me not to be afrai —

Scott: Your Honour, I must object!

Robertson: In the Thomas Scott acquittal yesterday this was permitted — what took place between the prisoner and others, and my learned friend has given evidence of the doings at Frog Lake and we already have evidence of the part Lone Man was taking in the insurrection —

Court: What was done on the 7th can hardly be an answer to what was done on the 2nd.

Robertson: The day has nothing to do with it. I am trying to establish what took place between the prisoner and others already proved to have been in insurrection, to show what the relations were between them. Mr. Osler yesterday —

Scott: I understand it this way, that the prosecution is entitled to use as evidence any statements the prisoner made in the nature of admissions as to what his intentions were: the defence may not show, in rebuttal, that he made other statements at other times.

Court: That is what I ruled in the Thomas —

Scott: The rule is extended to give evidence of admissions made by others with whom he was associated.

Robertson: My learned friend cannot have stated that correctly. Where a prisoner is charged with treason-felony, how can what he said not be used as evidence to indicate the part he took with others proven to be in insurrection? What he said to these others in trying to influence their conduct is evidence, not of admission, but of his *conduct*, that is, of his *intentions* in the business. The whole case is one of intentions!

Court: Your argument would be very good if your date was the 2nd of April; unfortunately it is the 7th.

Robertson: Then at two o'clock a man may talk like a traitor and at half past two he may not?

Court: Yes, and at three he may turn around again and talk like a traitor again.

Robertson: That is matter for the jury to consider, for that surely is evidence of the man.

Court: No, I don't think it is evidence.

Robertson: I must bow, of course, to your Honour's ruling, but does your Honour mean to say I am not at liberty to show that the prisoner endeavoured to prevent the Indians from doing these things, by word of mouth, by speaking to them?

Are we to pretend in this court that Indians habitually communicate by written orders, by *letters of intention*!

Court: Perhaps it would be as well to waive the rule, to allow the question to be asked, now that I have ruled it is not evidence.

Robertson: What did Big Bear say to you in Lone Man's tent at Frog Lake on April 7?

Halpin: He shook hands and said I could stop at his tent if I wasn't comfortable there. He said that this thing that happened is not my idea, it was not my fault, and we talked about a few other things, nothing really about this business here today.

Robertson: Were you present at Indian councils, when Big Bear was present?

Halpin: Yes, I was at several of them.

Scott: Are you going on with that, right straight through?

Robertson: If his Honour allows me.

Court: Go on.

Robertson: What part did Big Bear take in these councils?

Scott: The jury can only take what part he took by what he said or what he did, and even that is not evidence.

Halpin: I don't suppose anybody could think he took any part at all, as I never heard him say anything.

Robertson: Were you at Fort Pitt on the 17th of April?

Halpin: No, I was there the 13th and 14th and 15th.

Robertson: The 13th?

Halpin: That was when we arrived at Fort Pitt, the 13th, the day after Sunday. Big Bear sent another letter to Sergeant Martin on the 14th, and the police crossed the river that evening.

Robertson: Why did you go?

Halpin: Well, I had to drive a cart for Lone Man and Big Bear thought if I went down, since I talk Cree and that sort of thing, if I wrote letters I might be able to get the people out of the fort peaceably and prevent bloodshed.

Robertson: Where was Big Bear, as you went to Fort Pitt?

Halpin: I was about as far back in the caravan as I could get, and he was there, away at the back.

Robertson: Riding?

Halpin: No, he had no horse. He walked all over that bad ground, all the way.

Robertson: Where was Big Bear while the pillaging was taking place?

Halpin: On top of the hill along with me.

Robertson: Did you see him at Frenchman's Butte on May 28?

Halpin: Yes, in the camp some miles beyond the rifle pits.

Robertson: What was he doing?

Halpin: He seemed anxious to get away. He was telling the people to get out as quick as ever they could.

Robertson: When did you see Big Bear next?

Halpin: The next time was at Prince Albert, in the cells.

Scott: Do you want to know whether he also showed surprise there?

Robertson: While you were prisoner, how did the leading men of his band treat Big Bear?

Halpin: They treated him with contempt altogether.

Robertson: Had he any control over them?

Halpin: I don't think he had.

Scott: This is altogether irregular, this sort of examination, and I object again. I have never gone to this length in cross-examination.

Court: This unfortunate man is an Indian and I have allowed an unreasonable stretch here, simply because he is an Indian, and I shall tell the jury why I have done so.

Robertson: Do you know Stanley Simpson, the witness here?

Halpin: Yes.

Robertson: Several days ago, did you have any conversation on the subject of Big Bear's trial with him?

Halpin: A little.

Robertson: What did he say to you?

Halpin: He seemed —

Robertson: What did he say?

Halpin: I told him I was called on the defence and he thought it was strange, very strange, any white man should get on the defence of an Indian. His idea was that Indians should have been hung.

.... I waited for a few seconds, and it was followed by another, and then there were several shots fired in succession, and I went out of the store and saw Big Bear running up the street, and he called out: Tesqua! Stop, Stop! two or three times, running up towards where Quinn was lying. I saw Quinn lying on the side of the hill, and I did not hear anything of him then till afterwards when Wandering Spirit was riding through camp on Quinn's white mare proclaiming, I killed the Sioux Speaker, that was their name for Quinn. I don't recollect anything with regard to the council at which Mr. McLean was present when Wandering Spirit was speaking against the white prisoners in the camp and agitating, as he often did, to kill them, and Big Bear got up and seemed really as if he pitied all the prisoners: he got up and spoke, and he says: I pity all these white people that we saved; he says: I don't wish harm should come to one of them; and he said: Instead of trying to do harm to them you should be giving them back some of the things you plundered from them. And another thing which goes to show the influence that Big Bear held in the camp is that, at one time, I heard Mr. Halpin complain that some of the Indians had complained — Halpin complained to Big —

Scott: I object to this.

Court: What did Big Bear do?

William B. Cameron: Halpin complained some things had been stolen from him by some of the Indians, and Big Bear said he had a blanket stolen out of his tent; and he says, When they would steal from me, the man they called their chief, he says, I can't be responsible for what they do to other people.

Robertson: He complained that his own blanket had been stolen?

Cameron: Yes.

Robertson: On several occasions he spoke in favour of the prisoners, that he was averse to killing them?

Cameron: Yes.

Robertson: I have a couple of other witnesses, much to the same effect, but I think perhaps, that your Honours and the jury are tired of them.

Court: I am not tired.

Robertson: I think it is clearly established, it is hardly necessary.

Court: Are you done?

Robertson: Yes, that is the defence.

(Stanley Simpson recalled.)

Scott: Is what Mr. Halpin said a few moments ago, about your statement to him, true?

Stanley Simpson: No.

Robertson: What was it you did say to Mr. Halpin?

Stanley Simpson: I told him that there were a great many Indians I would like to see hung, and that there were a great many I would not like to see hung.

Robertson: You told him Big Bear was one you would like to see hung?

Stanley Simpson: No! If you ask Mr. Cameron, or any of them, I said today I would not like to see the old man hung at all.

Robertson: You said that *today*?

Stanley Simpson: Yes, and I said it before.

Robertson: On the occasion Mr. Halpin speaks of, you remonstrated with him for being a witness for the defence?

Stanley Simpson: No, I did not remonstrate with him. I said — I asked him if he was a witness for the defence and he said yes, and I said, it is a strange thing, after the trouble that you had, that you would be on the defence. That is what I said to him.

Why couldn't Big Bear speak for himself? Past the projecting corner of the wall and through the high, tiny window hanging down, open to the air blown wispy with cloud, Kitty could hear cranes flying south, though she could not actually see them. Throughout that long day she was certain, she thought, she heard them, certainly she heard them, her ears were perfectly sharp and clear, no stumbling witness or lawyer argument about horse cases, who cares about horses, or even Mr. Justice Richardson past whose head she must look to see Big Bear, why should that prevent her hearing the cranes pass outside in the smoky fall air. She could hear them perfectly; their squawky boom crossing between gaps of words and sometimes past the chipped corner she had an impression she thought of the line of them drawing away, though of that — she was too close behind the judge and his partner, almost on their backs, it was the only space left and she had come all the way from Winnipeg, begged herself along with her father and as the unending questions crept on, yes, no, no, I don't know, she found herself trying again and again to focus Big Bear through the outside edge of the judge's egg-shaped glasses almost as if she were ignorant of how glasses worked, past the whitish bristle of his sideburns, but anything she could finally distinguish through them was smeared as if the room were submerged, a swamp of milk. Again and again she pondered the problem: what could anyone, even a judge, see looking through that, gold lines creased into his temples as if grown there. What profound vision, what special — but largely he was an unfocused bristle wiped away; Big Bear. She heard absolutely everything anyone said and the cranes too, for after his thundering laugh he talked to her. Silently, his hands moving while the nervous witnesses he could not understand, except Mrs. Simpson, were made to talk and talk, aloud about him as if he were a child and not sitting there, until in a few moments they seemed to forget what they had once certainly seen, their minds, she could see that even of Stanley Point-nose Simpson, pouring out empty under questions like water pouches slit by a knife, he should that liar. Understand Cree. But not Papa, of course; what could a wigged Canadian lawyer do to a graduate of Edinburgh University. Mr. Robertson explained everything and not one sound from Big Bear, again, fingers whirling under the jury's nose as if such meaningless gestures would finally make them understand, lean arms swinging between her and the box where he sat so small now, blinking. As if his eyes

said over and over to juries here, and every time I have repeated it his Honour has taken care to tell the jury that the law is the same for white man and Indian. Yes, that is the law, but I say you cannot draw the same *inferences* from the conduct of an Indian as from a white man, a white man accustomed to live under our forms of Government. A white man knows he can move easily because the law protects him, that anywhere in the country, however large, he may find a home. But the Indian, apart from his little band, cannot live. He is not free, when he sees mischief done, to say, I will leave here, go among other people. His life is his band, and what else has my learned friend to rest this case upon except that Big Bear was with

the grey, unbuttoned prison shirt and the cheap blanket, matted cotton not even a horseblanket, his chest showing dark out of it, his face as if hammered down to the point of his chin and his eyes, even in the dim courtroom where the light shifted grey as wind spread out the autumn smoke, his eyes tight as slits. Blinking sometimes as though they suddenly refused to see for him. Only when he talked to her, sometimes the smallest gesture which she understood immediately, did she see light startle from his eye as if he were still there, somewhere, perhaps inside the almost unrecognizable huddle on that chair in the black box with the decorated stump of policeman over it. The tiny room was stuffed tight with black-bearded pale faces, the black sleeve of Mr. Richardson's arm was moving a pen across more paper, she could have reached over his thick shoulder and plucked it like feathering a goose but she couldn't read a word, more words slurred goose tracks over white paper as the day bent towards evening and she began to feel what she could not remember ever feeling the two months they were prisoners, even when there was no sun to sink under the spring drizzle: she began to feel only evidence is what Stanley Simpson has asked us to believe, after what he has shown us in that box of what he knows of Cree. Mr. Stanley Simpson, gentlemen, has been ill from what he has endured, and I am as sorry as anyone for his suffering, but are we to convict on the basis of guesswork like that, influenced by a strong animus as shown by what he said to Mr. Halpin, when he says it is a strange thing that any white man should be called as a witness for the defence of an Indian? Strange, gentlemen, strange for a white man to give an Indian the benefit of the truth!

I must object

his sharp nose, face drawn white as leeched lime staring ahead at the jury and only once his good eye flicking to the judge and then her glare hooked him and he certainly never dared turn her way again, not even when Mr. Richardson asked about sign language, it wasn't hate for Immaculate's lies — understand that after four years of using his fingers only to pinch his nose shut high in the air! — which startled her into an awareness of it, though after she thought of it for a time she understood that was where her feeling began. While the long afternoon wore away it had gradually come to her it was fear she felt, as her body deadened sitting on that bench, and this had nothing at all to do with Simpson who sat beside Cameron now looking merely sick. Her enormous certainties had somewhere leaked between her fingers, almost suddenly, she could not tell whether — she thought in a revelation it was the monthly blackness seeping through her and momentarily she would feel dampness, she was certain she felt it, once, and when she could look at herself there would be the dark worm crawling between the blackish hair inside her leg out of that unstoppable entrance into herself, she could never squat now as she had as a child and not feel herself opened uncloseably, forever unlocked unless she sat tight down on the gentle ground, not on this straight horrible bench behind all that powdered, bristling, hair. Even though the date was quite wrong, she finally remembered that. Words for Friday, the 11th of September were piled so tight, so deep in this small room that everyone seemed stretched up, craning for space to breathe but the ceiling moved steadily shorter with the sun sunk below the open window, and in this shrinking orange box, with the memory of any clean sound or air soaked up by the drone of English voices, there was nothing but the inevitability of this frightful orangeness tightening, down on them, squeezing him with them into one indistinguishable, tiny squashed cube and it was obvious that the only voice that could prevent it could never be allowed to utter a sound for there was no air left here, had there ever been any, to carry the running beauty of Cree

> not justified in acting upon any impressions derived from anything but evidence given here in this box! You must know, as I know, the multiplied and outrageous reports we heard about this old man, all the sins of his tribe, and a great many they never committed, laid upon his shoulders in the public print —
> Pardon me for interrupting you, did Mr. Scott mention Big Bear?
> He did. He said it was well known, and he particularly referred to the massacre at Frog Lake, that it was very well known.
> Go on.

I would have, if your Honour had not interrupted.
You referred to me.

I was saying gentlemen, you *must* set aside altogether such impressions, and if you had your
minds prejudiced by any of these former impressions you would not have been fit, in the eyes of the
law, to sit on this jury. You must think only

his hands were speaking again. Lifting themselves, heavy in
the heavy light, moving bright globs of it as only Mr. Houri
shifted his head slightly and watched with her, and Horsechild
of course, he was talking to Horsechild. Not to her, though he
obviously wanted her to see what he said, that it would not be
long now, when the sun was gone they would let them stand
up, and perhaps go to their places to eat since they needed
light to write and there was no place here to make a fire. They
were just talking among themselves now, the bosses, and they
would understand soon. Horsechild had sat there beside Kitty
behind the judge all day, his cheeks round from the prison food
he shared with his father but his motionless leg against hers
seemed fluttery. Flabby almost, like grease as if the hard limbs
that had run and straddled horses with Duncan had loosened
like his face, there was nothing to use them, it, on, though as
she looked at him he seemed much larger than she remembered, his shoulders heavy and his eyes bright on his father
past the judge's white fringe with perfect attention as those
hands, dark now, flickered, explaining it was just the long
heavy way whites had to do their things because everyone that
knew him and spoke knew he had done nothing, that what a
few bosses who had never seen him before said he had done
could not have happened to any People leave alone himself
since he had never so much as seen the Grandmother

McLean shows also that friendliness on the part of the prisoner and his band was to the Hudson's Bay Company alone, and not extended to the Government. For centuries the Company has been the protector of Indians for the purpose of cultivating their trade and making a profit, and clearly they have succeeded, but Mr. McLean by the way he gave evidence today shows he does not want to hurt a hair on the head of any person, was nevertheless forced to admit under cross-examination that the prisoner thought he had a grievance against the Government. That he was continually grumbling, which we also hear —

That is not what the witness said. Mr. McLean said that on one occasion he heard him make a complaint. Mr. Robertson, you should not interrupt.

Could Mr. Parks refer to his notes, your Honour? Perhaps I misstate it. I understood him to say Indians were always grumbling. Now, gentlemen, I admit there is strong evidence that the prisoner intended to save the lives of prisoners; however, the question is did he continue to associate with those who pillaged and

lives far away beyond the Stinking Water and would never visit us when we were still rich, and now we couldn't welcome her, now we have no buffalo to feast her properly with raw liver and tongue, so there is nothing true when they say I tried to steal her hat. How could I do that? Or knock it off, as Poundmaker said they told him, by throwing sticks at it. Poundmaker said that himself behind the bars, you heard him — what did he mean? At first she thought he was repeating his beginning laughter but his face was so monolithically set, it made no sense; as if he had suddenly changed by half a degree all the sign language. But Poundmaker wasn't with them in the Regina cells anymore, he was convicted and in Stony Mountain Penitentiary north of Winnipeg, she had seen them all herded off the train and him gaunt with his waist-long hair there weeks ago, what was he talking now about a hat and Peter Houri's really laughable struggle to translate "her crown and dignity" — had he actually no sense of what was happening, as it had happened to Poundmaker here too, that this was grinding on and there was no — I didn't know she had a hat and I never wear hats, what would I want it for to make me steal it, women's hats are nice but a man would be drunk — she was trying to catch his eye, to make him see her talking to him over the judge's head, but he was not aware of her any longer; the welcome he had signed to her and the bits of memory, a day and rocks and black sand and story, untraceable in the crushed shale visage, those blinky slitted eyes — was he laughing? Again? Surely he must be, he couldn't possibly be so without comprehension of all things white. It was impossible. He had always understood every — her thoughts stopped with a terrible lurch that shook the very bench they sat on; Horsechild sat there as if carved. It was the abrupt, momentary endless silence of the court, silence complete, with everyone, oddly, sitting there black and white and not so much as breathing. The boy was staring at his father and Kitty was staring at Big Bear too. Suddenly devastated. In this silence, now, his great voice, he must now — understanding at last she could not understand him — a woman's hat with feathers, what fea — not in the least. The last red edge of the sun slashed across his closed, monolithic face.

.   .   .

Mr. Justice Hugh Richardson, the Court: Gentlemen of the jury: This prisoner is charged with participating in rebellious acts against the constitution and the Government of the country. I must point out to you that it is a cardinal doctrine of law that "the king" means "the people," that their interests and his are inseparable. Where we have in an Act of Parliament the Queen's name, it means merely that the offence, if such, is against the people. It is true, as we have seen but too plainly, that the prisoner is not a white man — what we term a white man — he is an Indian, but although he is an Indian, I cannot give any other view — put it any other way to you than to say that between white people and Indians there is no distinction whatever. The law is there and it is binding upon the Indian, or at least he is entitled to as much protection and receives as much protection from Her Majesty as the white man; the converse is also true that from him is due the same amount of respect and allegiance as is due and we enforce from the white man. True it is that the Indian, as a rule, has not the amount of enlightened education and has not, perhaps, so much civilization as white men, what we call civilization, but I have yet to see the Indian in the year 1885 who does not know the difference between right and wrong. Innocence or ignorance at any rate is not shown in this case and I tell you as regards the man himself he is there to stand the consequence of whatever acts he may have done, of which he is charged. What wrong I may have expressed in the opinion of any young gentleman has nothing to do with this case. I have always understood that, speaking generally of the law, rebellion is wrong, and I have declared it so in each case put before me, according to my oath, without fear or favour whether the prisoner is black or white, Indian, halfbreed or any other colour or nationality at all. I don't claim to be old by any means, nor too old to be instructed in law from my juniors, no matter how young, but my du —

Robertson: Perhaps your Honour would like to know I am thirty-five. That's old enough with eleven years' practice at the bar to know something, and to do my duty. The crime of being a young man I am not ashamed of.

Court: I must notice interruptions because they stop my addressing you, but that won't at all shake me in anything I have to say; but now we are apprised of a fact which, perhaps, I did not know before.

Robertson: Which is very important in the case, of course.

Court: Now, my duty is to tell you what the law is, and express an opinion as to what portions of the evidence you should and should not consider, as to law, and to leave the question of credibility to you. So, if the evidence of Mr. Halpin, Mr. Pritchard and Mr. Tompkins is to be believed, a state of rebellion existed prior to the 2nd of April last and the prisoner knew it. Now, if he knew it, what was his duty? His first duty was the same as yours and mine: not to be found in the rebel camp but where law and order prevailed. That was his first duty, and the only excuse which the law recognized is this: "the present fear of death is the only excuse. Suffering or any injury less than would deprive of life is not a justification of a traitorous act."

Now, then, was he there? Was he with them and was he under any constraint short of what I have told you? We know that he was at Frog Lake when the thing broke out, was he then at Fort Pitt? And if he was at Fort Pitt, and the protection part of the Government had to leave, why wasn't the prisoner with them? That may strike you. It has struck me. The same thing will occur to you when they got back to Frog Lake, was he with the rebels or was he not? I simply submit to you a class of questions which should enter your minds. Well then, when we come on further, where was he after this fight that was spoken of? Was he with the peace party, the prisoners and the Wood Crees, or why was he with the other party?

If you answer these questions affirmatively, as a conviction created in your minds beyond all reasonable doubt, then I say your verdict should be one of guilt. If, from the evidence as presented, you feel that it is so unreliable as to create a reasonable doubt in your mind as to its veracity, why, then you ought then to give him the benefit of that doubt, and acquit him.

In the conduct of the case you may, perhaps, have been struck by what you heard me say, that in strict law certain things should not here be offered as evidence. Yet I felt that in a case of this sort, with the class of man who stands there, the widest possible limit should be given to anything he had to say, or that any witnesses who might be called might have to utter, that there might be no doubt they had the full benefit of bringing everything before you. The evidence is now before you, and you will come to a conclusion of guilt or innocence. If knowledge of the rebellion was brought home to him and participation after that, without excuse that I have told you of, then he has come within the pale of the law.

Now, you will retire, gentlemen, and consider it, and let me return into court for your determination upon it.

(The jury retires.)

Robertson: There is one thing that I would ask your Honour to tell the jury, and that is, that although the prisoner was there, if they are satisfied upon the evidence that he was not willingly participating in what was being done, he is not guilty.

Court: I have told them that.

Robertson: I understood your Honour to say if he was there when the fight was going on, nothing short of the fear of death would free him.

Court: I did not say that. The onus of freeing himself from responsibility lies upon him.

Robertson: But if the evidence satisfied them that, although he was there, he was not acting with them, his being there is not enough upon which to convict him.

Court: I think I have put it fairly to the jury.

Robertson: Will your Honour tell the jury now that if they are satisfied that although he was there, if he was not aiding or abetting them, then he ought to be acquitted?

Court: Oh, I think the jury may be brought back, yes.

(The jury returns to court.)

Court: Gentlemen, I have brought you back because of some question as to my having put the remarks I made in a proper light to you with regard to this prisoner's presence in what may be termed the rebel camp. Now, I read to you what the law was, but I am asked to go further and to suggest to you to consider whether upon the evidence there is not sufficient to excuse him; whether a sufficient explanation has been given for his presence; that you should consider whether he was there compulsorily — I think I have got that right now to suit Mr. Robertson — or whether he was there against his will, and acting solely in the interests of peace.

Robertson: If they think, though he was there, he was not actually aiding and abetting them, if they are satisfied on that, then they ought to acquit him.

Court: And if he was there against his will and giving no assistance whatever, then he would be entitled to an acquittal. I must, however, declare the law on this subject, and it is this: If men band themselves together for an unlawful purpose and in pursuit of that commit murder, it is right that the court should pointedly refuse to accept the proposition that a full share of responsibility for their acts does not extend to the surgeon who accompanied them to dress their wounds, to the clergyman who attends to offer spiritual consolation, or the reporter who volunteers to record their achievements; the presence of anyone in any character aiding and abetting or encouraging the prosecution of unlawful designs must involve a share of the common guilt.

Robertson: Aiding and abetting or encouraging, your Honour. I wish the jury to understand distinctly.

Court: Now, gentlemen, you will retire again. I have given you the addition. I thought I had placed it plainly before you when you went out. You have it now though, and you can retire again.

(The jury retires, and returns in fifteen minutes.)

Clerk Watson: Gentlemen, are you agreed upon your verdict? How say you, is the prisoner "guilty" or "not guilty"?

Jury: Guilty, with a recommendation for mercy.

Clerk: Gentlemen, hearken to your verdict as the court records it. You find the prisoner "guilty, with a recommendation to mercy," so say you all.

Court: Gentlemen of the jury, you are discharged, and I might tell you, gentlemen, that your recommendation shall have all the weight that it can reasonably have. I shall not pass sentence tonight.

. . .

III

The room was the same as it had been, twice longer than wide
but not crowded this time. Momentarily to him it appeared
empty, his eyes blinking simply darkness and his nostrils still
holding the outside air, the bluish savour of smoke laid along
the horizon in upward thinning layers of haze that directly
above him was almost the washed blue of evening sky, the
rattle of wheels under him, the horses' hooves crunching and
lifting in the grass beside the wagon-track and he could almost
feel their muscles bunching, shifting between his legs, feel the
endless flow of his bay stallion down the dip of the dry creek
and up over the flat earth in the autumn hunt and stretching
out up the next rise so gentle its tilt was imperceptible and the
black sprawl of *mus-toos-wuk* emerge into the greyblue of fire
running somewhere beyond the horizon still, if he pulled up
he would see more and more of them, endlessly buffalo. If his
eyes were what — for buffalo they would be as they had always
been — but that was a train there, crawling on the prairie so far
away he could see only its black line, stubby and belching.
These huge fires in the autumn grass came from that, sparks
flying from that white fire inside them. Piapot's reserve by the
lake was burning the police guards said, there were enough
rifles surrounding him but it was only policemen bumping
along erect and stiff on the running horses, a fire so big the
biggest boss of all, the Governor-General travelling around
and giving presents to any Indians that stood up and held out
their hands, and they all stood up if they weren't in jail, presents were always good for something, sometimes even edible,
the scout riding with the Governor-General who came from
where the Queen lived got lost in the valley, the smoke was so
thick the police said, and the big man had to ride half a day on a

grey horse before they got him to the right place for him to say his words. Let it burn; the buffalo were far beyond this fire.

He was in the wooden box again. The evening sunlight seemed brighter now, bright enough to distinguish again the pocks on the steel ball as he placed it carefully, it moved almost noiselessly for him after three months of contemplation and waiting together, between his feet. He raised his head, out into the room and one policeman was gesturing; so he stood and Peter Houri came up beside him again, paler now, as if he had never left the spot since they placed him in here the first time: he had been there for Poundmaker and One Arrow, long before him. Big Bear smiled at his wide, gentle face. Talking with his hands to him, They give you plenty to eat at this work, eh, and Peter grinning back while a door opened and the short judge with his glasses and white hair came in as if his black sack floated him over the floor, signing, There are almost enough People being led to this box to make me fat! Everyone in the room stood, the little dry man shouting aloud as if his voice were intended for open prairie. They they all except one sat; his English sound began.

Mr. Scott: "I move the sentence of the court upon Big Bear."

Mr. Justice Richardson: "Big Bear, have you anything to say why sentence should not be pronounced upon you for the offence of which you stand convicted by a jury of your — were convicted on September 11. I am ready to hear anything you have to say, now."

Big Bear watched Peter's pale face moving, hearing the good Cree sounds, and then he stood up. He pulled his blanket tighter with his left hand, it felt wrong and he stared down at himself: it was the shirt. It seemed too heavy for his right arm to lift, he could see nothing of his arm, only his hand clamped tight on the wood, sinews like bulging roots there from his arm under the shirt straining, as if he had no power now to lift that thin, dingy cloth. He contemplated his right hand in the yellowish light: his fingers on the wooden box: that was the problem; his fingers would have to let go, it was necessary, and after a time slowly they loosened until his arm felt better. He could throw back his head; words began to rise.

"It comes to me perhaps I have a few words here. Some small words," he paused, watching the light glint on the glass over the judge's eyes, "that will not take long to say. After all the words that have been made about me. I think I should say something, perhaps about them too. After I have been sitting all summer where the sun couldn't come, waiting, with iron on my leg. Though there were always enough men around to give me food, far more than enough men."

Peter Houri was grinning as he translated but no one listening to the English seemed to understand, so he continued directly: "It has been said here that I wanted to make war. If I had wanted to do that, I would have painted my face. I do not remember anyone saying here I ever had paint on my face. I threw my paint away long ago because, as you can see, my face is too old now to be helped by painting."

There was laughter then, round laughter of River People behind him where others of his band and some Assiniboines waited to hear their sentence after him, and a scattered white laughter too when Peter translated. Big Bear's arm came up, so easily:

"At Frog Lake when the leaves were coming out I heard shots fired; I heard warcries, but I knew little before that happened. I never called a councillor to a council. The angry warriors in my band did not listen to me and they poured out the blood of people I wanted to protect. The warriors who did that and wanted to give themselves up afterwards are in

Battleford now, I know, and long ago I saw what would happen to them; others who did it are over the Line because they did not want to give themselves up. There were enough soldiers going places to make the trees shiver and if I had wanted to fight I would not be standing here. No army captured me. I came in and talked to the police at the place where I wanted."

His voice lifted, against the walls of the small room.

"Did anyone stand here, can anyone stand here and say I made words against a priest or an agent? Can anyone say I touched his feather or his blanket? It was said here by people I never saw before that I encouraged my people to take part in the trouble. I never did. Long before any white men listening to me now saw this country I had been given to see some things; before I met the Governor Morris winters and summers and autumns ago I saw beside the Tramping Lakes that my people would die with their blood swollen in their faces and I said to that Governor, when he wanted my mark on his paper giving up the land that was ours from The Spirit Alone, If any man has the right to put a rope around another man's neck, some day someone will get choked. I said that to him, on the hill above Fort Pitt, and he said there is only one law. I know about that law now, but I never wanted to know what I know now because I never needed it. My heart sank when those white men at Frog Lake were killed; I had eaten with all of them and some of them were my friends, but when some came to my people with news of the fight at Duck Lake, my young men ignored my words. I was away most of the winter, hunting and fishing for my family north in the Moose Hills and when I got back the day before the killing the young men despised me because I would not talk with our half-brothers. I did not so much as touch a white man's horse. I always believed that by being a friend to the white man I and my people would be helped by those who had wealth. I always understood that it pleased the Great Spirit for men to do good. But this summer, with this round iron around my leg, my heart is stretched out on the ground.

"I look around me, here," he turned his lowered head slowly and it seemed to him now the room was packed, full, filled to the very ceiling with all the white men he had ever known. Sitting there, those he had liked and those he had sometimes hated and all the others passed in a somehow dirty blur of unending movement, saw them as if piled in wooden layers with their white wooden faces gleaming at him and the few River People and Assiniboines standing chained behind him, listening where he could not quite see them: the yellow light at the tiny windows would pour over them, melting like hot fat into pemmican into their ruddy faces, and his heart staggered for all the great goodness now gone, gone altogether.

"I see this room crowded with — handsome faces — faces handsomer than mine even when I was young. I have been the leader of People in this country for a long time; People rode from four directions to hunt with me. I never put a chain on anything. I stand here an old man, and I will be sent somewhere with this chain. No doubt these handsome faces I admire will know how to care for the land. No doubt, better than I. Perhaps they will also be able to care for my people, now that I am gone. My people are hiding in the woods, terrified — those are my children, and they are starving, driven from the land which was our great inheritance and they are running, somewhere, in the darkness, afraid to show themselves in the big light of day. Oh, when I stand on the ground with the sky over me I pray to That One whose finger drew us from Earth and spread it out for us like a big blanket, Forgive them, they are hungry and terrified, forgive them!

Have you no children? Have they never asked you for food? Is there nothing but punishment in the Grandmother's law? When a young man of the River People leads other young men rashly into a bad raid and one of them is left on the plain, that leader returns to camp and falls down before that father, that mother, and he cries for forgiveness. Then the mother touches him, the father lifts him and holds him to his breast and there is a son again in that empty lodge to make them happy, to care for them when they are old. Who can say here why the dead are dead? Who can give them life again? I say there will be a time soon when the Grandmother will be very happy for every one of my people that live in the North West. I plead with you, chiefs of the white law, have pity! Pardon the outcasts of my people!"

The judge had no eyes. On the motionless head the egg-shaped glasses sat glazed gold.

"There are only a few words left," Big Bear said, softly. "This land belonged to me. When I had it I never needed your flour and pork. Sometimes I was stiff with Indian agents who looked at me as if I was a child and knew less than a child. Before many of you were born I ran buffalo over this place where you have put this building, and white men ate the meat I gave them. I gave them my hand as a brother; I was free, and the smallest Person in my band was as free as I because the Master of Life had given us our place on the earth and that was enough for us. But you have taken our inheritance, and our strength. The land is torn up, black with fires, and empty. *You have done this*. And there is nothing left now but that you must help us.

"I have heard your many words, and now you have heard my few. A word is power, it comes from nothing into meaning and a Person takes his name with him when he dies. I have said my last words. Who will say a word for my people? Give my people help! I have spoken."

For a moment the thunder of his voice battered the room; the answering sound of River People rose behind him, almost as if for an instant the old man stood again in the strong circle of his council. Then Peter Houri's voice spoke and the English voice came immediately, quiet as always, but now more than ever as he would not expect it from so thick a body, though covered with black; thinly hard like steel:

"Big Bear, you have been found guilty by an impartial jury. I have no objection to hear what you have to say, but on one point you must be corrected. This land never belonged to you. This land was and is the Queen's. She has allowed you to use it. When she wanted to make other use of it, she called you together through her officers and let you decide which of the choicest parts of the country you wanted, to reserve them for yourself. Your people can live there because the Queen has graciously given it to them. The land belongs to the Queen.

"Now, grey-haired as you are, you cannot be excused from all responsibility for the misdoings of your band. You have been found guilty. Much as I dislike to punish an Indian, much as I dislike to punish, to pass sentence on anyone, I should be wanting in my duty to the public and the Crown if I did not place such punishment upon you as would make you feel it, as also to make other Indians of the country know what would become of them if they followed a bad example. As for your people who have committed no crime, they will be looked after and cared for as if nothing at all had happened. The sentence of the court upon you, Big Bear, for the offence of which you stand convicted is this. That you be imprisoned in the penitentiary of Manitoba at Stony Mountain for the period of three years."

Mr. Justice Hugh Richardson had been careful to speak very slowly, pausing at the end of each sentence, however short, so Peter Houri could get it absolutely clear. But Big Bear was not looking at him anymore. He seemed to be leaning forward, peering through the half-open window, very broad under his blanket, hair straggly about his crushed-stone face, into the smoky sky. When it came at last, the sound of his voice seemed to growl up from the earth itself.

"I ask the court to print my words and scatter them among White People. That is my defence!"

"Next," Richardson next, "Next!" Hammering.

IV

Toronto: Major Samuel Bedson, who distinguished himself in the Canadian Militia and is now Warden of the Manitoba Penitentiary at Stony Mountain, being in Toronto on a visit, a reporter called on him in order to learn something of the prison life of the Indians and Half-breeds who were punished for complicity in the recent rebellion. Most of the Indians are handy with tools, they can make themselves useful and the intention is to teach them such trades as will make them useful on the reserves. Poundmaker, tall and stately of person, with a solemn and not ill-favoured countenance and a dignified manner, moves from shop to shop, watching and issuing orders to the Crees over whom he exercises a sort of general superintendency. Big Bear is learning to be a carpenter. He lies his saw and hammer with dogged steadiness, and it would be hard to read in his deep black eyes the longing for the wide plain, the swift shaganappies, and the trusty rifle. One Arrow is engaged in the prosaic task of making shoes. There are in all about 43 Indians in gaol. They are amenable to discipline, but pine for their old wild life, their wives and children — family affection appearing to be very strong among them. The Half-breeds are docile, tractable, expressing regret....

— *The Globe*, Wednesday, December 9, 1885

Battleford: Robert Hodson, who hanged the six Cree and two Assiniboine murderers here in November last, has been appointed public hangman for the Dominion. He sold out his business here and left for the railway on Sunday week, intending to go to British Columbia where his services will be required shortly. He neglected, however, to pay some debts due here, and was followed to the Eagle Hills by a sheriff's officer and brought back, and after adjusting his affairs took passage south by stage on Wednesday. Hodson was at one time a pupil of Calcraft, the English hangman. Prior to the rebellion he served as cook to the McLean family at Fort Pitt, and suffered the two months Indian captivity with them.

— *Saskatchewan Herald*, Monday, January 11, 1886

Winnipeg: As has been mentioned several times in previous letters, it is within the range of probabilities that trouble with the Indians will arise again at the most critical time — when the flowers bloom in the spring. Upon pretty good authority it is learned that the American Indians are sending runners to the Blackfeet, and further north amongst the Cree around Battleford. No grave apprehensions are felt, however, of an uprising. The absence of the leading chiefs, in their visit to the east, and the presence of a large military force coupled with the fact that the Indians really have no personal griev-ances, are not conducive to an uprising. Besides, Pound-maker, who is to be released shortly, has just written Crowfoot that he wants the Crees and Blackfeet to create no more trouble. Poundmaker is Crowfoot's adopted son and without the countenance of these two big chiefs, representing the two largest Indian tribes, there would not be much chance of an outbreak of any importance.

I went out to see Poundmaker the other day at Stony Mountain. He has not been well lately, and is now suffering from a severe cold. He told me that he was well treated by everybody, especially by Warden Bedson, but that he felt lonesome and wanted to get back to the prairie. His hair had not been cut, and he had lots of tobacco. All that he lacked was liberty.

Just then Big Bear came in — a small-sized weazen-faced chap, with a cunning, restless look — and I interviewed him, but without much success. He said he liked the place well enough, only they made him work, and it was evident he was constitutionally prejudiced agianst that sort of thing. He wanted to get home again, and when released would return to his reserve. His Grace Archbishop Tache had been out a few days previously baptizing a number of prisoners, but Big Bear had declined to be christened. He wished to get home.

"What did Crowfoot and Red Crow say to you when you wanted them to join you and raise trouble six years ago?" I asked.

"An officer asked me that at the time," Big Bear answered, "and I told him there was no truth in the matter at all. We were gathering to have a feast, and it was told all over the country that we wanted to fight."

"Didn't Riel want you to join him and the Blackfeet, Sioux and Half-breeds in a general uprising in 1879?"

"Riel? I saw Riel one spring, it may have been after that and there was talk. Riel wanted me to raise all the men I could, but of course I wouldn't."

"What was Riel's scheme?"

"Yes, he had a lot of rum which he was selling, but it ran out and I went back buffalo hunting. I only stayed one day."

"He didn't tell you he would have the North West for the Indians and Half-breeds and drive the white men out?"

"Oh no."

"What did he want you for?"

"I don't know what he wanted to say to me. There were so many there."

"He didn't send for you just to sell you some rum, surely?"

"Riel came to me, and I went back with him."

"What did you go for?"

"Oh yes, I always listen to what I am told and say yes. I was told I was wanted, so I went there."

"Riel said he wanted you in Montana and you went?"

"Buffalo — I was in Montana hunting buffalo."

Then he contradicted himself again and said that Riel did send for him, but that when he started to go he met some friends who advised him to stay away.

"What did he say?" I asked.

"Riel didn't say anything, only about trading."

"Other Indians tell me he did."

"Yes, they say that?"

"Crowfoot told me he did, and so did Crowfoot's interpreter."

"It is six years since I saw Crowfoot, when we had that feast. I never remember saying anything. Many wanted to fight in 1879 too but of course I stopped them. Riel and Crowfoot may have met, but I don't know anything about that."

"Perhaps Riel didn't ask you to go into the late rebellion," I suggested. He unblushingly remarked:

"That's right, he didn't. I never knew anything about the trouble till Mr. Halpin of Cold Lake told me. I was going to go to Cypress Hills when the fighting started. I wanted to, but someone needed my horse and so I had nothing to ride. I didn't know till the man who had my horse came back that there had been fighting."

"Why did you capture Mr. McLean at Fort Pitt?"

"I didn't," he unblushingly answered. "I sent him a letter and he came out."

"But you detained him."

"Oh yes," he replied, without moving a muscle, "I was afraid he would get killed, and didn't like that he should go back. It was only to save the lives of those people, and not to harm them, that they were detained. Were any hurt?"

"Perhaps you weren't on the warpath at all?"

"Yes you're right," he coolly remarked. "I wasn't. I was half a day away when the soldiers started shooting."

Poundmaker smiled significantly several times during this interview, and it was plain to be seen Big Bear did not propose to tell anything at all. We all knew that he was lying, and he knew that we knew it. Finally I jokingly asked him if he had been in the North West last spring, and at last he admitted that yes, he was, that he was taking care of his women and children, as they lived there. I then suggested to him that perhaps he hadn't heard about a rebellion out there at all, but he said:

"Oh yes, I heard them talking about it, a lot."

And that was all Big Bear knew about our little five-million-dollar unpleasantness. When he is released, it is believed shortly, he should secure the appointment of Winnipeg correspondent of some American newspaper. He has one pre-eminent qualification for the job.

When he had retired, I remarked to Poundmaker that Big Bear hadn't been telling the truth. The chief smiled and said it was sometimes hard to say what the truth was, but his looks told more than his words.

"Didn't Riel want you to join him six years ago too?"

"I never saw Riel till I met him in Regina last summer. We stayed in the same house there."

By which I gather he meant the gaol. But a bell rang signalling time was up, and Poundmaker wandered off. G.H.H.

— *The Toronto Mail*, Saturday, February 27, 1886

v

The white mare Little Bad Man had given him was between his legs; he could feel her hide creak shifting over her ribs. Perhaps too big a black stallion had got on her that summer, her belly sagged lower than drying meat on a string and he couldn't see her head, barely her withers in the whining snow. He tried to stretch forward in the lee of her neck, to get his legs completely back against her hide, but they wouldn't lift, wouldn't so much as bend and the wind cut up under whatever it was he wore, furrowing into his spine like a hot knife. The wind had been partly held along the creek between Cutknife and the Eagle Hills, it had been possible there but now on the prairie it seemed to hurl them south; as if the mare no longer had ground under her feet, simply flung between the trees that grew in short clusters everywhere. They hadn't been there when he hunted buffalo and now the wind used them to wait behind and gather itself and slam him with steel doors, hoisting the white mare off her feet into nothing, her hide against his face cold iron and he could not find his breath. They were getting that too, they were at last, and a bell rang.

"The blankets are there, won't you lie down?" He heard that as gentleness, and he could understand words; they were gentle too. And all wrong for he was standing already as he must, groping about for the grey pants he had certainly folded up properly but there seemed to be nothing, no iron bed and it was Horsechild, would he ever forget the face of his last son and his hands on his shoulder, "Will you lie down?"

"The basin — water, I have to —" but this was really Horsechild, yes. And the walls around him pushed out. Logs and his son's eyes held him firmly out of the wind; there was the heater with his feet beside it burning cold as if on fire, and he gathered his words together, holding hard to the strength in the dark eyes holding him. "Forgive me," he said, and he saw his own hands clamped to his son's shoulders, and could feel that too. A shoulder almost too hard for a boy with fourteen such winters. "I can't lie down yet," he said.

So he was sitting on a blanket by the tin heater with a fire so loud inside it could almost be heard above the storm tramping endlessly over the roof. The fire gradually died in his feet he thought, and it was Horsechild kneeling over them, rubbing them, he could see that and he knew there was no one else in the house which was almost as good as a buffalo lodge, though it could not split the storm around it like a buffalo lodge and of course couldn't be moved either. The Magpie wasn't there; she was outside this house, somewhere, wherever it was she had as much shelter from the storm as she wanted and could run after and he was too ashamed to say a word to his last son who knew that as well as he; to say anything. He watched the boy far away slowly, gently, work on the two poles that were his legs stretched into the distance; the year and a half in those black tunnels had killed his legs, he couldn't sit like a Person now and when he had let them hang over the iron edge of that iron bed and known that, it had come to him that he was getting closer to where he would have to go anyway now that everything he saw everywhere was dying too. And he was almost resigned sometimes, momentarily, sitting like that.

But his son's strong hands warmed him, he could feel his legs again and so he could ride more easily before the wind, the withers of the mare not so much now like a canoe-bow tossed about white water. When the storm grew worse he could walk now and lead her, keeping warm. He had about bent his knees to do that when it came to him there was no cold along his back; that his legs felt so good he could barely feel them and a lightness something like dawn, not howling snow, swam there ahead of him. He rode on, his heart lifting and the mare steadier on her feet and the Tramping Lakes must be there stroked smooth between the round hills and then he was on a ridge, the hills reaching down like the spring green legs of sleeping buffalo, down to the level blue earth, green legs tipped with blacker green hoofs under bright sky quite empty of sun. He rode down there, heat loosening his frozen face and the mare already quick, her head nodding, swinging easily down and he was among the submerged, inverted trees dipped in buds like yellow syrup and saw the green hills across the water between them, the water one sheet of light and swung his leg over the grey mare's withers and knew it before his feet touched the ground. The thunder of *mus-toos-wuk* running the earth. At last, again; here. He stood feeling it, motionlessly listening. They were there, coming, the bulls bellowing in happiness as they ran side by side and the spring calves by their mothers and the dust of their numberless hooves roiled up wherever the horizon would reach and his body was with them a living wand thrust into the earth, shivering to the drum-roll of the charge coming to trample him into itself. He knew, immensely, that whole thunder his thunder and from him burst the roar with its arms stretched open wide, jaws agape and clamp into that arched neck, heave and tear the crushed body behind those daggered horns, and through his roars, echo upon echo to the prairie's thunder, slid the thin steel of a tinkling bell.

"I think she heard that at Little Pine's," Horsechild said. "Will you lie down now?" But the bell kept on ringing, a sound so tiny that no sound he would ever make could stop it if it did not wish to stop by itself and he knew by now it would never do that. Finally he said to the endless tall white men all black around him, the tall warden with his black beard and the round black hat that covered his white hair, and all the black robes clustered blacker than so many judges and with tight white collars holding their heads stiffer than any judge, Taché with the huge silver crosses and Lacombe with his snowy hair wiped back from the glistening dome of his head and all the others craned over him while the bell rang. "Yes," he said finally, "I know now it's what you tell me, Poundmaker was with his father Crowfoot and there he has choked. He died too because he had no breath. I know. Yes, you can do that to me now if you want."

The bell rang immediately and water was sprinkling upon his head; he could barely feel that as he faced the black toes just sticking out under the edge of black dress scuffed dusty and singing above him with the sharp smell of something burning far up in the gloomy rafters and he lifted his head to the sounding face melting slightly above him, almost discernible, and told it directly just as its eyes hardened and held steady, "Yes, and John McDougall would have a word for People here. I want him to do this too, he'll have that much, that little water left for me too," with the white face soughing into hesitation, its incomprehension melting it like fat and its sound stretching down, down into a long snout of laughter dripping between tiers of teeth. Black fur lifted laughter.

The mare's hide nevertheless was almost glossy white. A song to her strength in the knee-deep grass lifted him riding south, the quick coulees; happiness, he was past the Tramping Lakes and Little Round valley and the sand hill where he had hunted white wolf once too often. The land laid its endless circle around him in distant bluish levels tilting and curving slightly against and over each other; he looked everywhere under the bright sky but there was no sun to be found. The brightless sat like a summer cap and here and there tufts began sticking out of the land almost as if clusters of giant trees sprouted now where wolf willow had barely grown before. He saw then that straight lines had squared up the land at right angles, broad lines of stark bleached bones had been spread straight, pressed and flattened into the earth for him to ride over, and sliced into hills as if that broad thong of bone could knuckle them down, those immovable hills. As far as he could see, wherever he looked the world was slit open with unending lines, squares, rectangles, of bone and between the strange trees gleamed straight lines of, he comprehended it suddenly, white buildings. Square inedible mushrooms burst up under poplars overnight; but square. He could not comprehend where he was. He suddenly recognized nothing where he knew he had ridden since he was tied in the cradleboard on his mother's back, where he had run buffalo since he could fork a horse. He was seeing; the apprehension which the settler-clustered land of Manitoba and Winnipeg's square walls and gutted streets had begun drove like nails into the sockets of himself and his place was gone, he knew Earth and Sun which had been his gifts to accept and love and leave to others were gone, all gone. Only Sky remained, overpowering brightness, floating pillars and tufts of cloud, laughing him into the horror of its final irony with no Thunderbird either; no more rain, the land dead with no Thunderbird to revive it, only the wolfish wind to lick dry and hound endlessly until there was none of it left, even dead, there would be — nothing, not even a hole — just nothing. He was hitting the mare, head, ribs, haunches with his legs and arms like unbendable clubs and she stumbled through the brittle grass, grasshoppers spraying, and he beat her staggering across the hard bleached bones, buffalo and People, yes he could see that, eyeholes in parts of skulls upon the scraped hillsides until he felt her breath sawing its last under him but he was on the hills then looking down, it was the South Saskatchewan — The Forks he recognized, unchanged! and he screamed his cry and hammered the mare down the long tilt of hill he knew he could never have walked, her legs braced and reeling as if she were drunk and he laughed aloud down to the crossing where the land whitened and above him stood Bull's Forehead Hill, flung with snow which the sear grass sprayed about the mare's floundering hoofs. Under the cottonwoods whorled black like snakes, but the mare refused to touch the river ice; stood shuddering. He battered her then as he never had any animal before, the horror of what he had escaped driving him beyond horror until she strained forward her bloody head away from his bloody fists and staggered out, slipping and almost falling but he heaved her to balance again and again with the sheer power of his shoulders, they still worked as they once had I yo ho, I yo ho, I am here now! and she was almost to the shadow of the hill when water, there is living water still in this river he roared, broke up black out of whiteness and he gave her to it with great happiness that by his final abuse of her she would find such a good, sweet end as she slid silently down the bending ice, under, and vanished, he lying there on the ice as it groaned and watching, his eyes wide open since the bell must ring now, certainly ring.

But it did not. Horsechild was talking to him, the warm softness of the First People, "You have to lie down now. She'll come back when she comes, you have to lie down."

"Yes...yes, I...." standing now for out of the reddish darkness faintly stinking, he was aware of that, coming towards him he saw at last what he had dreaded so long. The hard boots of Little Man, his white child's clothes and stiff black hat, it was clearly Hodson with glass over his snout making two oval reflections where his bulging eyes should have been. And behind him came the procession; six shapes coming relentlessly and he saw them as he had seen long ago, and knew them in their steady pace, their hands tied behind their backs. Miserable Man lifted his great pitted face and his lips were moving for his hands could not, I want to eat and then be shot, not like this, you tell the boss; old Bad Arrow came head down, and behind him Round The Sky, his kind young face staring where sky should have been, somewhere, but Wandering Spirit was a skeleton still asking Mrs. McLean if he could be forgiven, crouched perhaps by a small fire and asking if punishment would last long, asking, asking, and Mrs. McLean certain that God always forgave everyone who truly repented of his wrong, he must now repent for what he had done and put all that away but the soldiers, now the white soldiers.... Little Bear's mouth gaped in warcry, his chin jabbing down at the still unhealed scars on his breast as he came in fury but it was his friend Iron Body alone who spoke aloud. He made very calmly, his lean face without any expression whatever, the longest speech of his life, and it seemed begging too: "We will need different shoes. On the white Jesus road it's a long way to the Sand Hills, and for that you should give us good Whiteskin shoes." He stood motionless and staring, unaware that he could no longer breathe, these six River men who had once respected and loved him, with whom he had once thought that something might be possible, that they could all stand together and build something together that was their own, theirs, of the First People, but for which the power, wherever it was to do those things he had once perhaps dreamed, perhaps impossibly, had never been given him or he had never taken it when it was there or there wasn't any to take or perhaps it would be a hundred years in coming, he had to face that he knew nothing of it now if he had ever known anything of it as he faced those six River men before him, standing where their individual bits of power had brought them pushing individually against massed whites, and not quite standing either for their heads bulged a little crooked to one side, he had eaten meat with their fathers before they were children, slightly swinging there in a row with blood swelling up, their faces bursting out disfigured in the reddish, stinking darkness and he was beating himself with his head and battering the walls and his head with the steel ball and chain for that bell, the bell, bell you have to ring, bell!

Horsechild was wiping his face. For an instant Bull's Forehead Hill leaning down on him was Stony Mountain forcing him under the stiff men with guns high and pacing endlessly between the barbwire sagebrush along its crest, but it was really Horsechild's hand upon him, the other wiping his face and he could not so much as raise himself under that thin hand's weight, but then he could and lunged up from the blanket beside the stove. After a time, sitting, he had enough air in his chest once more too, with that sick stench gone.

"Tell me again," he could say then, "everything, about the People, still breathing, start with . . . Poundmaker."

"Crowfoot buried him on the hill above Blackfoot Crossing."

"Ahh. That was where, his mark on the treaty. Crowfoot. And Sitting Bull?"

"They say he's shooting his gun in a tent and Whiteskins pay to see that. With a Buffalo Bill."

"Buffalo, there are none of those now, Dumont?"

"He's in there too, they say, shooting."

"Yes. And Little Poplar, who showed his wide bare ass to soldiers."

"Soldiers shot him outside their camp in Montana. He was sitting on the wrong horse."

Big Bear found he could not so much as throw his head back, leave alone find breath to make a warcry for his sister's son, dead perhaps like a warrior. He whispered, finally, "He always loved many horses. Lone Man —"

"He was riding the wrong horse too, Cowan's horse from Fort Pitt and a policeman saw him in Edmonton. They say he's in . . . that place. . . . "

"I know that, I saw him," said Big Bear. "They pushed him down that black tunnel, where they push everyone, there's no time, I want to know about Kingbird. And his son, tell me."

Horsechild said very slowly, "You know, Kingbird and his son are in Montana with . . . his brother and other River People, down there."

"With Little Bad Man, whose name now is Little Bear?"

"Yes, that one."

"What do they eat?"

"They . . . hunt, in the Bearpaws. . . . "

"There is nothing to hunt in Montana. How does Little Bear feed The People?"

"They. . . . "

"What!"

"Live around the towns in winter. They eat what Whiteskins throw away."

Big Bear was able to whisper, after a long time, "He became a great warrior, that day on Belly River, facing Bloods all bloody."

"But that kept in a clean place," Horsechild said quickly, "it's here. There under the rafter where I put it, it's there, Kingbird gave it to me when he and Sits Green and the boy had to go south and he said Chief's Son's Hand had to —"

"When you see Little Bear, tell him I remembered at the last hunt there, how he said the Bearpaws was the place for People."

He was looking his apology for interrupting, he had to hurry now and he added as soon as he could, "If you want to, you tell Kapay-tow-aysing he's welcome to her. Maybe he can find where she has kept her softness."

Big Bear said that, and he was going to say something more to his last son silently facing him, waiting for his word; he was going to say something about Chief's Son's Hand, keep that among the People for they have nothing left, and it seemed that he was actually thinking again those long, long thoughts of power and confederation and of his people living as they would wish, not with buffalo for they were gone, but as People still, somehow, the proud First People. But the bundle given him by Great Parent Bear, the songs that had guided him in his long life, where were they all now? Where were they for his son who might have to live a long time yet? There had always been too much, there was too much he could not understand, leave alone know. He had lived some things wrong and some things right and that was what he had lived. It was time now. To lie down; to finish the long prayer to The Only One that was his life and when he had decided that he stood up from beside the black water easily and walked over the river ice, up between the hills, climbed between the folded hillocks through the hollow of blow-outs streaked with running snow and steadily, strongly, up the sand hill. On the top he stood erect and slowly turned in the circle of all that had once been given him. Above him the ghost dancers flamed like torn curtains springing fearfully beautiful out of their own vanishing again and again. He cleansed his hands with sweetgrass, its smell sharp as a good woman in his nostrils. Then he said:

"You Only Great Spirit, Father. I thank you. I thank you for giving me life, for giving me everything, for being still here now that my teeth are gone. So now I have to ask you this last thing, and I think it's like the first thing I asked but maybe you'll forgive that, since you have already known for a long time how hard it is for me to understand and learn anything, even in all the time you gave me. I ask you again. Have pity."

After these words he was going to lie down immediately but then he felt a warm weight against his soul. He looked down and saw Chief's Son's Hand hanging from around his neck, on his chest, each great ivory claw curved, there, the fur silky against the bright scarlet flannel. Such happiness broke up in him then he had to turn the complete circle to see everything once more in the beautiful world that had once been given him. Then he was going to lie down, and realized that he had no robe or even blanket to spread on the sand. He would arrive naked in the Green Grass World. Well, they would have an immediate opportunity to feel good by showing him their kindness. So he lay down then on the sand, his head to the north. It was very cold. He rolled onto his left side, pulled his knees up against the yellow claws. It was so quiet he could hear sand grains whisper to each other as they approached. For a long time he stared at the tiny world coming to him and for an instant he thought he would see, at last... but what he saw was the red shoulder of Sun at the rim of Earth, and he closed his eyes.

He felt the granular sand joined by snow running together, against and over him in delicate streams. It sifted over the crevices of his lips and eyes, between the folds of his face and hair and hands, legs; gradually rounded him over until there was a tiny mound on the sand hill almost imperceptible on the level horizon. Slowly, slowly, all changed continually into indistinguishable, as it seemed, and everlasting, unchanging, rock.

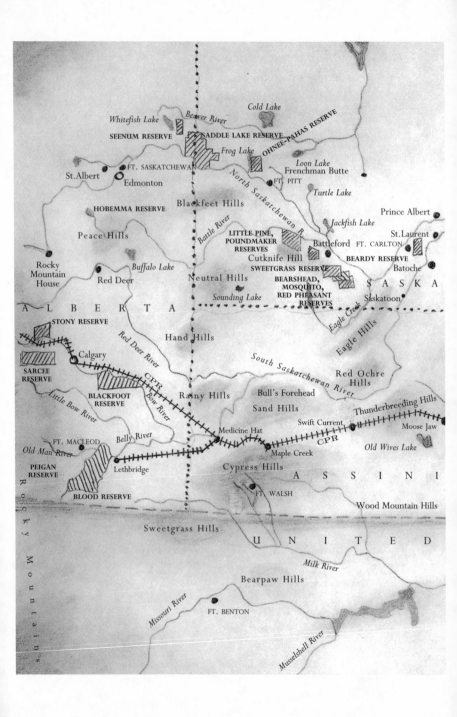

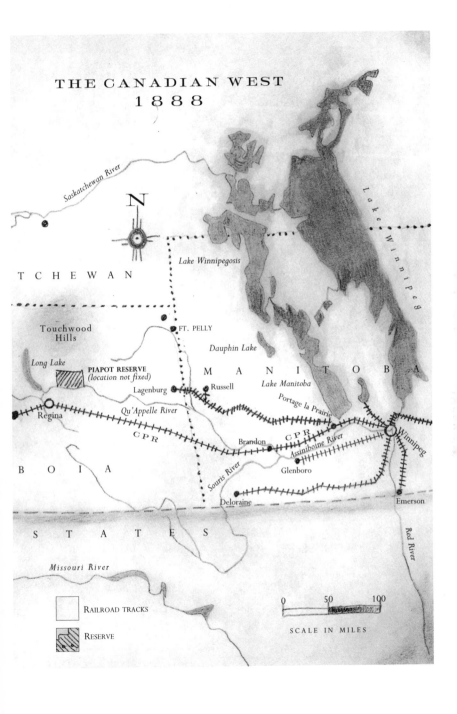

THE CANADIAN WEST
1888

Saskatchewan River

N

Lake Winnipegosis

Lake Winnipeg

T C H E W A N

Touchwood
Hills

FT. PELLY

Dauphin Lake

Long Lake

PIAPOT RESERVE
(location not fixed)

M A N I T O B A

Lagenburg

Russell

Lake Manitoba

Portage la Prairie

Regina

Qu'Appelle River

CPR

CPR

Winnipeg

Brandon

Assiniboine River

B O I A

Souris River

Glenboro

Deloraine

Emerson

S T A T E S

Red River

Missouri River

RAILROAD TRACKS

0   50   100

RESERVE

SCALE IN MILES

ABOUT THE AUTHOR

RUDY WIEBE is the author of several short story collections and essays, including *River of Stone*, and eight novels, including *A Discovery of Strangers*, winner of the Governor General's Award for Fiction. His most recent book, co-authored with Yvonne Johnson, the great-great-granddaughter of Big Bear, is *Stolen Life: The Journey of a Cree Woman*, which received the Viacom Canada Writer's Trust Non-Fiction Prize, the Saskatchewan Book Award for Non-Fiction and the Alberta Book Award for Non-Fiction (the Wilfred Eggleston Award). Rudy Wiebe lives in Edmonton.